MIAMI GOLDEN BOY

MIAMI GOLDEN BOY

by

HERBERT KASTLE

Published by

BERNARD GEIS ASSOCIATES, INC.

For Rhona, who loves Miami

"March fifteenth, and as if on a signal the vicunas and the chinchillas are leaving. The migration is over. They are due someplace else. . . . The package plans are flooding the beach. The cloth coats are returning. Somehow I resent them. The men look out of place here after the rich have left. . . . Women look better than men, but not like the tall, furred goddesses of February . . . Everyone is too nice."

Room 306 Doesn't Tip!
by William Price Fox, Jr.
Holiday Magazine (1967)

"So what is Miami Beach? Steve, Miami Beach is the only natural we ever had. But *what* a natural!"

—Miami pioneer Carl Fisher
to his contemporary,
Steve Hannigan.

MIAMI GOLDEN BOY

CUBAN PROLOGUE

The dark blue Chrysler Imperial blended into the heavy shadows of Biscayne Boulevard's palm-lined center parking area. Miami's main street, three lanes wide on either side of the service road, whispered softly under the wheels of an occasional car. It was two A.M., a humid Wednesday in December, with New Year's and the start of the season still three weeks away. Ivan Cesar Lamas sat beside his chauffeur, smoking a thick Havana cigar. They spoke in Spanish.

"A soft night," Lamas said, pursing heavy lips, blowing heavy smoke out the window. "Almost like home." But it wasn't. Nothing was like home.

"We shouldn't be here, *patrón.*" The chauffeur gave the title its full Latin value, pronouncing it *pah-tron.* He was a big man, hard and dark and sharp of profile. He had done many things for his employer, but always with vital reason, vital purpose. This seemed purposeless. His eyes roved up and down the wide avenue. "It's not good to take chances like this, a man of your importance."

Lamas smiled faintly. He had a small, round face and eyes of the palest blue. His fingers, rolling the cigar back and forth, were delicate, the nails buffed and polished. His body was also delicate, clothed in soft gray slacks and dark blue jacket. There was something vaguely dated about the clothing, or the way he wore it. His lips pursed again, blew smoke again. The lips weren't delicate. They were full and sensual, strong and expressive. "My mother used to say things like that to my grandfather. My grandfather used to say, 'As important as Comrade Lenin?'"

The man beside him nodded, but looked blank.

"My mother was an émigrée." The faint smile flickered again. "A refugee, as are we. She and her father got out of Russia with a handful of family jewels. In Cuba she felt safe again, at home again."

"But in Russia, the weather—so different than in Cuba, *patrón*."

"The feel of the people. My father's estate, his cane fields, his workers." Lamas looked at the big man. "You remember your father, Jorge?"

"Of blessed memory, of course, *patrón*."

"My mother was comforted by men like him. She felt safe in Cuba. Perhaps it was best she died before Fidel came."

The chauffeur muttered a ritual obscenity followed by a ritual, "Forgive me, *patrón*."

Lamas said, "Now I must ask, 'As important as Comrade Castro, Jorge?'"

The chauffeur sighed and made a sad face. Lamas said, "Of course, things must be different when we return. The workers must have more dignity, more land." That was *his* ritual. It was some years since he had actually believed the Cuban émigrés would return to their homes, except on Fidel Castro's terms. But then, a few days ago, had come the news of Senator Christopher's Miami visit, and it had revived the old plan in Ivan Lamas's mind. The old *dream*, really. A dream because, on the surface, it was so farfetched, so risky.

And yet, it was based upon reality—the most obvious reality in American politics: the Wheeler clan.

The ex-President, Michael Blaine Wheeler, whose daughter was married to the current President, Jonathan Everett Standers. Mike Wheeler, who had married off another daughter to the prime contender for the Democratic presidential nomination, Senator Richard Bernard Christopher. Old Master Mike, who had never been reconciled to giving up the power of his office; who had attempted to run the nation through his daughters and their men; who was still trying to do so, he and his millions of dollars, even from a wheelchair. Iron Mike, who could change the direction and destiny of the United States if he wanted to—or was forced to.

Lamas went through the plan again—a dream no longer be-

6

cause he was no longer willing to just dream. Only details remained to be worked out.

Ivan Lamas had confidence in his ability to plan, to foresee, to work out details. Hadn't he done just that before leaving Cuba? Hadn't he sold the estate, the far-flung fields, the three smaller houses, the mills, the hotel, the casinos, *everything*, when Fidel was still just a *campesino*'s mountain myth? A little loss in value, yes, but what was a hundred thousand or so in the debacle that followed? Before that, he had tried to make his friends understand it was necessary to depose Batista, but they couldn't see it, or were more afraid of the secret police than of an intellectual bandit. They didn't have foresight. They didn't have a Tsar, his Ochrana, and his eight million bayonets in their family backgrounds.

"Democracy," Jorge said. "We will have Democracy, *patrón*, as in the United States."

Lamas nodded, and wondered if Jorge was as one-dimensional as he seemed. Or was there the lurking tiger in him, too? One could never trust out of one's class; in that, Marx had been absolutely correct. *Democracy, as in the United States.* That was Democracy predicated on enormous national wealth. Let the national wealth disappear and what the Negroes had done in their ghettos would be as nothing compared to what the white disinherited would do all over the land.

"There," Jorge said, pointing. He reached for the ignition key, glancing at Lamas. Lamas shook his head. Jorge sighed. "This is not our way, *patrón*. You laughed at this plan."

Which was true. His own plan would be far more complex, and meaningful. But watching this little exercise would reassure him that there were men to carry out the meaningful operations; men who could help him bring the old life back, the sweet life back, the life that was so much more than just money.

Some two hundred yards in front of the Chrysler, on the bay side of Biscayne, was the Wheeler Alcove. A stocky man carrying a large suitcase, a very heavy one judging by the way he walked, was approaching the curved stone wall with its engraved message: *The Torch of Unity, Dedicated by the Committee of Latin Americans for Democracy to Michael Blaine Wheeler, President of the United States.* Jorge began to point again, to speak again. "Ramon Pedras . . ." Lamas said, "*Sí,*" drawing out the word heavily. Jorge grew still. The *patrón* wanted no further interruptions.

Two more men had appeared, crossing Biscayne from the Northeast streets. Both carried tanklike objects in their arms, and were running to avoid a cab approaching from downtown. Lamas knew that the tanks were fire extinguishers.

Suddenly, all three were together at the Alcove, at the pillar topped by a metal cone, moving frantically, arms and legs and heads jerking in all directions, in a way reminiscent of old-time silent movies. Lamas laughed, drawing a surprised look from Jorge. One man detached himself from the group and ran to the wall that swept in a half-moon toward the pillar. He began waving his right arm widely. Jorge said, "A message. He's painting a message with a spray can, *patrón.* He should be with the others at the flame."

"The gesture is nothing without the message, Jorge. He's writing, 'The blood of Cubans, dedicated to those who died at the Bay of Pigs.' The paint is red."

Jorge peered. "How can you see, *patrón?*"

Ivan Lamas didn't answer. He had composed the message. Anyone could have, but the leaders of this particular activist group had given him the honor in return for his generous donations.

The other two men had been busy with a folding metal ladder taken from the suitcase. The stocky one, Ramon Pedras, was already up the ladder at the top of the fifteen-foot pillar, pumping a steady stream of foam into the torch-shaped metal cone from which flickered the eternal flame. The flame continued to burn. He tossed the tank to his left, onto the grassy border, and the second tank was handed up to him. This one was more effective. A moment of pumping and the flame went out.

Despite several pole-mounted floodlights, a sudden darkness

seemed to fall on the Alcove. Everything came to a halt, the three men staring at the dead torch. Then the man on the ladder came down, sliding, almost falling, jumping the last four or five rungs. He and his assistant at the torch left their equipment and began running back across Biscayne. A car heading north swerved sharply, rubber shrieking against asphalt. Jorge said, "Let's go, patrón! Now!"

Lamas nodded. Jorge had the car started and moving forward simultaneously. The third man dropped his spray can and dashed toward Biscayne. Jorge swung the Imperial hard right and onto the main section of road. The third man was crossing directly in front of them, and raised his head. Lamas saw a teen-ager with a pinched, frightened face. What could such boys know or care about Cuba, he wondered, and gave the boy a salute. The gesture was either not seen, or was misread. The boy bent his head, legs pumping furiously. He disappeared from sight as Jorge sent the car surging forward.

Later, crossing the Julia Tuttle Causeway to Miami Beach, Lamas said, "It will at least serve to notify people we are still here. People outside Miami, that is. *The New York Times* will carry it and people in Washington will wince."

"But most Americans love Wheeler. Won't this make them angry?"

Lamas was silent. The warm night air took on a smell of sea from blue-black waters on both sides. They left the causeway for Arthur Godfrey Road; then Lamas said, "The people can be angry with us, or support us, or ignore us. It means nothing. Only the man, the family that leads the country, only they matter."

Jorge glanced at him as they pulled up to a stoplight. "No Batista here, patrón."

"That's right. No Batista. Just a Wheeler."

"The old President? You think he'll help us?"

Lamas lit a fresh cigar. "He hasn't helped us yet. Nor his son-in-law, the *great* President. Nor any of them."

"That's what I mean, patrón." Jorge was pleased with himself.

"Then again, Jorge, they haven't had any *reason* to help us."

9

Jorge was puzzled. Reason? Fidel was a Communist. What better reason than that?

Lamas looked out the window, but his vision was directed inward. Only a handful of people would be involved. No organizations; just individuals. Individuals free of strong attachment to any one group, or even to the Cuban liberation movement in general. Professionals. Mainly non-Cubans. Those who would take orders without question, without discussion.

Those interminable discussions at the liberation group meetings! The endless bickering. The endless disagreements. Splinters and factions within the already highly fragmented cause.

None of that. One plan to completion and success. One will, his own. No matter what it cost him.

They turned left on Collins Avenue, street of hotels and motels, pulsing main artery of the narrow strip of sand between bay on the west and ocean on the east that was called Miami Beach. They came to the Fontainebleau, the largest, the first in the section of contemporary hostelries that made up Hotel Row, that started at 44th Street and left everything below in slow deterioration. Fontainebleau, Eden Roc, Montmartre, Doral, Bal Metropole, Hilton Plaza, and others, all the way to the Deauville and Carillon at 67th and 68th, and beyond to the Americana at 98th. Between 44th and 98th, Miami Beach glittered and surged with tourists all year long, but especially during the winter period that was The Season. A cheap type of glitter to Ivan Cesar Lamas, but then again he recognized it was the lifeblood of the entire Miami area. A vulgar surging to Ivan Cesar Lamas, but then again business was business and he had money invested in several new resorts and condominiums. A glitter and surging that he had learned to ignore, turning eyes and mind away from the *nouveaux riches* and the spurious rich when driving down Collins. But tonight he looked out at everything and muttered, "Slow," when they reached the curved whiteness of the Bal Metropole.

"Just think," he said, turning his head to keep the glittering giant in sight. "Just think of that wonderful old man, Michael Blaine Wheeler. Sick, yes, but still a power, still spoken of with respect, almost with fear. That proud old man, with one son-in-law in the White House seven years and another ready to take the Democratic nomination next year. That ambitious old man determined to continue ruling this nation as he did when President, through the politicians he chooses for his daughters' husbands." He straightened in his seat. "I would like to know more about him than is written in the newspapers and magazines. A man like that, there is always much more to know than is written —even more than is whispered." He took a leather-bound notebook and thin gold ballpoint from his breast pocket and wrote briefly. Mr. Vine of Vine Investigations would get a call in the morning.

Jorge resumed normal speed. They passed hotels and left Miami Beach proper and entered Surfside, legally a separate township but still very much a part of Miami Beach. It was Miami Beach all the way to the bridge beyond the Americana, where Motel Row with its honky-tonk air took over. Beyond that was Hollywood, dominated by the Diplomat Hotel, and beyond that Golden Beach with its section of beautiful houses, prime among them that of Ivan Lamas.

"Richard Bernard Christopher," Lamas said, as if thinking aloud, "brother-in-law of President Jonathan Everett Standers, will be honoring us with his presence. Did you know that, Jorge?"

Jorge nodded. "At the Bal Metropole. In January, I think. There's going to be a picket line."

"No," Lamas said, still musing, "there will be no picket line."

"Ramon Pedras said—"

"We will find some way to change their minds about a picket line. There will be nothing but smiling faces and applause. He will be relaxed, and his security man will be relaxed, and why not? After all, he is not yet the President. He is only a United States senator, and very well liked."

They reached the tree- and brush-lined driveway to the Golden Beach home, not on the sea because Lamas could get neither the piece of land nor the privacy he required on the sea. And not in Indian Creek Village or any of the other millionaire preserves scattered along the Gold Coast because he wanted no one to guess just how wealthy he was. At home, wealth had been a badge to be worn with honor, but as a proven anti-Batista refugee it could prove embarrassing, even dangerous, considering some of the fanatics in the liberation movements.

"What do you think would happen," Lamas asked, "if the President's brother-in-law were abducted?"

Jorge smiled. It was a joke.

"Were abducted and only Michael Wheeler and the President were to know and all the rest of the world to think he was taking a quiet holiday for reasons of health? Were abducted and Wheeler and the President were informed he would be released safely if Cuba were invaded, and killed if Cuba were not invaded?"

Jorge opened his mouth, then closed it. It had to be a joke.

"I know," Lamas said, stepping from the car, "there are details to be worked out. But Cuba is so small a country, so small a matter compared with the beloved flesh and blood of such a family's ambition. No one any longer seriously believes the Russians would go to war, atomic war, for Fidel. Not if they weren't forced to. So an invasion of Cuba by Cubans—or men not easily and immediately proved to be other than Cubans—gets a foothold, and this time the American aircraft do a little work, and the hot line is used to inform the Russians the Americans will be less touchy about some sensitive area in *their* sphere of influence. Then the great American public, seeing there's a good chance the invasion might succeed—the great American public, hungry for some sort of victory over Communism after years of choking on Vietnam, will clamor for active intervention. And the President's brother-in-law goes home. And so do you and I, Jorge." He walked toward the house.

Jorge jumped from the car and ran ahead to open the door.

"That," Ivan Cesar Lamas said, entering the chill of air-conditioning, "is *our* plan."

Jorge waited until his employer had left the entrance hall before crossing himself. *"Madre de Dios!"*

12

BOOK 1

The Season Begins

1

TUESDAY, JANUARY 3, A.M.

Bruce Golden noticed the difference as soon as he entered the lobby. First of all, he didn't get the hot-eye once as he crossed the carpeted rotunda and climbed marble steps to the desk area. Not that the place was empty of females. There were quite a few—young, old, and in-between. But they weren't the package-plan, budget-wise secretaries, schoolgirls, matrons, and widows he had met in the past eight months. Furs and jewels and good living and artful cosmetology made a rich middle ground of their ages; and while a few glanced his way, there were no obvious signals. These women were accustomed to have their men do the signaling, the chasing.

The difference extended beyond women, though Bruce tended to notice women first in most situations. A line of people checking in—all adults. No one checking out. Their luggage, on carts near the doors and elevators, didn't have a composition bargain among them. Leather and brass fittings, mainly, with stickers from some of the world's great resorts.

He slowed at the desk, nodding at Bob Lewin, assistant manager. For the first time in their acquaintanceship, Lewin didn't find time to nod in return. He was busy being charming and efficient, greeting a couple by name, making sure the others in line didn't feel as if they *were* in line. There were three men on the desk, and then a fourth appeared from behind the pigeonhole partition—Manager John McKensil. McKensil shook hands with a squat man in an exquisitely tailored blue silk suit that almost managed to hide his corpulence, and bowed at a tall, lean woman whose simple yellow dress whispered "original." The woman saw Bruce and interrupted McKensil, her voice carrying. *"That's* what this hotel's needed. A work of art."

McKensil laughed, and nodded at Bruce to indicate he should

reply. Bruce said, "I keep telling him that. Now perhaps he'll listen." McKensil introduced him to Mr. and Mrs. Melvin Fine.

"Golden," the tall woman murmured. She was about fifty, and clearly she had once been quite a dish. Now there was more strength than beauty in her long face, more humor than desire in the wry set of her lips. "You don't look it."

"My apologies. Neither do you."

The squat man said, "I married a *shiksa*, Mr. Golden. What's your excuse?"

"It's an old English name, too, you know. And my father happens to come from a long line of old Englishmen."

"Ah, so we have a Golden Goy here," the woman said, and smiled. "I'm sure you've heard that one before."

Bruce nodded, though he hadn't. At the office Lou had started everyone calling him Golden Boy, and that he liked. It suited the image he had of himself, and it was legitimate enough. He was six feet one, add a quarter of an inch. He was broad in the shoulder, lean in hip and waist. His face at twenty-five was better than it had ever been, and it had always been good enough to bring the girls in droves. He might use an occasional blond rinse when he wasn't able to get enough sun to keep his hair the right shade, but this, like the importance he attached to the right clothes, right wheels, and right pad, was serious business.

"Tell me," Marjory Fine said, "how does it feel to be a Gentile with a Jewish name?"

"Never thought of it," Bruce replied. "You tell me, *Mrs. Fine*."

They both laughed. Melvin Fine said to McKensil, "I'll be here four or five days, Marjory four or five weeks, longer if she feels like it. You'll be able to accommodate her?"

McKensil's eyes flicked to a ledger open before him. "The original reservation was for sixteen days, Mr. Fine."

"You know Marjory."

Mrs. Fine said, "Marjory doesn't know Marjory. I just decided while riding down Collins. Miami smells like fun this year."

McKensil said he was sure they could work something out. Fine said "something" had better be the eighth-floor ocean-front suite they'd had last year, or he'd switch his patronage back to the Americana.

Bruce was certain all prime rooms and suites had been reserved, with the usual cash advances, long before today. The Bal Metropole was not only one of the newest and biggest on Hotel Row, with a solid line-up of star entertainment from early January through mid-March, but this season the publicity accompanying Senator Christopher's visit and the appearances of two of the country's best-known show-biz personalities in honor of that visit had made it Miami's hottest attraction.

McKensil said, "She'll have *a* suite, that I promise."

Bruce understood then that McKensil listed the Fines among those few guests whose patronage he valued so highly that reservations would be kept open indefinitely for them, or other accommodations juggled so that they could have what they wanted. He murmured his good-byes, and Mrs. Fine said, "Stay available, Golden Goy." He said he would and walked away.

She was a sharpie, a shrewdie. That question—what did it feel like to be a Gentile with a Jewish name. She was establishing common ground there—because, of course, he *had* thought of it, hadn't been able to avoid thinking of it. Arthur Miller had once written a grim little novel in which the protagonist, mistaken for a Jew, suffered insults, beatings, near-death, and a final realization of the special agony of the American Jew. That was in the 'thirties in Pan-Germanic Long Island. It was somewhat different now, especially here in Miami Beach. Being a Gentile with a Jewish name meant being invited to seders (and learning what a seder was), having Yiddish and inside Jewish jokes thrown at you, and extricating yourself from the kindly clutches of parents who had just the right daughter for you even if you didn't *look* Jewish.

He walked toward the marble staircase, past the bank of elevators, watching the bellboys loading passengers and luggage inside, noticing the differences with which they treated, and were treated by, this moneyed breed of guest. No conversation beyond a murmured, "This way, sir," and, "Careful, madam." No response other than a glance, a cool smile, or a nod. Yet the bellboys were functioning more sharply than ever. And with good reason. Their eighty to a hundred a week in off-season tips would now begin to climb; would mount to as high as six hundred a week, with bell captains going well over a thousand.

"I could get you into one of the hotels we service," Andy had said. "As bellhop or cabana boy you'd make a hell of a lot more than the hundred twenty I'm paying." Bruce hadn't hesitated to turn it down. He said he was looking at the long-range picture. And he was, though not in the way he'd allowed his boss to think. As bellhop, cabana boy, bell captain, or even one of the hotel executives, his actions would be limited; he would be labeled a servant type among those he had to meet as an equal. The long-range picture was not one of jobs, big or little. It was one of sudden riches.

He climbed the curved stairs to the upper lobby, then turned to look down. The Bal Metropole had a lobby that more than matched the Fontainebleau's or Americana's, with "art work" to equal the Doral's. When he had first seen it, Bruce Golden, as many another newcomer to Miami Beach, hadn't known whether to laugh or cry. He had stayed, however, to grow accustomed to what Andy called the Beach's three great themes: BIG—OR-NATE—MORE.

He walked along the balustrade to huge wormwood doors fully fifteen feet high, doors that might have graced a medieval castle, complete with iron fittings and life-sized wolf's-head clapper. There was also an incongruous little plastic plaque, white on brown, reading, "No Admittance." He took a last look into the lobby. Sound rose in a rich, heady wave, different from any human sound he'd ever heard.

The season. He had waited for this. The money was arriving. New money, mainly, without heavy locks on it. Where a Golden Boy might wilt and die outside the magic circle in Palm Beach, he could flower and triumph in Miami. The money was arriving. The women with money were arriving. Somewhere among them would be his bride.

He opened the door easily—far too easily for it to be solid wood

—murmuring, "Sir Lancelot cometh"; then he saw the girl. She was sitting on the black leather couch to the left of the desk. Perhaps twenty-five, perhaps a little older, it was hard to tell with her kind of face—small and very perfect in feature—and with her close-cut boyish cap of light brown hair. But one thing was certain—she was damned attractive. She wore a touch of eye shadow and a touch of pale lipstick and a checkered minidress. The whiteness of skin showed she was new to Miami, or else a dedicated exception to the ubiquitous sun worshiper. Good chest and good legs. Good face, *marvelous* face, but not a very good expression on that face.

"Ah, Guinevere," he said, and walked smiling to the armchair opposite. McKensil often interviewed job applicants here. Bruce envied him this one. "Waiting for John McKensil?" he asked.

She nodded, gray eyes evasive. He let his own eyes drift appreciatively over her. It had no effect. He took cigarettes from his pocket and extended the pack. She shook her head. "Then what can we do to pass the time?" She laughed, briefly and not too convincingly. He said, "I had faith you were alive. You a friend of John's?" She hesitated, as if the answer required thought, and shook her head. "A relative?" Another negative shake. "His mother?" The laughter came again, even more briefly. Then there they were, sitting and looking at each other.

Something about her face, her eyes, warned him to let it go at that. He ignored the warning.

"*Parlez-vous français?*"

Nothing.

"*Sprechen Sie Deutsch?*"

A movement of the lips that might have been the beginning of laughter.

"Talk a little straight English, baby?"

She stood up. "Yes. If you want to get laid, ask the bell captain. He has contacts." She stalked out, the huge door swinging shut behind her.

He sat still a moment, then lit a cigarette and blew out smoke. "You win some, you lose some," he murmured. But he hadn't lost any in quite *this* manner before, and it left a bad taste in his mouth.

McKensil came in a few minutes later, an impressive man of fifty who must have been picked for his looks as well as his managerial ability—six-three, lean, with crisp graying hair and a thick mustache to match.

"The ad was second-rate, Bruce. Badly placed and shlaggy looking."

Bruce spread his hands. McKensil and owner Claude DeWyant had insisted on heavy copy: purple prose covering everything from the sub-level ice-skating rink to the roof garden and not a feature left out, including those found in second-rate hotels. There hadn't been *room* for any sense of style, of taste. And it would happen again and again, because most of the hotel owners had been raised in a school that demanded they get as much for their money as possible.

McKensil sat down at the desk. "Actually, the way we're booking, we don't really need ads. If we had another two hundred rooms . . ." He stopped suddenly. "Where is she?"

"If you mean a chick in a minidress and bad humor . . ."

"I mean Miss DeWyant."

"DeWyant," Bruce Golden repeated. Oh yes, you win some, you lose some, and some murder you.

McKensil was staring at him.

"She a poor relative?" Bruce asked, and even before McKensil spoke knew it wouldn't be that easy. He had heard of Claude DeWyant's daughter, the mysterious Ellie who came out for a few weeks during the season and spent the rest of her life in New York.

"She's a rich daughter," McKensil said.

Bruce Golden stood up. "Tell me where Miss DeWyant hangs her crows. I'm going to eat a dozen."

"What's that supposed to mean?"

The phone rang. McKensil picked it up. Bruce walked to a watercolor of palm trees and a dock. He wondered if he was finished with Andrew Stein Associates. In Miami, all Poppa had to do was call the boss and say, "Get rid of that bastard, my daughter doesn't like him," and it was done. If Poppa owned a hotel. And the boss's office was in the lower lobby of that hotel. And the boss depended on Poppa for a good hunk of his business.

McKensil said, "Of course, Miss DeWyant. Oh, I don't think he was aware of any such . . . Yes, good-bye."

Bruce was facing him.

"She said to apologize to you for the way she acted."

Bruce found he could breathe again.

"She also asked if there wasn't some way, some *subtle* way, I could make sure you didn't cross her path again."

"Subtlety is your middle name, John."

McKensil didn't smile. "See to it, Bruce."

Bruce showed his teeth and told himself to be thankful it had ended so quietly. They talked a while longer and he left. He had more hotels to visit, more publicity to promote, more women to case. No one chick could stop Bruce Golden. He was going to fall in love soon. Like Momma in the movies always said, "It's as easy to love a rich man, my dear daughter, as a poor man, believe me." Dear Daughter never believed her. But Bruce Golden did. So what was one Ellie DeWyant more or less?

Still, it rankled, and he drove the XKE like a novice and ground the gears badly while downshifting. A few minutes later he noticed the sweet redhead on, of all places, a bench waiting for a bus. He pulled sharply over, earning a grim look from the cabbie he cut off, and opened the door. "The only kind of bus you'll get in Miami Beach is spelled with two S's."

She dimpled. "If you're that archaic, I guess I'm safe."

He took her home, and home was an efficiency motel on Harding, which was budget land. Still, her hip reactions to his discourse on such "safe" archaisms as *Fanny Hill* and *My Secret Life* and her thanks-so-much and response to his squeeze-of-the-hand added up to an IOU payable the next night. And a boy had to think of his health as well as his career, didn't he?

2

TUESDAY, JANUARY 3, P.M.

"Something wrong, honey?" The girl was looking up at him, and Dan Berner had to answer and couldn't, not during the long seconds it took to fight back his screams. The pain had struck suddenly, excruciatingly, deep and low in his right side and back.

He shook his head, sucking in breath, and the pain subsided. *Talk about the wrong time and place!* "Little stomach ache," he said.

She still looked worried. "You got so pale so fast, I thought maybe . . ." She didn't finish. She didn't have to. He wondered how many of these girls, dealing almost exclusively with middle-aged and elderly men as they did, had customers die in the saddle.

He felt himself going soft and bent his elbows, lowering himself down over her until their bodies pressed together. He kissed her cheek and murmured, "Where was I? Oh, yes." She laughed, lifting her big buttocks as his hands slid under them. He had been delighted when she'd come to the room. He loved a big-bottomed woman. This one was in her early twenties, pretty, with fair skin and a heavy rope of blonde hair down her neck. She had a scattering of pale freckles across her nose and a baby pout to her lips and was altogether charming in a Nordic way, like a Swedish farm girl. Her breasts and buttocks, where protected by what must have been something more than a bikini, were creamy white compared to the pale tan of the rest of her. It had excited him and he had begun immediately. Now the pain was almost gone and he was with it again.

He didn't rush. He used professionals occasionally, when new to a place and its women, and he always tried to bring them to orgasm. At one time, in his innocent thirties, he hadn't thought this possible, but he had learned much since then. Whores who were part of a pimp's stable were generally immune to the rare customer who thought beyond his own pleasure. The pimp was their sweetheart, their one and only lover, and their contempt for the "John" was so deep as to make him less a man than an animated fee. But call girls who were part of a big operation, who used a switchboard and paid off to a district racketeer, were closer to normal in their relations with men, including customers. If the "John" knew what to do, he could overcome contempt and gain status as a man in their eyes.

Dan moved slowly. He kissed her mouth deeply. He murmured to her, but stayed away from any reference to her profession; he concentrated on describing her beauty in real terms, in terms she would understand and accept.

"So hard, baby . . . such hard, round tits . . . great legs . . . not long but perfect . . . and that ass, everyone must tell you about that ass."

She laughed a little, and one hand rubbed his neck. "You always talk when you do it?"

"Yes, if the girl's worth talking about. You could be a show girl. Do you dance or sing?"

She laughed again. "You're going to get me into show biz, huh?"

"That's not my field. I write ads and speeches. But I know models, singers, actresses. I know what I see when I look at you. I know what any man would see."

"Speeches? For who?"

That was what he'd been waiting for. It was necessary to establish an image. It was necessary with any woman. Women saw men, not only as they looked, but as they functioned. A famous actor had ideal status for a woman. Politicians, industrialists, men of wealth had similar status. Artists, musicians, writers had a different kind of status, not always top-grade with whores. But Dan Berner didn't play the romantic poet.

"For Senator Christopher."

Her eyes fixed on his. "No kidding? That's why you're here?"

He moved a little faster, a little stronger, and his mouth came down and his kiss was demanding. When he raised his head, she said, "What's he like?"

"A man. Like his brother-in-law. Like any other man. Who'd go crazy—" he filled his hands with her buttocks and squeezed until she winced— "over you. Baby, tighten your legs . . ."

He worked and worked, and she asked a few more questions, and he answered curtly, with an insider's lack of respect for the great political family, and all the time he was waiting for some sign that she was catching fire. She said, "I'd like to meet him," her voice a little strained. He said, "Sure . . . give him a freebee." She laughed hard then, and he stopped to laugh with her, and during the seconds of laughter it began to happen.

He worked very hard after that. He felt perspiration trickling down his sides, felt her body dampening, felt their bellies sticking with each pump. He kept watching her face, and after a while her eyelids quivered and she sighed, "You about ready, baby?" He didn't answer. They often resisted the onset of pleasure, feeling they would probably be left hanging when the customer satisfied himself, and the rules of their game didn't allow for personal requests. He pushed a finger between her buttocks and felt her move up and away from it. She giggled nervously. "No, daddy." He persisted, driving, driving, and soon she settled back down and said, "Oh God!"

He began to tremble. *She wanted him!* With that he lost control and forgot everything but his own pleasure . . . until afterward, when he went on the moment longer she needed.

She got up and said, "*Well!*" in a satisfied way and went into the bathroom. He expected her to be a while, but she came right back with a wet washcloth and a towel. She sat down at the edge of the bed and washed him, the cloth cool on sweaty skin. "You're in good shape, you know that? Most of the men here, you wouldn't believe it. The bellies and all." She lowered her head to his stomach, the spray-crisp hair tickling him. "Twenty-five more?" she murmured. "That's the lowest I can go on an afternoon gig in season."

He considered it. But even as he stroked her breast and told himself he was fine, a little tired but fine, he felt the pain—a dull throbbing that not only ended all chance of a second bout but robbed him of the pleasurable afterglow of the first.

She moved her head further down. He sat up, gently disengaging himself. "I'm not a tourist, I'm a working man. Some other time."

She said to remember to ask for Cerise and went back to the bathroom. He walked to the closet, fingered a bathrobe, then let it go. Nude except for socks, he walked to the picture window, a lean, firm-muscled man of forty-five with thinning black hair combed forward in a modified Caesar. He could see himself in the thick slab of glass, and as always he was surprised. He had been such a plain youth, such a plain man. When had he changed? His early thirties? Later?

Whenever it was, whenever he had approached a woman and made it with ease for the first time, it was then he had truly begun to live. It was then his wife had ceased to mean anything to him.

He flexed his muscles, at the same time testing for pain. He looked out at the sun and bright blue sky hanging over a sparkling Atlantic and remembered another ocean-front room, and Verna. Poor Verna. They had come to Miami Beach six years ago—a "second honeymoon," she'd insisted, and the start of her "health campaign." From then on she had smoked no more than half a pack of cigarettes a day, filters, and always the ones the *Reader's Digest* rated lowest in tars and nicotine. Within the year she learned she had cancer of the left lung; and after the horror of having it removed, the dread blotch showed up in her right lung. That was the beginning of a three-month "terminal" nightmare. Doctors, hospitals, more doctors. Begging for hope and no hope anywhere and he aiding her search for life when he knew she was already dead.

And what was it throbbing deep in his right side, spreading its pain out into his back? What was it that he had felt before, yes, definitely before, milder but still before, last week, last month, last year? What was it eating away . . . ?

Crap! He was hale and hearty, and had royally fucked a woman and nothing was wrong with a man who could screw to a fare-thee-well and make a whore come. (Comforting, rugged Anglo-Saxonisms. Full-blooded words—and words were his strength, his talismans, and would exorcise the fear.) Nothing was wrong with Dan Berner and there was no reason to think of doctors and hospitals.

But he did think of doctors and hospitals, initially to help defeat the fear, and then because the memories evoked refused to go back into that soundproof, emotion-proof closet in his mind.

He'd had a checkup three years ago because the agency insisted that its new VP's show a clean bill of health. He'd been given just that, even though he'd felt nausea all through the exam. The smell of the place, Fifth Avenue private clinic notwithstanding, had turned his stomach—the smell of a place where human beings became bodies, defective machinery on its way to the junkyard. It had let loose that carefully secured memory of Verna, drugged and dying, mumbling away in a dim hospital room. He had sworn to himself, "*Never again! Not until they carry me in!*" He had found a doctor near Grand Central who did nothing but write prescriptions for pill addicts (and seemed an addict himself), and when the agency asked for another examination the following year, he had paid the pill man fifty dollars for a written report covering a nonexistent examination. He had done the same a few months ago.

Was something growing inside him, something that would have shown up in a legitimate examination?

He turned abruptly from the window, trying to think of the speech he was going to revise for Dick Christopher. Work would end this hypochondria. Work was why he was here, though he had come a week early and would stay two weeks after the Senator had gone. He didn't have to be back at Grigson & Layle until the thirtieth, time that included the vacation he hadn't taken last summer due to the usual office crisis. Old Grigson had suggested this winter vacation himself, impressed by the President's brother-in-law ("wild-eyed leftist Democrat" though he was) trusting a third major policy speech to G & L's copy chief. Old Grigson was just about ready to change Dan Berner's vice-presidency from junior to senior. There would be more money, a better stock option deal, a bigger cut of the annual bonus pie. Not that money was a problem. He had been making better than fifty thousand for the past three years, and there had been only himself to support for the past five. But there was always that dream of becoming big enough to have his own shop. One solid account . . .

The girl emerged from the bathroom fully dressed. He went to the closet and took out his robe. "Don't do it for me," she said. "I like you better this way." He put on the robe, saying how much he had enjoyed her. She hesitated, and he put his arm around her waist and moved her to the door, thinking she was going to ask if she could come back tomorrow. Instead she said, "You take care of yourself, hear? I thought sure you'd had it, your face was that *white*."

He patted her rear. "So is this, and it's healthy." She went out laughing.

He showered and put on bathing trunks, a terry-cloth shirt, and canvas shoes. He left the room and went down the red-carpeted hall to the elevators. A couple was waiting there, the man ridiculous in grass-green shorts that fell from protuberant belly to knobby knees, exposing hairy pipestem legs. The woman was stout, but had enough sense to dress for it, wearing a loose beach dress of bright yellow with a wind cone over her high hairdo. They all murmured hello's. The elevator came, and they rode down together. The woman said, "It's lovely today, isn't it?" Dan nodded. She said, "I hope we don't have any more of those sun showers, as they call them here." The man snorted. "Sun showers! It rained like hell three straight days. And at eighty bucks a day—" The woman said, "Max!"

They stopped twice, picking up a carload of passengers, most of whom got out at the lobby. Then they rode to a lower lobby called the Arcade Level ("Guests in Swim Attire Please Use

Arcade Level for Beach-Pool Access") and stood talking near the elevators. The pool was visible through a curved glass wall on the left; a subterranean street of shops and services began on the right. The couple introduced themselves as Mr. and Mrs. Max Prager of Philadelphia. "I'm in shirts," Max Prager said. "Maybe you've heard of Maximilian Originals? That's my sports line. My dress line—" Mrs. Prager touched his arm. "Max," she sighed.

She invited Dan to join them for a snack and he said some-other-time and they parted.

He walked away, holding to the differences between himself and Max Prager, who couldn't have been five years older than he. He was in the prime of life, in the best condition. He could run between five and seven miles at a stretch, and longer distances if he pushed himself. He ate moderately and wisely; he drank lightly; he smoked not at all. How ridiculous to think that anything could be seriously wrong with him and not with a wheezing tub of lard like Max Prager! In fact, looking about as he walked to the pool, he felt it was ridiculous to think that he could be in poorer health than just about any of the males present. Then he saw the young giant lounging negligently in a canvas chair near the three diving boards, and quickly excluded him.

A really big man that, solidly heavy in arm and thigh and chest. A type of man Dan Berner had never liked to see because it made him feel less the man *he* wanted to be.

He came closer and realized that the man was wearing the fishnet T-shirt and white shorts with the M-symbol of a Metropole employee—lifeguard or pool boy or cabana boy. He felt better. The lowly position mitigated much of the man's strength. And he wasn't as young as these boys usually were. The dark hair wasn't quite as thick as it might have been; the pale gray eyes were underscored by fatigue shadows; there was a weariness, a petulance about him.

"Leech! Leech!" a girl's voice shrilled, and the big man raised his head slowly, unwillingly, from contemplation of his thick-fingered hands. The girl was poised on the center diving board, the high-dive—young, supple, bikinied, obviously frightened. "I'm going to do it! Now, Leech! Watch me!"

"Yeah," the big man muttered, and nodded. The girl dived, legs coming over too far. Leech laughed, as if relieved she'd failed, and looked around. "Olympic champ," he said to Dan.

"Not too bad," Dan replied, feeling a weakness here and exploiting it. He was rewarded by a quick flush that rose under Leech's tan. The big man rose and strode to the high-dive ladder. He climbed with simian ease—a pause, forward trot, bounce, and the board twanged as he launched into space. The dive was a clean swan, executed with precision, with skill, but not with artistry.

Leech swam to the edge of the huge pool and hauled himself out in one corded-arm movement. His handsome, lowering face swung to Dan, a little boy's bragging, daring face.

"Not too bad either," Dan said, and smiled, no longer aware of the man's size and strength. Too many things canceled it out.

Leech made laughing sounds and flicked water from his eyes, seeming to shake off anger with the gesture. "Just check in today, sir?"

Dan nodded.

"I'm Jerry Leech. If you'll give the boy at the pool office your name, I'll see to it you have a lounge every morning. It's a dollar a day, five a week." Dan said fine and turned to go. "Leech the Beach, they call me."

Dan stopped, wincing a little, smiling a little. Leech the Beach, after Murph the Surf. A man's heroes are revealing.

As if he'd read Dan's thoughts, Leech laughed and shrugged. "They laid it on me and it stuck. My friends. Not that I heist anything. Used to do some surfing at Santa Monica, in L.A. You ever get out there?"

Dan said he did, occasionally, and had seen the surfers.

Leech grinned. "Man, for a while I was a name out there. I mean, I had one of the longest rides . . ."

He went on, and Dan nodded quietly and felt that this was a

man who had to get the hell out of his job. He was too sensitive to the pecking order.

Dan interrupted with, "See you," and walked across the vast concrete deck covered with hundreds of brown wooden lounges lined up in rows. To the north and south, curving in gay pastel backdrop to pool and deck, were the cabanas. Lounges and cabanas were almost empty now, but according to the Metropole's brochure they could accommodate between six and seven hundred sun-worshipers at a time, and there were more available on the beach itself. Where the cabanas ended, a waist-high, white-bricked wall began, running in two long sections toward wide flagstone steps. Beyond that was the sea.

He walked up the beach, broke into a trot, then settled back to a walk when he suspected the beginnings of pain. A moment later he had convinced himself there had been no pain. It was just that he'd had a long, exhausting day. He had never been a good traveler, and the flight down had been unusually rough. They had run into jet turbulence and worn their seat belts all the way. A white-knuckle flight, followed by that long sex bout. So he was exhausted. Exhaustion could lead to all sorts of symptoms. He would take it easy this evening—have a light dinner and get to bed early. Tomorrow he would swim and run. Tomorrow the pain would be forgotten.

3

TUESDAY, JANUARY 3, P.M.

Max Prager came out of a cabana and strolled to the pool, eyes following the man just walking down the ramp to the Arcade Level. Jerry Leech left a group of young people and said, "Mr.

Prager, how're you doing?" Prager answered heartily that he was doing very-well-indeed, and they ambled away together. Prager murmured, "That's the speechwriter."

"Big man," Leech said. "Anyway *he* thinks so."

"You spoke to him?"

"Sure. It's my job."

"All right, but be careful *how* you speak to them—the people *we're* concerned with, I mean."

Two women came toward them, the younger bronzed and voluptuous in a print bikini, the older sagging and ridiculous in the exact same swimsuit. Leech said, "Hi," and Prager nodded. When the women were gone, Leech said, "Perfect double date for us, Max." He laughed when Prager gave him a hard look.

"You better concentrate on business," Prager said. "What do you know about the hotel owner's daughter?"

"Miss DeWyant? A dish. I'd like to—"

"Has she been down here yet? Have you spoken to her?"

"Me? I never speak to her. Neither do any of the other boys. Nothing except good-morning or can-I-get-you-a-lounge or things like that."

"She's unfriendly?"

"It's more like . . . like she doesn't see people."

"A strange person, you'd say?"

Leech shrugged. "With all the weirdies you get in the hotel business . . ."

A bikinied girl ran up behind them. "Leech honey, show us that groovy dive again, *please?*"

Prager's nod was just perceptible. Leech sighed. "Anything you say, doll." He put his arm around her waist, the hand low on her hip, and winked at Prager and moved her back toward the pool. She smiled up into his face, no more than seventeen and pretty in the unaffected sun-washed way of her generation. Leech's hand slid lower.

Max Prager felt sudden anger. Her parents shouldn't allow her to hang around . . .

He caught the thought, surprised. "Tension, tension," he muttered, and went back to the cabanas to find a card game and relax and, of course, to think about what had to be done.

4

TUESDAY, JANUARY 3, P.M.

Her father was in the kitchen of the spacious two-bedroom suite, a room hardly ever put to the use for which it was intended. He was taking a handful of cigars from the refrigerator, which held five or six boxes of the long, thin, custom-made Havanas that had become his trademark. He got them through an official of some sort of refugee agency who made regular trips to Cuba, and flatly refused to trust them to the humidor in the hotel's smoke shop. Since he was Claude DeWyant, a despot not always benevolent, no one dared suggest he might be making a mistake. Except Ellie, who didn't care enough about cigars to bother.

Ellie could have told him anything and he'd have listened. Not only was he her father, not only did he love her, she had given him his life—the Bal Metropole. He was one of seven people, besides herself, who knew where the money for a controlling interest had come from. There had been rumors about Mafia money —in Miami there were always rumors about Mafia money, from the Fontainebleau on down—but she was certain that in this case they were wrong; that only Ellie DeWyant money and bankers' money had built the Metropole.

"How are you, darling?" he asked, and came to her and kissed her neck. "Mmmm, you smell nice."

She sat down, snug inside her long bathrobe, nodding and smiling. How strange it was to remember his kissing her the same way, on the neck, always on the neck, when she had been a little girl fresh from her bath. And calling her "darling," always "dar-

32

ling," for as long as she could remember. How strange that it went on that way when so much else had changed.

"I'm wonderful, Daddy. I feel like you look."

He sat down across the table from her, immaculate in his "uniform"—dark trousers and double-breasted gray jacket with thin blue box-stripes. He had a dozen such outfits, differing only slightly in color and cut. His pencil-line mustache was still dark, while his full head of wavy hair was absolutely white. He said, "Now, darling, I'm serious. All the way from New York you've been avoiding serious conversation."

She smiled, thinking how his serious conversation had improved. He'd grown up to his position of hotel owner and Miami Beach personality. He'd done well in the past thirteen years—especially well in the past three with the Metropole. Mother would have been pleased.

But that was an unnecessary thought, and she had to avoid unnecessary thoughts. She stood up. "I'm feeling much better, honest. I'm going to get dressed and you're going to take me to dinner. Is there any chance of beef Wellington?"

"Of course." He was already moving to the wall phone. The chef in the Vale Room would have his work cut out for him tonight. Then he stopped. "I don't want you to be disturbed, but there's something you should know. We have a convention here next week—managing directors of eastern investment funds. A real coup for the Metropole—two hundred of the most influential men in the country. And they'll be addressed by various speakers." He paused. "Among them—"

"I know, Daddy. Dick Christopher. Right down the hall."

"And still you came?"

She said nothing.

"That's a good sign, a healthy sign, darling. That's a sign of strength. As you might guess, the old man is also coming."

That she hadn't known. She smiled for him and left the kitchen, walking through the large living room, with its bar, into her bedroom at the opposite end of the suite from her father's. The smile remained fixed on her lips. How strange it was, living with her father and talking with her father and he not understanding a single thing about her—as he hadn't understood a single thing about Mother. Dick Christopher bothered her, all right. She hadn't known about his coming here until an hour ago, when she'd read it in the *Miami Beach Reporter*. But even if she had known, she would still have come to Miami. She wouldn't allow Dick or Wheeler or any member of the Wheeler clan, not even Jonny, to keep her from this hotel, the closest thing to a home she'd had since Mother died.

She closed her door and went to the drapes and opened them. The view was, in her opinion, far superior to that of the coveted ocean-front rooms. She had chosen this suite—one of the Premier series renting for upwards of two hundred dollars a day in season —as their permanent home, though Father was the one who actually lived here. Her windows, as all windows in the suite, faced south, down Collins. From fourteen stories up the Atlantic was a glittering sheet of gray-blue on her left, Miami Beach and Miami a vista of green and blue and white, of vegetation and water and buildings, on her right. Beautiful "Miamah," her home town.

Ellie DeWyant was that rarity on the Beach, the native. Raised on talk of the tourist season and hotel doings and Dade County schools and Paul Bruun's highly flavored and ungrammatical columns. Grown beautiful on sunshine and water sports and her father's superb cooking—he had been a chef for the Algiers and other hotels, way back when. Grown hopeful, in the way of youth, despite a mother who hadn't left her Surfside house for almost four years before her death. Grown ripe early, ready for love early. Grown old early, ready for death early . . .

An unnecessary thought. She had to counter unnecessary thoughts. "I have everything," she said, and went back inside and lay down to rest. And had more "unnecessary thoughts."

That blond boy in McKensil's office, that irritating fool, his face was before her. She *hated* it—smug face, assured face, laughing face! (Like Jonny's? Was that why she hated it? Was that why she had struck out at him in McKensil's office? Like Jonny thirteen years ago?) And the blond hair and the glib words. And

34

the strong eyes, flickering up and down, probing at her skirt, lifting it as he would have liked to lift it . . .

She looked down at herself. Her robe was open and her hand was rubbing, touching, and even as she watched, feeling as if it were a stranger's hand at her body, the fantasy took hold.

He came across to the black leather couch and stood over her. She told him to step back, but he opened his trousers and forced her head to him and she cried out, choking . . .

She jerked her hand away and sat up. She hadn't felt this way in months, and what sort of person was she that a man she disliked should be the one to set her off? Yes, she wanted some fun, that's why she was here; but with someone she could admire, someone she could *like*. Even her fantasy had been one of violence, of ugliness and crudity . . .

She went quickly to the bathroom and washed her face and began dressing. She chose what she knew was a provocative outfit, the frothy pastel-flowered dress even shorter than her checkered minisuit, and daring in the neckline. She looked at herself and she was beautiful. Someone would come to her. Someone who would help pass the time, help pass this season in the sun, help her to remember that she had everything.

It was terribly important that she remember she had everything.

They had beef Wellington in the hotel's best dining room, the expensive supper club called the Vale Room. She concentrated on the food, enjoying it, not allowing anything else to get in the way of that enjoyment.

"Someone would like to come to our table," her father said, looking across the gay room, the perennially springtime room decorated in greens and flowers and branches.

She shook her head. "Not tonight."

"Marjory Fine. The one who gave those exciting parties last year."

Last year had been a bad year. Last year she had returned to New York after eight days.

"It would do you good to speak to her. She's a very interesting woman, full of fun and life. You'd enjoy her parties. Will you meet her?"

"Yes, but not tonight. I'm suddenly very tired. The trip and all. I'll meet her tomorrow."

"Promise?"

"Yes."

He excused himself and left the table. She didn't look after him. She beckoned Charles, the maître d', and ordered a small cream pastry and smoked until it arrived. Then she ate it slowly, sipping coffee between bites. How good the food tasted tonight! It was a joy and a refuge.

She finally looked around. At a table nearby, a man in evening clothes was appraising her. He raised his eyes from her legs and began to smile, but she turned away. He seemed nice—mature and strong and nice—but she just wasn't ready.

Another man, across the small dance floor, was also looking at her. Younger than the first man, taller and thinner, he sat with an elderly couple and tried to catch her eye. She looked down at the remains of the pastry. He too was nice. Miami Beach was full of nice men, men eligible for anything she had in mind. But not tonight.

"Miss DeWyant . . . no, please go on eating. We just wanted to say hello. I'm Max Prager and this is my wife, Ruthie. I'm in men's shirts. Maybe you heard of Maximilian Originals?"

Ellie blinked at them, too surprised to respond. The stout, parental couple nodded and smiled. The woman said, "I told him not to bother you, but Max is so, how you say it, *impulsive.* Just sees someone and wants to say hello." The man said, "How else do you tell a pretty girl she's pretty, by saying good-bye?"

Ellie murmured thank you and that she was pleased to meet them. The man said, "The reason we came over like this . . . if we didn't say hello now, we couldn't later. I mean, you and your father'll be so busy with the mob coming in next week and Senator Christopher and all. You know."

She began to say she didn't have anything to do with running the hotel, but stopped as his eyes seemed to narrow, his smile to change. She was imagining it, she knew, as she imagined so many unhappy things, but still she wanted them to go away.

He said, "Who knows, maybe even the President will come." He leaned forward; his voice dropped. "I myself didn't vote for him, but what an honor, right? If he came? That handsome young President of ours? I'll bet if he saw *you*, he'd be here tomorrow!"

The woman said, "Max!" and he chuckled and said, "Well, maybe not, with that First Lady of ours. But for *my* taste . . ."

She was beginning to shake. His eyes were hard and cut into her like knives. His smile was a mask and she was afraid of what lay behind it. His words; his weighted, sneering words . . .

Suddenly they were gone, the woman saying motherly things about eating and getting rid of "that paleness" and joining them sometime for a long talk, the man just walking away. Gone, and her father was there. "Did those people *bother* you?" he asked, staring at her.

She made a smile for him. A *chaindle*, Mother used to call that putting-on of little-girl cuteness, in her rarely used Yiddish. A *chaindle*, the word dropping sweetly from the soft mouth, the sad mouth, the mouth that poisoned itself first with whiskey and later with barbiturates.

"What is it, Ellie, darling? What happened? What did they say to you? I'll throw them out!"

She said they had been a sweet, friendly couple and she was just tired and nothing was wrong, nothing at all. He asked a few more questions, and she answered cheerfully, determined not to allow her imaginings to spoil this evening. Now that the Pragers were gone she was sure they were exactly what she'd told her father they were—a friendly couple, gregarious people who didn't understand the finer points of social behavior or a desire for privacy—but harmless, certainly. And what the man had said— foolish chitchat.

Her father said he had spoken to the Fines and Marjory was giving a farewell party on Saturday for her husband, who was re-turning to New York. He had promised that Ellie would be there. "Now how about catching the show at the Platinum Room?

We'll meet Endora Gray—you've heard her records—and a very funny comic—"

"No, I don't think so."

He was worried. She could see that. "Then the midnight show," he pleaded. "It'll be fun."

She said all right and that she'd rest until then. She left, smiling back at him to prove that everything was all right. At the door, Charles and the two captains bowed and murmured their good-nights and she went out into the lobby. It was surging with people. They wore furs, gowns, jewels, tuxedoes. They smelled of every great scent, male and female. Their sound was a boiling of words and laughter. They had money and energy and were in Miami Beach, and they were determined to make the most of it.

She fled. She took the elevator to the fourteenth floor and went to her room and her bed. She would rest, and then she would go back down and become part of the surging throng. She would find a man, *tonight*. A man to help her move and live and laugh with the others. A man to help her forget that the world was a ravaging jungle where a mother could die of alcoholism and anguish and where a girl could be stripped of love and purpose at eighteen. And with that she was lost to Miami and the soft night and beautiful sky outside her window. With that she was slipping down the black spiral shaft of her own special reality. Yes, she would find a man—a man to help her forget that the world was a place where busy Nazi ovens had consumed eleven close members of her family and where the books her mother collected gave clear evidence of man's bestial nature, from Genghis Khan and his pyramid of skulls to Auschwitz and its cordwood piles of bodies to Vietnam and napalmed villagers to American cities and blacks killing whites and whites killing blacks to the Bible and exhortations from God himself to spare not the pagan babes in their cribs. A place where each morning's newspaper, each evening's television, brought fresh horrors, whether in China or Africa or Newark, New Jersey. Where men died in the thousands by intent, and in the tens of thousands by accident. Where the good died young, the bad died young, and no one was sure which was which. Where people called upon Christ and saints and angels in Heaven to help them murder other people and age devoured those lives miraculously left untouched by the general carnage. Where drugs were often more necessary than bread because people—perfectly sane, successful people with everything the world could provide— couldn't sleep, couldn't get through the day without two martinis at lunch and three at dinner and a little red pill at night, and when they finally realized *why* they had to have this they ceased being sane and saw the ravaging jungle that was their New Frontier or Great Society or Standers' Reunion of Peoples. Where the only *truly* sane approach was to withdraw into psychosis, and reason demanded you discard reason and curl into fetal position and sleep, sleep . . .

She was on the bed, curled on her side, hands over her face, when her father came in, saying, "Ellie, it's time, darling. Ellie . . ." He put on the light, and she managed to say, "Tired . . . ate too much . . . tomorrow . . ." He wasn't fooled. He came to the bed and stood looking down at her. "Why?" he whispered. "Just a few hours ago . . . why, darling?"

How could she explain? It was so complicated if you didn't feel it, if you didn't live with it.

He asked about her pills and she pointed at the lamp table. He opened the drawer and got water from the bathroom. She took the pill and grew less anguished. Later, when he had gone, she sat up, a little foggy but able to use the phone, to call New York and Dr. Iglesias at his home. He spoke to her a few minutes. He said, "Now we decided this was silly, didn't we, Ellie? We decided it was just *one* approach, and a very destructive one, when there are a dozen others, just as valid, just as descriptive of reality. We decided to stop such unnecessary thoughts, to remember that you have everything a girl could want." He went on a while, and it made her feel better in the same way the pill had, dulling the truth.

But she wished he could know *everything*. She wasn't allowed to tell him everything. That would be breaking the Agreement. That would mean the end of the money. And perhaps the end of her life.

She thanked the doctor, and he said he would see her in April. "Not before then, understand, Ellie? You're to enjoy Miami. Then we'll get together in April and I have a feeling I'll lose a very good customer." He chuckled, and they said good-bye.

Well, maybe he was right.

She undressed and fell asleep, and dreamed of the blond boy in McKensil's office. This time when he approached her she told him her age—not the lie she told most men, that she was twenty-four, but the truth, that she was thirty-one and had been married when she was eighteen. He was opening his trousers and stopped and looked at her and said, "Hell, who needs an old bag like you?" He went away. At first she was glad, but then she saw herself in a mirror and she was old and her mouth was poisoned with whiskey and drugs and she wept for him to come back because he moved her, and he was the *only* one who moved her. . . .

5

TUESDAY, JANUARY 3, P.M.

"Yeah, Lou, it's fine." Which, while not exactly an accolade, was about all anyone, including Lois Degano, ever got from Andy on an ad for a fur shop or bank or any of Andrew Stein Associates' non-hotel accounts. He reserved his *wowowees* for promotions like Bruce's underwater Treasure-Chess game in the Metropole's glass-walled pool and his own wild prank of having a sandwich-sign man walk up and down Collins Avenue advertising Benny Barker's opening in the Fontainebleau's La Ronde, the sign man being Barker himself. The obese comic had turned down a similar idea this year for his Metropole appearance, saying he'd thought of something much better: "Have Wally Jones shine my shoes on Collins. Not only will it be a gas, it'll be *realistic*." So they hated each other. So she still refused to laugh at racist jokes.

"Your enthusiasm overwhelms," she said, rising from the red armchair in the all-red office—red carpet, red walls, red ceiling. It flipped the clients, and it wasn't bad aesthetically. Especially that slender red-leather desk, behind which the slender man in his blue suit sat frowning at nothing. Andy Stein looked remarkably young for fifty-one, this despite a beautiful head of scalp. "It's the clean life you live," she'd once told him. "Your dedication to the simple verities of our town—put on, put down, and put away." He'd been able to put away enough to open this new office on the Arcade Level of the Bal Metropole, which pleased Claude DeWyant and gave Andy a unique business address. He was making out in a business where, despite publicity to the contrary, few people really made out. In addition, he was a doll, a sweet man to work for, and she wondered what she would do if he ever tried to make out with *her*. Sooner or later, every man she knew did try.

He looked up then, and she smiled and turned away. He said, "You must be getting older, chicken. That skirt of yours is barely five inches above the knee. What happened to the *real* minis?"

"I figured they were bothering you, taking your mind off your work."

"Well, I'm willing to sweat a bit for the good of all mankind, if you're willing to risk a most unusual cold."

She said, "You'd be surprised what I'm willing to risk," and he leaned back and said, "What a lousy time to remember I'm married," and she said, "You'll forget again. All men do." And he smiled and murmured, "I suppose so." She left, feeling—strange. It was the closest they'd come to sex talk in the two years she'd been his creative girl Friday, handling media and doing a little copy and, recently, a little art. Such as the ad she held in her hand—a quiet little bit for Bronsor's Fur Salon, with a mink draped over a luncheonette stool, the counter in the background, and the caption reading, "No Longer a Luxury." Nothing to worry Doyle Dane Bernbach, but it would make Mr. Bronsor happy.

She walked down the hall, a tall girl with long legs, generous hips, and chest to match. A big girl with a big face, honest and open and handsome. A young girl who wore daring skirts and dresses to the office because it was her kick, and because she had always worn daring things, done daring things.

Lou Degano had had it all, tried it all, the Hollywood bit and the Greenwich Village bit, starting at seventeen by leaving her New York home for Los Angeles, returning at nineteen a veteran of the tea party, the acid hop (all good trips), the casting director's couch, and the Central Casting blues. In New York, but not at her parents' Queens home, she'd move in and out of the Village hippie movement, still reaching to taste things, try things— painting and writing, La Mama's and the Private John (a fully integrated love-in club where, as she put it, they called a spade a spade and made love to him), peace marches and civil rights marches, and all the time reading, thinking, trying to find her bag, trying to place herself in this big, juicy, exciting but sometimes frightening world. She'd ended up confused, too confused to stay in New York, and a quick vacation to bourgeois Miami Beach— "The Boor Pit," "Water-*Crass* Gardens," "Borshtville in the Palms"—had unexpected results.

She found she loved the climate—far more so than Southern California's. She found a lack of pressure, perhaps because the young people weren't with it, weren't moving with the times, but then neither was she at this point. She found she couldn't get back on the jet when the vacation was over and the money almost gone, so she took a job as a waitress and used it as a base to find a job with some style.

She stayed away from Coconut Grove and the few local hippies and artist-types. She roomed with a square, stolid chick named, naturally, Mary, until Mary surprised her by getting pregnant (don't you know about the Pill, you nit!) and rushing home to Kansas for help. Now she was set in a converted guest cottage on what had been an estate off Pine Tree Drive. Now she was over the Hobbits and Holden Caulfield and Kesey and Bob Dylan and entering the land of the real people. What more could she ask for?

As she reached the opening to her frosted-glass cubicle, Bruce Golden entered the hallway from the reception room. She stopped and said, *"That's* what more." He said, "What private reverie have I entered now?" It was amazing, the way he read her. She began to lose some of her cool, and tried to retain it. "Reverie Number ought ought and ought. A nothing scene." He leaned against the wall, took out cigarettes, and lit one. His eyes went to her legs. Most men's eyes went to her legs. He said, "Why don't we go into your office and you'll sit down and cross your legs and I'll *drool?*" She said, "Because, sir, I'm far too young." He changed his grip on his cigarette, holding it now like the villainous German in a late-show movie. "Und vat *iss* your age, Liebchen?" She kicked at the ground, hung her head, and lisped, "Twenty-three, mister, but I used to be much older." He laughed. She forgot about retaining her cool. His laugh did things to her. She wanted to trace his lips with her finger, feed him shirred eggs, pour him libations of beer, tell him who she really was. He said, quickly, "You have any objections to dating a co-worker?"

"None." At last at last at last at last—and to hell with knowing he was not for her and hung up somehow.

"Tonight then? Seven-thirty? Your place?"

"Sure."

"I'll bring some Scotch."

"Bring a few joints instead."

His smile was uncertain.

"My only vice," she said.

"Let's hope not." He thought a moment. "I'll have to see a man. Might be a little late."

"Better late than no tea party."

He glanced up and down the hallway, then stepped close and leaned into her. "I'm glad we had this little talk, Miss Degano. I think our firms can do business." His hand worked her rear in a very expert feel.

She said, "Mmmm, yessss," and watched him walk to his own cubicle, directly across from Andy's office. She was very excited, and a little sad. The sad part angered her. What did she expect, marriage in the church around the corner? A cute little home with two cars in the garage and sly sex with the neighbors on weekends? Ugh!

It was eight-thirty before he arrived. She showed him around the large studio room and he nodded and said nice things about her furnishings and then they sat down on the sleeper couch. He took out a crumpled pack of L&M's, put them in her lap, and kissed her long and hard. "Want to light up now or after?"

Just like that, the bastard. And she knew it was deliberate—his way of being honest. She pushed away anger, hurt, all the stupid feelings, and said, "Now, baby, so it'll be *nice*." He didn't like that, and she smiled and asked if he was hungry. He nodded. She got up and went to the kitchen. She filled two large plates with *boeuf Bourguignon* and two glasses with dark Heineken's and put it all on a tray with a basket of French bread and a stick of butter and some silverware. She served it on the coffee table in front of the couch, and when he tasted the stew he looked up and grunted, his eyes wide in admiration.

And that was the nicest thing that happened to her that night, even though they turned on with a joint each and opened the bed and got into it and he was as beautiful as could be and she moaned, "Out of sight—oh, out of sight, baby!" and came twice before he was through, which wasn't something she could re- member ever doing before. But there was that sadness in her, that feeling of being less to him than he was to her. He had been sure of his make and dug into her as he'd dug into the *boeuf Bourguignon* and enjoyed her in much the same way. Which was what she wanted, wasn't it? She didn't play the bashful- virgin game, never had, always insisted on the equality of wanting, and loving. But—it was something less than it should have been.

But but but but but! She rolled over to him and took him in her hand and said, "Get 'em up."

He sighed. "Patience is a virtue, and a necessity in these matters."

"And a pain in the ass."

"Tough guy, huh?"

"Shit, yeah."

He laughed, and she kissed him on his laugh and put her whole goddam self into the kiss and didn't say the cursed word, *love*, but it was pressing at her tongue and she shoved that tongue into his mouth and ground against him. He stiffened in her hand, groaning, but pushed her away and held her away, looking at her. She said, "Like what you see?" He nodded, but thoughtfully. She said, "Then take it." He said, "Easy, Lou," and she flushed as if that were the foulest thing ever said to her, as she had when a boy had whispered "Fuck" into her ear at the tender age of twelve. She put down her head, making like laughter, but her chest ached with shame and fury and tears. He read her! He knew, damn him, he knew! She didn't know what to do. She wanted to jump out of bed and leave him with his erection, to hurt him back. But she needed him too much for that and waited until his arms came and drew her close again. It was better this time, because he felt pity.

When she returned after washing, he was stretched out blissfully in the middle of the bed, eyes closed. He said, "I can use your razor, but do you have an extra toothbrush?" She said, "Sorry, no, you can't stay the night." His eyes flew open. "Why not?" She busied herself putting on a bathrobe and hunting under the bed for slippers. "I'm frigid," she muttered, and stamped out to the kitchen for more beer.

He was dressing as she brought in the tray. They drank and she lit up a second joint. He shook his head when she extended the pack with the lone remaining stick. She inhaled deeply, feeling the lightness rise in her. She began to relax. She loved a good joint—so superior to martinis or other liquid poison. And your kidneys didn't wince and your liver rot. "Where do you come from?" she asked. "I mean, I know home is Westchester County, but what was it like?"

45

"What's Westchester like? Like all the movies about West-chester." He said some other cute things and then he was quiet—glum and quiet. She held out the joint again, and this time he took it. They smoked, and he said, "It was fine for a while. The first fifteen years were a ball."

"And then?"

"And then the great American tragedy—a car accident."

"Your parents?"

"And my brother."

"How bad?"

"Dead, all of them."

"Terrible," she murmured.

"But ordinary. Everyday."

He was right. She had known two girls in L.A. who had lost family in car accidents, and a successful studio composer who had been widowed four days after returning from an Acapulco honeymoon. And the more she thought of it, the more people she recalled who'd had accidents, or had family and friends who'd had accidents. "Fucking cars," she said. "They'll wipe us out."

He smiled faintly. "I dig cars." He smoked, dragging deep, slouching beside her on the couch-bed, which was once again made up for sitting. "I had my first car in college."

"Most kids have them in high school."

"I was out of high school at sixteen and into Brown at seventeen. And you?"

"I was out of high school at seventeen and into life at eighteen."

He nodded, but she felt some sort of criticism implied.

"You think that was a mistake?" she asked.

"It depends upon your circumstances."

"My circumstances were average." She tossed the ball back to his court. "I gather yours were better than that."

"While my parents lived, yes. My father had a small piece of a stock brokerage firm, and a fat salary. After he died, the piece was bought out for cash—all legal and as stipulated in the partner-ship, but a bad deal for the survivors, namely me. There was also the house in Tarrytown and some life insurance. But his will named my mother and hers named him, and before the probate buzzards were through there wasn't a hell of a lot left."

They smoked a while in silence. He took her hand and rubbed the back with his thumb. She said, "Golden Baby," looking into his face, the pot loosening her grip on herself, the love bit coming through. He touched her hair with his lips. It was just what she wanted, and she melted against him, head down, breathing in the sweetness of him mixed with the sweetness of pot.

He said, "Two-thirds of what was left went in the next six, seven years—two years living in Manhattan with my aunt and uncle, my father's sister and not well off, and then four years in college."

He was back to the hang-up, money. She straightened and flicked ash off the joint. "And I'd guess the rest went for that mile-long Jag and that ocean-view pad and those groovy clothes and all those broads."

He smiled. "The broads are free, haven't you heard?"

She answered the smile, but she was bugged, oppressed by something. "You have a thing for money, haven't you?"

He nodded slowly, spoke slowly. "Yes, I have a thing for money. Hasn't everyone?"

"No."

"Oh, you don't want it? You work for Andy for the fun of it?"

"I work for Andy for my living, and for the fun of it."

"All right, for your living. And if you had more money than you needed for your living, then I suppose you'd go right on working for Andy for the fun of it?"

"Maybe. I don't eat, sleep, and dream money. I live day by day, for people and talk and joints and food and the fun of it."

"And with superior insight, based on knowing me a few months and this one night, you've decided I'm different."

"Yes."

They were looking at each other, and she felt he didn't like her very much at this moment. Then he laughed and said, "How come you're not one of the flower people?"

"Who says I'm not? I just don't wear flowers. Lots of us work in offices and don't wear flowers, or ponchos, yet we see the stupidity of our age, the—"

"Spare me the lecture on conformity and war and the big put-on of modern life." He was still laughing, and she seethed inside for having been backed into a corner like that. Because she *wasn't* one of the flower people, didn't dig the empty-headedness and acid parties. Didn't dig withdrawal from society, not any more. Preferred Montoya and Menuhin to The Grateful Dead. Preferred all sorts of real things to the shoddiness of Hashbury. All of which she wanted to tell him, but he ground out the butt and said, "I'll leave the roach for you. With that philosophy of yours, you'll certainly need all the leftovers you can get."

"You expect maybe a *touché?*"

"No, just a cup of coffee." Which was de-escalation, armistice, *kamerade.* She went to the kitchen and plugged in the percolator. She let it brew strong and dark, smoking the joint until it singed her lips, then using crossed toothpicks to smoke it to a quarter-inch roach. And still she felt down, way down.

She brought him a cup and asked, "Cream, sugar, acid?"

"Nothing." He drank it straight and stood up.

"Yes, I know. A lovely evening, and thanks for the gash."

He sighed. "You come on a little too strong as the emancipated woman."

"Really? I thought I played it for laughs."

"Good night. Great dinner. Great everything."

She nodded, curled on the couch.

He went to the door, hesitated, said, "Hey, it really *was* something. See you tomorrow, right?"

"Right."

Still he hesitated. She smiled for him. "You don't have to have a tender exit line. Everything's great."

He went out, being careful to close the door softly. She lay down with her face in the cushions and wanted to cry. But it had been so long, she had forgotten how.

6

TUESDAY, JANUARY 3, P.M.
TO
WEDNESDAY, JANUARY 4

Bruce went into the S-turn without slowing, the good scream of Michelin tires splitting the air. Lou Degano was far from ESP when reading his ambitions. She didn't know him at all, despite the patter about money hang-ups. She thought he rated money first, money second, money last, but she was way off. He rated *living* first, second, and last, and was determined to begin the process before youth was gone.

The girl he landed, the rich chick he managed to love and make love him, would have the best life any chick had in all this world. No cheat. No shortchange. No racket in which every other broad was fair game. But a real thing, a deep bit, a lifetime affair in which they grew together, using all their lovely hours of freedom to build a tremendous friendship. He was a fortune hunter, but ready to give his life to the woman who gave him her fortune—a romantic searching for one great love, with the stipulation that she be wealthy enough to buy them both out of the rat race.

Lou couldn't know this, and he suspected she wouldn't understand it even if she did know it.

He used Abbott to avoid Collins, entering the main artery when the two streets joined near the Americana. He crossed the bridge, slowed by the increase in traffic, a large percentage of it rental Caddys and Continentals. The hotels and motels were booming. Which made him think of his major account, the Bal Metropole, and that in turn brought back the unpleasant bit in McKensil's office.

The edge had worn off his anger and discomfort; he could think of Ellie DeWyant with a degree of objectivity again.

Pretty woman. Too bad he hadn't known who she was—though, then again, he might not have played it much differently. Definitely a prospect. Her father was good for at least half the worth of the Metropole, and the Metropole had cost almost thirty million to build and had increased three to five million in value since then. Ellie was Claude DeWyant's only child. More important, it was said that she drew a private income, a legally defined income, from the Metropole. Andy Stein guessed (and his "guesses" were usually facts) at forty thousand a year, not counting her use of the hotel itself.

He took another sharp turn, testing himself for effects of the pot. His high was fast disappearing, was about at a one-martini level now. Still, he slowed, not liking the way opposing headlights danced in his eyes. He had no intention of ending as his parents and brother had.

He reached Hollywood, and drove just over the line to the new hi-rise apartment house on the shore. He parked in the basement garage, nodding at the night security man, and took the elevator to the third floor and his one-bedroom flat. The tariff was steep, close to four hundred a month on a three-year lease, with a painful six-months rental as security—which was where the last of his inheritance was going. But it was a necessity. He had to have the right place to bring his prospects. They had to see him as an equal, as least in the initial stages before love took over.

And this place, he was assured as he turned on the foyer lights, was right. The furnishings were far from the usual bachelor-pad thing; he'd been insistent upon a degree of originality when briefing the sprightly little faggot decorator Andy had recommended. And Marco Renier had done a marvelous job.

The living room was lean couch, lean armchairs, and lean lamp, and a contrasting coffee table of pink marble that ran almost the length of the couch. The bedroom was teakwood, almost black, with everything massive and oversized. There were drapes—heavy, northern-clime drapes that could cut off the blazing sun and glittering sea that lay just outside the windows without impairing the effectiveness of central air-conditioning—and paintings, two originals of the Hudson River school that were part of his inheritance, and several others picked up at Coconut Grove art shows. The kitchen was large and held a square, glass-topped table of wrought iron and four wrought-iron chairs with space to spare. He enjoyed eating there, when no Lou Degano was available to provide *boeuf Bourguignon.*

He carried a glass of milk and a handful of cookies to the prim little telephone table in the foyer and sat down on the prim little chair. He called his answering service, another luxury-necessity that was bringing him closer to stony-broke each day. The girl said, "Marjory Fine at nine P.M. Return her call any time before two A.M." She gave the Metropole's number.

Ah yes, the shrewdie. The sharp-eyed, sharp-tongued matron with the big-businessman spouse. He wondered what her particular turn-on might be.

He finished the last swallow of milk, dialed, and asked for Mrs. Fine's suite. She answered, and after the amenities said, "I got the number from John McKensil. You don't mind, do you?"

"Not at all." She hadn't seemed the type who hunted young stud, but he threw out a test line anyway. Voice just a *little* playful, he asked, "Now what can I do for you?"

The answer came straight over the plate—no curves. "I'm having a farewell party for Mel Saturday at five-thirty. I'd like you to come."

He said he'd be delighted to, and that was it. He still wasn't sure about Marjory Fine, but he hoped she was just a friendly lady.

Was *anyone* just a friendly lady, or gentleman? Whatever he'd learned about the inner workings of *genus Humanus* stacked the odds against it. If she wasn't, it could prove embarrassing. In a sense he was an employee of the Metropole. He had to walk softly where guests were concerned, especially important guests. But he couldn't see himself servicing aging ladies. That was cabana-boy stuff. That was Jerry Leech's speed.

He checked in early the next morning, leaving his car with the park boys, and walked away from the lobby, around the side to the ramp that led directly to the Arcade Level. He went past the big shop with "Arnoud Clothier" on the window and nodded at Arnold Klein, who was "Arnoud," and past Kitty's Specialty Corner (her specialty was charging three and four times what a ceramic ashtray was worth). Across from Kitty's were two sections of plate-glass window with a door in the center. The windows were covered by interior drapes of deep gray and had "andrew stein associates" stenciled on one and "publicity and advertising" on the other. He opened the door, red with a brass mail slot, and stepped into a narrow reception room that ran the length of the windows. Jackie wasn't at her desk yet, but he heard the new Royal in Andy's office.

Lou wasn't in. Manny wasn't in. Patricia (not-so-lovingly called "The Mick") wasn't in. If he'd been serious about this job, he'd have made noises outside Andy's closed door to show that he was here at eight-forty and pin-a-rose-on-me-sir. He slipped into his cubicle and sat down and hummed a little and checked his schedule.

When Andy went to the john, Bruce went into the all-red office. When Andy returned, Bruce threw a few ideas at him, most made up right on the spot, and got pats on the back and a promise of a raise "just as soon as we land the new restaurant account." Bruce made happy sounds because he was expected to, and returned to his desk. He began setting up his day's appointments, phoning the list of hotels and businesses on his schedule.

Half an hour later he leaned back in his chair and shrugged. Only two of nine scheduled appointments would be kept. He had most of the day to himself.

He phoned Gail Yolles, the redhead he'd picked up at the bus stop, and she was *sooo* pleased to hear from him. He said, "I was just thinking, why wait until dinner?"

"Why indeed?"

"We'll lunch at the biggest fish house in the Miami area."

"Marvey-do! I love fish! What about afterward? I mean, how do I dress?"

"Casual. Very casual. Slacks or shorts, if you like."

"For the biggest fish house in Miami?"

He grinned and said yes.

He went to Lou's cubicle. She was at her file cabinets, tilted back against the wall in a chair, reading a long media listing, her miniskirt really *mini* and covering almost nothing. He said, "Like wow." She smiled a little without looking up, murmuring, "Like busy."

He came into the reception room and said, "Jackie, sweet Jackie, when are you going to give me a smile?"

The statuesque blonde with the vacant-looking face tucked her legs under the desk, protecting them from his view. "Good morning, Mr. Golden."

Jackie didn't approve of him. And, in truth, he didn't approve of Jackie. Her favorite topic of conversation was last night's television. Which was an example and a warning. He mustn't make the mistake of thinking he could get along with *anyone*. Jackie could have had ten million and it wouldn't work.

He strolled the length of the Arcade Level, glancing into Vance Cooper's window ("Your Portrait in Eternal Oils") where the thin artist was doing still another delicately aging woman. He took the elevator to the main lobby. McKensil had left word he wanted to talk a fall publicity campaign and brochure.

The desk was even busier than it had been yesterday, but the rest of the lobby was almost empty. Late sleepers, this in-season crowd. He saw McKensil beside Bob Lewin, caught his eye, and went up the marble stairs.

He didn't enter the office right away. McKensil would be a while. He looked down at the lobby, shook his head, and wondered at a man with Marco Renier's taste and reputation putting together anything like this. But of course, Marco had been under orders; Marco had known that the job called for BIG—ORNATE—MORE.

The Metropole was head-of-the-class in all three. A circular lobby of two hundred eighty feet diameter, carpeted in bright blue, walled by alternating sections of marble and glass, the glass looking out at gardens (color-spotlighted at night) and lily ponds as well as at Collins Avenue and Indian Creek. Dead center, and enclosed in a glass funnel that went up to the ceiling of the upper lobby, was a waterfall dropping onto a lush tropic garden inhabited by colorful birds. Louis Quinze chairs and sofas stood comfortably enough with Italian Renaissance tables and lamps. Along the marble sections of wall was a polymorphic display of statuary, and between the statues a series of palette-knife paintings of the Metropole's attractions—its three night-clubs, three dining rooms, rooftop ballroom, two outdoor bars, and lush snackery.

It should have been a jumble. It almost was, at certain times—because the Bal Metropole looked different at different times of the day. Bruce had seen it at its worst, untidy, jumbled, bare of the leavening element of guests, at four A.M. with the cleaning crew moving through under the night manager's weary eye. He had seen it at its best, swinging at eleven of a Saturday night when visitors from cheaper hotels and busloads from the package tours joined the guests in milling about and then moving off to the various bars and clubs. He had seen it crisp and efficient of a bright morning—but never crisper than it was now, with McKensil marshaling everyone for a best-foot-forward effort; never more the "Dream Hotel of Your Dream Vacation" as promised in the last ad.

Two women at the desk caught his eye. The younger one wasn't much over thirty, quietly blonde, with a rather wan look. The coat, clothes, jewelry, and luggage, however, were far from wan. The older woman, stout and efficient, seemed more a servant than a companion. She saw to everything, except the actual signing in, at which point the younger one took over.

Then came a thin, plain girl in nurse's cap and uniform, pushing a man in one of those folding aluminum wheelchairs. Bruce wouldn't have watched them any further, except for the effect they had on the desk. Lewin and McKensil both rushed to serve, McKensil coming around front and practically bowing as he spoke to the wreck in the wheelchair.

Bruce opened the door to McKensil's office; and for the second time in two days was unprepared for anyone being there. Another girl. Another knockout. But very young—perhaps seventeen—and, he was sure, Cuban or South American. She was dressed in what, compared to Lou's mini, was a modest skirt with matching jacket. Her hair was shiny black and fell straight to her neck. Her face was round and brown, appetizing as a fresh-baked pastry. Her figure was very mature, just short of lush.

"I'm thinking of setting up housekeeping in this office," he said, moving to the armchair since once again the dish was on the couch.

She smiled, as if she understood him. With only the faintest trace of accent, she proved she did. "Mr. McKensil must see many women here."

"And a few lovely girls."

"You don't think I am a woman?"

"Cut out my tongue if I ever said that. I meant, at sixteen or seventeen—"

"Eighteen, almost nineteen."

"What this climate does for a girl. By forty you might look old enough to drink."

She shrugged. "Drink?"

"I agree. There are more exciting things to do when you're an adult."

Her eyes flickered. "I'm still too young to understand *that*."

He laughed. She had a fine thrust, a nice parry. He asked her business here.

"I'm a secretary. I was told Mr. McKensil could use a secretary."

Bruce said McKensil had a secretary. The girl looked around, as if to say, "Where?" Bruce explained that this was McKensil's hideout, his place to be alone, his on-the-run office, and that the executive offices were on the main floor, along a corridor behind the dining room. The girl nodded. "I was told he *would* need a secretary. Maybe the other girl is leaving? Or maybe he's hiring an assistant for her?" Bruce said maybe, and that he was rooting for her to get the job. She asked what *he* was doing here, and he explained, and they exchanged introductions. Her name was Violetta Murillo. "I'm thinking of changing it to Violet Murray." Bruce said he would hate to see that happen. "Violet Murray is just another girl. But Violetta Murillo is romance, mystery . . ."

"Rice and beans in the Cuban section." There was little humor in the way she said it.

"I guess everyone has his problems."

"No problem," she said. "But no romance or mystery either."

They smoked and he looked at her and she looked straight ahead. The message was clear if not loud. *Nothing doing.* He wondered if he changed into a pumpkin or something when he entered this room.

McKensil came up and spoke briefly to the girl and turned to Bruce, lowering his voice. "Did you see who just checked in? President Wheeler. But it's off the record. No guards, no entourage, just a nurse." He glanced at the girl as Bruce commented that the old man wasn't recognizable without his ten-gallon hat and looked far gone. "Don't be fooled," McKensil said. "He's a fighter, a mover of men and events. He won't be finished until he stops breathing." He glanced quickly at the girl and said, "About that brochure and promotion. Let's wait until an ad is formulated, then integrate the two." Bruce didn't say "but" and "you specifically told Andy," or anything else. The girl was looking at McKensil and McKensil obviously liked the *way* she was looking at him, and if Bruce didn't know John was happily married and too aware of his position here to be susceptible to pitches he could have sworn the manager wanted to be alone with this *chica.* So he left, saying "tsk-tsk" to himself but not really believing John would fall for the pitch and give her a job.

He went down to the lobby and toward the doors. And was face to face with Ellie DeWyant. Startled, he said, "Oh . . . I . . ." She walked right on by.

Bruce went outside where he smoked and paced, waiting for

the boys to bring his car; then he drove off, grinding the gears again.

The bitch! The evil little cold-hearted bitch! What the hell was burning her ass?

He told himself to forget her; the Jag couldn't take much more. He made his two calls, picked up Gail Yolles, drove across the Julia Tuttle and out along U.S. 1 to the Rickenbacker Causeway and the Seaquarium.

He laughed as she bit into her cheeseburger, looked through the glass wall of the main tank, and said, "The biggest fish house in Miami. Very clever." She enjoyed the cheeseburger and chocolate malt. She enjoyed the monorail ride and then walking to everything they'd seen from the air. She enjoyed the tanks and arenas, the shows with seals and porpoises and whales. The one thing she didn't enjoy was watching fins cut through the murky waters of the 750-foot snaking Shark Channel where, to quote the brochure, "scores of vicious predators splash and slash for food and survival." The food today was large hunks of sea bass lowered into the canal by rope. The gray shadows surged; the rope jerked and went limp. Gail shuddered and pressed against him. "If anyone were to fall in!" she whispered. "Could we see something else, Bruce?" He said of course and put his arm around her waist.

They moved through the crowds and the sunshine, their bodies touching. The friction was delicate, but he made sure it was insistent. At a picnic table during a rare moment of privacy he took her chin in his hand and kissed her. "I just can't wait for dinner," he said. She smiled. "After two cheeseburgers and a giant malt?" He kissed her again. "I'm not talking about food." She surprised him. She dropped her eyes and murmured, "We can go now, if you'd like." He waited until she looked up again, and their eyes met, and he said, "Yes, let's go."

Bingo!

7

WEDNESDAY, JANUARY 4, P.M.

The child was hungry. That was why he had driven her to a Royal Castle at the end of Motel Row. The *only* reason, John McKensil told himself, ordering two superburgers and two malts at the take-out counter, ignoring the frankly curious stare of several customers and the boy waiting on him. The Royal Castle didn't get many people dressed as he was. And that was why he was here. He wasn't likely to meet anyone he knew.

Still, he was nervous. He checked the price list on the wall, took out the exact amount, bill and change, and glanced through the window at his black Continental. The girl was waiting there. The pretty Cuban girl with the naïve eyes and unspoiled body.

All right, he could appreciate a lovely child. But he wasn't looking for trouble. Certainly not!

He repeated, "Certainly not," to himself several times, thinking of Los Angeles and his fourteen-year-old niece and the fine position at the Sunset Arms he'd lost when they forced him to leave the state. "Leave California," Derreck had raged, after Millie begged him not to call the police. "Leave California, *tonight!*" Not that it had hurt him in the long run. Millie had handled the sale of the house, and he had found a job as assistant manager of a residential hotel in New York and soon after was running one of the Catskills' better resorts and soon after that was brought to Miami and the Metropole. Onward and upward, and so he should be grateful to Derreck and Anita. . . .

He saw his niece as she'd been that night, her sweater up and the budding breasts and her skirt up and the still-sparse thatch of brown hair and her struggles, both authentic and specious, and her voice, both frightened and desirous, and his own voice, full of anguished hunger because she was clean, she was untouched, she was unspoiled, and all women, adult women, no matter how young, were already turning toward rot, toward putrefaction. He had stopped at that last moment, despite the liquor and the passion, to give her the chance to break away and save them both. He had stopped, and she had whimpered, "Uncle John, please don't, *don't*," and not moved and looked at him with luminous, burning eyes and the moment had passed as both had wanted it to pass, the child and her uncle, and he had taken her in her own bed and it had been the one sexual satisfaction of his life, truly the one and only despite Millie and his two children and the girls before Millie and the occasional woman after Millie. All a sham except for Anita. All a sham except for his child-bitch, his infant-whore, who had lain beside him afterward and laughed and explained why there was no blood. At fourteen she had already had three men, or boys. It hadn't spoiled things. He had wanted her the more. Because spoilage didn't come from other men, it came from *years*. A child was beautiful and innocent no matter what happened to her. An adult was rotten and dying no matter what *didn't* happen to her.

His order was handed to him in a white paper sack. He paid and turned to the door, his eyes already fixed on the child in the Lincoln Continental. Older than Anita, but not by much—not by as much as she claimed. She was no more eighteen than he was. His eyes, and more importantly his instincts, assured him of that.

He walked outside and opened the door and got in. He handed her the sack and said, "We'll drive and eat," because that was safer yet, though there was no reason for his being so cautious. He could buy a prospective employee a lunch, couldn't he? He certainly wasn't going to do anything else. He had learned his lesson once and for all with Anita!

The sweater up and the dress up and the low moans and the burning eyes and the feel of the body pulsing under his, the child's body, the unspoiled body, when all else was corruption . . .

He backed away from the parking curb, then swung forward into Ocean Boulevard, the northern extension of Collins Avenue.

She took two hamburgers from the sack, folded back the wax paper on one, and handed it to him. He nodded, smiling at her, and began to eat. She also began to eat, and crossed her legs. The flash of thigh struck into the corner of his eye and brought his head around. She wasn't being careful of her skirt. It wasn't *very* short, but like all skirts nowadays it required cautious handling.

The skirt up and the olive skin revealed and the black thatch and the desirous struggles and the moans—"Mr. McKensil, *please don't*"—*and then their bodies* . . .

He returned his eyes to the road, feeling perspiration on his upper lip. He wiped it away when he took his next bite of hamburger. This lunch was a mistake. He had work waiting at the hotel. And he had far too much to lose now to even *dream* of risking it with a girl like this!

She sighed and said, "That was good," and opened one of the containers of malt. He glanced at her as she drank, tilting back her head, her neck smooth and round, the throat rippling. She took a deep breath and turned to him, her upper lip wet, her breasts pushing out. She had full breasts, the equal of most adults.

"Now tell me the truth, Violetta, how old *are* you?" She began to answer and he quickly added, "I'm thinking of hiring you. I know you have to say you're eighteen, but if you tell me the truth I promise not to allow age to be of any consideration."

She murmured, "But I *am* eighteen," and looked away and it was a plain admission that she wasn't. He finished his hamburger and asked for a napkin. Instead, she used one to wipe his extended fingers, then leaned over and delicately dabbed his lips and mustache. He thanked her, and said, "About your age?"

She dropped her eyes. He put out his hand, covering her hand where it rested on her knee. "My dear child, if you're as nice as you appear, and can of course handle the work, you have nothing to worry about. I've long been dissatisfied with my present secretary." Which was true, in a way. He couldn't stand looking at Miss Bayleth any longer, that corrupt, aging mass of fat and skin blemishes!

She still didn't answer. He tightened his grip on her hand, and felt his fingertips touch the flesh of her knee. She wore no stockings. He moved his hand a little, as if involuntarily, while talking. "Now come on, Violetta. I thought we'd decided to be friends, not just employer—prospective employer—and employee. You *have* to answer me." And on that "have" his hand jerked a little, went above the knee a little, the pinkie brushing under her skirt.

She whispered, "Fifteen, Mr. McKensil," then turned, leaning toward him intensely. "Remember, you promised!" The abrupt shift and movement brought his hand over her hand much further up her leg than it should ever—in normalcy and innocence—have been. And immediately afterward she jerked *her* hand away, to gesture as she said, "But I have papers to prove I am eighteen and I will never admit I am fifteen, so please, Mr. McKensil, you must keep your word. I need a job very badly!" She said more, and he tried to listen and understand, but his right hand now rested high on her bare left thigh, and in her excitement she didn't notice and kept gesturing and shifting about on the seat, and his hand moved over the firm flesh, touching the crevice between the thighs. When she shifted yet again, sliding forward as she talked, his pinkie touched, just barely touched, the heated bulge of cloth.

She stopped then, looking down, face almost comic in its expression of shock. "Mr. McKensil," she whispered, and sat absolutely still. He had to take his hand away. He knew that, and muttered something in apology, and was relieved when she nodded. But he didn't take his hand away. All his life he had hungered for but one thing, the thrill that lay behind that heated bulge of cloth, that had come to him with Anita and was waiting here with Violetta. He drove, and his right hand twitched —just a spasm, an involuntary, minuscule spasm—and the pinkie pressed the bulge.

"Mr. McKensil," she said, voice so low he could barely hear it.

"Now don't tell me a beautiful girl . . . boys must be after you all the time . . . almost old enough to . . ." He laughed and drove faster, passion clouding his mind, his judgment, his fear.

She took his hand with both of hers, but gently, and lifted it and put it on the seat. She lowered her skirt and dropped her head and sat there. He kept glancing at her, charmed, charmed, aching and yearning and charmed! How sweet! How fresh and pure and sweet! Full of desire and innocence and shame and passion. All the drives of budding womanhood, all the doubts of childhood. How unbearably charming!

"You are not angry at me, are you, Mr. McKensil?"

He angry at *her!* He took her hand and squeezed it. "Of course not. You could be angry at me."

"Oh no," she whispered, eyes still down. "A man like you . . ." She shook her head, and withdrew her hand. They drove on a while, and he saw a clock on a gas station wall. He had to get back to the Metropole. He was in Golden Beach, and swung into a quick U-turn. He asked for his malt, and she held out the container. He tapped the lid. She said, "Oh, how stupid of me!" and opened it. She held it to his lips, tilting it to just the correct angle. He said he'd had enough. She replaced the lid and put all the trash into the paper sack and put the sack on the floor.

"You're very neat," he said. "You'll be an asset to the Metropole."

At first she didn't understand. Then she looked at him, and her mouth opened. He smiled, and she said, "I'm hired?"

"You can start tomorrow. You'll assist my regular secretary." Until he was sure Violetta could handle the job, and then he would dump Miss Bayleth. It would be a pleasure having Violetta around. He wouldn't allow himself to be alone with her again, but it would be a distinct pleasure to see her each day.

She touched his arm, smiling—a truly radiant smile that lit up her child's face, a toys-at-Christmastime smile that made her even more beautiful than she was.

He wondered how she would smile if he gave her that lovely pendant emerald he'd been looking at the other day on Lincoln Road. He wondered if she would come to him, kiss him . . .

No gifts! No being alone with her! No taking chances with his position at the Metropole! And while Millie had accepted his story of being too drunk to know what he'd been doing with her brother's daughter, and nine years had gone by since then, and there hadn't been a single solitary incident in all that time, she would certainly leave him if anything even remotely like it ever happened again. Not too great a loss in terms of passion and affection, perhaps, but real enough in terms of comfort and position. And she would take his children.

He could, in effect, lose *everything* by forgetting himself with this child.

Of course, she seemed far from the hysterical personality that had been the fourteen-year-old Anita. His niece had been caught nude in a park with a high school senior, and in an attempt to escape punishment had blamed her status as a fallen woman on her uncle's evil influence. Lord knew how many men had made love to children younger than Anita without being found out. It had only been the worst of luck. . . .

He glanced at Violetta. Her radiant smile remained. He drove, basking in it, his determination not to think of her except as a secretary weakening. She leaned forward to look at something, leaned back, and in the process her dress slid up. Shortly afterward she crossed her legs. Again he saw her thighs. Again she smiled that radiant smile.

Charming! Utterly, unbearably charming!

WEDNESDAY, JANUARY 4, P.M.

Eve Andrews had been much too busy after checking into the Metropole to react fully to her surroundings. In fact, she had been much too busy the past six days to react fully to being nurse-companion to Michael Wheeler. Imagine, the ex-President!

President Standers' father-in-law! Senator Christopher's father-in-law!

She still couldn't believe it had happened. She had left Bannesville the day of her father's death (that man who had *appointed* himself her father) and fled the insular Pennsylvania town for Philadelphia. She knew a few people—girls from her nursing class who had gravitated to the big city—but hadn't contacted anyone. She had spent one full week sleeping and eating and sleeping and going to movies and sleeping. She had concentrated on eliminating the exhaustion, near-total exhaustion brought about by nursing her father eighteen and twenty hours a day from the morning he entered Bannesville General Hospital with what looked like another example of his hypochondria to the night he died of cancer.

She had also concentrated on wiping out, although unsuccessfully, the memory of things he had said to her the last two weeks of his life. Then she had registered with an agency and been sent to the palatial residence of Michael Wheeler. And been hired!

This morning had been the most exciting of her life. There was the flight, her very first, and the pilot had come to their seat to say hello. Then the cab ride to the Bal Metropole, the sun shining and water all around and people tan and laughing, while in Philadelphia there had been five inches of snow on the ground! And finally this suite.

She hadn't had time to really look around. First there'd been Mr. Wheeler's therapy—hot bath and massage and a brief walk, shuffling slowly around the living room, supporting him with her strong right arm. Then his medication, a light massage of his neck muscles, and into bed. He had been exhausted by the trip, a dangerous exertion for a man in his condition. He had barely spoken since they left Philadelphia, and the paralysis in his right side, the result of a stroke, seemed more pronounced. After he had fallen asleep, she'd gone about the business of turning the one-bedroom suite into a nursing home.

Mr. Wheeler's daughter—the one called Piggy, married to an

engineer and, like the unmarried one of the four Wheeler girls, Kitty, uninvolved in politics—had wanted him taken to a nursing home in Fort Lauderdale, which she had chosen after careful investigation. But the old man had refused.

The daughter had enlisted Eve's aid. "Dr. Cormond insisted you get away from the cold weather. Ask Eve if that isn't so."

The doctor *had* said a change to a warmer climate was often useful in treating CVA's with hemiparesis, and so Eve had nodded. But Michael Wheeler hadn't been called Master Mike for nothing. Voice still retaining elements of his Oklahoma upbringing—where an even dozen oil wells had begun his father's fortune—he had said he would go to Florida. "But not to . . . damn dying home! And not . . . Palm Beach! Want to . . . see Dick . . . and Bunny. Bal Metropole. Want to . . . see *life!*"

Mrs. Claver, the daughter, had said Bunny, the youngest Wheeler girl, wasn't accompanying her husband from Washington to Miami. The old man had shrugged. "Don't . . . blame her!" However, he had made up his mind to be there. Mrs. Claver had then suggested a male assistant for Eve. The old man had refused with a spastic shake of the head and a glare from his one good eye, just as he had refused, absolutely, to allow his Secret Service agent to remain after the stroke. ("Who'd want . . . to kill . . . dead man?")

Eve had said she could handle the situation; she was strong (not adding that you *had* to be strong to survive thirteen years in the St. Theresa Home for Foundlings). The daughter had finally capitulated, anxious to have the old man on his way. "Well, if you're willing . . ." she'd murmured to Eve.

Eve had been more than willing; she'd been delighted at the opportunity to escape Pennsylvania and memories of Bannesville General. She had also been delighted to partake of luxury and wealth. But, she insisted to herself, these were merely side issues. As a nurse she was trained to concentrate on the patient in her care. Mr. Wheeler's health was the prime consideration. (It was! She wouldn't let what had happened with Father—with Mr. Andrews—change anything!)

She had phoned the desk to arrange for delivery of foodstuffs for Mr. Wheeler's special diet, begun unpacking the four suitcases, received the foodstuffs from a bellboy, stocked the refrigerator and pantry, finished unpacking, changed the position of Mr. Wheeler's head on the pillow for unobstructed breathing —and only then had taken time for a cup of coffee.

Now she rose from the kitchen table and walked out into the living room. It was all in pale blue and had a sleeper couch that she would use. She went down the foyer to the hall door, examined the large entry closet, and opposite it discovered another door. It wouldn't open, though she operated the turn-bolt, and she realized it was locked on the other side. That meant it led to another room, or suite, which could be added to this one.

Senator Christopher's suite?

She returned to the living room and stepped onto a narrow patio-porch, then put her hands to her face—a long, plain, generally somber face now suffused with delight. She was fourteen stories up, suspended, so it seemed, out over the ocean. The sky was an intense blue, the sun an intense gold, the air at once soft with sun and tart with sea. She lowered her hands, braced herself on the rail, and leaned out as far as she dared. "Lord God Almighty," she sighed.

As if in answer, Mr. Wheeler called her name, voice choking.

For an instant she didn't move. For an instant she heard her father calling over and over for her, his nurse, his adopted slave . . .

Mr. Wheeler cried out inarticulately, a sound of terror. She whirled and ran inside.

He had turned on his stomach again, his mouth pressing the pillow, and was gasping for breath. She rolled him onto his back and smoothed his wispy gray hair. "It's all right. You can't smother yourself. You have far too much control for that."

The blue eyes—one still bright and incisive—looked at her, losing the dark of fear. She used a washcloth to wipe sweat from his forehead. He licked his lips, the tongue slow, uncertain. He had told her it felt as if he'd received an injection of Novocain at the dentist's—thick, numb, barely manageable—and that the entire right side of his body felt that way.

He had been President of the United States for eight full years (though he had left the White House eleven years ago and that was all before Eve's time and she thought of him as "Mr." and not "President" Wheeler). He had gone back to managing the financial empire he, and his father before him, had built. He had come to Philadelphia, leaving behind oil and ranches, to be close to steel mills and stock exchanges, and to the dozens of businesses he controlled. Eve had seen pictures of him taken before, during, and after his term as President—thickset and handsome, with a touch of the brutal about his wide, large-featured face. It was hard to believe this was the same man.

"Please . . . be here . . . when I need . . . you," he whispered, fighting for clarity of speech.

She nodded. "You'll eat, and then we'll go down to the beach." She pushed him to the kitchen and served him and helped him to feed himself. She had a sandwich and talked about how he was going to regain the use of his right side, and after a while he smiled in that lopsided way and reached out and touched her hand. She stopped eating. He said, "Good . . . girl." She smiled, though what she wanted to do was pull away. The man who had called himself her father had done the same thing, said the same thing—at the *beginning* of the four long months of illness.

It was almost three when they went up the hall to the elevators. She had dressed him in white duck trousers and a blue-striped, short-sleeved shirt. (He had lots of good clothing, vacation clothing, though most of it was large on him now.) He refused his western-style Stetson, feeling people would recognize him because of it, but insisted on having his heavy black cane slanted into the side of the chair.

She was wearing a yellow two-piece bathing suit under a short yellow beach robe, both items purchased just for this trip, but she was glad no one else was in the hall. She was a lean, flat-bodied girl of twenty with an awareness of her plainness, her lack of sexual projection, sure of herself only with the sick or old. When a young intern had thought to use her as an easy thing, a quick toss in the hay to relieve the tedium of long hours and short pay, she had recognized the insult and rejected him and her own hunger. *Pride,* she'd told herself. *A girl has to have pride.* It had been her one and only chance at a man.

The elevator came and she pushed Mr. Wheeler inside. They went down, stopping several times, and the elevator filled with people. They looked at Mr. Wheeler and at her. She stayed cool and professional, secure in her role as Angel of Mercy. Besides, no one seemed to recognize the ex-President.

They reached the lower level and she let the others out first and followed with Mr. Wheeler. They went up a ramp to a door, held open by a tall young man. She said, "Thank you," in her professional voice, and he nodded and looked at Mr. Wheeler and seemed about to say something, to ask a question, but she kept going, right past him into the sunshine. There was an enormous pool and an enormous sun deck and the sound of the ocean beyond. Mr. Wheeler said, "Ah . . . the air."

They went along the side of the pool and paused to watch people swimming, diving, and sunbathing. It wasn't at all crowded, but she guessed there were two or three hundred people around, most lying on adjustable wooden lounges made comfortable by blue mats. There was a blend of sounds—voices, laughter, transistor-radio music, splashing, occasional shouts—that would have been a roar indoors, but here was only a steady hum. There were many, many good-looking women—and some good-looking men. It was a bright, happy, colorful scene.

The sun was hot. She wanted to take off her robe, and when she realized she was afraid to she stopped and slipped it off and hung it on the push-bar of the chair. For a moment she felt absolutely naked, then she glanced around at all the bikinis and was reassured.

She wheeled on, relaxing and beginning to enjoy herself. She looked at everyone, at everything. Off to the left, amid the lounges, her attention was caught by a big, handsome man standing with a middle-aged couple. She had never seen any of them, but the middle-aged man, short and dumpy and ridiculous in swim trunks and gaily flowered shirt, smiled and nodded at her. He said something to the handsome man and the handsome man smiled at her and came forward. They must have recognized Mr. Wheeler.

As the handsome man approached, a woman called to him from a lounge, a woman Eve guessed to be close to forty but still like something out of the movies, blonde and with a long, ripe figure that was almost nude in a skimpy white bikini. "Oh, Leech, could you please—" He said, "In a minute." Then Eve had to stop because he was standing right in front of the chair. He nodded at Mr. Wheeler. "I'm Jerry Leech. You need help, here, in your suite—" his eyes lifted to Eve— "any place, any time, just call on me." He smiled, not a nice smile, perhaps even a little frightening, but it made her breathe more quickly. She decided he was not a gentleman, and murmured, "Thank you. If you'll let me by . . ."

He didn't move. His smile stayed on her. "You're welcome. It's my job, sort of." His eyes flickered a little, moving over her, and she wondered what it could mean, with that blonde waiting and all those other women, those rich and desirable women, waiting.

Mr. Wheeler said, "Go . . . on."

Jerry Leech stepped aside. Voice low, he said, "Hope you enjoy yourself, Mr. President. We'll see no one bothers you." So he *did* know. She began pushing. Leech said, "You, too . . ." He walked with her and she had to give him her name. He said, "Be seeing you, Eve. Don't forget. Anything that needs muscle—" that ungentlemanly smile again— "yell for Jerry Leech." He waved and was gone.

She felt the heat in her face, and it wasn't the sun, and she was annoyed with herself because there was no reason to be blushing. He wasn't interested in her, no matter how he smiled. It was Mr. Wheeler. It was her rich, famous employer.

At the end of the pool she turned toward the ocean. Mr.

Wheeler said something. She came around front. "What was that?"

"How'd he . . . know me?"

She wondered if he was beginning to show signs of paranoia. Sick people often did. "*Millions* of people know you," she said, smiling.

"No . . . not now. Own wife . . . wouldn't know . . . me if . . . she came back . . . from dead!"

"Then the management informed certain employees, in order to serve you."

"Management . . . instructed . . . to keep . . . quiet. Otherwise . . . I'll need . . . damned agent."

"Would you want me to ask Mr. Leech? I'm sure he'll be glad to explain how he knew."

He hesitated, then sighed. "No. Just habit . . . of checking . . . everything. When I . . . ran country . . . companies . . . Jonny's campaign . . ." He made a never-mind gesture with his left hand. "Useless . . . habit . . . now."

She said he would find use for all his good habits again, soon. He didn't answer, but his eyes probed hers for belief. She went quickly around the back of the chair. She, along with his doctor, had little hope that he would be able to lead anything like a normal life again. If he could learn to walk with twin canes or a wheel-pen, it would be a major triumph.

They went to the steps leading to the sea, and stopped. Mr. Wheeler said, "Want to . . . walk . . . sand." She began to say it was much too soon, the day had been far too exerting, but he said, "Please . . . try," and the hunger in his voice ended her argument. She stood looking at the beach, wondering how best to get him there.

That question was answered when Jerry Leech appeared beside her. "You want to go down? I think I'd better carry him." He reached for Mr. Wheeler, who made a sound of protest. Leech said, "I'm no beginner at this sort of thing. I've worked around hotels eight years now. You can trust me."

Mr. Wheeler said, "Yes . . . but want . . . *walk*."

70

Leech looked at Eve. She nodded. "Between the two of us."

That's how it was done, Mr. Wheeler dragging his feet from step to step, Leech's powerful right arm around his waist, Eve holding her patient's arm on the other side. And as they progressed—a step and pause and step and pause—she became aware of Leech's knuckles pressing her bare side, of his breath laboring close by, of his thickly muscled legs and massive chest under the fishnet T-shirt. She exerted herself only slightly, but by the time they reached the sand she was breathing as heavily as he was. Leech said, "All right, Mr. President?" Mr. Wheeler said, "Yes . . . thanks . . . but don't . . . call me . . . that. Mister . . . *Wheeler*." Leech said he understood. "I'll keep an eye peeled for when you want to come up again," he said, and left, nodding at Eve's thank-you. A moment later she was moving slowly toward the sea, right arm around Mr. Wheeler's waist, left arm held across her body as a rigid support for both his hands. They paused frequently, as much for her sake as for his, but he was making better progress than she had expected.

"Sorry . . . wearing . . . shoes," he panted, looking at the sea.

She said that tomorrow he would walk barefoot in the sand, and wade in the water. His hands tightened on her arm. "Yes! Feel . . . better! Feel . . . a chance!" She looked at him. He was moving his head, following a motorboat as it raced along some two hundred feet from shore. "My . . . boat," he said. "*Bigger*."

She was startled. For a moment his face had seemed different— more like those photographs in his home.

Jerry Leech was waiting when they returned to the steps. The trip up was quite difficult, but Leech did most of the work. Halfway there, he paused to shift his grip, and his hand touched her thigh. She made believe she didn't notice, but hadn't he glanced at her at that very moment and hadn't his smile flickered briefly?

Her patient safe in his chair, she said, "Good-bye, Mr. Leech. Mr. Wheeler will take care of you at the proper time." Leech said, "Right," and she began moving past him. And then, close beside her and so softly she couldn't be sure she'd heard him correctly, "Will *you*?" He was gone before she could react.

They weren't in the suite five minutes when the phone rang. She had made it clear Mr. Wheeler was not to receive calls from anyone but his family. All others must leave their names, their numbers, and their business with the switchboard. Mr. Wheeler would decide whether to return any of them.

She said, "Yes?"

The hotel operator's voice sounded strangely excited. "The White House calling."

Eve said, "Yes, wait, I'll . . ." She turned to Mr. Wheeler, who lay on the bed with his trousers open. She'd been about to undress him. "The White House," she said.

He held out his left hand and she gave him the phone. It slipped from his hand. He said, "Must . . . hold it . . . for me." She sat down on the bed and held the handset to his ear and mouth.

"Hello," he said, and listened, and said, "Yes," once or twice. She was leaning close. The voice at the other end was the President's; there was no mistaking that high, vibrant tenor. Nor was there any way of avoiding what he was saying. He was telling his father-in-law to take care of himself, not to exert himself, not to push too hard for recovery. Mr. Wheeler said, "Why . . . not? What can . . . happen? I'll . . . get sick?" He laughed a little, and the President said there was something else, the real reason for his call. The Secret Service, in talks with Dade County Police, felt there was some danger of violence being done the ex-President. "If putting out the torch of friendship last month is a barometer of local Cuban feeling . . ."

"They . . . kill me . . . they waste . . . good . . . bullets."

The President ignored that. "I intend to reassign you your agent."

"No! Don't want . . . flatfoot . . . hanging around . . . in my . . . way." His gaze flicked to Eve. "I . . . forbid it!"

The President said that was the wrong attitude, as was pushing too hard for recovery. "Recognition of *facts*, Father, was always one of your strong points. Now you're ignoring—"

Mr. Wheeler's face got pink, and he interrupted with, "I'll

push . . . harder'n . . . hell! Don't want . . . to live . . . this way!"

The President's voice rose, and he reminded Mr. Wheeler of his obligations to the family and the country. Mr. Wheeler's good eye glared. "Obli . . . gations . . . my ass! Man has . . . one . . . obligation. To . . . *himself!*" The President said that wasn't what his father-in-law had told him thirteen years ago, and that it only confirmed his opinion that it had been a mistake not to go to a regular nursing home. Mr. Wheeler tried to say something. The President said it was obvious Mr. Wheeler wasn't in "the proper frame of mind for constructive conversation" and that he was glad Dick and his bodyguard would soon be at the Metropole to see what was going on. Mr. Wheeler put his lips up against the mouthpiece and said, "Go play . . . with your . . . country!" then turned his head away.

"Mr. Wheeler!" Eve whispered, frightened.

"Hang . . . *up!*" he said, and now it was his voice that shocked her. She hadn't realized he could sound so violent.

She wanted to say something; at least good-bye. It didn't seem right to hang up on the President of the United States. But Mr. Wheeler jerked his left hand, and she hung up. "Talk to . . . me like . . . I was . . . child! Made him . . . President! Gave him . . . delegates . . . issues . . . everything! My mind . . . still better . . . than his!"

She undressed him. His shirt was damp, his undershorts, too. She decided to give him a sponge bath.

Always before when she had bathed him, he'd closed his eyes. Several times he had dozed. Today, as she moved the sponge down over his hairy chest to his stomach, she was aware of his gaze. She looked up and smiled. "Does it feel good?" He nodded slightly, and she returned to the bath. She worked the warm sponge around and under his genitals. He made a sound. She looked up again, inquiringly, but now his eyes were closed. As she continued, he said, "When young . . . nurse once . . . hit it . . . with finger," and he laughed. She said nothing. Eight or nine months ago she had bathed a teen-age boy in traction. He had retained an erection despite her striking his penis three times in the accepted fashion. The poor kid had pressed his face into the pillow and said, "I'm *sorry!*" But even though she'd assured him it was all quite normal, he couldn't have been more embarrassed than she. No matter what she'd been taught, a stiff penis was something she just could *not* treat as casually as, to quote Head Nurse Valence, "a stiff joint."

She finished and turned to get his pajamas. "Wish," he said, "you had . . . to hit it . . . now." There was no laughter from him this time. He sounded bitter, and tired. A moment after his pajamas were on, he was asleep.

She made coffee and sat down with a cup in front of the television. Sound, faint but audible, reached her from somewhere— outside or another suite or down the hall. Laughter. Men and women laughing together. And music.

She switched on the set and found a game program. She loved a good game program. But after a while her head turned to the windows, to the sunlight and the sea, and her thoughts turned to Jerry Leech.

9

WEDNESDAY, JANUARY 4, P.M.

Eunice bustled around, unpacking and making enthusiastic comments, and for this May Krasmer was grateful. It filled the void into which her fears might otherwise rush. But the servant's very presence posed problems, as May had known it would. Still, it had been her decision and hers alone to bring her along.

A complex matter. As was the whole trip. As was her whole life.

Yet simple, too. Seven years without a man was simple, wasn't it? Seven years since your husband had last made love to you was simplicity itself. And called for a simple solution—another man.

But that was where simplicity ended. Harold was good. Harold was lost without her. Harold had threatened suicide and had actually attempted it the one time she'd packed to leave. Equally important, she had no one else, no one who meant a thing to her. Not in Chicago.

There was someone in Miami Beach; someone right here in the Bal Metropole.

Her heart began to pound, and she wanted to call him right now and couldn't because of Eunice and was glad she couldn't because what if he didn't remember her? It had been sixteen years since they'd last met. She'd heard about him every so often through old friends, had heard about his triumphs in advertising, his wife's death, his connection with Senator Christopher. And a month ago, when she'd heard he would be coming here, she'd made her plans.

Sixteen years, and he had no old friends to tell him about her and she'd been in Chicago all that time and would he even recognize her?

She showered, and her stomach grumbled because she had been too tense to eat since last night. She came out, and Eunice was in the kitchen. "What's the use of a kitchen, Mrs. Krasmer, if we're on that American plan and eating three meals a day downstairs?"

May thought quickly. She said it would be nice to have coffee when they wanted it, and orange juice and biscuits, too, in case they decided to sleep late and skip breakfast. "And cream and sugar for the coffee. And jam for the biscuits. And a loaf of bread for toast."

Eunice said yes, it *would* be nice. May said, "Why don't you go down and find out where there's a supermarket? Take a cab. Get a few crackers and chips and things for TV snacks. And a bottle of Scotch. Do a little shopping."

Eunice said, "Now?"

May knew she was looking forward to getting into a bathing suit and trying the pool. She had talked of nothing but swimming and sunning all the way down. But she nodded firmly. "I think it would be a good idea."

As soon as the hall door closed, she ran to the phone and asked for Mr. Berner's room. The phone at the other end rang and rang. The operator said, "He doesn't seem to be in." May's hands were damp with perspiration. She took a deep, steadying breath. "I'll leave a message. Tell him Mrs. May Krasmer . . . I'm sorry, make that May Jacobs. May Jacobs would like him to return her call." She read her extension number off the phone.

Then she slumped into a chair. She'd done it. She'd started the thing. Now it was only a matter of time, of hours or a day, before they would speak.

It was much less than that; the phone rang two or three minutes later. "May?"

She wasn't sure. "Danny?"

He paused. "No one's called me Danny in years. Sounds strange." He laughed a little. "Well, how are you?"

"Oh, I have my problems . . ." She stopped short. All the hurt, all the anguish, had rushed to her tongue. Sixteen years, and in the first minute she'd been ready to tell him everything! "It's so nice to hear your voice. You sound just the way you did back in New York."

"I'm still in New York."

"Yes, I know. I mean when we were both in New York." (So stiff, so stiff. Their conversation was creaking, and they used to *babble* to each other for hours.) "And how are *you*, Danny? Or would you rather I called you Dan?"

"No, it wouldn't sound right from you, May. I'm all right."

She waited for him to ask when they could see each other. He asked, "How long are you staying?"

"I've got reservations for a month. I might even stay longer."

"Husband with you?"

That was why he hadn't asked to see her! "No, just a servant."

"Ah. Sounds like success, May. Your husband's doing well, I gather."

There she didn't have to hold back. "He does reasonably well in his business. I do better in mine. I have a chain of costume jewelry shops."

"A chain? Sounds impressive." (Now he would ask to see her.) "It was wonderful talking to you, May. We'll have to get together soon."

She was stunned. He was going to say good-bye. He wasn't going to ask to see her.

She heard herself say, "Yes, real soon. Say in half an hour, for cocktails?"

"I . . . sure, but make it an hour. Do you know the bars in this hotel?"

"No. Name one."

"The Orbit. That's at the rooftop ballroom. Two o'clock."

They said good-bye and she went to the bedroom. She had to dress now. She had to get ready to meet the man she had once loved. But she was afraid. He hadn't wanted to see her. She'd had to force his hand.

She wore a youthful sheath in pale blue with a deep-cut neckline. She looked through her jewelry and decided on the small diamond earrings. Eunice came in as she was touching her neck with scent. May explained that a business acquaintance had phoned and asked her to cocktails. "After you put away those groceries, why don't you try the pool? I won't be back before five . . ."

She hoped it would be much later than that.

She was standing at the glass wall that ran the length of the bar, looking out at Biscayne Bay and the city of Miami, when he came up beside her. She glanced at him, then back at the view. She felt his eyes on her and wanted to look at him, to see if he was as attractive as he'd seemed in that one glance, and said, "This is a really incredible view." Her voice was steady, which both surprised and gratified her. "I have a suite on the fourteenth floor, facing the ocean, but I think I've been cheated."

"I think I've been cheated too," he murmured, and now she looked at him and he was examining her. "You're a beautiful woman, May."

She smiled. "Don't sound so surprised."

He took her hand and turned to beckon a waiter, and she was able to look at him. He had changed. All for the better, it seemed. Of course, that open hunger, that boyish vulnerability, was missing, and she had once been stricken by it, hooked by it. And his hair was thinner, though the way he combed it, all forward, suited him better than his full head of back-combed hair had.

They followed the waiter to a little glass-topped table at the end of the long window-wall. She couldn't help it; she squeezed his hand. He looked at her, smiling, but now she noticed lines under his eyes, a touch of something grim around the corners of his mouth.

Seated, she asked, "Working hard?"

He nodded. They ordered—he a sweet vermouth (he had never drunk much), she a Scotch and water.

"Tell me about that chain of stores," he said.

She took out cigarettes, and he picked matches off the table and struck one. She leaned forward, feeling the wicked vamp as she did, because she knew how much she was showing. Blowing smoke, she said, "It started with one costume jewelry store in a shopping center near our Chicago Heights home. That was seven years ago. It grew, roughly, by a store a year. I now own seven. End of success story."

Their drinks came. He raised his glass. "To the facts behind that success story." She smiled. Oh yes, the facts behind that success story. She drank, and felt the liquor warming her empty stomach. She began to relax, to unwind. She asked him to tell her about his wife, about his job, about Senator Christopher. She had another drink, and he talked, and she leaned forward for a light, and his eyes went to her breasts and then to her face. She met his gaze. She held it. He blew out the match. "About your husband?"

She was high now. She was almost drunk on just two drinks.

Not eating and tension and seeing him and knowing she wanted him—oh yes, she wanted him—all this made her drunk. She ordered a third Scotch.

"Harold is a very fine man," she said, and smoked a while. He knew something was coming, and he waited. Her drink was served. She took her first sip and looked into the glass. "He just can't make love."

He said nothing. She took another sip, and raised her eyes. He was staring at her, his expression positively grim. "Don't let it bother you," she said, smiling. "It's nothing new. Happens to many men, for either mental or physical reasons. Seems Harold's reason is mental. He's even tried other women, with my blessing."

He still didn't speak.

"I'll tell you something else, something you might not believe. I've never had another man."

"I believe it," he said, and the way he said it made her laugh.

"You're remembering me the way I was."

He nodded. "There was no shaking your conviction that sex didn't exist outside of marriage."

"It's shaken now." She put back her head and drained the glass. She asked for another drink. He hesitated. She said, the words thickening, "I know, Danny. I'm not holding it well. But it's all right. I'm not worried about anyone taking advantage of me."

He ordered the drink. She looked out the window, her head spinning, wondering if it was going well. Was she wrong to lay it on the line this way?

Too late if she was. She had never been good at dissembling. Not when marriage had been all important, and not now when love—when sex with someone she could care for—was just as important.

"Are you wealthy?" he asked. "Seven stores can be a fortune, or it can be a living."

"I net something more than a hundred thousand a year."

"*Net?* After taxes?"

"After everything. I consider that a fortune."

"I do, too." He was impressed.

Her fourth drink came. She took it, sipped it, smiled into it as his knee brushed hers. She wondered, briefly, if the dimension of her success story was helping him change. If so, she was a little sorry for it. She had never been concerned much with money as a girl, and she wasn't concerned much with it now that she had it. Love and children and helping your husband make his way were the things that had mattered to young May Jacobs, and they were the things that mattered still. But that road was blocked. Another road had to open.

She drank. He took her hand. "It's strange that we should meet now, isn't it, May?"

She finished her drink. She leaned forward to put her other hand over his and said, "No, it's not. I came for you. I knew you were here. Danny—" her eyes found his— "Danny, you're the boy I remember." Her voice grew weak. "Am I the girl you remember?"

He said yes, his eyes at her breasts, and she wanted his hands and lips there, wanted him with a sudden wave of heat that made her slightly faint.

"Would you like to leave?" he asked.

She nodded, afraid to trust her voice.

He called for the check. She rose carefully, wondering if she would spoil it all by staggering or falling on her face. He came around the table and took her arm.

They went down in the elevator, and she smiled at him and he smiled back. There may have been other people there, but she didn't notice. They got off and walked down a hall, and he opened a door and she stepped inside. "My room," he said. She walked to the window and looked out. He came up behind her, and his arms went around her, and one hand cupped her breast. She said, "Danny, hello . . ." His head came around and her lips were covered. She turned and locked herself against him, feeling the stiffness press her lower belly. "Do it," she groaned. "Do it do it . . ."

80

Again his lips sealed hers. His hands were at her bottom, and then at her zipper. He was quick about it, and her dress came off and her brassiere and pants. She was sitting on the bed and he was standing over her, his clothing dropping away. He brought the stiffness to her mouth. She looked up at him. His expression dared her to prove she had changed. She kissed the throbbing, hot skin and took it into her mouth. But she had a hunger of her own, and as he groaned and grasped her head, she pulled away and put her arms around his waist and pulled him down with her. He landed on his side, raised himself, bent over her breasts. He sucked them and bit them, and she was saying no no no and it was an affirmation of something beyond expression.

When his fingers entered her, she dug her face into his chest and screamed. He stopped. She kissed his chest. She'd had an immediate orgasm. "Go on, Danny, go on."

He went on. He went on and on. She was ready to scream again, but she wanted him in her. On her back, looking into his face, she reached for and grasped the stiffness, then quickly changed position and straddled him. A moment of fumbling, another moment of experimental movement; then, with a roll of her haunches and a quavering sigh, she sent him deep up into her.

She bent forward on stiff arms. Slowly, slowly, instinct and long hunger making her lascivious, she rotated her hips, her pelvis, massaging the root of her pleasure. But she was also thinking of him, and contracted the muscles that contained him, beginning a rhythmic churning, looking into his eyes, murmuring his name.

His body moved. He worked up and down. And while commanding herself to wait for him, she was unable to, and fell forward and bit his lip. He grunted and twisted his head away, and she was sorry for that but she was exploding and the screams of pleasure were rising and she had never screamed when Harold was potent, never felt anything like this before. It was almost worth the seven long years of famine.

She went back up on her arms when it ended for her, not only because she had to bring him to his orgasm, but because there was no real end to her need. Seven years' wanting was being fed now.

He moved again, but not strongly enough, and then stopped altogether. His eyes were closed, his mouth set in a strange, tight line that made her think of pain. She worked on. She told herself not to worry; it was just his way.

She pumped faster, trying for the churning effect inside her. He began moving more strongly, gripping her waist, and his eyes opened and stared past her, and that strained, pained look intensified. And then he gasped, and she thought he was coming and pumped harder. He said, "Stop!" his voice choked, and held her hips rigid with hands that dug painfully into her flesh. At the same time, she felt him shriveling inside her.

"Danny?" she murmured, waiting for his smile, his kiss, his sign of love's crisis passed.

He moved her to the side and slid out and away from her. She was kneeling on the bed and he was disappearing into the bathroom. Was that also his way, leaving without a word?

She got off the bed and went to the closed bathroom door. "Danny?"

"In a minute."

She touched herself. She was wet, yes, but it seemed no more than a wetness of her own body. She returned to the bed and lay down.

When he appeared, he seemed pale. She smiled and held out her arms. He went around the bed and got his shorts and put them on. She said, "Danny," and he came to the bed and sat down. She wanted to hug him, to draw his head to her breast, but he took both her hands. She said, "Do you remember Prospect Park, that time we went to a party in Brooklyn? How I wish I'd said yes. It might have changed our lives."

He nodded. "It's almost four."

"I don't have to be anywhere, do you?"

"As a matter of fact, I do."

She stared at him. He wanted her to leave. "All right. Just a cigarette and a little talk."

"Must you smoke those damned things?" he muttered, and got up to find her bag.

"If you'd rather I wouldn't . . ."

"It has nothing to do with me," he said, and took the purse from the window ledge and brought it to the bed. "It's *your* life, not mine."

"I won't smoke," she said, mortified to hear her voice choking. And then, shaking her head, trying to smile, "Why are we quarreling about a silly thing like that?"

He tossed the purse into an armchair. "A silly thing like that cost my wife her life."

He began picking up his clothing, straightening and folding, keeping his back to her. She suddenly felt cold—and naked. She drew up the blanket. "Danny, why are you . . ."

He turned. "Why am I what?" His face was bland, empty of anything resembling affection.

"Why are you being so . . . mean to me?"

"Listen, May, I don't know what you expect from a man."

She sat up. "Not from a man. From *you!* We just . . ." She faltered, seeing what was happening, understanding from his expression that she was doing just what he wanted—giving him a way out.

But why? What had she done to make him want out? If this had been going on for a month and he was afraid of becoming involved, she could understand it. But *now*, at the very beginning?

"We just screwed," he said, and he seemed more than cold, he seemed angry. "That's what you wanted, wasn't it? That's why you looked me up and insisted we see each other today and got drunk and came here with me and pushed, pushed . . ." He was leaning forward, glaring, almost shouting, and she got out of bed and ran to where her clothes lay on the floor.

Her hands shook and her stomach twisted and she thought she was going to throw up, but she fought to dress, fought to get out of there. He despised her. He had made love to her *and hated it!*

She couldn't get the zipper up, and kept fumbling with it while sticking her feet in her shoes. She ran her hands over her hair and went back to the zipper and still couldn't get it up.

"Let me," he said. He helped her and she went to the door. There her fear, her shame, her anguish made her say, "Why didn't you tell me you'd turned homosexual?"

"May," he said, face tired, voice tired, "get the hell out of here."

She got out. She walked to the elevators. She was on the eighth floor and took it to the fourteenth. A woman looked at her. She knew she must be something to look at. A real mess.

But then again, she couldn't have been much better even at the best of times, especially with her clothes off.

Her defenses crumbled and the question struck like a white-hot blade searing her brain: Was Harold's incapacity her fault? Had he lied about being incapable with other women?

She was in her suite. She undressed and showered and scrubbed and washed her hair without regard for its set, and looked in the full-length mirror. What was it about her that made men lose desire?

It couldn't be! She looked normal. She *was* normal. And attractive enough. It had to be Harold.

Danny, too? Because he hadn't come. She knew that now. He had left her in—disgust!

Yes, both of them were incapable! The only two men who had ever made love to her, and both were sick! Yes, it had to be that!

She turned from the mirror, her body wracked by sudden sobs. She went into the bedroom and locked the door, went to the drapes and drew them, got into bed and pulled the covers over her head as she had when a child and frightened. She cried there, in her dark cave of misery, until Eunice knocked and asked if everything was all right. May said she had a splitting headache and would nap until dinner.

Eunice moved around, humming. May wiped her eyes and blew

her nose. She wanted to go home, but home wasn't in Chicago with Harold. Home was somewhere she hadn't yet been, some place she hadn't yet found.

She got up and went to the closet and looked at her clothes. She chose the most daring of her dresses. Tomorrow she would shop for more, and they would be dresses neither May Jacobs nor May Krasmer would dare to have worn. She was going to shock Eunice, and shock herself. She was going to *swing*.

She had to find out.

10

WEDNESDAY, JANUARY 4, P.M.

The drive-in movie was near Dania. Violetta Murillo and Jorge were parked far back where the cars were sparse, watching the James Bond thriller. A rental Caddy came up the aisle, passed them, stopped, and backed into the left-hand space beside Jorge's four-door Plymouth. Jorge reached for the speaker hanging on his door. He turned the volume down but not off.

The stout man got out from behind the wheel of the Caddy and took the remaining speaker off the pole. As he did so, he looked into the Plymouth, eyes flickering past Jorge to Violetta. "Good movie, Jorge?" Jorge said, "Get in, Mr. Prager. Your wife and Mr. Leech, too."

Prager said, "There's more room in my car," hooked up his speaker, and slid back behind the wheel.

Violetta began to open her door. Jorge said, "No." He turned the volume of his speaker back up and began watching the movie. In a moment, Max Prager got out of his car, and so did his wife and Jerry Leech. With his left hand, Jorge turned the volume down again; with his right he reached under the seat and threw a switch.

"Why so touchy?" Prager said, smiling affably. He got in the back seat, followed by his wife and Jerry Leech. Leech closed the door.

Jorge said, "It's the way I want it, and I am paying for what I want."

"You," Prager murmured, still smiling, "or the man you work for?"

Jorge shifted in his seat, turning to face full around. "You must learn to believe what I say, Mr. Prager. You have a job. Nothing but that is your business."

"That and the payoff."

Jorge took two envelopes from his jacket pocket. He peered at them, and handed one to Prager and one to Leech.

"And staying alive and out of jail," Prager added, opening his envelope to count the money inside.

"Max," his wife murmured.

He looked at her. "You're beginning to live the part."

She shrugged. "Why make waves? We're in or we aren't."

"And you're in," Jorge said.

"Never too late to have second thoughts," Prager said.

Leech said, "What is this? I thought it was all decided. I mean, if we're going to do it . . ."

Prager chuckled and patted Leech's knee. "Just probing for weak spots, Jerry. Of course we're in. Haven't we been working hard the last few days?"

"Tell me," Jorge said.

Prager looked at Violetta.

"She will be Mr. McKensil's secretary."

Prager said, "I thought *I* was coordinating everything in the hotel?"

"This was done another way. When the time comes to *use* Mr. McKensil, you will handle it."

Prager grunted. Leech finished counting his money. He put

it in his pocket and rubbed his hands together. "The old man's nurse looks easy. I think we'll be real tight."

"It's a certainty," Prager said.

Leech shrugged, grinning. "Another break. Wheeler's got no guard."

"That will give us access to the Senator's suite on the south," Prager said.

"And the other side?"

"A woman named Krasmer. May Krasmer. She knows the Senator's speechwriter, Daniel Berner. But she's not as easy as the nurse."

"She's married," Ruth Prager said, "and spent time in Berner's room. She looked bad when she came out. Whether there's some way of getting leverage on them—together, I mean—isn't at all clear. I rode up with her in the elevator after she left Berner, and couldn't break through for a hello. But Max has something else working."

"Through Jerry," Prager said. "A woman who gives parties. Marjory Fine."

Leech said, "Real freak-outs."

Jorge frowned. "What?"

"Wild parties," Prager said.

"She invited me to a few last year," Leech said. "She needs guys. There're always more women than guys. And the action is good. I mean, I always picked up tips and stuff. Sometimes a hunk of jewelry, with no complaints afterward." His hand dropped to the pocket where he'd put his money. "But good-bye to hand-outs and peanuts!"

"If all goes well," Jorge said.

"It'll go well," Leech said, face suddenly tight and determined. "I'm gonna get that payoff. It'll go well if I have to do it all myself."

Prager patted his knee again. "That's the spirit, Jerry. That's the spirit that'll get you killed."

Mrs. Prager said, "Leech honey, play it cool. Always cool. The blueprint Jorge gave us is the right one. No lone-wolf actions. The odds against any *one* plan working are worse than those in *bolita*. So we try as many different angles as we can. And when C-Day comes—no honey, not the C-Day *you're* used to." Leech laughed, and glanced at Violetta. She watched them all impassively. Ruth Prager said, "When Christopher Day comes, we pick the one plan that's developed best, use bits and pieces from the others, and keep an alternate plan ready in case things go wrong. And take it from an old con artist, something *always* goes wrong."

Which was why, Jorge thought, Lamas had looked so long and hard for a Violetta. If need be, she alone could make the plan work. With the manager of the Bal Metropole in their grasp, they could do almost anything.

"About that party," Prager reminded Leech.

"Yeah, well, like Max told me, I asked Mrs. Fine if she was looking for real swingers for her parties, and when she said sure I told her about Christopher's speechwriter. That she liked."

"A social lion," Prager murmured.

"And I said there was this big businesswoman without her husband, probably looking for action."

"May Krasmer."

"I got them invited, too," Leech said, jerking his head at the Pragers. "At the beginning this Fine dame throws big blasts and she'll try anyone. Later on she starts pairing people off and makes the groups smaller, but oh brother!"

"Mmmm," Ruth Prager said, snuggling up to the big man. "I'm going to pair off with you, honey."

Leech chuckled. "Remember your husband."

"Remember we're not really married," Ruth replied.

"Finally," Prager said, "there's Miss DeWyant. She reacted to my talk about the President, all right, but I'm not sure exactly *how* she reacted. Isn't it time you told me what he was to her?"

"We are not certain yet," Jorge said. "But we know there is something there. Keep testing her. She is a hysterical type and might let it all out under pressure."

"An educated guess, Jorge?"

Again, Prager was needling him, reaching out for the man behind him. Jorge merely nodded. The *patrón* now had *three* detective agencies working on the Wheelers and on Ellie DeWyant's past. Little bits and pieces of information kept coming in, but the *patrón* wasn't ready to draw any conclusions.

"If we could get hold of *her*," Prager murmured, "the possibilities would be endless."

Again Jorge nodded. "What else, Mr. Prager?"

Prager smiled. "What we gave you isn't enough?"

"No, it's not."

The three in the back seat looked at him.

"What about the singer? The Negro. Can't anything be done with him?"

"Wally Jones?" Leech asked incredulously.

"Yes, that's the man. A Negro is always open to certain leverage."

Ruth Prager laughed. "That's like asking Jackie Robinson to help kidnap Nelson Rockefeller. Jones supported the President and the Senator in all their political campaigns. He's coming here only because he wants to honor—"

"A Negro is always open to certain leverage," Jorge repeated, knowing he was right because the *patrón* had said it. "When he comes, something should be tried. Find an approach, Mr. Prager. That's what I'm paying for."

Prager smiled. "How'd you make all your money, Jorge? Stock market? Manufacturing? Retailing?"

"If there's nothing more to talk about . . ."

"Ah, Jorge, if I only had your wit, your brains."

Jorge said, "Mr. Prager, *do your job!*" He was angry at the needling. So Prager understood he was only a middleman. So there was no reason to keep bringing it up.

He almost hoped Prager did something wrong, did something to endanger the *patrón*. Then he would get the chance to repay him.

Prager said, "I am doing my job. I just like to know who I'm working for. After all, we're taking all the risks. Knowing the employer is insurance."

"Don't think of it," Jorge said. "Insurance is just what you would need."

"Aha, the muscle emerges."

Ruth touched his arm. "Max, don't. The pay is the best ever."

Leech said, "Yeah, let up, Max. We're going to make enough to retire." He grinned. "One job. One job and I'm through kissing—" he looked at Violetta— "hands."

Prager nodded, smiling slightly, looking at Jorge. "And all from our millionaire friend here." Before Jorge could respond Prager opened the door.

Jorge put out his hand, stopping the fat man. "Do more," he said. "Think of that Negro singer. Think of other things, *everything*. Remember, we must have as many plans as possible so that one can work out. As many as *possible*."

Prager nodded and got out. The other two followed. They got into the Caddy, Prager slinging the speaker back on the pole, and the Caddy drove off.

Violetta spoke in Spanish. "It doesn't seem possible, with people like those. All they want is money. When the time comes to risk their lives, will they act?"

Jorge nodded. "They want their final payment. And that is the big one. Also, I will be there at the end. And someone else who is not just interested in money."

"I could be there," Violetta said.

Jorge smiled.

"*I could be there*," Violetta repeated, and the way she said it made Jorge look at her.

"You want to go back to Cuba?" he asked.

"Cuba? I know nothing about Cuba except what they tell me."

"Then why?"

"You are paying me, remember?"

He nodded, and waited for whatever was burning inside her to work its way out.

"I want Americans, those Americans who could have helped us

and didn't, I want them to *suffer.*" She kneaded her small hands. "My father. My brother. My father's brother. All at the Bay of Pigs. I didn't know or care anything about the invasion. I was a baby. But now I know and now I want them to suffer." She looked at Jorge. "Better not have me there after all. I would kill him."

Jorge wanted to say something. He wanted to tell her that people all over the world lost fathers and brothers and uncles in wars, and that no fifteen-year-old girl should own such a hate. But he reached down and snapped off the tape recorder, then unhooked the window speaker. Lamas had found this girl, was using this girl *because* of such a hate. And Jorge's work was done for the night.

Violetta said, "Must we go right now?"

Jorge looked at her.

"Couldn't we see the movie? I like James Bond."

A fifteen-year-old girl in spite of such a hate. "I like him, too," Jorge said, and put the speaker back. He wondered what Violetta would do if by some chance she *was* present for the abduction. Maybe not what she thought she would do.

He bought her a bag of popcorn and a Coke and she jumped up and down in her seat. A *child*, he thought. But later, stopping before her home in Coconut Grove, she said, "Come in. My mother works nights. We have an hour or two."

He shook his head.

"You don't like me, Jorge?"

"But so young!"

She shrugged. "And what about Mr. McKensil?"

"I don't like to think about that."

She smiled and patted his hand. "Maybe afterward," she said, opening the door. "Maybe when you see the pictures."

She laughed at his expression, said, "*Buenas noches,* Jorge," and went into the dingy frame house.

Jorge thought of her all the way to Golden Beach. And after the *patrón* had heard the tape, he thought of her in his room.

He finally made a call and left the house at two A.M. The one sure way to forget a woman (a *woman!* that *niña!*) was with another woman.

11

THURSDAY, JANUARY 5, A.M.

Bruce Golden awoke feeling edgy, trying to remember a dream, a bad one, and failing and remembering instead the way that DeWyant girl had walked past him with stony eyes. Immediately, he substituted Gail Yolles, but that didn't work too well because Gail herself hadn't worked too well yesterday afternoon. Not for him. Though *she'd* enjoyed it. But he hadn't really wanted her once they'd gone to bed. He didn't know why. No reason, really. She was nice enough in the raw, but the chemistry had failed.

He showered and shaved and ate, and was left with plenty of time to spare. And found himself thinking of Lou.

That had been a *great* scene, physically.

Gail should have been a great scene, too.

Maybe he was toning down. Maybe he was peaking out as far as enjoying every single piece of ass on God's earth was concerned. He'd certainly had enough to reach the stage of selectivity!

He lit a cigarette, thinking of Lou and the pot and the *boeuf Bourguignon.* If only she hadn't talked so damned much. About him.

The cigarette tasted bad. The vague memory of something unhappy—that dream?—lingered. He tried again to remember it, and again remembered Ellie DeWyant.

He went to the phone, dialed, said, "Hey, I thought I'd act as your alarm clock this morning."

Lou Degano said, "Bruce?"

"Yes. We should talk. Tuesday was really something else again."

She was silent.

"Wasn't it, Lou?"

"I don't know *what* it was."

"I do. Look, it's not quite eight. Dress and get down to the hotel and we'll have coffee."

"I'm dressed. And I'm just about to leave."

"Great. The Bon Bouche in twenty minutes?"

She was silent again. He began to speak. She said, "Not the Bon Bouche. It's a beautiful morning. Out on the deck near the pool."

"I'll have to call room service . . ."

"It's all taken care of."

He should have known right then what he found out twenty minutes later. Walking out of the Bal Metropole's lobby and around the curved ramp, he saw Lou in a gray minisuit at a poolside table. With her, wearing white slacks and a Hawaiian-type shirt, was Jerry Leech. Leech was leaning half out of his chair, drawn up close to Lou, with his arm around the back of her chair. He was talking and grinning.

The grin died as Bruce said, "Good morning," and, looking at Lou, "I didn't know this was going to be a threesome."

"Neither did I," Leech said. "So why don't one of us sort of disappear, huh?" He tried to make it sound light, but lightness wasn't his forte. It sounded ugly, and Bruce sat down and took a piece of toast from a center plate and said, "How do I get a cup?"

Lou pushed hers over toward him. "I'm finished. Or are you afraid of catching something?"

He poured coffee from a silver pot and sipped and looked at her and smiled. "It's a little late to worry about that, isn't it?"

She took a cigarette from a pack on the table. Bruce reached for his lighter, but Leech was there first with matches. Bruce put the lighter away and spread jam on his toast. "And what subject is on the agenda for our little *tête-à-tête?*"

"Me," Lou said, and smoked. She didn't smile. She hadn't smiled once, or come anywhere near it.

"Yeah," Leech said, and he looked at Lou and he looked at Bruce; then he seemed to make up his mind. He lowered his voice, as if hoping to exclude Bruce, and murmured, "So what about it, Lou? I mean, it's been a long time between invitations, like they say. A few drinks and a few laughs, tonight after work, right?"

"I'll have to check my calendar."

Leech nodded, but he wasn't happy.

Bruce washed toast down with coffee and cleared his throat. "Funny thing. I was about to ask the same question, more or less." Lou's eyes came to him. "But it wouldn't be cricket to cut in on a compatriot."

"Since when have you played cricket?" she muttered.

Leech laughed, trying to get in on the conversation. "Yeah, he can't even play . . ." He thought hard. "Hopscotch, right?"

Bruce nodded, smiling. "That's right, Jerry. Never played hop-scotch. Only grown-up games, as Lou—"

"And dirty pool," she interrupted.

"This is clean pool, is it? What did you anticipate, a bout of arms to determine your champion?"

Her quick flush showed him he'd scored. But he wasn't pleased. This was a bad, childish scene—something he hadn't expected of Lou Degano.

Jerry was leaning toward him. "What's that supposed to mean, huh?" He was getting ready to flex his muscles, to push for a physical confrontation, because how else could he come off well?

"Look it up in the *Britannica*," Bruce said, finished his coffee, and rose. "Have a ball, you two."

Leech stared a moment, then looked pleased. "Yeah." He became magnanimous. "Take it easy, Bruce. See you around."

Bruce began to walk away. Lou said, voice tremulous, "A chicken by any other name would still cackle."

Bruce stopped and looked back. He shook his head. "That's not the girl *I* knew."

"Sure," she said, the blood still in her cheeks. "Oh sure, Prince Valiant."

"You've got your prince," he replied easily, but put a little bite into his smile.

She jumped up. "For what *you* think I want, any hunk of gristle will do, won't it? Why be choosy?"

"Let's not fight, baby. Enjoy your gristle in good health."

Leech was lost. "Listen, Lou, I got to change for the trade. You'll let me know if we're on?"

"We're not," she snapped, and stalked toward the lobby.

"Dames," Bruce said, remembering his late-late shows, and left Mr. Leech.

In the office, he checked Lou's cubicle. She was yanking open desk drawers and taking out papers.

He said hey. She didn't answer. He said, "Games people play. I play them, too, sometimes. Why don't we stop playing games and get together and be what we were Tuesday night?"

She continued with her paper bit. He waited patiently. Finally she looked up. Her color was more normal, and she sighed and then smiled slightly. "I'm sorry, Golden Boy."

"That's the girl I knew," he said. "Care for a tourist's-eye view of Miami? Say dinner at a big, expensive joint and then go-go at the Castaways?"

She shook her head. "Try again. And again. And again. When I'm convinced it *means* something to you, I'll say yes."

He shrugged. She nodded sadly. "You're all broken up about it, huh, baby?"

He spread his hands, said, "Peace," and went to his office. The morning's action had been good for him. The bad dream was gone; the gloom was gone; he was ready for work, and for that search for the right girl.

12

THURSDAY, JANUARY 5, P.M.

Jerry Leech was busy. More guests out for the sun today. He placed mats and chatted with flirty broads, and watched for Michael Wheeler and his nurse. Prager came by and he set out mats for him and Ruthie and Ruthie gave him a once-over that worried him a little; it didn't look much like kidding to Leech. He wondered if he'd have trouble with her at Mrs. Fine's party. Not that she was *that* bad in a bathing suit. Her chest was bigger than he'd thought and her legs thinner. But still, she was just another aging Jewish broad.

About one-thirty McKensil came out to the pool, and with him was Bruce Golden. Leech watched them while arranging lounges. Golden saw him and nodded. A cool little nod, the prick! And that business with Lou Degano this morning—something about that had left a bad taste in his mouth, even though chicks were no problem, not with *this* job, and he'd only been looking for a little change of pace. Still, something about Golden's smile—his goddam superior smile!

The two men walked to the end of the pool, conspicuous in their business suits, McKensil waving his arm and pointing out things, Golden nodding, answering, pointing once in a while himself.

The *big* men! The fat cats! Talking ads and other shit. Thinking they were so goddam hot! And neither of them ever getting his hands on *real* bread.

What could McKensil make? Twenty grand? Twenty-five tops. And Golden was working for peanuts—a hundred fifty a week, maybe. He'd never have the guts to make it the way he, Leech, was going to make it.

He only wished they could know just how *big* he was going

to make it. He wished everyone could know, but especially
Golden with his goddam superior smile and smooth talk. He
wished it could be in the papers.

Leech the Beach Snatch Rocks Nation!

McKensil was talking to the lifeguard. Golden was walking
down the ramp to the Arcade Level, and heads turned, watching
him go. *Women's* heads.

"Joe College," Jerry muttered, and slammed a mat onto a
lounge and wished he could slam that smooth face instead. Not
that Golden had ever *done* anything to him. Not that he *could*,
with all his smooth talk! But it was the way he looked at you,
the way he talked, the way he—hell, just the way Joe College *was*.
The way so many of those bastards were.

He saw Eve Andrews pushing the old man up the ramp from
the Arcade Level. No more time to waste on Joe College. Opportunity knocks. He'd missed that knock once or twice in his
life, but not this time. No sir, not this time!

He sauntered up and said hi and she said, "Could you help
us again, Mr. Leech?" So she was going to make out yesterday
had never happened. He grinned. "Be glad to. How're you today,
sir?" The old man said he was feeling better, and Leech said,
"That's great!" and remembered when Wheeler's face had been
in the papers and on TV and now here he was nailed to that
chair and old and finished and it didn't seem possible it was the
same Wheeler, the President. He laughed inside, thinking,
Tough shit.

He helped them down to the beach and managed to grab a
little leg toward the end. Eve thanked him. He said, "For what?"
grinning when he saw her redden. She knew what was happening.
Her pants were warming up, all right. He just hoped she wasn't
as damned *dull* looking with that suit off as she was with it on.

Later he helped her up the stairs to the deck. The old man was
trying to say how much better he was doing, gobbling away like
a chicken on the block, and Leech took a real good feel of Eve's
ass (while shifting holds, of course). And was surprised at how

much there was to feel. She kept her eyes down, but that red hit her face again. He said, "I'm sorry, honey." She nodded, so stiff he was afraid her neck would crack.

When the old man was back in his chair, Leech said, "You ever give this nurse of yours a day off, sir?" Wheeler gobbled about sometime soon, and Leech said, "Well, I'd like to show her the sights," and Eve muttered they would see about it, her face still red, and began moving away. Leech came up behind her and murmured, "What time does he go to bed nights?" Her head snapped around, and she looked at him with eyes big as saucers. Her lips moved but nothing came out. He whispered, "What time, Eve?" and the old man gobbled and she turned and said, "It's a little too soon for *steak*, Mr. Wheeler." Leech stayed behind her, but she wouldn't look back and wouldn't answer, and the big blonde who gave him the stiffs was waving and calling. He figured she needed time to think, a square chick like that. She'd answer tomorrow.

He went to the blonde, Mrs. Manary, stretched out on her lounge. He said, "Yes, baby doll," and pushed his knee into her thigh. That was because Mr. Manary was in one of the game rooms playing gin for more money than College Joe Golden would see in a month, maybe a year. She said, "Now *now*, Leech," and rearranged those long legs and pushed up those big boobs and looked like she was about to pop out of that white bikini. He sat down at the edge of the lounge and let his fingers brush her arm. She said, "Would you be a dear and order me a drink? A screwdriver." He nodded, looking her over closely, and murmured, "A *screw*driver, you said?" She said, "Now *Leech*," and he stood up, close to her, feeling hot and doing a little crotch bulging. She dropped her eyes. He continued to stand there. She raised her eyes and wet her lips. "Be a good boy," she murmured. He laughed. He went to get her a drink, still laughing. She had a ton of bread, but she was ass, not class. She would get all the *screw*drivers she wanted, but she would pay for them. All these rich, bored, itchy broads would pay for whatever they got from Jerry Leech. He was a professional.

Only Eve Andrews would get it free. Or it would look like free, anyway, until payoff time came around.

He found that he was angry. He was angry at that blonde hunk and all the hunks looking him over like a side of beef and wondering if fifty bucks over the regular tip would do it, or maybe sixty or maybe seventy-five. Or a dinner when hubby was in a big game—a dinner and a gold wristwatch. (And that's why he needed a straight date once in a while, a Lou Degano.)

Still, what the hell was wrong with the way he was making it? How many guys got *paid* for what all guys wanted? How many times had he congratulated himself for graduating from the back seat of a car to the best beds in Miami—the best beds and the best broads and a little envelope with fat green as a thank-you?

Besides, it would end soon. He was going to graduate once again. With a hundred grand he could open a club, a bar, a restaurant.

LEECH THE BEACH'S, the neon would read, with a surfing symbol, and he standing in tux and cummerbund greeting guests, and all the top people from the top hotels making *his* scene because he'd have a rep by then, a mysterious rep as a guy who'd made it no-one-knew-how. . . .

He was glad when six o'clock came and his tour ended. Mrs. Manary was heading for the Arcade Level and said, "Charley's going fishing off Bimini one day next week, leaving the night before, he says. I'd like to go to the dog track and dancing." He nodded. "I'll start training now, baby doll." She smiled with all her beautiful white caps and gave him a great view as she swung away.

He went around the south side of the pool and through the woodslat door marked "No Admittance." He went down the narrow flight of steps to the alley-like area, opened the heavy steel door marked "Employees Only," and down more steps into the hot dimness of the basement. You couldn't smell the sea and perfumed bodies here—only a mixture of food and machinery, an oniony-oily smell that turned his guts inside out. The locker room was just around the corner, no more than twenty feet from the stairs. A break, not having to walk through much of the base-ment. He hated hotel basements. He'd walked through too many of them. They were all alike in one way, one lousy way. They were night to the upstairs portion's day. They made you know who you were, but good, like a dirty pair of overalls.

He changed into tan slacks and a gold Banlon polo shirt and slung his brown jacket over his arm. Jess Boyle came in, eighteen and tickled pink to be working as cabana boy at the Metropole. Jess said hey-man-what-a-*great*-day and he said yeah and got out. It was Jess's first season in a major hotel. If he went on to col-lege like he said he was going, he'd always think of it as a great day. If he stayed on, like some did, he'd stop thinking of great days and after a while begin looking for ways out. Because tip money, no matter how big, wasn't real money. After the season came the long summer—which included fall and spring—and there was little bread then, and the guys jumped from hotel to hotel and took time off between jobs to lie around the beach like the tourists. And somehow the money was always gone. Of course, you lived good. You lived better than anyone anywhere—as long as you could make it. But just how long could you make it?

Leech was hungry, but he couldn't see going to the employees' cafeteria tonight. He wanted a little privacy, and felt he could afford it. With the second advance payment from Jorge, he had himself another two grand. Four grand in two weeks! Jorge wasn't kidding. Jorge—or whoever was behind him—was going all the way. And so was Jerry Leech.

He went quickly back to the stairs, trying to hold his breath. Goddam basements! They made him sick! (They also made him afraid, because deep down inside where he lived, really lived, he was sure he was going to end up sweating with the Spics and Coons some day—some godawful day when he was too old to look good in bathing trunks and make it with the rich, bored, itchy broads.)

He got his '65 T-Bird from the car park and drove to the smorgasbord place where he usually ate when he couldn't face the cafeteria and there was no broad to take him to dinner. It was reasonable, and you could eat as much as you wanted for one price, and with his appetite the management always took a beating. He sat alone at a side table, and a guy he'd known at the Singapore called to him and he nodded and didn't encourage the guy to come over. Tommy Something. About forty-five and beginning to look it and scrubbing out the pool at one of the crap motels and making less and less and with fewer broads each year to take him to dinner or give him a little green.

He started on his third half of chicken and spooned in mashed potatoes and green beans, but his appetite was gone. He was thinking there was only one thing a guy like Tommy would be able to do in a few more years, and that was sweat in the basement.

And what if the kidnap didn't go through? What if he ended up like Tommy?

He drove south on One. He wasn't going to end up like Tommy, or in the basement, because long before that time arrived he'd make his play. The kidnap wasn't his first chance at the big time. Every year a contact or two from the jewel-heist mobs wandered through the hotel and gave him an eye. He could always nod. He could always make a haul that way.

All right, so it was smaller than this. But a few good hauls . . .

It was smaller, and after a haul or two your rep stank and you couldn't get into a top hotel and the contacts used other guys. And maybe you got your cut and maybe you didn't. And if you made waves you could end up in Biscayne Bay with a hole in the head.

He turned west and reached Peachtree Drive and the quiet middle-class street of mostly private homes. He parked in front of the two-story apartment house near the end of the block and got out. It was completely dark now, and the sky was full of stars. He lit a cigarette, thinking how lucky he was to live in Miami when back home they were freezing their balls off and the guys at the Stamford Tool Works were skidding all over the place getting to and from work.

He went inside the apartment house, to the second floor and the room-and-a-half in the rear. Furnished in one of those package deals from a downtown department store, two hundred fifty bucks complete. He'd dump it all the minute the snatch was over.

He poured a stiff rye and watched television. A sports program —professional football highlights from last weekend. He stretched out on the couch, closed his eyes, and remembered football in high school back in Stamford. He'd been a medium-sized kid up to twelve or thirteen, but then he'd grown fast. As a sophomore he'd been as big as his old man, and as rough. He made every team, but he wasn't making good grades. And he wasn't the top man on any team. Good, yeah. Great, no. But he had the potential, and he was sure that if he got into college he'd bust loose in football, maybe baseball, too, and end up a pro.

He thought he would get his chance. So his average was barely C. Still, an athletic scholarship . . .

In his senior year he got stopped for drunken driving, and like a jerk he panicked and ran away. They had his license number, and he was caught at home the next day. He spent the night in a big cell with three old bums and one tried to feel his cock. He slugged the guy. The others let him alone.

He got a suspended sentence. Damned lucky, his father said, and time he began to earn his keep. "But what about college?" he asked.

The old man laughed. "Sure, they're beggin' for you. And with a police record . . ."

His mother insisted he graduate, and he did. But there was no athletic scholarship. He went to work in the tool factory with Pop, learning to pull a lever and watch a little hollow doohickey turn over and over, getting shiny, until it fell out the end, and then he lifted the lever and watched another doohickey drop in and pulled the lever and watched it grow shiny and fall out. And the light bulbs behind the wire fixtures and the green-painted concrete walls and the cold that seeped into the place winter mornings and by eleven worked its way into his thick-soled shoes and by noon was up into his legs. Even after lunch it was there, and he hated the cold, hated the factory and the bowling team and the doohickeys turning over and dropping out and hearing about Billy Wurtough in State Teachers and Pete Wyola on the track team at UCLA and other kids, so many other kids he'd known, making their lives over in college.

He hated the bastards!

He left the factory and his home when he was nineteen and drove to the West Coast and worked in an airplane plant, but except for more sunshine and a little more bread it was the same thing. He saved a few bucks and joined the surfers that summer at Santa Monica. He did all right, living with different chicks and sometimes on the beach until every last cent ran out and it was September, and, except for the hard-core bums, everyone started going some place.

He stuck it out until November, then drove east. He didn't know just where he was going. He ended up at his home, but never even stopped. It was a cold, rainy day and it wrenched his guts to think of Mom and Pop and the Stamford Tool Works.

He drove to Miami. He got a job in a small hotel and after three months switched to the Casablanca. It was fine, hardly like work. Sun and swimming and good tips and a place of his own and all the ass he wanted. He took a little time off every so often, jumping to the Deauville and Singapore and Carillon. And then the Fontainebleau for a long stretch. And then the Bal Metropole.

He opened his eyes. The television was showing an intercepted pass in slow motion. He watched, but didn't really see anything.

Now he was thirty, almost thirty-one. Now he was scared of the basements. And no use kidding himself—he couldn't forget that one night in jail with the old bum trying to feel his cock and he ready to scream for help because they were tough old bums and he wasn't tough, not inside where it counted. That was why he was no good for the jewel heists or any other rough stuff.

This kidnap was the roughest stuff ever. *This kidnap was the President's brother-in-law, Wheeler's son-in-law, maybe the next President of the United States!*

It didn't seem that way. Prager and Ruthie weren't like the jewel-heist contacts. No hard talk and cleaning the nails with shivs and bulges under the jackets. No Mafia clearance and pay-offs. Jorge wasn't like the strong-arm characters who came to big opening nights like Sinatra's at La Ronde.

He would do whatever Jorge and Prager said he should do, because the payoff was one hundred thousand dollars and one hundred thousand dollars was going to remake his life. Like Billy Wurtough and Pete Wyola had remade theirs by going to college.

He felt better. He had avoided thinking it out since Prager first recruited him. He had avoided thinking of *himself*, and so the doubts had built and the fear had grown behind the cocky exterior.

Now he was sure he would do whatever he had to do.

13

FRIDAY, JANUARY 6, A.M.

His arm ached from all the needles that had been stuck into it. His head ached from all the thoughts that had been flitting through it. He lay in the hard bed in the strange room and couldn't sleep. Around his left wrist was a clear plastic bracelet with a paper inset. On the paper was printed, "Berner, Daniel G., 15910 M43H," and centered under that, "M-SP-Sochall." He wondered what the numbers and letters meant. One of the M's probably designated him as male. Male, at least for the present.

How incredible that he was here, in a North Miami Beach hospital! How quickly it had all happened!

Yesterday, Thursday, he had gone to see a urologist recommended by the druggist on the Arcade Level. Dr. Sochall was tall, dark, athletic looking, and very persuasive. After a long and thorough examination that included a variety of horrors from urinalysis to prostate massage, and a forty-five-minute wait for results of testing of "specimens," the doctor had ushered him into his paneled office.

"Prostatitis, Mr. Berner, a comparatively minor infection, is most commonly associated with the general type of pain you've experienced. But then there are other symptoms—hematuria, dysuria . . ."

The explanations had led Dan to understand that he had closed his eyes to far too many signposts. Then had come the bombshell.

"I'd like you to enter the hospital this afternoon." Sochall had raised the phone and dialed. "Three o'clock. That should give you time to return to your hotel for pajamas and toilet articles."

Dan had tried to protest.

"I know I have a bed available now, Mr. Berner. I might not have one the rest of the week. And the sooner we determine exactly what is wrong with you, the sooner we can begin to treat it."

"But—a hospital!"

"Just for tests. I want a complete GU workup. I want to check your spinal cord, along with kidneys and prostate. One day should take care of it all."

Dan had felt sweat running down his sides, but hadn't asked the questions pushing at his tongue—the terrifying questions, the questions he later told himself were foolish. *Minor* infection, Sochall had said. And what Dan was thinking of, sweating over, wasn't minor.

So here he was, with gray light filling the windows and the room's other occupant snoring softly behind the partitioning screen. Here he was with the terrifying questions still lodged in his mind.

Here he was, and here he remained until the hospital came awake and the little colored nurse entered and said, "Ten minutes to wash up, Mr. Berner. No breakfast. We like you nice and empty for your next series of tests."

He brushed his teeth and sipped a little water, and a male attendant came in with a wheelchair. "Mr. Berner?" He said yes. "Sit heah, please." He said it wasn't necessary; he could walk. The attendant, a short, husky youth with a mild Southern accent, said, "That's the rules, suh. You gotta ride to X-ray." So, feeling like a fool, he got into the chair and was wheeled into the hall.

It wasn't too bad until they entered the elevator. It held visitors, civilians, people from the outside world. They looked down at him pityingly, especially a cute, brown-eyed girl in a cream minidress. Sitting there that way he was low and they were high and he felt reduced, at a terrible disadvantage. He wanted to say something to the attendant, to make some joke about the chair so the girl would know he was perfectly able to walk and was here only for a day's testing. But the elevator stopped and the girl got out, and as the doors closed she glanced back at him as if to say, "Poor old man." More people got on. He stared at the floor. His pajamas and robe felt loose, empty, as if he had already begun to waste away. His mouth tasted vile. And just as the elevator stopped, his stomach rumbled cavernously.

The attendant wheeled him out and around a corner. There they met another attendant with a chair, entering the hallway from a door marked "Radiology 2." The second wheelchair held a withered, sunken-cheeked crone. Side by side they picked up speed, the attendants saying hey-man and how's-things and choking back laughter. Dan chuckled and said, "I could use one of these hot rods." His attendant turned left and drew to a stop. "Change in the dressing room, suh. Wait for your name to be called."

Dan stood up, and the man was gone. He was at a small, open waiting room with two curtained cubicles on the right. He entered the first cubicle and changed into a long, loose, wrap-around robe of crinkly white paper. He had to check to make sure it didn't flap open in back as he walked to a plastic chair and sat down. A middle-aged woman whose lipstick seemed unnaturally red against the pallor of her face and the whiteness of her robe was seated two chairs away. They exchanged a quick, shamed glance. *Her* stomach rumbled cavernously.

Please, he prayed to a God he didn't believe in. *Please get me safely out of this.*

14

FRIDAY, JANUARY 6, P.M.

Leo worked steadily, seated at the writing desk, crumpling sheet after sheet of hotel stationery and carefully burning them, one at a time, in the metal wastebasket. Ruthie had seen him planning before, but not for so many hours, so many days. They'd collaborated on at least a dozen jobs, from a very profitable Angola mining corporation (stock sold at ten dollars a share and they'd collected twenty-three thousand before leaving their backer with the bag) to a simple little hot-furs con that made them eight grand in two weeks as well as expenses at three fine Bahama hotels.

"Flush it," he grunted, tapping the wastebasket with his foot.

He was a meticulous worker, a top con, but this was his first try at a snatch job.

She took the wastebasket to the bathroom, flushed the ashes down the toilet, and rinsed the basket out with water. When she came back he was burning still another sheet of paper. "Leo, let it go for now."

He looked at her. She quickly said, "*Max.* Let it go for now." She touched his face. He didn't move or tell her to go away, but the way he sat there made her withdraw. Eleven years ago, on their first collaboration, they'd spent more time in bed than with the mark. Leo—*Max* had aged fast since then. He admitted it. And it was the reason he had taken on this wild job. His pay-off would be one hundred and fifty thousand, a score to end all scores. He could retire on it.

She'd been staying with her sister in Brooklyn when he called from Miami. He didn't tell her what the job was. He only said, "Expenses and eight, ten grand in advances for you *personally*. A fifty-grand payoff for you *personally*." Ruthie had saved quite a bit from jobs with Leo (Max, damn it, Max!) and from odd jobs with Chick Evans and Ben Hirsch. She was pushing fifty and had never spent a day in stir. She had just about decided to call it quits.

But ten grand in advances, and a fifty-grand payoff—where did you find dough like that? Still, she'd almost got back on the plane when Max outlined the job. He hadn't muscled her. He'd just said he would have to tell his contact he'd spelled out the job to a woman and she'd turned it down.

She understood. She would be in trouble. Maybe they would do nothing, and maybe they would send a little bullet her way one cold Brooklyn night. So that plus the money plus Max saying they would make it like old times had swung her.

Only they weren't making it like old times.

She sighed. She should've married Bernie when she'd had the chance. Fourteen years since he'd proposed, and then he'd met a widow from Jersey and she'd set him up in the catering business.

Max said, "Yeah," and hunched forward in his chair the way he did when he liked something. "Two for sure and maybe all three."

She came over to the desk. Before she got there, he folded the sheet of paper and stood up. He went into the bathroom and closed the door. She said, "We got plenty of toilet paper, Max." He barked a brief answering laugh. The toilet flushed. He came out, along with a sharp smell of smoke.

"So even when you get it down you burn and flush it."

He smiled. He tapped his head. "No one's going to burn and flush this."

"Except if you keep sweating that Cuban fellow. He's a hard baby, Max. I can feel it."

"A shmuck," Max said scornfully. "A messenger."

"A messenger, maybe, but an interested party. Forget about who he works for. You don't need to know."

"I've forgotten," he said, in a way that told her it was the last thing in the world he'd forgotten. He checked his wristwatch. "How about a pastrami on rye at Pumpernik's?"

It was almost midnight, and pastrami wasn't what she wanted. She said, "Okay, I'll slip into a decent dress," and whipped off the print she was wearing. He didn't turn away, so she took off her brassiere. "The sun makes them itch," she said, and rubbed them a little.

"They get bigger all the time," he murmured. So she took off her panties and went to the dresser. He caught her as she bent to the drawer.

Even so, she had to work half an hour before he was ready. And even so, he didn't do her justice.

It was sad, she thought, lying beside him, listening to his heavy breathing. Sad the way a man went down just when a woman was reaching her peak. She had never liked it more, never been better at it, and all the men her age were slowing to a crawl.

That Marjory Fine was about her age. Those parties she threw, they must be tied in somehow with getting what she wanted. When you had dough like Marjory Fine—Max said her husband was a millionaire—you could play it exactly the way you liked it. But Max wasn't sure what it was Marjory Fine liked, and neither was Leech, who'd known her a while. Her husband brought her down and then left after a few days, and she threw parties that got pretty wild. But no one knew if she was making it with anyone.

Max said, "The girl," quite clearly.

She looked at him. He was dead asleep. "The girl, Max?"

"The President," Max said.

"The President?"

"No one figured," he said.

"Figured what?"

"An out."

"Out of what, Max?"

He cleared his throat. He mumbled. She tried to understand and couldn't. It bothered her a little. This whole job bothered her. Then she was thinking of Leech and that party. . . .

15

SATURDAY, JANUARY 7, P.M.

Bruce Golden pressed the chime button to the eighth-floor ocean-front suite. It was a quarter to six. He expected to be among the first arrivals, and he was. No one showed up at a party, especially a hotel party, less than an hour late. He gave his name to the deeply tanned man in stiff-looking blue suit and tinted glasses who opened the door, and glanced past him into the living room of the Premier-A Suite, the largest the Metropole had to offer. The music was light—Henry Mancini? Four people were at the bar in the corner. Marjory Fine and her husband sat on the candy-striped sofa, talking to a stout man who stood in front of them, hands behind his back, rocking slightly on his heels. And that was it.

The doorman, or butler, or private cop (which was what he most resembled) was checking a guest list. "Yes, here we are, Mr. Golden. Won't you go in?" He had slicked-back brown hair, a lean face, and an interesting accent—Cockney tempered with Middle American. Bruce had never seen him before, but reasoned he must be a hotel employee. The Metropole offered every possible service to its guests.

"Well, *hello*, Golden Goy," Marjory Fine said, and put out her hand. She wore a colorful shift, predominantly red and fashionably brief. Her hair was frosted, her face nicely tanned, her smile wry but pleasant. He smiled in return, liking her, and paid his respects to Melvin Fine. "Meet Max Prager," Fine said, and Bruce shook hands with the short, stout man who could have been Melvin Fine's brother. Fine and Prager resumed talking men's clothing. Marjory got up and said, "Mel honey, remember, you've got fifteen minutes." Melvin Fine said, "Did I ever miss a plane?" and turned back to Prager. "Cloak and suiters, like everybody else, have grown too big. Sales up, profits down, that's the slogan of our age. I was making more six years ago with twenty percent less help . . ."

Marjory drew Bruce away. "Buy me a drink."

Bruce said, "The guest of honor is leaving his party fifteen minutes after it starts?"

They were at the small bar. "Gimlet," Marjory said to the young Cuban in green jacket. Bruce ordered a Jack Daniel's and water. They carried their drinks to the window and looked out at the ocean. It was a gray day, cool and overcast—a perfect day for a Miami Beach party. She said, "Will you miss him?"

He glanced at her. She sipped her gimlet. He said, "I don't know him well enough to miss him."

"Neither does anyone else." She patted his arm. "Excuse me now. More guests arriving. Eat, drink, and be patient. I'll introduce you to a few people, and they'll be worth knowing."

He watched as she went to the door. She greeted two men and a woman, and then a woman who entered alone. The lone one was the wan, not-too-blonde whom Bruce had seen checking in at the same time as Michael Wheeler and his nurse. She was wearing what looked like a Pucci print, pink and clean and sexy as hell. Yet that touch of sadness, fragility, whatever—that wan look—was still present. Also present was a diamond bracelet about two inches wide that sent blue-white signals all across the room.

Bruce downed his bourbon and moved toward her, deciding

not to wait for Marjory Fine's introductions. This one was obviously worth knowing.

The man at the door studied his list and said, "Yes . . . Mr. Berner," and Dan went into the music and smoke and laughter and voices, wondering who his hosts were and looking for someone to tell him. Then he saw May and considered leaving. Not so much because he was ashamed of how he'd treated her, which he was, and not because he dreaded speaking to her, which he did, but because she reminded him of just what he wanted to forget—at least until Sochall's report reached him.

He walked away from the bar. He was forbidden liquor anyway. He slipped by individuals and around groups and made it to the windows, then felt he had to have a drink, just to be holding something, to be doing something. He looked back at the bar. May and a tall blond man were walking toward him. He turned his back and edged to the rear of the room and then around to the bar.

He asked for a beer. The bartender said, "Dark or light, sir?" He said, "Dark," surprised, and then, "Could you point out the hosts?" The bartender poured Heineken's into a slender Pilsner glass and tried to look over the heads of people hemming him in. He smiled apologetically and turned to fill another order. Dan sipped his beer, and saw a familiar face. He moved to where the man who owned Maximilian Originals (which helped Dan remember the name) was just lighting a stubby cigar. They greeted each other and Dan asked after Mrs. Prager. "She's around somewhere. Ruthie likes to mix at parties. Me, I like a shot of rye, a good cigar, and some quiet talk. Only anything quiet is becoming impossible here."

He was right. More and more people were arriving, and the music had changed from bland and tinkly to hot and jazzy. Dan asked about their hosts, just to keep Prager talking and help himself forget May and pain and the hospital and how he'd sweated to get out this noon after being kept an extra night.

Prager pointed out Marjory Fine, and said he was going for

a refill. Dan stood there, nursing his drink. The music had grown louder, but the raucous rock-and-roll was somehow hypnotic.

A very pretty girl moved across his path. He stared. Really stunning! He followed her. The music pounded. Every step brought him into and between people. He smiled and others smiled and voices filled his ears and through the voices the pounding beat of music. The stunning girl was at the bar. He pushed in beside her and said, "Can I get something for you?" She nodded. "A gin and tonic, please." He tried to get the bartender's attention. It took a while, and then he waited until the drink arrived before introducing himself.

"Eloise DeWyant," she replied. He took her arm, moving her away from the bar, looking for a place to sit. There was, of course, no such place. They stood near a door and talked. Or rather he talked. She drank and her eyes flickered about the room and he built his image. She nodded and smiled and didn't ask for whom he wrote speeches. So he worked around it a little and said, "When the Senator read that first one, he laughed. Seems I had taken a vital portion of his approach to Southeast Asia and aborted it, just enough to place him amidst the opposition."

"What senator is that?" she asked.

"Richard Christopher."

She finished her drink.

"Can I get you another?"

She nodded, handing him the glass, eyes moving about the room.

He went to the bar. The young Cuban looked pale and sweaty. He finally got the drink and returned to the door. Eloise De-Wyant wasn't there. He waited, looking for her, but the room was jammed and the light fading from the windows and he couldn't make out faces more than a few feet away.

The music pounded. He felt it as well as heard it. He said the hell with Sochall and sipped the gin and tonic and wondered why someone didn't turn on a few lights.

Ruthie found Max in the shadowy confusion. People were beginning to dance in the gloom. She said, "Are you going to need me for anything?"

He shook his head. "Jerry arrive?"

"Yes. Give me a few hours, okay?"

He nodded. "Good luck."

She made her way back to the bar. Jerry was talking to a slender woman who laughed and said, "Oh come on now, really!" Ruthie squeezed in on the other side. "Bartender." The man leaned close. She asked for a Scotch on the rocks. He fumbled around under the bar, muttering in Spanish. She said, "You ought to turn on a few lights." He said, "We try. They don' work. I don' know what happen pretty soon!" She took the glass in her left hand. Her right was busy.

Jerry turned abruptly to the bar. He kept his face to the woman, but he was no longer talking. She said, ". . . to hell with San Juan and flew back to good old Miami." Ruthie sipped her Scotch and hummed softly. Jerry said, "Yeah, well, uh, here's my friend," and turned to Ruthie. The woman looked shocked, then angry, then left. Jerry looked down at Ruthie, his big face determinedly bland. She stroked him through his trousers and murmured, "As I was saying, honey." He whispered, "For Chrissake, someone'll see." She shrugged. "Then let's go." He said he'd only just come and he wanted another drink, "And besides, you shouldn't . . . I mean, a mature person like you." Which meant she was old and getting fat, and which she'd known she would have to overcome. She ordered a double rye, and opened his zipper. He pressed up against the bar, looking around. The rye came and she gave it to him. He gulped half of it and breathed heavily and lit a cigarette and looked away from her. But then his head swung around and he whispered, "Baby, easy, easy," and one hand came down on her shoulder and slid to her waist. He looked around again and it was really getting dark and he bent his head. They exchanged a long kiss. His hand went from her waist to her rear and he murmured, "Momma, it's still good and tight." She murmured back, "And not only *that*."

He laughed huskily. She zipped him up again and said, "Drink up." He didn't bother. They made their way to the door. The guard said, "Leaving so soon?" Jerry said, "It's getting so dark in here, you can't see what you're doing." The guard said something about the power having failed, but out in the hall everything was bright.

Walking to the elevators, Jerry looked at her and said, "Maybe we shouldn't have left so soon. Maybe we're missing—"

She said, "You're missing nothing, honey. *They're* the ones missing something." She kissed him, letting him feel her educated tongue. He said, "Hey, not here," and came along like a good boy.

There was another slight cooling when she undressed, but a few minutes later he was making all the right sounds, and after that it was just what it was supposed to be. Except that toward the end she found herself thinking of Bernie. Of Bernie and his slight stammer and his shyness. A real *yutz* . . . but how he had wanted her.

The place seemed to be exploding with music and talk and shrill laughter, which occasionally sounded like screams. And what had happened to the lights? Ellie tried to push past a cluster of people and someone put an arm around her waist and spoke drunkenly. "This one feels good." He put his face in her neck. "Smells good, too." She broke away and blundered into a woman and the woman said, "Miss DeWyant, I was looking for you." For a moment all she could make out was the glint of eyeglasses. The woman said, "It's Marjory Fine," and laughed. "I know . . . something wrong with the lights. I finally had to put on my glasses, and even so . . ." She took Ellie's arm. "But it's sort of fun, don't you agree? Everyone free of the restraint of seeing too well, of being seen too well?"

Ellie said she supposed so and thanks for a lovely time.

"You're not *going*," Mrs. Fine said, and it wasn't a question. "At least not until I introduce you to someone." She looked around. "*If* I can find him. Ah, there's the handsome fellow."

Ellie expected the man would be close by, but Marjory Fine led her clear across the room to a spot near the hall door. How had she ever managed to see anyone that far away? It was actually *dark* now!

The man had his back turned and was talking to a woman. The woman was leaning against the wall, laughing. Marjory Fine said, "Sorry to interrupt, but here's someone you should meet."

The man turned. He was smiling, and then he wasn't. Marjory Fine said, "Bruce Golden, Eloise DeWyant. And this is . . . ?" The woman said May Krasmer. Bruce Golden asked, "When are you going to get some light in here, Marjory?" and Mrs. Fine said, "Does it really bother you?" He said not really, and she waved her hand at the room. "It doesn't seem to bother anyone else, either. I think I'm going to grab a handsome young buck. He won't be able to see what he's getting." They all laughed, and she was gone.

Bruce Golden took out cigarettes and offered them to May Krasmer. She accepted and he offered them to Ellie. She'd been smoking all evening. She didn't want another cigarette. But neither did she want to reject him again, even in so minor a matter. "Yes, thank you." He lighted May Krasmer's first and the flame illuminated her face. She was looking at Ellie. Ellie leaned forward and lit her cigarette and Bruce Golden moved the lighter to his own cigarette. "Three on a light," May Krasmer said, and blew out the flame. Golden said he wasn't aware that particular superstition was still alive. May Krasmer said, "Oh yes, very much alive among we survivors of the Spanish-American War."

Bruce Golden chuckled. Ellie inhaled deeply. She glanced at Bruce and he glanced at her. May Krasmer asked how long she was staying in Miami. Ellie said a few weeks, probably. Bruce explained she was the hotel owner's daughter. May Krasmer said, "And so very lovely. How lucky to be young and the hotel owner's daughter and so very lovely." She sounded strange—sad and strange. Bruce Golden didn't answer, because he was staring at Ellie and Ellie was staring at him.

She remembered her dream. She remembered how she had

wept for him to come back because he was the only one who moved her. In the growing darkness with their cigarettes brightening and dimming and brightening she seemed trapped in the dream again, couldn't move away as she knew she should. She had interrupted these two, and May Krasmer was looking at her and she and Bruce Golden had locked eyes and she couldn't unlock, couldn't do anything but stand and smoke.

So like Jonny. And he had taken her to the motel and into the shower and said he wouldn't wait until they were married, no, and he hadn't . . .

She turned away from Jonny and Bruce Golden. She said, "Good night," and he came after her, saying, "Don't go. Please. We were just chatting." He took her arm. "Stay and talk with us."

She knew it was wrong. That woman liked him and would be hurt. But she turned back with him.

The woman was gone. "She'll be back," he said, but he didn't mean it. And he didn't care. Their eyes had locked again. She moved carefully to the wall where May Krasmer had been standing and leaned against it. "What do you do for my father, Mr. Golden?"

He began to tell her. She listened, and she understood, but she also heard and understood another voice, Jonny's voice, explaining what he did and how he would be important, very important, and she would be his wife.

She didn't want to confuse Jonny and Bruce Golden. She tried to separate them, concentrating *hard* on what Golden was saying. But still the confusion remained, so she put out her hand and touched his wrist, to make him different from Jonny, to make him real and solid and Jonny just a memory. Bruce Golden stopped talking. She said, "And besides advertising?" He said, "Besides advertising there are the yearly brochures, the convention material, the special mailers, the promotions . . ." She kept her hand on his wrist. His face was very close to hers. His face was very serious and very close and very much a face she liked. Jonny began to dim out. Bruce Golden laughed as he explained a silly publicity stunt, and she found herself laughing with him. He grew quiet; then he murmured, "That's a very beautiful laugh, Miss DeWyant. You should use it more often. It might cause a few aches and pains among the more romantic, but that's the price romantics have to pay."

"You don't pay that price, do you, Mr. Golden?"

"Not usually. But I'll make an exception in this case."

"You're putting me on, but beautifully, Mr. Golden."

"No." He leaned closer. "No, I'm not."

"It's the darkness and the crazy music and all the people laughing and whatever you've been drinking. It's Miami Beach, Mr. Golden, we both know that."

"No," he whispered, and his hand took hers and his lips brushed her cheek. "It's us."

She laughed. "Love at first sight. Another battered survivor of the Spanish-American War."

"I don't know about that. At first sight you hated my guts. After that first sight I hated yours. I don't know about love, Miss DeWyant, not at this stage of the game, but I do know about chemistry. I know we have it for each other, and I know it's strong."

Laughing, she stepped out from the wall and past him. "For this I need another drink."

She expected he would hold her hand, or follow, but he let go and she was in among the dancing, laughing, screaming people and the glowing cigarettes and the pounding music (so loud!) and when she turned she was lost.

She understood. She had struck out at him in McKensil's office and ignored him in the hall, and how could he be sure she wouldn't do something like it again? How could he be sure she wouldn't have him fired if he pursued her?

She wanted to go back to him. She stood there, trying to re-orient herself, and hands clamped onto her waist from behind. Before she could think of what to do, she was pushed into the rocking darkness, across the room. A joke, she thought. Bruce Golden, perhaps. And she tried to look back. But then she slammed into a wall, a corner, her face hitting before she could raise her hands. She cried out, but it was lost in the music, the voices, the mélange of noise.

The voice was close to her ear. It was thin and high—a false voice, a disguised voice. It said, "Wouldn't our handsome President like to be here in the dark with you, Miss DeWyant? Wouldn't he enjoy . . . ?"

"Who is it?" she whispered, and again tried to turn. But the hands kept her from turning, one pressing her head into the corner.

"Remember, Miss DeWyant? Remember our handsome President? I could call him. He'd come to you, wouldn't he? *Wouldn't* he?"

She reached back then, trying to grab the hands, trying to gouge the hands, but one left her head and a sudden, crippling pain pierced her right kidney. She bent over, or tried to, gasping, striking the wall with her face. The hand returned to her head, the other maintained steady pressure on her back. She stopped attempting to struggle, sick from that searing pain, and from fear.

The voice said, "We both know *why* he would come, don't we, *Miss* DeWyant? We both know and you're going to say it. Confession is good for the soul, Miss DeWyant, so *say* it! *Say it!*"

"Because," she said, beginning to sob, beginning to fall apart. "Because . . ."

Her head was again slammed into the wall, her face hitting hard. She felt salty wetness run from her nostrils. "Because *why!*" the voice hissed, and it was infinite evil and infinite menace and it already knew and if she spoke it would let her alone.

"Because . . . he knows I could tell . . . and then everyone would know . . ." She broke down, weeping, and the hand gripped her hair, drawing back her head, preparing to smash her face into the wall, really smash and crush her face, and the voice said, "Say it all now. Say it once and you can go. Say it *all!*"

"Everyone would know," she wept. "And they're not supposed . . ." She choked on her tears and sobs and the hot wetness from her nose, choked on her terror. Someone shrieked laughter. And on that sound Ellie began to shriek laughter. The hands yanked her away from the wall and threw her into the darkness and she wasn't laughing she was screaming, and someone else screamed and she bumped into people and she was running, running, leading the chorus of screams. Running with the hands directing her.

Except that the hands were gone. But she wasn't fooled. The infinite evil and infinite menace were there and had always been there and would always be there, waiting for her as it had waited for her mother, and screaming was good because it burned out everything, every thought, and if she kept screaming long enough, it might burn out her very brain and she would be through with thought and through with living. . . .

The smash across her face stopped her. And in stopping she heard other screams and realized light was pouring in from the open hall door and people were pushing toward it and voices were asking what was wrong and to please, *please* let them out. She looked for Bruce Golden, thinking he had struck her and ended the screams. But he wasn't there and no one was looking at her and everyone was trying to get out.

She went along with the crowd and out the door into the hall. Bruce Golden stepped forward and took her arm. "Are you all right?" She nodded, eyes fixed on his face. He led her away from the elevators, to the end of the hall where there were no people and no noise. "You mustn't shake that way. Some silly drunk panicked and it became general. Nothing, really." He used his handkerchief on her face, her nose, then pressed it into her hand. She looked at it and it was red and she held it to her nose and tried to think who the voice, the hands, could have been.

The one who had come to the table the other night and made silly talk about the President?

But he had come with a sweet woman and they had been a sweet stupid couple and no one knew . . .

She stood there, shaking. Her nose stopped bleeding but she kept shaking, kept fearing.

120

"Ellie," Bruce Golden said. "Ellie, let's go. We'll get some air."

She said yes, they'd get some air.

They rode down in the elevator.

Maybe it hadn't happened. Maybe she had imagined the whole thing. Maybe she had simply bumped into the wall. Maybe she was flipping, absolutely.

She took his hand.

"One thing," he said.

"What?" She looked hungrily into his eyes, hungry for sanity—for comfort and purpose and sanity. "What, Bruce?"

"At least we made friends. It took a near riot, but we finally made friends."

She smiled. She hoped it wasn't as close to crying as she felt it was, but kept smiling.

She was sitting on a couch in the lobby because she couldn't face Eunice and television and the thought that she might as well pack up and go home. Then she saw them—Bruce Golden and the hotel owner's daughter. They walked from the elevators and out the back doors. All right, so he *had* wanted to dump her for the girl. She'd half expected it from the moment he'd approached her, a handsome man like that, because she'd also seen Dan (before it got too dark to see anything) and remembered what he had said and what he had done.

Someone sat down beside her. A rumbling voice said, "Mind if I . . . ?" She turned, and the voice died out in a funny way that made her smile. What also made her smile was that she'd expected a man of middle years from that voice, and it was only a boy. Big enough, from the way his knees came up as he sat there, like a high school basketball player. Big enough and very well built, but still a boy.

"Of course not." He seemed to be staring at her. She wondered if something were wrong—her makeup perhaps. "Enjoying your stay in Miami?" she asked finally, to break the silence.

"Not too much," he said. He finally dropped his eyes.

She took out her compact. She looked herself over while talking, and could see nothing wrong. "I guess there aren't many people your age in the hotel this time of year."

"I guess not." He leaned back, right arm going across the top of the couch, hand resting near her. "But even if there were, it's no guarantee I'd enjoy myself."

"No, of course not."

"Because I've yet to find a girl in my age bracket who's worth a damn, sexually, emotionally, or intellectually."

She was momentarily shocked. He glanced at her, as if to assess just what effect his words had had, a touchingly childlike glance that took her back to the New York days, to shock words and looks and the importance attached to them years ago with Dan, with other boys . . .

Her silence must have worried him. He took his arm down, murmuring, "If I said too much . . ."

She smiled and shook her head. "I didn't expect such maturity from so young a man."

He liked that. He looked down at his big hands, flexing them a few times. "Maturity isn't anything you can judge by *years*, is it? I mean, you know immature people much older than you, don't you? And mature people younger than you?"

She said of course, and how old was *he*?

"Near nineteen."

She wanted to ask *how* near, but it might embarrass him and he was a fine boy, mature enough—and why bother?

He said, "In fact, I've always mistrusted words like 'mature.' And words like 'young' and 'old.' "

She began to feel something. " 'Young' and 'old' are a lot more specific words than 'mature.' At eighteen, you *are* young. At sixty, you'll be old."

His head snapped up and around so quickly that his long brown hair whipped in back. His face was large, lean, and at the moment intense. He was a debater seizing on a weak point. "You're talking years again. Are *all* boys of eighteen alike in being young? Are *all* men of sixty alike in being old?"

How *important* he made this silly conversation seem. In spite of herself, it began to seem important to her too. "No, but in general—"

"Not in general. In specifics. Specifics are what count, Miss ..."

She should have said, *"Mrs.* Krasmer." He had certainly noticed her wedding band. She said, "May, to you," and smiled. He said, "Al, to you . . ." and seemed about to say her name and then didn't. Again it was touching, and flattering.

Had he been staring because he found her attractive? An "old" woman like her? She laughed. He flushed, thinking she was laughing at him. She said, "I just remembered someone—" Harold—poor old Harold— "he's as old as a man can get, and yet he's only forty-three."

"There. That's what I meant." He rubbed his hands together, and charged on, nonstop. "Take a woman like you. You're barely thirty, I can tell, but even thirty is a lie when describing how *young* you are." She began to murmur, "Thank you," but he wasn't through. "Your looks, and it's more than that—I mean, I've known pretty women before, but some of them don't have the—the special *glow* of youth." That was a television cliché of the most obvious sort; and even so it didn't prevent the warmth from taking hold of her. "We're sitting here talking," he said, turned toward her now, animated and excited and more than a little apprehensive, "and I feel as if I'm with someone I could date and like and—"

"And marry," she injected, laughing. She'd had to say it, to make him see that she wasn't a complete fool.

"Biologically," he murmured, "there's nothing wrong with it, you know."

She heard herself say, "I know," and laughed again.

"The only reason you expected me to lose face . . . I mean, I know what you were doing—reminding me of the social taboos. But social taboos are falling left and right, aren't they?"

She nodded. "If you promise not to propose tonight, I'll allow you to take me for a walk."

He grinned, and sobered quickly. "I'll have to . . ."

"Your parents?" she prompted, and the concept of parents intruded on the game.

"It's all right," he said firmly. "They're in the Platinum Room. The show doesn't end for a while."

They stood up. He was tall and broad and very good-looking. He was the dream of what she had wanted in a boy back in New York, when such dreams had been all of life.

They walked to the back doors. She felt discomfort, and glanced around to see if anyone was watching them. But even if they were, they would think them a boy and his mother.

No, not his *mother*.

At thirty-eight she could easily have an eighteen-year-old son.

She was relieved when they left the lobby. It was cold, but that was good, too, because there weren't many people outside, just a few figures moving in the darkness. She asked how come he was on vacation this time of the year.

"I'm waiting to get into a good college. I hope for Berkeley . . ." His parents had insisted he accompany them. "I didn't have anything better to do."

"No girl friend?"

He shrugged. "No *one* girl friend." He looked at her as they reached the end of the concrete deck. "And I meant what I said about girls in my age bracket." His voice grew playful, but not entirely free of apprehension. "Now if *you'd* been back home . . ."

She leaned on the railing and smiled out at the sea. She was shivering, but inner warmth was there. He said, "That's not much of a dress. I mean, it's terrific, but not much to keep you warm."

She nodded, not thinking, just feeling.

"For medicinal purposes only," he said, his deep voice threatening to slip upward into areas of childhood. She felt his jacket placed around her, his hand press her shoulder.

Still without thinking, still only feeling, she put her hand over his. She said, "Thank you, Al," softly, as she might have said it back in New York.

They stood there a while, his hand growing warm under hers;

then she turned from the sea. "Let's walk. Tell me about yourself."

He did. In detail. In all the exciting detail that young people see in their lives. They walked in the deeper shadows of the cabanas, and stopped to look out at the sea again when they reached the brief section of end-railing. He said, "I can babble on this way for hours. But what about you, May?"

She told him about Chicago and her stores, and he said, "Really? Can I pick them or can I pick them!" She avoided speaking of Harold, waiting for him to ask. He asked what she liked to read, what she liked to do. He didn't ask about the ring, and after a while she understood he wasn't going to.

Now they had defined the limits, the boundaries of the court, and could play their little game within them. For as long as the game lasted; which might be this one night.

She warned herself about that. He liked her, yes. Bruce Golden had liked her, too, until someone else had come along. Only with this boy it didn't matter. How could it? His parents were probably looking for him right now.

She asked how long he was staying.

"My father's an investment broker here on convention. He'll stay for Senator Christopher's speech. My mother wants to stay on longer, if I'll stay with her."

She said nothing.

"How long are *you* staying?"

She said she wasn't sure.

"Well," he said slowly, "if I knew I had someone interesting to talk to, to play a game of tennis with once in a while . . ."

"I play tennis."

"Great! You ever fish?"

She shook her head.

"I can teach you. There're piers and charter boats . . ." He talked and rubbed his hands together and strode ahead every so often and turned, facing her, still talking as she caught up. She smiled and nodded and they reached the pool. The thought struck her that they would see each other in swimwear. Her bikini was close to nothing. How would he react to her in close to nothing? As Harold did? As Dan did?

The feeling was bad, and she had to end it. "Don't wear me out with sports, Al, or there'll be nothing left for moonlight walks."

He stopped talking then. She looked at the pool. He suddenly laughed and put his arm around her shoulders, and playing it fast and funny, said, "There's always plenty left for *that*. That's the name of the game, isn't it, May?" And kissed her quickly on the cheek and pulled her toward the lobby, gagging it up in case she should protest.

When he finally stopped laughing and practically running, she said, "Yes, it is." And met his look, let him see he had nothing to fear.

He quieted. He kept his arm around her and they walked slowly across the deck. But his breath came quickly and his arm trembled. He was terribly excited.

"Tomorrow morning, May? About nine? Near the pool?"

She nodded.

They reached the lobby and he put on his jacket, fumbling with one sleeve until she held it for him. "I'd better go," he said. And then, whispering as he opened the door, "You're *beautiful!*"

Now it was her turn to tremble.

Both lamps were on, and Ruthie lay on top of the covers, her nightgown rolled up to her belly. He came over quietly. The bed looked as if the Green Bay Packers had held scrimmage there. "Ruthie?" She sighed and rolled over on her side, big bare ass to him. He turned away, frowning. And remembered how exciting she had once seemed. Now . . .

He shrugged, moving to the desk. A younger, finer woman would still excite him. And he would get one, soon. Not with his looks. He chuckled as he sat down and put on the desk light. He had no illusions about his looks. With the money, the *fortune*, he was going to make in the next few weeks.

He took a sheet of hotel stationery and the hotel ballpoint and drew a few lines through the neat *Bal Metropole* lettering. He wrote:

DeWyant—$150,000 *up.*

Jorge's boss—$150,000 *up.*

Total—$300,000 *minimum.*

He drew several neat lines through each of the three figures. He drew circles and boxes and triangles. His eyes didn't see them. His mind clicked along, bringing up possibilities, eliminating others. Then he wrote, "Eloise DeWyant and President Standers. Affair? Not enough for her fear, or her payoff. Child as result of affair? Maybe. But would Michael Wheeler allow such child to be born? Secret marriage? Another maybe."

He carefully crossed out all the sentences, and wrote, "Bastard or secret marriage. Records should exist for either. Alert Jorge to search for such records? Then I lose exclusivity. Hire researchers myself? Even if I get right answers, an agency will also know, a private eye will share exclusivity."

He crumpled the sheet of paper and put it in his jacket pocket, then took a fresh sheet and crossed out the heading and printed in big capital letters:

ASSUME BASTARD AND MARRIAGE, AND WORK TO ISOLATE ONE FROM ELOISE DEWYANT.

He crumpled the sheet of paper and put it in his pocket with the other.

He thought of Jorge's boss. He didn't have to write that out. He'd already done so, the day he'd met Jorge and realized there had to be someone behind him. That someone didn't want to be known. That someone had lots of dough. That someone would eventually pay not to be known.

Blackmail was the word. A dangerous word, and a dangerous ploy. Leo Skein knew that well. Ruthie didn't have to tell him about it. But he was fifty-four (Ruthie thought he was fifty) and his heart was acting up. Nothing *really* dangerous, but the doctor at Harkness Pavilion, where he had spent most of the take on his last job, wanted him to "definitely slow down. Play more golf and lose some weight and get plenty of rest. If you're in the position to retire . . ."

After this was over, he'd be in a perfect position to retire.

But dangerous? Hell, yes.

He went to the closet, looking back to make sure Ruthie was still asleep. He took his large suitcase down from the shelf, opened it on the floor and removed the cloth-wrapped bundle. A moment later the cloth was back in the suitcase, the suitcase back on the shelf. He went into the bathroom and locked the door. He burned the crumpled sheets of hotel stationery and flushed them down the toilet. Then he sat on the closed toilet, wiping excess oil from the gun with tissues from the wall-set dispenser.

He didn't like guns. He rarely carried one, except when the going got tough. The going would be tough from here until the end, and the end wouldn't come until he was out of Florida and out of the States.

He finished and sniffed the gun to make sure there was no heavy odor of oil or powder. Smell as well as bulge could give a weapon away when dealing with professionals. And there might be professionals behind the scenes.

Bulge was no problem with the Colt .25 pocket automatic. The overall length was four and a half inches, the weight only thirteen ounces, yet the blued miniature fired a magazine of six bullets. Up close, and loaded as it was with soft lead, it would stop the toughest strong-arm.

He put it in his jacket pocket. He would carry it from now on. At the pool or beach, it would be in his smoke-and-accessory kit.

He returned to the bedroom, sat down on the edge of the big double bed, and backhanded Ruthie's ass. She said, "What . . . oh, how'd it go?" He nodded, and picked up the phone. "Get this bed fit for sleeping. Turn the sheets or something." The operator came on, and he read the number Jorge had printed into his address book.

It was, as he'd expected, an answering service. "Mr. Eight" would receive his message. He hung up and Ruthie was stretching and rubbing her eyes.

"I see everything went okay for *you*," he said.

She got up and walked into the bathroom. He moved to the window, not wanting to hear anything. Lately, she disgusted him.

She came out nude and began stripping the bed. He said, "Put something on, for Chrissake," seeing her reflection in the window. He closed the drapes. When he turned, she was pulling a nightgown over her head.

She didn't look at him, didn't say anything. He smiled placatingly. "Sort of nervous. That party—damned music and all."

She remade the bed in silence. He walked to the desk and considered writing Chuck, and couldn't think of what to tell him. He hadn't been able to think of anything to tell him for a long time now. Anyway, the kid hadn't been answering worth a damn the past two or three years. He lived in Dayton and had a stepfather and was going to high school, and it was all a million miles removed from the father he had known until he was five and seen only twice since then and not seen at all in the past three years. They had nothing in common any more.

When he made his killing, *then* they would pick up again. He'd invite him to Buenos Aires, where he might settle down, and they'd have a fine time together.

"I could go for a hamburger," Ruthie said.

"Haven't you had enough meat for one night?"

He'd wanted to make it funny, but it didn't come out that way. Ruthie got red. "Now listen, Leo—yeah, Max. I wish you was Leo again. The old Leo. If you want me in a separate room, say so."

"I'm sorry."

"So am I. I know you don't like it any more. I got the message. So after this job we're finished. But until it's over, stay off my back."

He was humiliated. He laughed and said, "I might not want to stay off your back the *entire* time. Like last night." He quickly added, "I was feeling rotten, but you misunderstand if you think that means—"

"Honey, when it comes to that I never misunderstand. I've got instincts as sharp in *that* department as you have in the con. If you don't want any, fine, only don't keep knocking it."

She went into the bathroom. He heard something, and instead of going to the end of the room drew closer to the door. She was crying.

It made him feel better. Why, he didn't know, but he knocked softly. "Ruthie, hey, let me buy you a steak instead of a hamburger. Get dressed—"

The phone rang. He went to the bed. "Yes?"

"Mr. Eight is returning your call," Jorge said.

"I think we'd better meet tomorrow instead of waiting for the regularly scheduled date."

"Why?"

"Problems. Just you and me this time, okay?"

Jorge hesitated.

Max said, "There's a good movie at the drive-in."

"All right." The line clicked.

Max rose, breathing hard. The second time tonight he'd breathed hard—the first time, when manhandling Ellie DeWyant. And he shouldn't breathe hard. It wasn't good for him. Besides, if *little* things excited him, what would happen when the action *really* started? It would be a hell of a note to drop dead before the payoff!

He laughed, just to hear the sound, and went to the bathroom door. "Ruthie?"

She said, "Okay. Let me get my face on."

He lit a cigar. Tomorrow at this time he might know where Jorge went to report. It wouldn't take long after that to know *who* he reported to.

"A filet mignon," he called. "The *best* for Mrs. Max Prager." And laughed, and walked up and back, thinking how Chuckie would love Buenos Aires.

"Thank you," Bert Cooper said, blocking the doorway. "We found the trouble ourselves."

The night manager said, "If Mrs. Fine would let the electrician here take a look—"

"Mrs. Fine is resting. It was just a loose fuse. Thank you." He closed the door, turned the lock, heard the electrician say, "Why didn't the air-conditioning . . ." The voice died away.

He walked across the room to the master bedroom and knocked. "They're gone, Mrs. Fine."

Marjory Fine came out. She looked around and made a face. "Unbelievable!" The room was a shambles; glasses and food and napkins and paper plates and ashes and butts on the furniture and carpeting; chairs overturned; a coffee table split in the center, forming a three-dimensional M. "Change the rest of the bulbs. Then I'll call for some cleanup help."

The man who had guarded the door during the party went to a lamp, took off the shade, and screwed out a bulb with a metallic cast. He replaced it with a normal bulb from a large paper sack on the floor.

"You'll be wanting your massage first, won't you?" he asked.

She bent to an armchair and brushed away cigarette stubs and ashes. "I don't know." She watched him awhile. "It was such a good idea. You agreed it was."

He was at a floor lamp beside the bar. "I did. Positively brilliant, Mrs. Fine."

"C'mon now, it's Marjory."

He replaced the shade on the lamp. "Sometimes it is, and sometimes it isn't."

"Well it *is*, from now on. Just how intimate do two people have to get before they exchange first names?"

He was working on another lamp, and nodded.

She rose and walked to the bar, where she picked up the tinted glasses she'd worn earlier. "If that stupid girl hadn't screamed . . ." She put the glasses on and looked around. "Now it's nothing; just like sunglasses. But with those infrared bulbs all over the room . . ." She took off the glasses and went behind the bar. "Scotch?"

"Yes, thank you, Marjory."

"So formal," she mocked. "Always so proper and British and formal."

"It's the way I prefer it," he said, changing still another bulb in a lamp near the hall door. "And if you're honest, you'll admit it's the way you prefer it, too."

"I guess so," she murmured, pouring Chivas Regal.

He replaced the pale yellow shade. "Of course. Otherwise, it wouldn't have been possible for us to continue as long as we have—four full seasons, and part of that first." He looked around, murmured, "Ah, that one there," and went to a lamp near the window.

"Do I pay you enough?" she asked, coming out from behind the bar with two lowball glasses filled to the brims.

"Quite enough. Any more and you'd find yourself considering it blackmail. Then we'd both be in trouble."

She stopped to sip a little from each glass. "Mmmm. Come get your drink."

He picked up the paper bag, now full of infrared bulbs, and went into the bedroom. She sat down in the armchair she'd cleaned. He came out, took the glass she handed him, bowed a little, and drank. "You mix a man's drink, Marjory."

She shook her head, muttering, "I think you get more warmth out of Mrs. Fine."

He went to an overturned chair, straightened it, and sat down facing her. Bert Cooper was a handsome man. Not contemporarily handsome. The slicked-back hair. The lean, long, somewhat-worn face. The old-world manners that were outdated even in the old world. But built beautifully—strong, tight, no waste on his five-foot-ten frame.

"We forgot the toast," he said. "To a successful season."

He spoke well, but he wasn't well educated. She hadn't pried into his past, but she felt certain he'd had little formal education. All she knew about him was that he had served in the

British Merchant Marine, in the British Navy in World War II, and had been working as a pool boy in Miami for the past nine years. He read a great deal, classics mainly, going slowly and painfully, then trying to share the insights and knowledge with whoever would listen. He had bored her several times with college-type lectures on *The Republic*, *The Life of Greece*, *Don Quixote*, and similar long-forgotten books from her youth.

"You've never really told me about yourself," she said.

He took two cigarettes from the worn silver case he had carried since she'd first met him while visiting a friend at the Trillon Apartment-Motel. He lit them and brought her one. "Very little to tell, Mrs. Fine."

Mrs. Fine it was.

He was back in his chair, still immaculate in blue suit (*always* blue; he must have at least six of them), white shirt, striped gray-and-black tie, and shiny black shoes planted firmly and respectfully on the floor. "Would you like to tell me about yourself, Mrs. Fine?"

She laughed. "If I ever decide to run away with a man, you're it."

He bent forward in a sitting bow. "If I ever decide to accept a woman's offer to run away, you'll be it." He drained his glass and brought it to the bar. "Would you like your massage now?"

She made a don't-know gesture.

"Why don't we try anyway? Remember the first party last season? We didn't have anything nearly as effective as the infrared lights and no one seemed to pair off properly and all that work with the two-way mirror came to nothing. And yet, talking about it during massage, you remembered a few items . . ."

"You still have the mirror, don't you?"

"Stored safely in my place."

"You'll install it next week. We can't have two electrical failures in one season." She ground out the cigarette. "I should have saved it for later on, when the guests were paired off better. Perhaps the third or fourth party. I didn't think it through."

"Still, you saw some interesting items, didn't you?" He came over and held out his hand. She shook her head. "I saw a few myself," he said, "and I wasn't able to move around like you. There was a couple dancing and the man bumped into another man, a smaller man. That interior decorator."

She looked up. "Marco Renier?"

"Yes. After they bumped, Mr. Renier said something in the man's ear and the man continued dancing and they came quite close to the door. And even though the glasses didn't work as well as we'd hoped, I saw that Mr. Renier was putting his hands on the man and trying to touch his organ without alerting the woman."

Marjory stood up. Bert took her arm and led her to the bedroom, where he put on a night-table lamp. She sank to the edge of the bed. "I did see something surprising. That dumpy little woman, Mrs. Prager, at the bar with Jerry Leech."

Bert said, "Oh?" encouraging her to remember more. He was on his knees and had removed her shoes. He reached under her dress to free her stockings of the garter belt. She lay back. He rubbed her thighs a little, encouraging her further, and drew off one stocking.

"Leech was talking with another woman and Mrs. Prager came over and stood beside him. I couldn't see at first what she was doing, but Leech finally turned to Mrs. Prager, ignoring the other woman, a much younger and prettier woman."

Bert removed the second stocking, once again chafing her thighs between his hard palms. "And then?"

She drew up her knees. She breathed more quickly, remembering the brief glance she'd had of Leech's organ in Mrs. Prager's hand. Bert was rubbing both thighs now, and she thought of how she was wearing no pants and how he could see everything and she lowered her knees and whispered, "Don't look."

"I can't help but look," he replied, and took her by both arms and raised her up. She stood still while he removed her dress and brassiere. She lay down on her stomach. He began working on her shoulders and back. "I'm compelled to look."

134

"Why?" she whispered, thinking of Jerry Leech's organ being squeezed by that fat little woman.

He worked his hands down to her waist, the fingers probing, soothing, digging, smoothing. "My peculiarity, Mrs. Fine. I look, and lust, and know I'll never experience the pleasure of having you. It hurts, yet feels good, too."

All familiar words. All things he told her at every massage. All things she believed while the massage was going on, and dismissed afterward. All things that helped her toward the rare moments, the prized and hard-won moments of pleasure.

"Do you want me now?" she whispered.

His hands kneaded her buttocks. "You know I do."

"How do I know?" She remembered a man and woman dancing together near the windows, the man's hand resting on the woman's rear. And another couple on the couch, kissing, thinking themselves unobserved, their hands moving, touching, and then a second woman coming along, calling a man's name, and the man on the couch disengaging himself to join his wife.

"I don't like to be vulgar," Bert said. His fingers moved lightly down between her buttocks, and she stiffened, and he moved quickly to her thighs, and she relaxed.

"Be vulgar this once."

He sat down beside her, on the pillow. He was very obviously aroused. She turned her head away, murmuring, "Poor Bert. Poor darling."

He rose. "What else did you see, Mrs. Fine?"

She told him about Jerry Leech and Mrs. Prager, in detail, embroidering a bit as he manipulated first one foot, then the other, making them feel as if they were coming free of her ankles. She told him about the dancing couple, and he said, "Over on your back please, Mrs. Fine." She obeyed and lay exposed, watching him through slitted eyes, waiting for his hands to leave her shoulders.

She told him about the couple on the couch, and his fingers brushed her nipples as he moved his hands to her rib cage. Lean-

135

ing over her, he pressed down with the heels of his hands, moving them up under her breasts until she groaned. He did it several more times, making her feel big-breasted and high-breasted and almost ready.

"What else?" he asked, hands growing feather-light on her sides and stomach. She giggled, and he moved to her hips. "Wasn't there anything else, Mrs. Fine?"

"That fool girl screamed . . ."

"I saw several interesting items," he interrupted. His hands worked from hips to thighs and back up to hips. His hands approached and skirted forbidden territory. Occasionally they trembled.

She forgot her anger over the screams that had ended her party. She watched him, enjoying his excitement. He said, "There was this man, a boy really, dancing with this woman, near sixty I'd say. She was seducing him right there while dancing. She was doing things to that boy . . ."

He went on, and she saw it in her mind while knowing he was making it all up. He worked on her thighs and calves and ankles. And back to her thighs. Very high on her thighs now. Dangerously high now.

Her hands moved down, reached her belly, stopped. He was saying, ". . . shifted her skirt around so the zipper portion . . ." then turned abruptly away.

She knew what was coming because it was part of their ritual— one of the most exciting parts. When he again faced her, his trousers gaped open. She rolled onto her stomach. Her hand reached down and worked. He talked about the boy and the old woman and massaged close to where her hand worked. She raised herself a little, panting, struggling to make it, to attain the elusive instant of release. "Now," she gasped, and came up on her knees.

His hands left her. The bed sagged under his weight and his trousered legs brushed her bare legs and she felt it, the heated firmness pushing between her buttocks. He said, "My dear, my dear," his voice ragged, trembling. "My *dear* . . ." And just when she thought he might forget himself, the bed bounced and she looked to see him standing beside her, handkerchief out, body crouched, hand moving rapidly. She tried. She tried so hard! But that scream lingered in her mind and she couldn't make it, not even when he threw the handkerchief on her pillow.

She gave up. "That bitch! That stupid bitch! Did you see who it was? I could kill her! All that work. All that planning and all that work! For nothing!"

He rubbed her neck. "Now, now." He picked up his handkerchief and went to the bathroom. She began to cry. He came back and gave her the pill and water, covered her, and drew up a chair. "I'll sit right here until you're asleep."

"Stay till morning," she begged.

"Mustn't chance compromising you. That wouldn't do at all."

"*Please*, Bert."

"You wouldn't like it when you woke up. You're no little chippie to get your name bandied about. They wonder about you, yes, but no one can say a word."

He was right, of course. She asked for her money. He got it from the false compartment in the suitcase. She took five one-hundred-dollar bills from the thick packet. (Another protection— cash, always cash.) He put the bills in his wallet, returned the packet to the suitcase and the suitcase to the closet. He put out the lamp and sat down beside her. "You're very generous, Mrs. Fine."

"Marjory," she murmured, beginning to grow sleepy.

"Marjory. And the next party will go better. You'll have your pleasure, I promise."

She held out her hand. He took it, pressed it gently.

"Did you see who screamed?" she muttered.

"No, Marjory."

"Funny thing. Prager running across the room with someone. Didn't get more than a glimpse."

"Mr. Prager and a girl, yes."

Her eyes were closing, but something in his voice made her

look at him. He was sitting there, the same as always. And when next he spoke, his voice was the same as always. "They seemed to be playing a game."

Her eyes closed. "I wish . . . I could play . . ." Quite suddenly she was crying again. Half asleep from the pill and crying. "Why can't I . . . be like other women? Why, Bert?"

He didn't answer, and she didn't expect him to answer, because there was no answer. Mel had ceased satisfying her very early in their marriage. Several affairs had proved to be failures. Erotic books and films had worked for a while. Now there was this, only this.

She wept and held his hand.

Bert Cooper closed the bedroom door quietly, went to the bar, and poured a Scotch. He sat down in the clean armchair and crossed his legs. He considered calling for a maid, then decided against it. It might wake Marjory.

"Playing a game," he murmured, thinking of Prager and the hotel owner's daughter, the girl who had screamed.

He had another Scotch and continued to think. It puzzled him.

It also interested him. It might mean money. And despite what he'd told Marjory, he needed money. But not money *she* gave him. Big money, free of any association with Marjory. Big money that would allow him to approach her as an equal.

He went to the bar, his face changing. He poured a fresh drink, for the first time showing emotion, violent emotion. He had been at sea twenty-seven years and in Miami nine years and had never really wanted anything in all that time except his freedom and his comfort. Now things were changing. Now he was past fifty and alone and finally unhappy at being alone.

Not because he was getting old. He was a strong man, in perfect health. He had always been able to do a woman two or three times a night, night after night, and he felt no weakening now that he was approaching fifty-two. The weakening was in his *raison d'être*, his reason for going on as he always had. The cause of this weakening was Marjory Fine.

138

A bit off, he'd considered her, when she first brought him into her employ, into her confidence. He'd laughed to himself and played his role and collected his money. He was used to serving the rich, no matter how exotic the manner of service. It didn't bother him. It was fun and games. But then the fun grew until it overshadowed all other fun, all normal relations with women, and the game became the most important part of his life, and he began to want Marjory Fine and to believe he could make her want him.

Not the Bert Cooper he was now. Not the servant. It was difficult enough for such a woman to accept a man under the best of circumstances, and impossible if that man was her inferior. Her husband was her inferior, in all the ways that counted —in education and intelligence and sensitivity and physical attractiveness. That's why she couldn't tolerate him. That's why she couldn't tolerate most men.

He had observed enough life and read enough psychology to understand more than the basic types—and she was no basic type. That was her problem. Her dream of love, her fantasy of copulation, was so superior to what she had experienced, that she could, in the end, turn in only one direction—away from herself to *other* people's sexual experiences, to voyeurism and masturbation. And even then she often failed because she had to forget what she was doing, and a girl's scream or any other unplanned element made her remember and spoiled things.

He could change all that. Freed of his role as servant, he could give her love, give her eroticism such as even her advanced fantasies had never offered her. They would play and play—hours, days!—and end in lovemaking that would break through her frigidity, her incapacity. He *knew* he was right. But right or wrong, he wanted his chance.

Prager and Miss DeWyant. They might free him. Prager had been playing a dangerous little game tonight. It was either for sex, or for money. He didn't see Prager playing for sex. For money then, and Miss DeWyant had *big* money.

He got up and turned out the lights and left. He hadn't the faintest idea of what he would do. But he would do something.

16

SUNDAY, JANUARY 8, P.M.
TO
MONDAY, JANUARY 9, A.M.

The Lincoln Continental came west on Abbott, pulling to the curb before the faded green-stucco house. It was six o'clock, and the heat of what had been a surprising scorcher, after yesterday's gray chill, still lingered. Surfside, even this close to Collins Avenue, seemed a sleepy Southern town on the Sabbath.

The big car stayed parked only a moment, its motor running. Violetta Murillo stepped out, said, "Thank you, Mr. McKensil," and walked up the concrete path between two browned-out patches of lawn. The car moved away. Violetta paused on the porch to watch it turn the corner toward Collins, then let herself in.

The combination living room-dining room ran the length of the house, with picture windows at both front and rear. It was furnished in cheap, worn bamboo-and-print, with a brown cotton hooked rug in the living room section. Through an arch on the left were a bathroom and kitchen, and through a similar arch on the right were two adjoining bedrooms. The air-conditioning was on.

Violetta went through the right-hand arch. One bedroom door was open. The other was closed and locked. She knocked. "Forget it," she said in Spanish.

The door opened. She put a hand on her hip, model-fashion, and burlesqued a step-and-turn for Jorge's inspection. She wore a

140

minishift of pink and gray swirls, a lovely dress that managed to emphasize both her sexuality and her youth. "See? I gave him my best. Tell Mr. Lamas he has wonderful taste in women's clothes."

"He will be disappointed. You said McKensil was going to be fast. We would like to get him working with us *before* the Senator arrives."

"He's more afraid than I thought." She came past Jorge and into the bedroom, smiling at the way he moved back from her. This one was also afraid.

The room was bare of furniture. The inside wall, shared by both bedrooms, had four cameras bracketed lens-first into niches cut from plaster and lathing. They ran from waist level a few feet from the door in progressive steps to ceiling level near a window. The highest was a movie camera. "Three days I've been working with him." She laughed. "*On* him. Three days he's been looking at me so hard I thought he'd go blind. So when he asked me to work on Sunday I was sure it would happen."

"Did you invite him in?"

"No. He has to ask to come in. Of course, if he doesn't ask, I'll have to invite. But not for a few more days. In the car . . ." She made a quick Latin gesture of bewilderment. "He was breathing so hard. And he knows I'm alone. Yet he said he had to keep an appointment." She moved back toward the door, coming very close to Jorge. "Maybe there's something wrong with me? Maybe I'm not woman enough, eh, Jorge?"

He stepped back again. She walked into the second bedroom. This one had a large double bed, two lamp tables and two dressers, all in inexpensive but attractive gray walnut. The bed was placed parallel to and under four Fragonard prints, set in unusual circular frames, running from door to window, low to high. In the ceiling was a cluster of modernistic cone-shaped lamps. Violetta threw the wall switch. The bed was bathed in white lights made to seem softer by two blues. "I will feel like a movie star."

He grunted. "Don't forget. Either those lights or the bed lamps. Even one lamp is all right. I have special film, if necessary."

She nodded.

His eyes slid from her to the bed. He turned and left the room. She followed, smiling to herself. "Would you like something to eat?"

He said no and went into the kitchen, to the phone on the low counter dividing table area from work area.

"Drink, then? I have Scotch, vodka, and rum."

"I know," he muttered, dialing carefully. "Who do you think did the shopping?"

She went around the counter to the sink and made sure he saw her taking one of the pills Mr. Lamas had given her when she'd first agreed to the plan. Everything for John McKensil's comfort and her protection. Jorge shifted position, looking at the table. She came back around the counter.

"*Patrón?* Jorge. No, he didn't." He listened. Violetta brushed him as she went by. He shrank against the wall. She rattled things in a drawer, came back, and put her hand on his arm. He pulled loose, shook his head, said, "And about tonight, with Prager?"

He listened again. She pouted up into his face, pressing him with her breasts. He finally shoved her away, mouthing violent words. She laughed and sat down at the table, crossing her legs as she did for McKensil. He faced the wall. She laughed again, because she felt he wanted her almost as much as the manager did.

Jorge said, "I will be *most* careful, *patrón*. End his prying, yes, *patrón*."

Violetta studied him. He was like a soldier, almost, standing at attention before his general. Even talking on the phone.

When he sat down at the table, he looked worried. She went and got the rum and poured some into a water glass. He took it without comment and drank. He lit a *cigarro*, almost as small as a cigarette, and rubbed his face.

"This is hard for you, isn't it, Jorge?"

He nodded without thinking, then caught himself. "Hard? Of course. As it is for the *patrón*. It is always hard for a patriot—"

"I mean this *criminal* thing."

142

"It is not criminal," he muttered, "if it is for the cause of freedom."

"*Viva*," she mocked.

"I do not joke."

She made believe she was yawning.

He finished the rum in one long swallow. "The *patrón* is also involved. Could you think of *him* as a criminal?" He laughed, as if it were beyond possibility.

She was annoyed. "What makes you think a rich man has to be a *good* man?"

"Rich? The *patrón* is more than rich. A man of importance. Of power and importance. And honor."

"Of money. The only difference between you and him is money."

He stood up, white with anger. "You are a stupid little girl. You know nothing about men, about life. The *patrón* . . ." He waved his arm. "He was like a *presidente*. He ruled thousands of people—houses and fields and *everything*. Do you think that was just money?"

She didn't want to quarrel with him. She didn't want to hurt him. She had merely wanted to make him admit that he was out for himself, like most people. All right—for revenge, too, like she was. To get back to Cuba, like so many others were. But also for money, and for *himself*.

"The *patrón* and his father ruled over me and my father and my mother. He took care of us, thousands of us. Good times and bad . . ."

"I'm sorry," she said. She still didn't understand how a man could feel that way, but she finally believed he *did* feel that way.

He stared at her, as if to determine whether she was mocking him again. Satisfied she wasn't, he sat down and relit his *cigarro*. "I know how it sounds to someone like you, brought up in Miami." He snorted. "This place. This country. No one cares for anyone else. Their families sometimes, yes. But their leaders?"

"They vote," she murmured. "They elect those leaders."

"Sure." He laughed. "Then they sneer at them. Crooked politicians. How many times have you heard that? Crooked politicians, the same men they elect." He inhaled the heavy smoke deeply, then jetted it through lips and nostrils as if purging himself of such folly. "When we rebuild Cuba, there will be democracy as in the United States. The *rules*, the *laws*—but not the *feelings*. We will live with *heart*, with *faith*. With Cuban fire and Cuban love. Not cold, dead, laughing at everything, mistrusting and hating everything." He jetted smoke again. "They do not know how good it is to *give* oneself to a leader."

She wanted to say, "Maybe that is why they are free," but rose instead and took his glass.

"No more," he said.

"Why? You don't have to meet that man until ten."

"My head must be clear."

She stood close to him. He sat stiffly. She said, "You don't want to relax, Jorge. Not with me. Why are you afraid to relax with me?"

He dragged on the remains of his *cigarro*.

"You think I am beautiful, I know it."

He ground out the little cigar.

"Can't you answer, Jorge? Is a grown man afraid to answer a stupid little girl?"

"Of course you are beautiful," he said, as stiffly as he sat. "That is why the *patrón* chose you. A beautiful little girl."

"Ah, thank you. Now look at me. Just for a moment. Is a grown man afraid to look? . . ."

"All right! I'm looking at you."

He was growing angry again. She didn't want him angry. Anger was a shield. She murmured, "Be patient with me, Jorge. It hurts me that you act the way you do with me."

"All right," he said. "I'm looking at you, Violetta."

She nodded. She smiled. His eyes tried to hold to hers, but she moved a little, her shoulders, her hips, and his eyes slid a little. "You want me, don't you, Jorge?"

He jumped up. "Must you play the whore *all* the time?"

"Is a grown man afraid to admit to a stupid little girl that he wants her, as he wants any pretty woman?"

He strode to the door. "You are not a woman."

"And you are a liar," she said, voice level. "And a coward. And because you are a liar and a coward with me I fear for what you will be when the time comes to be honest and brave for our plan."

He whirled on her. His mouth opened. His lips moved and nothing came out. The pride of a male in the Spanish tradition—*machismo*—was involved. She put her hands on her hips and pushed her chin out at him. "Tell me it is not true. Tell me a thousand times. I won't believe you. I know what I know. You know it too."

He came across the room to her. She kept her stance, but grew frightened. He slapped her so hard, so fast, she never saw it coming. As she cried out and began to fall, he caught her and held her close and kissed her cheek beginning to redden from his blow, her eyes beginning to leak tears, her lips trembling with shock.

"*Niña,*" he murmured against her ear. "*Niña,* fifteen years old. You are right, I want you. But it is as wrong as McKensil wanting you." He kissed her lips. "Now you've made me admit it. What good has it done?"

His third kiss was long, and she opened her mouth under it. He stepped back as quickly as he'd slapped her, and again she almost fell. "What good to make me admit it, *niña?*"

"But . . . we can be together."

"How could we? You belong to the *patrón,* to McKensil, to the plan. I would have to ask the *patrón*'s permission. Can you see me doing that?"

It was her turn to grow angry. "*His* permission? I belong to no one but myself! My permission, Jorge! *Mine!*"

He went to the door.

"Jorge." She was through teasing, through playing games with him and with herself. It was she who wanted him. She realized that now. Those kisses on her cheek, her eyes, her lips had been sweeter than any she remembered. She wanted him.

145

"Jorge, stay with me. Never before . . ."

But he was gone.

The reason for an "emergency" meeting was thin, Jorge felt, even though Prager talked about the party and asked whether there was anything more on Eloise DeWyant.

The *patrón* had received a report only last night. There was good reason to believe the DeWyants had come into money thirteen years ago.

"How much money?" Prager asked, seated beside Jorge in the Plymouth. On the screen, Julie Andrews danced and sang.

"Enough to change their lives."

"A hundred fifty thousand will change mine."

"More. A guess would be about a quarter of a million. Another guess would be that large amounts continue to come each year."

"These guesses—"

"Based on the way Claude DeWyant paid for his hotel."

"Then it might not be the *girl's* money. It might be her father's."

"Or her mother's, willed to the father and daughter. The mother was Jewish. She had family killed by the Nazis in Germany. It left her . . . sick, in the mind. The daughter seems the same. She has been in mental institutions."

Prager barely seemed to be listening; he watched the screen, smiling at the actors' antics. But he murmured, "Is Miss DeWyant still under some sort of treatment? Still sick, that is?"

Jorge said he didn't know. "And is it important?"

Prager shrugged.

Jorge said, "The money the DeWyants get—Claude DeWyant mentioned reparations made by Bonn for business and property lost by his wife's family. But it seems a great deal for reparations. And would payments keep coming all these years?"

Prager said it was possible; he had heard of such things. Jorge asked if he'd been able to talk further to Miss DeWyant about the President.

146

Prager shook his head. "I think we're wrong there. Besides, we don't really need her. We can enter the Senator's suite from his father-in-law's, where Leech will use the nurse. We'll also be able to enter it from the other side, where Mrs. Krasmer lives. And once you have the manager . . ." He waved his hand. "Everything else is just frosting, games to play until we pull a relatively simple snatch."

"If it was that simple, we wouldn't be paying you—"

"We?"

"A way of saying—a figure of speech."

Prager nodded, and let it drop—which put Jorge on his guard even more than if he'd pursued the subject.

"Once we've got the Senator in his suite," Prager said, "*then* we begin to earn our money."

"You've worked it out?"

"A dozen ways. The trick is to find the right way. Do we move him in his father-in-law's wheelchair, drugged, head down and face covered? Do we put him in a large trunk and let the bell-hops carry him? Do we explain that his father-in-law's life is on the line and he has to *walk* down?" He paused. "Do we kill him quickly, without mess, and dispose of—"

"He is *not* to be killed."

"You'd get the same results, without having to hide him."

"We wouldn't. The Wheeler clan is not a collection of morons. They'll want proof he's alive."

"Before doing what?"

"Paying the ransom, of course. You are asking foolish questions, Mr. Prager."

Prager shrugged. "Have you learned anything more about the Senator's security?"

"He travels with a bodyguard, once of the FBI and now self-employed. Sometimes he's given extra security by the President, usually when he leaves the country. But you should plan for *two* guards, just to be safe."

"That's the sort of thing you can't plan for at all. You can *expect* it, but what happens once you start to move . . ." He smiled slightly.

"Haven't you even *thought* of how to handle it?"

"Of course. We'll try drugs the night of the kidnap. We'll try women and booze. We'll try everything. But we might still have to use simple violence. You know that. You promised there'd be help."

Jorge nodded. "I'll do what I promised. It seems to me you're not doing what *you* promised. Trying and trying. Looking for *many* approaches."

"I simplify it for you, Jorge. As opportunities arise, I explore them." He opened the door.

"Is that all, Mr. Prager?"

"That's it, Jorge."

"I thought we decided the emergency number was to be used only for emergencies. This was just an extra meeting."

"If I'm not clear about things, it constitutes an emergency. And I wasn't quite clear about things."

"Now you're more clear?"

"Right." He got out and walked around the front of the Plymouth to his Cadillac. A moment later he drove off.

Jorge turned up the sound of the window speaker, muttering curses in Spanish. Prager had contempt for him! He hadn't even bothered to make up a decent excuse for this meeting! He thought he was dealing with a complete fool!

He'd show him who was the fool.

He reached under the seat and switched off the tape recorder. He leaned back with a *cigarro*, enjoying the thought of Prager parked somewhere near the exit, straining to make out each car as it emerged. He enjoyed it so much he stayed through the intermission, thinking how difficult it would be for Prager to be sure he hadn't escaped in the rush. When the second feature started and the exit was empty, he drove out.

He didn't spot the Cadillac until entering the section of A1A called Ocean Boulevard, with motels lined solidly on the shore side. He smiled, watching the big gray car complete the turn that had revealed it in his rear-view mirror, then disappear again into the solid mass of traffic a few hundred yards behind him. Prager had no way of knowing that what he wanted was back in Golden Beach, which they'd passed twenty minutes ago. It had taken that long not because of the mileage but because of the heavy in-season traffic, worsened by weekend visitors from metropolitan Miami and other local cities.

They approached 163rd Street, a major thoroughfare in its own right, made even more of a bottleneck by the Castaways Motel on the east corner and its famous Wreck Bar and marina on the west. Jorge inched up to the three-color light, saw that it was turning yellow, and shot across the intersection. Behind him, everything came to a halt. He stepped down on the gas, taking advantage of an open stretch of road as A1A curved through the darkness of Haulover Beach Park. He knew Prager must be sweating that he would get away, but he had no intention of losing him.

On the rise of the bridge approaching the Americana, his mirror filled with a solid, blinding mass of headlights released by the traffic light. He slowed. One pair of headlights was cutting in and out, and finally surged ahead of the others at what must have been a tremendous rate of speed. He went over the rise, and slowed even more. The speeding car mounted the rise a moment later, then rocked forward on its springs as the brakes were applied. Jorge smiled. He laughed aloud when he saw that the light at the end of the bridge had gone red. He rolled up to it and stopped. The car behind him had a clear lane in which to pull alongside. It didn't. It was the gray rental Cadillac.

Horns began blasting. The Cadillac was stopped eight or ten car lengths behind Jorge; the driver seemed to be reading a road map.

The light changed and Jorge moved forward. The noise of horns increased. The Cadillac stayed put, as if stalled, and traffic began to flow around it.

Jorge drove quickly, until the splitting of A1A into Harding and Collins. Now the jam resumed, and was intensified as they entered Surfside. Now they moved at ten and fifteen miles an hour, when they moved at all. Jorge no longer saw the Cadillac, and no longer cared.

It took nearly half an hour to reach the wide, modernistic section of Collins where most of the great hotels congregated, their upper lights reflected in bordering Indian Creek. Jorge pulled into the left-turn lane, stopping at the red arrow. When it flashed green, he drove across the northbound lanes and up the ramp to the Metropole.

He was in a phone booth with a view of the lobby when Max Prager entered—entered from the *rear*—and stood close to a statue. He stepped out, walking quickly, and when Prager saw him, raised his arm and called, "Mr. Prager, hello." He walked over, taking out his *cigarros*. Prager refused the smoke, his smile strained. Jorge lit up. "I like to visit the hotels once in a while. Can I buy you a drink?"

Prager said no, he was tired, he was going to bed.

"Sleep well, my friend." And he allowed the man to see his smile, and his inner laughter.

Prager went to the elevators. Jorge smoked and watched until the heavy man entered a car and the doors closed. Then he returned to the phone booth and called the *patrón*, keeping his eye on the elevators and the stairs to the upper lobby.

He explained why he was so late. The *patrón* seemed preoccupied. "Yes, thank you, Jorge." The line clicked. Jorge finished his *cigarro* in the booth, and left. He took side streets as far as he could, then turned off at a Haulover entrance, cut his lights, and waited ten minutes.

He didn't think Prager would try to follow him again. He felt that the man had been humiliated, that he knew he wouldn't get away with it now. But there could be no letup in his vigilance. The *patrón*'s own security was at stake.

It wasn't often the *patrón* entertained in his home. A bachelor, he visited several women in the Miami area, at *their* homes. Matilde Humes was the only exception Jorge knew of. And he knew why. She was marvelously beautiful, and very proud. The *patrón* assisted her, but he could not control her. He enjoyed this. Again Jorge understood why. Every man, no matter how important, had to have someone on his own level.

Mrs. Humes had been born into a family almost as wealthy as the *patrón*'s. At sixteen, she had been married to Arturo Humes, an M.D., and when the doctor decided to cast his lot with Fidel, she accepted the tremendous changes in her life without complaint. Two years ago, Dr. Humes was jailed as an agent of the CIA, and within a month had died of what the prison authorities called "physical collapse." Matilde had been brought over to the United States as part of the continuing, though unpublicized, Cuban immigration handled by a worldly and discreet bishop of the Catholic Church.

The *patrón* had very few hard and fast rules, but one of them was that no one was to enter his three-room private complex consisting of study, living room, and bedroom when he was entertaining Mrs. Humes.

Jorge was pleased when Maria told him. The *patrón* needed his pleasure like any other man. Perhaps more, with his problems and responsibilities. Jorge went to his room over the garage, played the tape for himself, felt it was hardly worth playing for the *patrón*.

At twelve-thirty, he came down the stairs at the back of the house. Maria was dozing in the kitchen. He woke her, saying, "What if the *patrón* should buzz?" She was fifty, and looked sixty. She muttered it was unfair to keep her up so late. "Don't I have to make breakfast anyway?" He ignored her. She had a nasty disposition. The only reason the *patrón* kept her was that she had worked for his family in Cuba.

At five to one, the buzzer sounded. Maria picked up the house phone. "*Sí*." She looked at Jorge, moved her head. He left the kitchen as she said, "*Sí patrón, leche y . . .*"

The *patrón* was in the study, stretched out in a deep armchair, wearing a gray robe over white, open-necked shirt and tan slacks. He was smoking a pipe. "Ah, Jorge. You showed our inquisitive friend a thing or two, didn't you? Sit down, sit down. We'll have cold chicken and milk and talk."

Jorge moved toward a straight-backed chair, but Lamas said, "No, the armchair. You've earned your comfort tonight." He relit the pipe. "You have the tape there? Good. Put it on the table. I'll play it later."

Jorge said it was hardly worthwhile. Lamas smiled. "If it taught him a lesson, it was worthwhile. If not . . ." His smile went away. "It would be very bad if we had to replace him right now. Later, it wouldn't matter. We could do without him in the final stages, the action stages. You and Leech and another man . . ." He waved his pipe and smiled again. "But why worry before we have to?"

Jorge hadn't seen the *patrón* quite this relaxed, quite this happy (though he was always an *easier* man after being with a woman). It must have gone exceptionally well tonight. On impulse, he decided to take advantage of it. There were questions he wanted to ask, and this seemed a good time to ask them.

"You'll forgive me, *patrón*, but how did you happen to choose this man Prager?"

Lamas puffed his pipe, looking at him. Jorge thought he wasn't going to answer, and quickly added, "I mean, I've wondered why you didn't get a different type . . . harder men . . . gangsters for a kidnapping."

Lamas suddenly laughed. "Now what would I be doing with gangsters, Jorge? It's difficult enough keeping Prager in line. Could you imagine the trouble we'd have with gangsters?"

Jorge nodded.

"Another thing, no gangster—no one from the syndicate of thugs and racketeers—would risk such a plan as ours. Not for any amount of money. They would say, 'The President's brother-in-law?' and laugh. They like only *easy* money, Jorge. The true gangster rarely risks his neck, deliberately. Only when his passions are aroused, as in a war over territory, over business, will he think of taking chances."

"Yes, I see." And as always, when the *patrón* explained things, he *did* see.

"Prager, on the other hand, has a history of clever swindles, and no convictions. That is very important, Jorge. No convictions.

He came highly recommended by someone very well known in upper-echelon crime. You would know this man's name, Jorge. Almost everyone would know his name. For gambling, mainly."

"This man, he understood *why* you wanted Prager?"

"Certainly not! I have dealt with him on occasion—in Havana as well as here—in order to invest in certain enterprises. Legitimate enterprises, Jorge, but controlled by hidden money." He put down his pipe. "Much of Miami Beach is controlled by such hidden money. This man can open doors, but I would not trust him with the name of my housekeeper, not to say information that could destroy me. Just as I won't trust Prager with the reason for the abduction. Or Violetta with the place we will keep Christopher. Or anyone with the complete plan."

They looked at each other, and Lamas nodded. "Only you, Jorge."

Jorge was full of pride.

Maria knocked and entered with a tray of fried chicken and a pitcher of milk. She served them and left. Jorge ate, even though he wasn't hungry. Finally, when the *patrón* put aside his plate and walked to the desk, Jorge was able to continue his questions.

"How was Jerry Leech chosen, *patrón?*"

Lamas answered while selecting, snipping, and lighting a cigar from a large cedar box. "By Prager. Leech is also known to the Miami underworld. Not as a member, but as a possible assistant. Jewel thieves need such assistants on hotel staffs. Leech has flirted with groups of thieves several times. He might even have helped in a robbery or two, though no one is sure." He blew smoke. "Would you like a cigar, Jorge?"

"I have my own, *patrón.*" He took out a *cigarro.* Lamas returned to his armchair. "The manager," Jorge said. "How could you know he would want Violetta, or any girl that age?"

"You are a true inquisitor tonight."

"Forgive me, *patrón.* If it is not meant for me to know . . ."

Lamas shrugged. "Why shouldn't you know? I am secretive by nature, but you already know enough to send me to prison."

"God forbid, *patrón!*"

Lamas drew on his cigar and let the smoke out along with his words. "When I first decided to implement our plan, I had everyone I thought might be of help investigated. In McKensil's case, the investigation led to Los Angeles and a niece—a twenty-three-year-old divorcée and alcoholic. During the course of a weekend spent in the company of a handsome young man, she was led to discuss her Uncle John, and with much merriment delivered him into our hands."

"He—his own niece, *patrón*? When she was young?"

Lamas nodded.

Jorge was silent a moment. "At times I feel unhappy that we must . . . with Violetta, a countrywoman, but still a child . . ."

"You should marry, Jorge. You are a man of morality, of ethics. Such a man should be married."

"I am not *that* moral, *patrón*," Jorge muttered. "With women . . ."

"Violetta Murillo is also a woman. Some females mature at fifteen, at fourteen—I've seen desirable *thirteen*-year-olds—while some are still children at eighteen." He stretched his legs. "You will have your chance to make things up to Violetta, later, when we have succeeded. You understand me, Jorge?"

"I am not sure, *patrón*. If you mean a man of thirty-eight marrying a fifteen—"

"Mrs. Humes' husband was forty when they married. They loved each other very much." He stood up. "I too feel responsibility for Violetta. I would provide a dowry that would make you the wealthiest servant in Miami."

Jorge also rose. "Thank you, *patrón*. I do not do such things for money."

They walked to the door. Lamas said, "Still, consider what I said about marrying. The Americans have an expression—to make an honest woman of her. I believe it would also make a happy man of you."

Jorge didn't intend to waste time thinking of it. And as long as he was awake, he didn't. But asleep, who could control the mind? Asleep, he thought of it so thoroughly that he awakened at four-thirty and took a shower.

BOOK 2

Christopher Time

1

MONDAY, JANUARY 16

The charisma sputtered a little, then caught as Dick Christopher left the limousine and strode into the lobby. That sputtering, that momentary failing, a result of the years of subjection to Jonathan and resentment of Father (who was Mike Wheeler and so much more important in his life than his own poor, lost, dead, unremembered father), that stammer in personality, that flaw, he despised it and hated it. As he hated Bunny Wheeler, who was his wife. As he hated himself for the weakness Mike Wheeler had exploited.

Also, he *feared* the momentary failing of charisma. It waited before each speech, each committee meeting, each appearance on his friend Benny Barker's TV show. It waited to mock him before the world.

But, of course, it wouldn't get the chance. He always defeated it. He walked or talked away from it, every time, and not since his second or third year of marriage had it caught him. As he walked and talked away from it now, smiling at the manager who rushed to greet him, asking after his father-in-law and not asking after but wondering about Claude and Ellie DeWyant. He hadn't seen them in nearly thirteen years.

Would Ellie be friendly? He supposed so. The fire must have been banked by now. Banked by Wheeler money. Three hundred thousand down, two hundred thousand a year as long as they remained absolutely silent. Buried by Wheeler money.

Bryan was instructing the bellhops which bags to take. Dick signed in and shook hands with the manager, filing away the name John McKensil for some future time, some future use, as he had been taught by Father. Everyone could be used, sooner or later. And should be—if you wanted to be President.

And he wanted to be President, didn't he? What else could he want if not to be President? He wanted to be President the way a laboratory mouse wants to solve the maze, without choice, following its implanted impulses. He wanted to be President to stop Bunny's talk and Wheeler's contempt, once and for all.

But he was here on vacation as well as political business. He had covered himself with Vance Alterson and expected no calls to committee. If Crowan tried to make Republican hay of his absence, he could fly back for any important vote. His secretary would practically live in the office for the two weeks he would be in Miami Beach, and would call every day as to developments. Which meant he could now move at only half the usual breakneck pace.

"My mother's ancestors were Welsh kings," he said, when he and Bryan were alone. "Your father's ancestors were Indian kings. This should be called the Royal Suite."

"Subchief. My great grandfather was a Chiricahua Apache subchief. He rode with Nana and Juh."

Dick smiled at the broad man with the face like a pale basketball. A wide, seemingly fat man who moved slowly, except when he had to move fast, who spoke slowly all the time. "Never admit to details like that, Bryan. My Welsh ancestors were probably servants to the king, but who's to tell? And who's to say my father-in-law's wrong in his claim that I go all the way back to Saint Patrick?"

"How can a priest, a saint, have children?"

Dick stretched all six-feet-two of himself out on the couch and put his hands behind his head. "First you take off your cassock . . ."

Bryan said, "Sure," and went to the bar. "They stocked your brand. You want it big, bigger, or biggest?"

"Just big, baby." He lay there, rubbing his pale brown hair, receding a bit in front and cropped short in defiance of political convention and current fashion. He was a big, athletic man with a big, unlined face, and when he spoke it always amazed his listeners that he didn't sound like a pro lineman being interviewed for all-you-fans-out-there. That he sounded like a combination of Adlai Stevenson and President Jonathan Standers absolutely astounded them. And converted them.

Bryan brought the drink. Dick sat up. "Make one for the chief."

"Indians can't drink firewater."

They'd been through this before. More often than not, Bryan refused to drink.

"Should I check if your father-in-law's in, Senator?"

"Yes, but wait until I finish this."

He drank the bourbon slowly, appreciating as always the searing smoothness of hundred-proof Wild Turkey. "What're you going to do, how are you going to act, when I'm the President?"

"As careful as I act now. Only I'll have more help."

"You going to be more respectful?"

"I'm as respectful as I can get without kissing your ass."

"You might try that, just once."

Bryan Whitelock nodded. "Sure." His round face never changed.

Dick laughed, and went to the bedroom. "Tell President Wheeler I'll be next door as soon as I shower."

"Right, Senator."

"Nana and Juh. Make it Nana and Geronimo and people will respect you."

"I respect me, Senator."

"Cut the noble-savage shit and make that call. And order me a steak." He was still in fine spirits, even with the prospect of seeing the old man hanging over his head. It shouldn't be too bad this time. Father was too sick to take off in usual fashion. "I suppose you want pemmican?"

Bryan Whitelock finally cracked a smile. "Sure." He went to the phone, opening the jacket of his baggy brown suit and loosening his tie, and revealing the shoulder holster and big .45 automatic. He drew up a chair and sat down carefully, as if afraid his broad rear might shatter the pseudo-antique. The shower went on in the next room.

159

Michael Wheeler's suite didn't answer. Bryan left a message and asked for room service. He ordered two sirloins, rare, fried potatoes, and coffee. Then he went to work.

He made a quick check of the suite, noting that it could be entered not only from the old man's suite through the door in the foyer, but also from a door on the north opening into the small bedroom, his bedroom. Barely thinking of it, he shifted the dresser to block the door. Nothing to stop determined people, but a complication. Bryan Whitelock always made complications.

He examined pictures, lamps, backs of furniture, drapes, edges of rugs, and assorted odd corners for bugging. Then he made another call. A local firm would do a scientific check later this afternoon.

The phone rang. It was Wheeler's nurse. Bryan gave her the message, and she said to make it forty-five minutes to an hour. Mr. Wheeler needed a bath, medication, and something to eat. Bryan mentioned that the Senator planned to eat with his father-in-law. "I don't think Mr. Wheeler will agree," she said. She must have covered the mouthpiece. "No, he prefers to eat alone. In one hour then?" Bryan said yes, and figured the old man was having trouble feeding himself.

Proud old bastard.

The charisma was almost dead here in this room with Father, with Bryan and the nurse watching as Jonathan and Doe and Bunny had once watched earlier humiliations. Dick smoked and smiled and winked at the nurse to show he was perfectly at ease, humoring an irascible old man, but inside he writhed under the lash of words and perspiration trickled down his sides and he could no more have convinced anyone he was fit to be President than he had ever been able to convince his father-in-law he was fit to be treated as a man.

The old devil's instincts, he thought. *Instincts that had trebled his inherited wealth. Instincts that told him something about his son-in-law—or had Bunny broken her word never to speak of their "problem," the reason they had no children?*

160

Only one thing helped: the speech he would give next week.

He sat on the couch with the nurse, and Bryan sat on a straight-backed chair near the windows, and the old man faced the couch in his wheelchair, rubbing that damned black cane. If he should lose his temper as he had with his male nurse . . .

Dick said, "I wasn't aware you still bothered with the mailings—" and the old man interrupted, as he did nine times out of ten: "I *bother* with . . . everything anyone in my . . . family does or says. That newsletter . . . you send to your . . . constituents is . . . most feeble excuse . . . for using congressional franking . . . privilege I've ever . . ."

He went on that way, suggesting Dick hire a journalism major to take over for him, detailing how Jonathan had handled *his* newsletter, comparing Dick to his counterpart in New York, talking and talking, the pauses so much shorter than when Dick had last seen him, his voice so much stronger, his general bearing so much stronger that it was hard to believe he had suffered a major stroke only a few months ago.

When he finally paused for breath, Dick said to the nurse, "You're doing a wonderful job. He's really coming along."

She nodded, dropping her eyes; and he flushed, suspecting pity.

The speech. Think of the speech. When the old man heard that speech he would have his second stroke!

She looked up again, and Dick fought to bring back the charisma, smiling at her and murmuring, "I know who *my* nurse will be if I ever need one."

The old man snorted. "You seem to . . . need one right . . . now. Nurse or . . . nursemaid."

The training, and fears, of sixteen years' subservience to Master Mike, of owing everything to the old Wheeler-Dealer, almost crumbled then. He almost articulated what he was shouting inside. *"You old bastard, I hate your guts! You old he-goat, I'm going to defy you as you've never been defied, smash you as Jonathan never dared smash you, spit in your face . . ."*

The speech.

The speech saved him. It would do the smashing and spitting

for him. And the nurse spoke quickly, sensing perhaps that he'd been pushed too far.

"Thank you, Senator. Is Washington as exciting a place as they say it is?"

He began to answer. The old man cut him off. "Exciting for those . . . who have inner excitement . . . to begin with. For others . . . it's just a place . . . to drudge away . . . their sorry political . . . lives. If you . . ." turning to Dick . . . "aren't careful . . . you'll end up . . . the senior senator . . . and senior bore—"

"I could provide some excitement, Father." It was he who interrupted for a change. "What would you like? A speech on the Soviet invasion of Czechoslovakia?"

The old man made a snorting, laughing sound, but his mouth tightened. Jonny had pulled a boner there. He had almost blown his re-election the last week of the campaign with an extemporaneous airport speech. He had supported the internationally sophisticated but domestically naïve position that there was no point in trying to intrude on the Soviet sphere of influence. He'd then tried to compare Czechoslovakia with Canada and Mexico, and lost a hell of a lot of votes.

Now that he had begun to counterattack, Dick couldn't stop. "Or perhaps excitement of another kind? For example, bringing home an unexpected bride?"

The cane thumped. "That's enough!"

Richard Bernard Christopher had to fight to keep from cowering. But deep satisfaction was present just the same. Then the satisfaction came to an end.

"At least . . . we know . . . he likes . . . women."

Dick lit his third cigarette, smiling thinly.

"He filled . . . the White House . . . with children. Where . . . are yours?"

Dick drew smoke into his lungs. "Ask Bunny," he murmured.

"She says . . ." He stopped, and Dick knew he was unwilling to go any further in front of Bryan and the nurse. But his hatred of Bunny burned high. She *had* broken her word! She *had* spoken to her father!

162

The bitch! The Wheeler bitch!

He smoked and calmed himself. Either he would become President, and could then ignore her—or he wouldn't become President, and could divorce her. (He almost wished for failure, because divorce would be so sweet, would surely destroy the old man and his goddam pride!)

Wheeler said, "All the world . . . loves a lover . . . and what better . . . proof of that . . . than fatherhood . . . at least among . . . the great . . . American unwashed?"

Dick sidestepped the continuing attack. "There's no such thing as a great American unwashed, Father. Not any more. It's the great American deodorized."

The old man cracked a thin smile—which was as much as Dick could expect—and he got up, hoping to be allowed a quick exit. "Feel well, Father. I'll drop in—"

"Sit down." He turned to the nurse. "Eve, take Mr. Whitelock . . . to the kitchen . . . for coffee." He waited until the two were gone, then wheeled himself to the open bedroom door and inside. Dick followed. "Close the door." Dick did, and faced him. "What do you . . . hear from Wenschler?" the old man asked, and Dick let out his breath. There would be no renewal of hostilities this session. The old man wanted to talk delegate politics. Dick sat down at the edge of the bed. "Nothing. I'm dealing directly with Bailey. . . ."

She must have been looking at him more openly than she realized, because he turned from the TV news program. "Say it."

"Say what, Mr. Wheeler?"

"Whatever has been . . . bothering you."

Eve shook her head, as if not understanding him. But ever since the Senator and Mr. Whitelock had left, she had been upset. No one should treat a relative that way—especially a son-in-law like Senator Richard Christopher!

Mr. Wheeler turned back to the news program. Eve went to the kitchen and wrote up a shopping list, then came back to the living room. She didn't like Mr. Wheeler as much as she had before the

163

Senator's visit. She valued the family relationship—parent and child—over and above most things in life, and having seen the way he misused his authority . . .

"Don't you love your son-in-law?" She was both frightened and relieved when she finally said it.

He wheeled himself to the set and turned it off. He took that heavy black cane from the corner of his chair and held it in both hands. Somehow, that bothered her. He said, "I suppose . . . I do."

"Don't you *know?* If you loved your daughter . . . you're sure of *that,* aren't you?"

"Is anyone?"

"You're joking with me, Mr. Wheeler! For parents not to love their children is—*unnatural!*"

"You're parroting . . . clichés. You're too . . . bright a girl . . . for that, Eve."

"Clichés? Well, maybe, as biology is a cliché."

He turned his chair to face her fully. "Biology dictates we . . . eat, sleep . . . copulate." His eyes, the right now almost as bright as the left, fixed on hers. He was making exceptional progress. He was walking straighter, eating better, speaking far more clearly.

"Those of us . . .' he added, "who can."

She flushed, remembering that today as she had bathed him there had been a mild but noticeable tumescence.

"To love," he said, "in an emotional . . . manner, as opposed . . . to a purely . . . sexual manner . . . is not biological."

"Mammals love their offspring."

He thumped his cane on the floor. "Walt Disney . . . nonsense! Research . . . indicates major emotions . . . are need for . . . territory, and desire . . . for opposite sex. And territory . . . comes first. Read *On Aggression . . . African Genesis . . . Territorial Imperative.*" He paused for breath, and to give her a chance to comment. She hadn't read any of those books, but she just couldn't believe he was right. "Offspring," he continued, "often end up . . . competitors in struggle . . . for territory . . . and sex."

She thought to make a joke and a strong point at the same

time. "Your son-in-law certainly doesn't compete with you *that way*."

"Quite the contrary. We were . . . competing for . . . you."

She stared at him.

"Unconsciously, of course. At least . . . on his part. I could feel . . . the struggle. Young man . . . handsome . . . though weak in . . . certain important . . . ways. Older man . . . sick . . . but much stronger . . . in those . . . vital ways. Young woman . . . observing both."

"That's really—" she struggled to find the right word— "stretching things, Mr. Wheeler!" She laughed, the blood suffusing her face. And thought of Jerry Leech and the call she had promised to make.

"Not stretching . . . at all." He came forward a little. "Am I . . . so completely . . . not a man?"

"No, of course not." She was shaking her head and leaning back away from him, a little frightened, remembering that tumescence, a problem she had never thought to face in a man of his age and condition. Of course, he was far from being *capable* of a sexual act. He was merely building his confidence—and it was her job to help him build it. "You're still a very attractive man. Your position, your strength—"

"All right!" His sudden coldness stopped her. "Don't treat me . . . like neurotic . . . or child!"

"I didn't mean to," she murmured, and her eyes fell and she felt inadequate. All the accepted things, the established and biblically right things, were suspect with him.

"Do you know . . . why I . . . chose you . . . for my nurse?"

She shook her head.

"Because of all . . . the nurses . . . I interviewed . . . only you . . . made me . . . feel comfortable."

They looked at each other. She didn't say thank you or anything else. He was angry at her. He wasn't complimenting her. She didn't want to hear any more.

"The others . . . were all so . . . *superior* to me. Their health

. . . their looks . . . their self-confidence. My male nurse . . . was too damned . . . strong, and horny. With me . . . lying in bed . . . he tried to seduce . . . cook's daughter. Standing in corner . . . grunting away . . . and me lying . . . helpless."

He was panting and white around the lips. She half rose, wanting to stop him, but he shook his head.

"Fooled him." He raised the cane in his left hand. "Called him over . . . struck him with cane . . . on head . . . good left arm . . . *hard*. He fell and I . . . beat him . . . until girl's screams . . . brought people." He laughed harshly, and lowered the cane. "They paid him . . . plenty not to . . . talk to newspapers. I wouldn't . . . have paid . . . a dime. I'd have used . . . the girl . . . to silence him."

She made no movement, no reply, heart beating slow and heavy.

"Same reason . . . I got rid of . . . my Secret Service . . . agent. Couldn't stand . . . his health . . . strength."

She still made no reply.

"You," he said, his voice growing quiet. "You, Eve. Helpless kind of . . . girl. Uncertain. Others made me feel . . . *less* than I . . . wanted to feel. You—"

She stood up. "Time for bed," she said, and was surprised that her voice was so steady.

"No, not yet. Not finished. Feel different now. You . . . changed things . . . for me." He wheeled very close, reaching for her hand. She moved it away from him. "Understand me!" he said, voice crackling. "Don't be . . . one of foolish . . . mass all your . . . life! You helped . . . me very much. Last week has been . . . tremendous experience! I used you . . . to grow toward . . . life. Use *me* to grow . . . toward maturity. Can have position . . . with me . . . for many years. Can have . . . money—" He began to cough and gasp for breath. She bent to him. He muttered, "As my . . . accountant says . . . I should . . . live . . . so long."

She took him to his room and undressed him. She made herself look at him, look closely. There was no tumescence now. The barrel chest and muscular legs and coarse, graying body hair were only remnants, vestiges of what had once been a powerful male-ness.

He was nothing—a patient and her job, but nothing to her per-sonally and she wouldn't allow him to hurt her as her father had hurt her.

She closed the door on his harsh breathing and went to the phone. She hadn't known that she would, but now she asked for the Burgundy Room. She waited while the phone rang in the lower-level bar and thought of Jerry Leech and of how he wanted to be with her. He had no hidden motive, no possible hidden motive. Unlike the intern at Bannesville General, he had at least a *hundred* women available for anything he wanted. And he wasn't at all impressed with Mr. Wheeler, she was sure of it. He just wanted to be with her.

Why? Why, with all the beautiful women? Why Eve Andrews?

"Hello?" he said.

"It's Eve."

"Hey, I was waiting and hoping you'd call! How's it going, baby? I mean, can you come down? Can we get together and talk a little?"

She didn't know what to say. It was seven o'clock, and Mr. Wheeler would sleep until four or five A.M.

"Eve? If you can't come down, can I come up?"

"Yes."

"Five minutes?"

"I have to see to a few things. Half an hour."

She went to the hall closet and took out her black dress. It was sort of formal, but it was the only one she considered at all excit-ing. She wanted to look exciting for Jerry. After what Mr. Wheeler had said . . .

It was only after she was dressed and waiting that she began to absorb some of the *compliments* Mr. Wheeler had paid her. She was still thinking of them, reassessing their conversation, when the door chime sounded. She ran across the foyer, frightened, having forgotten to tell Jerry to knock softly. She got there before he pressed the button again, and opened the door, gasping, "*Shhh!* Mr. Wheeler . . ."

He nodded and walked inside. She closed the door softly. She had just turned to listen, to make sure Mr. Wheeler was still asleep, when Jerry's arms went around her and his mouth pressed her neck. She was taken by surprise—both by him and by her own emotions. She felt his breath in her ear, felt her heart hammering. "You look terrific," he whispered. "That dress . . . clean lines, honey, not like the overripe broads I see all season. Clean lines and a sweet baby face." His lips came down over hers. She remembered the brief kisses, the groping hands, and frantic haste of that intern at Bannesville General. She tried to keep the memory sharp in her mind, tried to keep herself prepared for the same knowledge of insult, of degradation . . .

She didn't know she was going to do it. She simply found herself coming up on her toes, moving her body against his excitement.

His arms tightened. He could have broken her ribs with those thick pillars of muscle. He could have done almost anything to her without her being able to stop him, but he merely held her as she wanted to be held and kissed her as she wanted to be kissed.

She was enfolded in Jerry Leech. She was gentled and soothed by Jerry Leech. She moved up and down in a pattern and rhythm taught her only by instinct. *She* did the advancing. *She* directed the mounting excitement of their bodies. *She* moved toward her seduction.

She finally sagged against the wall, knees shaky.

"Evie? Are you okay?"

Evie. Little Eve. Her father—that man who first made himself and then unmade himself her father—had called her that. Her mother—that woman who had stood by, weeping, but unspeaking —had called her that. Evie . . .

She began to cry.

"Hey, no reason for *that*, baby. Let's sit down, huh?"

"It's nothing to do with you, Jerry. It's personal."

"And I'm *not* personal?" he chided, leading her to the living room and the couch.

"Oh, yes . . . I only meant—"

"Just kidding, baby." He looked around. "You want a drink?"

"If you mean alcohol, I don't drink."

"Mind if I have one?"

She said no, and he went to the bar and looked behind it. He came up with a bottle and said, "Scotch. Try some, huh?"

She put her fingers to her lips, pointing at the closed bedroom door. He lowered his voice, saying, "TV's louder than we are. You play the TV, don't you?"

He was right. But she was frightened of that old man. She remembered what he had said about beating his male nurse for doing just what she and Jerry had been doing in the foyer.

He came back to the couch with two glasses. "For that personal problem. Bottoms up." She hesitated. He said, "C'mon now, it's not *your* bottom I'm talking about." She looked into the glass and saw it was only an inch or so of liquid. She sipped, and choked. He said, "You really *are* teetotal, aren't you? I don't think I ever met one before."

Her eyes were wet, either from the tears or from that burning whiskey. She sipped again, then gave him the glass. He poured what was left of hers into his and took it all in one swallow. "Ummm. The old boy knows his Scotch."

"He's not allowed to drink any more. He keeps a few bottles for guests. Not that we've had any, except his son-in-law."

Jerry's arm went around her. She leaned back against it, feeling the liquor heating her insides.

"You mean the Senator?" he asked.

"Yes. Mr. Wheeler isn't very nice to—" She stopped, shocked at herself. She had no right to reveal anything about a patient's private life!

"Yeah?" Jerry prompted.

She shook her head. He bent over and kissed her. She touched his lips with her tongue, experimenting, wanting to know what a "soul kiss" felt like. A moment later she found out. His mouth opened over hers and their tongues mingled and the intimacy was so strong that she trembled, feeling all restraint deserting her.

His hand was at her legs. He said, "Evie, baby, I can't help myself!" But he paused, the weight of that big hand resting just above one knee. She knew then she could stop him, at any point. She knew then he was concerned for what she thought of him, concerned not only for tonight but for tomorrow and the day afterward. And this was so good, so much what she wanted and needed from him, that she whispered, "I know, Jerry. Me, too."

She felt that weight move. It slipped under the black silk and stroked her bare thighs. It was so warm, so deliciously warm. It moved up and down, sliding between her legs and under them. She didn't know when or how he removed her panties. She didn't care. The breath sobbed in her throat and his lips nibbled at her lips and the hand was everything good she had missed, everything warm she had wanted.

His finger entered her. Her breath froze. He said, "Evie, I'll stop when you say stop. But I'd sure give something to have you!"

She said, "Jerry, don't, please," but weakly because that finger was turning her insides to liquid fire.

He kissed her. "I won't hurt you, Evie, I promise. I'll give you a great big beautiful present, baby. The present of being a woman."

Now he was moving her and laying her down and going at her, but not like the intern. Because all the time his voice gentled her, his words told her the truth. Not that he loved her above all women, which she would have known was a lie, but that she was someone he wanted, had wanted since he'd first met her, found lean and clean and unlike the riper fruit that generally came his way. This she could believe, needed to believe because it gave her stature as a woman and overcame the fear that she was selling her sacred heart and soul and person cheap. This and her desire made it right, and she did as he said. He moved between her legs with the light still on and his face clear in her eyes.

He stopped to touch her face with his hand and to say, "Sweet little girl, good-bye. Beautiful woman, hello." She smiled, amazed at how consistently he was able to say the right thing, do the right thing, and realized he had much experience and was glad he had much experience.

He was entering her. She squeezed her eyes shut. He stopped and muttered, "By God, there it is." She shook her head, not wanting to hear the details. He left her and she opened her eyes. He was standing and looking around. He said, "The bathroom?" She said, "You can't. It's off the bedroom—Mr. Wheeler's room." He said, "I'll need something under you. There might be blood." She closed her eyes. Again the details. She began to feel a loss of desire. And spoke a little too loudly, through forgetfulness or impatience—or need to be rescued. "Behind the bar. Towels in a drawer."

He said, "Hey, easy," and turned to the bar. Mr. Wheeler made a sound. Jerry stopped. Mr. Wheeler cleared his throat and called, "Eve. Eve . . . come here."

Jerry looked at her. She jumped off the couch, pulling down her dress, and saw her panties on the floor and put them on. She pointed at his trousers, also on the floor. He made a despairing face, but picked them up.

"Eve . . . I heard . . . voices."

"Only the television, Mr. Wheeler." She went to the set, putting it on. "I've turned it down now."

"My throat . . . hurts. Eve, I'm sure . . . I heard . . . voices."

"The television . . ."

"Dammit, come here! Why are . . . we shouting through . . . closed door!"

Again she remembered his story of beating the male nurse, and motioned at the hall door. Jerry pointed at the kitchen, made a head-on-pillow gesture to indicate Mr. Wheeler would soon be back asleep. She shook her head violently.

"Eve."

She ran to the bedroom, looking back. Jerry was buckling his belt and moving past the bar. When he entered the foyer, she opened the door and went in. "Did you have a nightmare?"

"Nightmare . . . hell! Heard things! Why did . . . you take so . . . long to . . ."

"Just you settle down," she interrupted coolly. "If you're dissatisfied with my services, I'll see you have another nurse first thing in the morning."

"Put on . . . light."

She was sure he would notice something about her appearance. "No. You'll be up for good. And you've had too exerting a day to miss your sleep." She turned to the door. "I'll fix you a glass of chocolate milk."

"Want . . . beer."

She hesitated. They had a six-pack in the refrigerator. She hadn't as yet allowed him one, but she'd spoken to Dr. Cormond last week and he'd said an occasional beer wouldn't hurt. "All right."

Jerry was gone. She shut off the television, first turning the sound up—as if by accident—to support her story. On the way to the kitchen, she checked herself in the closet-door mirror. Her hair was mussed, but except for that she looked perfectly normal. It astounded her. That she could do all those things and not be *drastically* changed!

She brought him a glass of beer, helped him into a sitting position, and watched as he drank. "Not too quickly now," she cautioned. She needn't have worried. He drank more slowly than usual, savoring every swallow, and swished the last bit around in his mouth. He put the glass on the night table and smiled that thin smile of his. "Nectar of . . . the gods. Life's little . . . compensations. When you haven't . . . had beer . . . in so long . . . it tastes like . . ." He shook his head a little. "Like nothing . . . on earth."

She fluffed up his pillow and helped him lie down, then turned for the glass. "Eve, please . . . your hand."

She gave it to him. He tugged a little, looking up at her, his face dimly seen in the light from the living room, the features softened, the harshness and brutality she had glimpsed earlier now hidden. "Sit with me a little," he said, the sentence unbroken, the first time he'd been able to manage one of such length. It changed him somehow. It made him less the sick old man.

"All right. If you'll close your eyes."

He closed his eyes. She sat down at the edge of the bed. His hand was cool at first, almost lifeless; then it warmed, and his fingers touched her fingers, exploring as a child's might. She was strangely touched. She told herself it was the excitement with Jerry. Her body, her emotions, were still aroused. He said, "You are a fresh . . . and uncorrupted thing," and raised her hand and touched it with his lips. He let go before she could think of what to do. "You'll have some . . . time off . . . tomorrow, if you . . . wish it. A party . . ."

She went out, closing the door. She washed the whiskey glasses and beer glass and made the sleeper couch and got into her nightgown. She went back to the bedroom door, and hesitated. Until now, she had felt perfectly at ease passing through his room to get to the bathroom. Until now, he had been—not quite human to her.

It was changing.

2

TUESDAY, JANUARY 17
TO
WEDNESDAY, JANUARY 18, A.M.

Eunice asked when she would be back.

May said, "Forget me for today. I'm in a rambling mood." She wore the bikini Al had helped her pick in the Arcade Swim Shop, and over it a shortie towel-robe.

"But what time—"

"Honey, relax, will you? You're free to do as you please."

She left the suite, worrying about Eunice. The woman seemed overly concerned about where she spent her time and with whom. She expected explanations.

Which wasn't possible. Those explanations wouldn't have made sense to Eunice or to anyone else, May supposed.

She smiled, entering the elevator—smiled with anticipation of an eighteen-year-old boy's greeting, of his voice and eyes and lips.

Al had kissed her yesterday, really kissed her for the first time. And it was as if it had been the very first kiss of her life! They had walked north along the beach, walked for miles, wading and swimming where abutments blocked their way. About an hour from the Metropole, between an apartment house and a small hotel, the sand had been less crowded, the water almost empty. They had swum far out, then treaded water. He had talked incessantly—much of it about his parents (his mother "choked" him, his father embarrassed him).

"I should meet them," she'd said.

"I suppose so."

Neither of them meant it. Neither of them wanted anyone, especially his parents, to observe them, to have the chance to guess what they were playing at, to laugh at them.

He'd suddenly pulled her close.

"We're alone out here, do you know that?" He'd laughed, as always, to make a joke of it.

She'd drawn back a little.

"That bikini is beautiful, May. I mean, of course, *you*—"

"I feel naked."

He'd seemed to ignite on the word. He'd grabbed her, both of them going under briefly, and when they kicked up again he kissed her, mouth full and open on hers.

She hadn't been sure whether he had touched her. His hands had seemed to press her backside and, as she finally turned away, her breast. But that could have been because of the continuous, waving hand movement necessary to stay above the surface. She had swum away from him, and he had called, "May, I didn't mean

174

. . ." his voice anguished. She had turned then, smiling, and blown a kiss at him.

Now she hurried toward the pool, experiencing delight, shame, and excitement—an intensity of emotion unmatched even in adolescence.

He wasn't there. Every day for a week she had met him near the diving boards and he had been waiting. Now he wasn't, and she couldn't believe it. She walked twice around the pool, looking for him. By then he was ten minutes late.

He was held up, she reasoned. His parents controlled his life and they had held him up.

But she was afraid. He had met a pretty girl his own age. He no longer cared to see her. He had been laughing at her all the time.

The pool and deck were jammed. There must have been close to a thousand people out today! And their talk and laughter and transistor radios were too much for her. She walked between rows of bodies reclining on lounges. She tried to look for Al and there were too many bodies, too much tanned flesh, and it all blurred into sameness and she couldn't distinguish anyone.

She kept telling herself his not being there meant nothing, the entire relationship meant nothing, and she was almost crying. Then her name was called, and she looked out at the beach and beyond at the water and saw a head bobbing, an arm waving.

She went down to the sand and shrugged out of her robe and entered the water. She swam toward him, and he began swimming north, almost submerged, an excellent swimmer who rapidly outdistanced her. He finally turned in toward shore and stood up. She reached him. "My mother," he panted, "wanted to meet my friend."

May felt a tightening of the stomach.

"She saw us yesterday. She was on the deck when we walked back. Today she said she would come down with me to the pool. She never gets up this early on vacation, but today she was up at eight, saying that you looked like an interesting person and asking what it was we talked about, me and someone as—mature as you."

"Yes," May said, and began walking out of the water.

"I told her we talked about books and sports and things we were both interested in."

"And she laughed."

He nodded. "I got mad and went out without waiting for her. But she came right after me, and I had to lose her in the crowd."

They walked along the beach. Three young girls swung by, glancing at Al. One, lean and fair and piquant, smiled, trying to catch his eye. None paid any attention to May. A mother, they probably figured. An older sister. An aunt.

"Perhaps we'd better not meet any more."

His fingers brushed hers and he took her hand. "I'll do whatever you decide," he said, voice thick. "But I *want* to see you."

"What difference does it make?" She freed her hand, suddenly tired of this nonsense—of avoiding his mother and Eunice and reality, of dreaming an adolescent dream. What she needed was a *man*, a good toss in the hay, proof that she was able to satisfy sexually. "We'll soon leave—"

"You're not *leaving*?" He stopped, his face and voice anguished. "You said you'd stay a month!"

"All right. And *then* I'll leave. Or you'll leave." She began walking. He caught up and took her hand again. "Al, please don't."

He let go. Whispering, so that she was barely able to hear above the background sound of ocean and people, he said, "I want to keep seeing you, May. I don't care if it's only a few more weeks."

She was moved. But she wanted out and said, "Yes, well, there has to be purpose to a male-female relationship. What possible purpose—"

She looked at him, and her voice choked off. He was blinking hard; he was fighting tears. He said, "I don't know the purpose. I just want to keep seeing you."

She took his hand. Her chest ached. Pain and joy. He turned

his face away. "I know what you think. I'm crazy. I *feel* crazy. I just have to be with you."

"I didn't really mean—"

"I want to do things for you. I don't know exactly what. I'm no fool. I want to show you things. But I can't seem to show you, and you're the only one—"

"Albert." The voice was behind them, thin with distance, and his head snapped around. May tried to pull her hand away. His fingers tightened, hurting hers. "My mother," he said, and turned, still holding her hand.

"Let go," she whispered, and saw the tall, well-shaped woman in a black, one-piece bathing suit.

"You think I'm a boy," he said, and now he was almost crushing her fingers. "You think there's no purpose—"

"Al, I *know* you're a man. That's why I'm with you. Let go!"

He let go. But the woman had seen. She came toward them, smiling thinly, saying, "I'm Mrs. Fortens, Al's mother."

"I'm May Krasmer."

"Yes?" The word was drawn out; the small blue eyes moved over her.

Al said, "Where were you going, Mother?"

"Oh, just walking along." She kept looking at May, the look both curious and antagonistic. She couldn't have been five years older than May, perhaps two or three.

"We were about to take a swim," Al said, and turned to the sea.

May hesitated. Al plunged into the water. Mrs. Fortens said, "He knows I can't swim," and laughed lightly. May said, "You should learn," and followed him. Swimming, she glanced back at the beach.

Mrs. Fortens was staring after them. May waved, and wondered at her own self-possession.

Later, they came into shallow water. Al put his arm around her shoulders, his big hand clamping on her forearm. He said, "I want to keep seeing you."

She nodded, watching water run off his broad chest.

"My mother, my father, everyone I've ever known—they don't mean as much to me as your little finger."

She held it up. "Doesn't look *that* important."

He took it and kissed it. She shivered. "I'm cold. Let's get out."

They walked, and he talked. He was a young boy and made her feel like a young girl. But she wondered if he would stop talking before they finally parted, if he would reach for her in the next few weeks. She wondered what she would do if he did, and how it would end.

And she was afraid all over again.

Dr. Sochall had tried to phone him three times in three days, but he ignored the messages. He was much too busy now that the Senator had arrived. He was feeling fine and had just about decided to postpone treatment, if any, until his return to New York. It was unlikely that a minor infection would cause any immediate problems.

He had worked on the speech last night. He had spent all day today with the Senator and his bodyguard—at the pool, on the beach, in the Senator's suite—and they had worked much of the time. Now they were leaving the main dining room and returning to the suite for more work.

The Senator stopped at several tables to speak to people. He signed a menu for an elderly woman who thanked him and said, "You'll be every bit as good a President as your brother-in-law."

"But I won't," he murmured to Dan as they moved to the elevators. "I'll be nothing like Jonathan, will I, Dan?"

Dan Berner understood perfectly. At this stage of the game, he was probably the only person who *could* understand. Richard Bernard Christopher would emerge after his Metropole speech as a man with a strongly individual and surprising—for one of the Wheeler clan—approach to the nation and the world. He was making a break with the powers that ran the Democratic Party.

"It's a declaration of independence," he said, leaning back in the couch and accepting the bourbon Bryan Whitelock handed him. "A risk, Dan, but a calculated one. And if I'm right, it will lead to the nomination."

"When did you make this decision, Senator? When we talked in New York—"

"After that. Though the possibility was present long before that. The possibility has been present since the strong emergence of the doves, since suspicion attacked the minds of the electorate that all that's American isn't necessarily right, since international iconoclasts like De Gaulle began kicking our sacred cows, since our cities began to burn." He drained his glass. "Most important, since cynicism has become at least the equal of naïveté in the people's approach to their government. Such cynicism is, of course, decadence. But decadence isn't necessarily evil when a nation has industry and weaponry such as ours. Decadence can be maturity, Dan, when it allows for responsibility in the genocide of the American Indian and the soul-destruction of the American Negro."

"You believe—your polls indicate that Americans actually accept responsibility for such events?"

"Unconsciously, yes. In great numbers if not in the majority, yes."

"But it's the majority that concerns a presidential candidate."

"We have a year to move the uncommitted. I can't see going any other way, Dan. I find an area of deep belief here, deep commitment."

"Your father-in-law and brother-in-law will be surprised."

Dick smiled, and said, "You have doubts about the *rightness* of what we're doing, Dan?"

"In terms of my own beliefs, no. As you put it last night, the country is beginning to stink. Our stated goals and our actual goals are drawing farther and farther apart. And this divergence is tearing *us* apart. We've either got to bring the actual goals closer to the stated goals—reduce the materialism in our lives, the idiocy of our anti-Communist crusades, the cruelty and blindness in our dealings with blacks—or admit that the stated goals are false."

179

"That's good. Make notes."

Dan worked with his pad and ballpoint, then said, "But in terms of practical politics, I don't think you can win."

Dick Christopher held out his empty glass. Bryan Whitelock came over from the bar. Dick said, "To quote Adlai Stevenson, 'I don't have to win.'"

Whitelock, who was pouring Wild Turkey, looked up then. Dick drank and said, "Let's work."

Dan picked up the speech from the coffee table and turned to the section on Southeast Asia. There would be no explanation from Dick Christopher. But Dan felt the explanation was clear. Dick didn't have to win the Presidency to win over himself—over his in-laws and himself.

At one-thirty Dan was in his room undressing, walking to the desk every so often to glance at the speech. The phone rang. It could only be the Senator, and he answered with, "I've got a hot idea about the cities—"

Dr. Sochall's voice said, "I didn't think a man of your intelligence could act so childishly. I wanted to sit down and explain this to you, in all its ramifications, all its complexity and detail, but since you're running and I might not get the chance again—"

Dan pulled over the chair and sat down.

"—I have to put it bluntly. You've got cancer of the prostate, Mr. Berner. Not usual in a man your age, but there it is."

"I see." But he didn't. He felt all right and cancer was synonymous with death and he was in the midst of life, in the midst of stirring a *nation* to life.

"We have to talk. I want a few more tests. The cancer might be localized in the prostate itself. If that's so—and I sincerely hope it is—we can avoid an orchiectomy. If it isn't localized, we face several alternatives—"

Dan interrupted. "You're *sure* of this, Doctor?"

"No! I like to call patients up at one-thirty in the morning and tell them they have cancer! For kicks!"

Dan waited.

"Sorry, Mr. Berner. I know what a shock this must be."

"Yes." But it wasn't. It didn't mean a thing. "I'm quite busy right now," he said, looking at the speech. "I'd like an appoint- for the week after next. He reached for his desk calendar. "Say Monday, the thirtieth."

"I'd insist on *tomorrow*, Mr. Berner, but I'll be in surgery all day. So it's Thursday, nine A.M."

"That's impossible. I'm in the early phases of a speech for Senator Christopher. I'll be tied up until he delivers it on Satur- day, the twenty-eighth."

"I wouldn't care if you were conducting peace negotiations for the United Nations. *Time*, Mr. Berner, is our greatest ally, and our greatest enemy."

"You obviously don't understand the importance—"

"*You* obviously don't understand!" The doctor was angry again. "We're entering a fight to save your life! Your life is the most important thing in all the *world*, Mr. Berner!"

Dan said, "All right. Thursday. Will it take long? I have to be back—"

The doctor's laugh held traces of hysteria. "Nine A.M., Mr. Berner." The phone clicked.

Dan turned pages, made a few changes, and was suddenly very tired. He undressed, and was even too tired to wash. He put out the lights, got into bed, and thought he was falling asleep.

But then he heard the voice and realized he was talking into the darkness. "Now me, Verna. Can you believe it? He's a good doctor, concerned, involved. I'm lucky to have him . . ."

The voice stopped. Its minor echoes—tiny carom shots of sound—died away. He strained to hear more. He said, "I didn't smoke. I didn't drink. You know how I stayed in shape. Can you believe it, Verna?"

He listened again, and when it was dead silent, tomblike, he sat up, stricken, wanting to be with someone.

That girl, Cerise. He had the number. They were used to getting calls at all hours of the night.

He went to the phone, but turned right around and sat down on the bed. He didn't want action. He wanted company.

May. He shouldn't have treated her that way. She cared for him . . .

Had cared. He couldn't call her. He couldn't ask her for talk or anything else.

Not that he wanted May in particular. Not that he cared anything for her. Not that he had cared for Verna. Or any other woman.

Love. He hadn't ever known it. He doubted it existed for the true intellectual. Except on a self-imposed basis. Such as he had imposed on himself in order to marry and find sex and, he'd thought, raise a family.

A daughter. If he'd had a daughter she would be with him now. She would weep for him . . .

He wanted no one weeping for him!

There was no one to call; there was nothing to do. He went back to bed. "Can you believe it?" he muttered, and he for one didn't.

3

WEDNESDAY, JANUARY 18

The phone was ringing. Ellie waited, hoping her father was still here and would answer it. But it continued to ring and she reached across the bed and lifted the receiver, hesitating between putting it down and finding out who it was.

It wasn't Bruce. She'd been with him Monday night and last night, and last night she had stayed until two and he'd said he would be a zombie today and wouldn't make a zombie of her. He would call at noon.

Could it be noon already?

The night-table clock read nine-fifteen.

She put the phone down on the table and rolled over with her back to it. She thought of Monday night and last night, and smiled. Bruce Golden was something special. Bruce Golden didn't press and didn't strain. He played his cards just right. He was an artist with women, no doubt about it. (The fact that she *knew* this was a mark against him, but a very small mark.)

She laughed a little. They had kissed just once Monday and just once last night. He had cooked for her—sole Bercy on Monday and cassoulet yesterday, the cassoulet taking over three hours and contributing to the lateness of her leaving. The cooking was fun; he'd allowed her to help. His entire operation was fun. He was playing her beautifully, carefully—and she loved it. She could almost predict when he'd be ready to bed her, and could almost be certain she would accept.

Last night they had listened to Debussy and played chess and she had read to him from *Flowers of Evil*, the Edna St. Vincent Millay translations. It was all so *un*-Miami Beach that it was funny. They had lain on his big bed and talked and touched hands and that was when he had kissed her, a long kiss and very good, and she had laughed inside as he withdrew with a cool grin and she had known that the next time the kiss would be even longer and the withdrawal less cool and that the time would finally come—two more beautiful evenings, three at the most—when passion would "overwhelm" him, that cool, cool cookie with the well-trained libido, and he would take her.

She shivered a little, her own libido not *quite* as trained, and heard the tinny electronic voice say, "Ellie? President Standers calling."

She froze, all the pleasure drying up. She *couldn't* have heard that!

She turned over and looked at the pink Princess phone. The tinny voice (whoever it was must have been shouting) said, "President Standers on personal business, Ellie."

A joke. A very bad joke by a very stupid person.

But who would know to make a joke like that?

Dick Christopher? He wouldn't. Not Dick. It was no joke to Dick.

She put out her hand and touched the phone.

"Ellie? Are you listening?"

She raised it and brought it to her ear. "Who is this?"

"You knew it wasn't the President, didn't you, Ellie?" The voice was pitched high and false. The voice was the voice in the darkness at Marjory Fine's party. She hung up, trembling.

It rang again. She went to the bathroom. It stopped. She washed and came out and chose a bikini. It rang. She went to it.

"Why don't you tell me what I already know?" the false tinny voice asked.

"Let me alone," she said, calmly. "If you don't—"

"You'll call the police? All right, call them. We'll talk about the President."

She hung up. She stood waiting, then went to the dresser and took off her robe and picked up the bikini bottom. The phone rang. It rang and rang, and when it stopped her head seemed to ring without it. She crouched nude, panting heavily.

The phone rang. She went to it. "He was your lover," the false tinny voice said.

He knew, and why bother to deny the truth? She wouldn't be *telling* him anything—just nodding, in a way, at his statements of fact.

She sank to the edge of the bed.

"Your lover and your husband. *Isn't that right, Ellie?*"

"Yes," she whispered.

"Father of your child."

She took the phone from her ear and looked at it, stunned. "You don't know," she said. And then, raging at her own weakness, her own stupidity, she screamed into it, "You didn't know! You—you tricked—"

There was speech. She put the phone back to her ear. "Of course I knew. I just wasn't sure about that one point. And that's not important now. What's important is how you must *hate* the whole Wheeler clan. As much as I hate them."

184

"No, I don't hate—"

"You'll get your revenge," the voice said. "I promise you. It might cost a bit, but you'll be happy then."

"I won't do anything!"

"You've always wanted to hurt them. It's the only thing that will make you happy, make you well. Money didn't change things, Ellie. You have to even the score, don't you?"

She shook her head, tried to think of an answer, and said nothing. Because he was right. Money hadn't changed things—not inside Ellie DeWyant.

But *Bruce* was changing things. She didn't need this evil voice counseling her. She didn't want it!

"Stop speaking to me! If you don't stop—"

"Who will you tell, Ellie?"

Again she didn't answer. She could tell no one.

"I'll let you know what to do, Ellie. Soon. If you do it, we'll both feel better. If you don't, the Wheelers will be told you betrayed your trust."

"You *mustn't!* It's not just me. My father—" She stopped. Again she was making mistakes. Again she was arming this evil voice.

"Yes, Ellie. I mustn't. So you'll help me." The line went dead.

She sat down on the bed. Who could she ask for help?

Only the Wheeler family—Mike and Dick and Jonny. The brutal Wheeler clan. And she wouldn't.

Yet she had to talk to someone; she needed someone.

Her father? He would worry. And, eventually, he would go to Mike Wheeler.

Bruce Golden. She could talk to Bruce. He would help her think it out, help her decide what to do. He would share the secret.

No, she wasn't allowed to share the secret. Only the Wheelers and that old lawyer, and the lawyer was dead, and so only the Wheelers and the DeWyants knew. Five members of the Wheeler clan and two DeWyants. Seven people in all the world because

185

the Wheeler millions had bought and destroyed the records, the Wheeler millions had wiped out tracks.

Maybe the man on the phone—it had to be a man, didn't it?—was just a crank.

But he knew. Even if he hadn't known before, he did now. She had told him.

Maybe if she agreed to meet him he would grow frightened and melt away. Yes, that was the way to handle a telephone nut. Call his bluff. Yes . . .

She went to the dresser. She looked at herself naked, and suddenly remembered Jonny coming into the shower that first time at the shabby Fort Lauderdale motel, centuries ago, life-times ago, thirteen years ago. She remembered him as few if any people in the United States could remember their President. Mr. and Mrs. DeWyant was the way he had registered, a gag and a harmless one, since no one knew the name DeWyant then and Jonny had already dated Bunny Wheeler a few times and served as legal counsel to some congressional committee and had his name in the papers. Because the old man—no, don't let that scene come back with the pencil jabbing the air and Dick sitting in the background and the smell of whiskey and the sure, smooth, western voice explaining what she would get and how there were no alternatives, except perhaps death—the old man had been President and before that a power in national politics, he and his three or four hundred million dollars. The old man had been using his muscle all those years to move people, to push people into doing what he wanted. And what he wanted was that his daughter would marry Jonny and that Jonny would become President. And what Master Mike wanted he got. What the Wheeler-Dealer wanted . . .

No, don't think of that. Think of Jonny, of Mr. and Mrs. DeWyant and the shower and Jonny laughing and saying sorry, he couldn't wait until they were married. And he didn't. Shoving her up against the cold tile with the warm water running from her hair and his big, smooth hands gripping her and lifting her so she seemed to settle on it, impaled, with the hiss in her ears and his breath in her ears . . .

The phone rang, shattering the memory, and she sobbed dryly and ran to it. If it was that voice again! . . .

"*Yes!*"

"Hey, you wake up real wild."

It was Bruce Golden. "Come up," she said.

"I'm on my way to a client."

"Don't make me spoil my sweet, ladylike image by telling you what to do with your client. Tell Mr. Stein my father asked you to come to his suite to discuss an idea or two."

"I won't tell him anything of the sort, but I'll be there."

She pulled a minisheath over her nudity and put on pale lipstick and a little eye shadow and a little scent. By then the chime was sounding. She let him in. He set down his attaché case and looked at her. "What's wrong?"

She'd been ready to sex him out of his mind, but at that she turned away and cried. He led her to the couch and she cried herself out.

"Tell me," he said.

She shook her head and went to wash her face. When she came back he was on the phone. ". . . cancel out for me, Andy. I wouldn't ask if it wasn't. Yes . . . thanks."

He came to her and held out his arms. They kissed slowly and she murmured, "Golden Boy." She hadn't been able to say it when he'd first told her what they called him. It sounded so— affected. But now, with his arms around her and his lips on her neck, she said it and it was right.

His hands moved over her back and over her hips and they kissed again, and then drew apart by mutual consent. He could have taken her then and they both knew it. "Put on underwear," he said.

"Why?"

He cupped her face with his hands, then moved away. "My Jaguar is close quarters. We're spending most of the day in it—

driving some place and staying a few hours and driving back. We're going to *talk*. We're going to tell each other everything."

She nodded, thinking, *almost everything*. "Sanibel Island, Bruce, off Fort Myers. Fishing and shelling and quiet."

He'd heard of it.

She ran to the bedroom, leaving the door open. "Four hours through Everglades country to get there, four hours to spend there, four hours back. Add an hour for lunch and an hour for dinner and we make Miami by midnight." She rejoined him, carrying her bikini. "Take a swimsuit. The Gulf is marvelous."

He said he kept a pair of trunks in his desk. They walked to the door. She said, "You're playing this one *perfectly*, Mr. Golden."

He said, "I know it, Miss DeWyant."

She laughed and hugged his arm. But a little something, a touch of regret perhaps, entered her laughter. Plans were important, necessary, but she wished he weren't quite so *good* at plans.

The eighth-floor suite wasn't as crowded as it had been for the first party, but then again this wasn't the same kind of affair. This was a noontime buffet, with cocktails, in honor of Senator Christopher, and Marjory Fine didn't expect much in the way of action, at least until the guest of honor left. Then, perhaps, heavy drinking and people she had asked to drop in after five might produce the right sort of "items."

The Senator was holding court near the windows, surrounded by a group of admirers. The Pragers were back. So was Marco Renier, standing outside the group around Richard Christopher, sipping a drink, shooting occasional glances at the handsome politician.

Marjory drifted over to him and murmured, "You're impressed, darling, I can tell."

"I'm impressed with men in general, as you well know, Marjory."

"Ah, but that one's special."

"My dear matchmaker," he murmured. "Match me, then."

He was looking at the Senator again, his smile faintly mocking.

"Are you getting any signals?" she joked.

He shifted his large, heavy-lashed eyes to her. "Signals? From the next President of the United States? That most aggressively male member of the Senate married to that most obviously female member of the Wheeler clan, the forthrightly named Bunny? Signals, from that husband par excellence, whose every domestic virtue is reported on in depth by the press?" The smile was matched by his tone of voice. "Signals would be unthinkable from that paragon of Amurrican virtues. Let's forget that statisticians insist one male in four has had a homosexual experience. The Senator a *queer*? Let's forget that the odds rise rapidly when a male passes thirty, and that Dickie is past forty and dominated by both wife and father-in-law. The Senator a *pansy*? Finally, let's forget that despite all conjugal publicity to the contrary, he gives this particular homosexual distinctly simpatico impressions. The President's brother-in-law *gay*?"

She wasn't amused. "There's just one thing wrong with—your set, Marco. They imagine every male is the same as they are."

"We're right twenty-five percent of the time, dear matchmaker. And that's by *official* figures. And since when have official figures failed to play *down* a frightening or embarrassing statistic?"

"It's a wonder we have any birthrate at all."

"Oh, I could have children, if I got drunk enough."

"I think I'd better do some circulating."

"When you have the time, allow me to tell you of my experiences in the central lockup of a major eastern city. Do you know the percentage of homosexuals in prison, Marjory?"

"You, in prison?"

"Surprised? Members of my 'set,' to quote you, are natural victims of the police. Still, prison is quite a revelation. The percentage of confreres is close to a hundred percent. They may revert outside, but while *inside* they're much in favor of democratic sex, each man doing his buddy and being done in return.

Which goes to prove that every man wants his cock sucked—"

She turned quickly away.

"—and isn't particular who does it."

Revolting little faggot!

But by the time she reached the door, where Bert was admitting the elephantine man in pale blue sports ensemble, she was beginning to be stimulated by the images Marco had forced on her. Wouldn't it be something if Marco's insinuations about the Senator . . .

"Mine hostessel," Benny Barker said in Yiddish dialect, "you grow lovelier with each season." He bent ponderously over her hand as she waited for the inevitable punch line. "Older, baby, but lovelier."

"Thank you, Ben. I think you've gained weight. Your nose is larger."

He straightened, a vast-bellied, moon-faced man with sharp gray eyes and straight blond hair. "So are my ratings. Now where's my Fix?"

She led him and his manager and a curvy, sloe-eyed young redhead to the bar and made the Fix herself: four parts brandy, one part sweet vermouth, a half part vodka, a dash of Angostura, quick-stirred with ice. Then two maraschino cherries mashed into the bottom of a tall glass, four or five ice cubes, and the mixture poured over it. Barker sipped, nodded, took down half the glass. The redhead said, "How to get bombed out of your skull! Remember the time I had two of them?" (Hearing the high, chorus-girlie voice, Marjory recognized her. She was among half a dozen beauties who introduced skits on the Benny Barker Show.)

"Yes. We became *good* friends that night, didn't we, Assy?"

"That's not nice," she murmured. Marjory agreed, but the girl wasn't talking about Benny's kissing-and-telling. "*Asty.*"

"Astrid," Benny explained. "But Asty has no rhyme, no reason. Assy, on the other hand . . ."

Marjory couldn't help it; she burst out laughing.

Benny glowed, reacting to her laughter. "Hey, I've got a dirty joke. Dirty jokes are my hang-up. I love them, but I can't tell

190

them on the air." He glanced toward the windows and the Senator. "And I can't tell *this* one to my liberal ole buddy, Dick Christopher. You'll understand why—if I have your permission to go ahead?"

She was about to plead the necessity of mingling when he launched into the joke.

"There was this skin-merchant, see? A real make-out artist. Two or three beautiful chicks a week was his quota." He finished his drink and looked at Astrid. She grinned, obviously having heard it before. "Well, he decides it's time he got married. He wants a home and children and all the rest of it. *But*—he wants a girl just like the girl that married dear old dad. A sweet thing. A heart tried and true. A virgin."

Astrid couldn't contain herself and turned away, laughing. Benny murmured, "She thinks *that's* the punch line."

Pete Shrager, the manager, said he saw an old friend and ambled away. Astrid turned back, saying, "I *heard* that. One of these days, *pow!* To the moon, Ben, to the moon!"

Benny said to stop quoting the competition. "Anyway, he keeps going with girls, trying to find the right one. And the way he tries is by operating just as he's always operated. Only now he's interested in those who turn him down. Not many do, you understand, because he's a big businessman and handsome and has everything, but *everything*, going for him. Still, a *few* do, and of these few one is gorgeous, educated, refined, and with enough dough of her own so that he knows she isn't interested in *his* dough. So he gets serious, and they date for a year, and he keeps trying to make her but he never gets close. Finally, when he's convinced she's a virgin and will never give in, he pops the question. She accepts and they get married. They fly away on their honeymoon, arrive in Acapulco, and check into a luxurious hotel suite. He orders a champagne supper, they eat and drink, and she excuses herself and goes into the bedroom. He jumps up and begins pacing. He's as anxious as if he were a virgin himself. Because this is what he's wanted all his life—love as he's dreamed it, love with a pure woman, his and his alone.

"Get the scene now. The bedroom door opens. There she is in a black silk negligee. She's stacked, gorgeous. He comes to her, drops to his knees, kisses her hands, tells her how happy he is. Then he takes off the negligee. She's something! The greatest! His hands are shaking so bad he can hardly get out of his clothes. But finally they're in bed together, and he's hornier than he's ever been in all his life. He's proud of being a man, you know. He's made a thousand broads and now he has his one and only and he's showing her what he's got. He makes her take it in her hand, and through her sighs and blushes she murmurs, 'My, what a cute eeny-weeny peewee.' "

Astrid was breaking up again. "If only you could tell it on TV!"

Benny grinned. "This isn't exactly what our hero wants to hear. Eeny-weeny peewee? It emasculates him. So, in his full manhood, he rises up over her and says, 'This, baby, is a *prick!*' With that, the dream of his life shakes her head and murmurs, 'No, darling, you're mistaken. A prick is ten inches long and black.' "

Marjory forced a smile. She needn't have bothered. Benny's enormous stomach was quaking in laughter; Astrid was leaning on his shoulder and gasping for breath.

When Barker recovered, he said, "Speaking of black pricks, has Wally Jones arrived yet?"

Marjory said not that she knew of, but he had an invitation waiting at his room when he did. Barker nodded. "I know, honey. I'm a Ku Klux bum." His smile was cool. "But I'm not alone. The rest of the country is rapidly catching up to me."

Astrid muttered, "You gotta live near them like I did."

Marjory said she had never lived near Negroes, knew nothing about them beyond what she read and, of course, her friendship with Wally Jones. "And Wally is as fine a man as I know."

"But you *don't* know," Barker said. "Another thing you don't know is why he is coming here. The little shine wants to out-shine me."

192

"Are you going to reveal whatever it is that lies between you two?"

Barker smiled and turned away. "*We* shall overcome, baby." He and Astrid headed for the Senator.

Marjory drank her first Scotch of the day, to wash away the taste of that "joke." Benny Barker had the eighth most popular show on television, and had been in the top ten for seven years. He could make things happen in nightclubs, at benefits, at parties, when he was in the right mood. People loved him and he loved people—if you excluded black people. It seemed to have escaped the notice of all but a few black militants, but Barker hadn't had a Negro guest artist on his show in years. And those that *had* appeared were either of the old New Orleans jazz group or particularly inactive in things pertaining to their race.

She went to the door and Bert gave her a quick rundown on the guest situation. Michael Wheeler had failed to show. On the bright side, Jerry Leech had arrived.

Marjory began looking for Mrs. Prager.

"Materialism in full flower," Lou Degano murmured, waving an arm at the crowded suite.

Andy Stein raised his glass. "To materialism," he said. "Long may it provide me with life's goodies. Long may it provide my employees with their share of my share of life's goodies."

They stood beside the bar and drank. She said, "Meant to speak to you about my share of your share, boss."

He smiled, looking at the heavy knot of people around Senator Christopher. Lou said, "I'm sorry I met him."

He was surprised. "I thought him rather nice."

"Yes, nice. But my previous social experience with Presidents comes from the movies. There they always have stirring musical introductions, and make majestic pronouncements that bring tears to all eyes. This one might be President. He's just a good-looking hunk of man. Terrible."

Andy laughed. Lou said, "I'm hungry."

He headed across the room to the table of hors d'oeuvres. She smothered a burp. Damned liquor. Gave her heartburn. Now if Bruce had asked her here instead of Andy, she'd have worked him for a few joints.

But Bruce hadn't asked her, and wasn't going to ask her. Not to big hotel parties, and not to private at-home parties. He had barely looked at her the past two weeks. She'd played hard to get, played for a real bit of emotion, and he hadn't come through. Now something was working out for the Golden Boy. That meant he was combining women and the hang-up, money. That meant the talk in the office about him and Ellie DeWyant was true.

"How's tricks?"

She turned and it was Jerry Leech. "With me or my legs?"

He looked up, grinning. "Hey, why don't you and me dance a little, Lou?"

"No one else is."

"We'll start things off."

Andy came up with a paper plate and nodded to Leech. Leech said, "Hi, Mr. Stein," then, to Lou, "Well, you want to?"

She said, "Later, maybe," biting into a caviar cracker. Leech nodded and swaggered off.

"Well-you-want-to what?" Andy asked.

She selected a cocktail sausage. "How can I put it?"

He laughed quickly.

She ate six of the hors d'oeuvres and held the seventh, a high-piled deviled egg, out to him. He reached for it. She moved it away from his hands, up to his mouth. He bit. She put the rest into his mouth and licked her fingers. He said, "He didn't really . . . ?"

A couple began dancing, and Leech and a stout woman joined them, and Lou took Andy's hand.

It was a fox-trot. Andy held her close, then closer, then suddenly tried to put some space between them. But she wasn't having any. He gave a brief, embarrassed bark of laughter, and muttered, "Sorry."

194

"When it *doesn't* happen, then apologize."

He laughed a good deal more than the joke called for. The music went on, one number leading into another. A while later he said, "Remember a conversation we had a few weeks ago?"

"About what?"

"About miniskirts and what you were willing to do for your fellow man, namely me."

"Yes." She hummed along with the music. "I'm glad it stuck in your mind."

"Something else stuck, too. Something about men forgetting their wives. I don't think I could do that." He quickly added, "Not that I wouldn't want to, temporarily. I just don't think I could."

"I don't think you could either, boss."

The music ended. They drew apart. "Like picking flowers," she said, "eating hors d'oeuvres, singing songs. You don't forget people doing *that*, do you?" They looked at each other, and slowly the worried look, the tense and guilty look, began easing from his face.

She took his hand. The older generation—what children they sometimes were. Later, thinking of Bruce Golden, she wondered when the hell *she* would grow up.

"I can't leave," Jerry said. "You know I can't."

They were still dancing. Ruthie was getting to him, sure, and he remembered how great it had been the second time, when he'd asked for a hell of a lot of service, but he was beginning to sweat about Eve. Only ten days before the Senator's speech—ten days until the snatch. He had to hook her good before then! Last night could have been the clincher—or at least the beginning of the clincher—but Mr. Wheeler had to go and ruin things. He had a hunch the old bastard would have tried to screw her himself if he wasn't nailed to a wheelchair.

"She's not coming," Ruthie said. "The Senator's gone and why would Wheeler come after his son in-law's left?"

"She might come alone. He promised her some time off."

Ruthie kept working on him. "A half hour, that's all, Jerry. You won't be sorry, I promise."

He stopped dancing. "No! I got to stay right here until the party's over! You're beginning to bug me, Ruthie!"

"Don't get mad," she said, and the way she said it killed his anger. Her face was pale. She looked like she was going to bawl. "I've had such a lousy time . . ." She stopped, shrugging and trying to smile.

"You and Max?"

She shrugged again.

"I thought you got along like you were really married?"

"Yeah, exactly like we were really married. For fifty years."

He gave her a little pat on the beam. "Anyone as good at lovin' as you don't have to worry about men." They began dancing again.

"That's not true, Jerry. A woman . . . it has to be more than just that. A woman needs a little friendship."

"Well, sure." The last thing he needed was talk like this from a middle-aged pig. "You'll find a guy."

"Have you thought what you'll do after the job's finished?"

Had he! "Open a restaurant or bar. Maybe a nightclub."

"Where?"

"Where else? Miami Beach."

She laughed.

"What's so funny?"

"You haven't thought it through very carefully, have you?" She put her mouth to his ear. "Once the Senator's released . . ."

"We've got nothing to do with that. We just pull the job, deliver him to the limousine, and forget it."

"Yes, but Max says the orders are no harm is to be done the Senator. Which means that Jorge and his group expect to free him. What happens once he's free?"

Leech thought of it. "I guess the deal will be they don't bother us and we don't bother them."

She laughed again. He began to feel uncomfortable.

"Well, what *does* happen?" he asked.

"They begin hunting down everyone who might have had a part in it. You and Max are going to be the two hottest things in the country, and I'll be a close third. If Jorge comes in on the action—"

"*If?*"

"Well, who knows? I mean, why risk his neck?"

"Why? For the same reason we are. Dough. We're getting plenty. He must be getting the fat-cat share of the ransom. Say half a million—he and his boss, if Max is right."

"Max is always right. And Max knows we can't stay in the country. Max knows we have to run, and that no matter where we go we'll have to sweat. Like Nazi war criminals, they'll never stop looking for us. Jorge must know it too."

"Some of those Nazis made it," Leech muttered, but he was thinking hard. "Why all of a sudden these questions? How come we didn't talk about it—you and me and Max—*before?*"

"Because I trust Max. Because I know he never goes into anything without a good chance of coming out okay."

The music stopped. They stood together, voices low.

"So? He's in this with us, isn't he? So there's a good chance of coming out okay, isn't there?"

"Not the way it's planned."

"Ah, you're dreaming up trouble. I oughta tell him—"

"Think of it, Jerry. You're not going to open a bar in Miami Beach, or any place else. You're going to have to lie low the rest of your life. Oh, you'll have enough money, especially if you go to South America. But you're a beginner at this. You'll need help to stay out of prison, or the gas chamber."

He stared at her.

"I can help you, Jerry. Together—"

"You're crazy," he said, voice harsh.

"Think of it. You'll have your hundred grand, but the nurse, the old man, the Senator—who knows how many others—will know you. You'll have to run and hide, and you don't know how, Jerry. Think of it. I've been around a lot longer than you, and always in the rackets. I could plan for us, protect us . . ." She paused . . . "Maybe get us out of this in case of a cross."

"What's that supposed to mean?"

The music started. She took his hand and they danced. "Can you see a top pro like Max going into anything stacked this high against him?"

Jerry swallowed dryly. "If he sees what you see, he wouldn't touch it."

"Exactly."

He stopped dancing again.

"I say Max won't put himself on the line when the action begins. I can't see how he can get his payoff without doing his part, but he must have an angle. He might even sell out."

"Sell out? But who could he—"

"Wheeler. He's the one who'll pay the ransom, so why wouldn't he pay Max a lot less to stop the snatch?"

"I want a belt," he muttered, and turned to the bar.

They had two drinks, and she warned him not to let Max know of their conversation.

"You're guessing, Ruthie. You're guessing all the way."

"Sure I am. But they're educated guesses. And they add up, don't they?"

He gulped his rye.

"We have to stick together and watch," she said. "We've got ten days and we have to talk every day. Max is off by himself most of the time now. We have to protect ourselves. If he's playing it straight, all right. If not, we have to find out before it's too late."

He nodded slowly. She said, "Excuse me a minute," and walked toward a door. She tried it and it was locked. She went to the other side of the half-empty suite and another door. She went in. He lit a cigarette and tried to think. It was too much for him. He wanted his payoff. He couldn't face living without his payoff! But—if it was a cross . . .

Ruthie was back. "You ever see the rest of this place, Jerry?"

They walked around the room. She said the locked door was a bathroom; she had used another one on the opposite side. Beside the locked bathroom was a bedroom. She opened the door explaining that it was the second bedroom. The master was on the other side and locked.

"You been casing the joint?" he muttered, a sense of depression, of doom, weighing him down.

She said it was habit. "My habits can save us both, Jerry." She stepped into the room, drawing him with her. He watched as she closed the door and pressed the knob-lock. He said, "We're not sure of anything. I got to be out there."

"And you will, Jerry. In just ten minutes."

He figured what the hell and went to the drapes. He almost broke the cord, then tried to pull them shut by hand. They wouldn't budge. He shrugged and went back to where Ruthie was wriggling out of her girdle. So the seagulls would see them.

Bert came over as Marjory was saying good-bye to Benny Barker, his manager, and his girl. She moved aside and Bert whispered and she glanced around. Max Prager was at the bar with Dan Berner. Marjory hoped he wouldn't start looking for his wife.

She hurried to the bathroom, checked quickly to make sure she wasn't being watched, and opened the door with her key (another little modification Bert had made). Inside, she locked the door, throwing the windowless room into darkness. But she didn't put on the lights. She stepped to the sink and leaned forward, peering at the long mirror above it. She looked through it and into the adjoining bedroom. Because of the open drapes (Bert thought of everything) she had a good view of the bed and the couple on it.

She reached under the sink, found the little dial and turned it to the right. It clicked, and there was the somewhat hollow sound of amplified voices. She kept turning until the whispers could be clearly heard. Mrs. Prager did all the talking. Leech merely groaned.

"Need you, honey," Mrs. Prager was saying. "Need each other . . ."

It could have been better. They hadn't undressed and it didn't last very long. But Mrs. Prager was an inspired performer, and within those few minutes brought Marjory Fine to a point where she was assured satisfaction at tonight's massage.

She waited until it was over and they were arranging their clothing. She was about to turn off the sound when Mrs. Prager said, "We're good together, Jerry. Forget looks. Have you ever enjoyed it more?"

He said no, buckling his belt.

Mrs. Prager touched his arm. "Remember, without me you're in bad trouble. Max will cop out, I'm sure of it. He's working on the DeWyant girl."

"But that's part of it," Leech said.

"No, for himself. Like wanting to know Jorge's partner."

Marjory turned the sound off. She put on the light and flushed the toilet, in case anyone was directly outside. Then she left, the door locking automatically behind her.

She wondered what they'd been talking about. Perhaps Bert would be able to explain.

The first thing he saw when he came out of the bedroom (after giving Ruthie a chance to blend back into the party) was Eve. He said, *"Keeerist!"* under his breath, and started toward where she was standing just inside the door, looking a little scared and lost. He wasn't ready for her. Not even to talk to her. But he waved and said, "Hey, what a break!"

She smiled. "Hello, Jerry. Mr. Wheeler said I could drop in."

"Great!" He turned to the bar. "Let's have a drink to celebrate your busting out."

"Coke for me, please."

He said sure and ordered a Coke and a Scotch. They walked to the windows. He saw Ruthie standing with Mrs. Fine, and silently cursed her. Max walked over to Mrs. Fine; then he and Ruthie started for the door, and Ruthie waved at him. He waved back, his curses drying up. If she was right, he would need her like a baby needs its momma.

"I can only stay half an hour," Eve said.

Half an hour was nothing, but if not for Ruthie it might have been enough. He could have showed Eve around the suite the way Ruthie had showed him.

He took her hand. She was no sexpot, but she looked okay. She was wearing her black dress and it did something for her. Not that it showed her best feature. Even her bathing suit didn't give more than a hint of that. Only when her pants had come off had he realized she had a grade-A ass, long-cheeked and smooth as silk.

He began to feel a stirring—slight but still a stirring. He squeezed her hand. She murmured, "I'm sorry about last night, Jerry. I know it wasn't . . . fair to you."

Dumb little broad. He sighed and muttered, "I couldn't sleep hardly a wink. Not because we . . . well, that too. But worrying that you might've got into trouble. I guess you didn't?"

She shook her head.

He bent toward her, trying to whip up a little steam. "When I think how we were, how great you looked . . ."

She got red and muttered she would like something to eat. He put his arm around her waist and moved her to the food table. They had lobster and ribs of beef, and when he put down his plate, she asked if they could go for a walk. "I've never been around the hotel. Without Mr. Wheeler, I mean. Just where his chair can go."

He reclaimed her hand. "You get the deluxe tour."

They went to the top floor for the Orbit Bar, the rooftop ballroom, the gym, and the solarium. "Solarium's got two separate sections. One for men, one for women. That's so you can tan all over. I mean stripped, naked." She nodded, eyes down. He murmured, "But I wouldn't want you to change that smooth white—"

She said, "Jerry," redder than before.

They went down to the lobby and La Chine, the Gold Room,

and the Platinum Room. He gave her the full spiel about how La Chine was mainly for Latin dancing with Chinese food as the specialty come-on; the Gold Room was for spot entertainment and ballroom dancing, with two nights a week for rock and roll; the Platinum Room was the third biggest nightclub in Miami, with top stars during the season. "Guess you know Wally Jones opens here Friday, Benny Barker Saturday. Then they'll take turns at the ten and midnight shows for a full week."

They looked into the huge club, dim and empty now, the tables rising in three-quarter-moon tiers from a circular stage. He glanced around, then drew her swiftly through the door and into the shadows. He kissed her, tried to bring her up tight in a real clinch. She murmured, "Someone'll see," and pushed gently against him. He let go. "Yeah, a time and a place, as the man says," and yokked it up and led her from the club. He was bouncing back now, but good!

He took her to the three dining rooms, and then the glittering snackery called the Bon Bouche. "How about a banana split?" he said.

"We just ate. Besides, I've got to get back." But she looked at the long Gay Nineties counter and the three dozen glass-topped tables and the good-sized crowd of early diners and snackers. She looked at them the way she had looked at everything he'd shown her, with longing. The poor kid hadn't seen a thing except the inside of that suite, a stretch of beach, and the old man's rotten carcass.

"Hey," he said. "I just got an idea. Call him up—"

"He can't answer the phone himself, and I wouldn't want to disturb his guests—his son-in-law and some politicians."

"Then just forget the time. So you'll be a half hour late. Or an hour, if we drive over to my place."

"How could I? He'd be upset."

"I'll bet he's forgotten all about you. I mean, with his guests there."

She shook her head. "He's not like that. He said the Senator

202

was leaving in half an hour and I was to be back. He means what he says."

He tried pulling her into the restaurant, grinning and saying, "Aw, c'mon, Evie."

She resisted. "He hasn't even had his dinner!"

He saw it was no good, and they went to the elevators.

"When then?" he asked.

"I don't know, Jerry."

"Now come on, honey. Last night . . . and now we're not even making contact! I'll come up tonight, after he goes to bed."

She wet her lips. "He was suspicious last night. If he found out . . ."

"You *afraid* of that old man?" He laughed, to show her how ridiculous it was.

"I just don't want to upset him. He's doing well and I don't want to hurt his chances of recovery."

He was getting desperate. "Then ask for tomorrow night off."

"That's too short notice. I'd need a replacement."

"The hotel has registered nurses on call. I'll tell Mr. Balson, the night manager—"

"He won't want a stranger, Jerry. This is a critical time in his convalescence."

"Well *how* then? How do I date a girl like you?"

She didn't answer right away, then spoke quietly. "Maybe you don't. At least not when she's on a case."

A car arrived and they went in together. There were other people with them. He tried to think of what he would say when they were alone.

It was nuts, but after practically making it last night he was stymied!

The rest of the car emptied at the tenth floor. He grabbed her, kissed her, held her against him. "I'm coming up tonight. I don't care what he thinks. I'm coming up!"

He let her go, briefly, as the doors opened at fourteen, then held her again when he realized no one was there. She struggled.

203

"Jerry, I'm late." The doors shut and they started down. He ran his hands over her body, and suddenly she was straining against him and whispering, "Oh I want you to, Jerry! I want you to!"

He grinned triumphantly.

"But not tonight. Not right after he was so suspicious. Next week, maybe. Monday or Tuesday."

"No, tomorrow."

"I'm afraid . . ."

He let her go, playing it by ear, by the way she had held him, by the expression on her face. "*Tomorrow*, Eve."

The car stopped. Two stacked broads got in, mink coats open over Paris originals and jewels. He recognized them from the sun deck, and they recognized him, nodding and saying hi. One turned to the other and said, "They want to plan their convention tonight, fine. If we had an escort we could go to the Kennel Club . . ."

It meant a few free bets and a late dinner and maybe a late-late piece of tail. But he ignored them. It was no contest. Eve meant a hundred grand.

They reached the lobby and the broads got off, looking back hopefully. He and Eve remained in the car. "You could have a nice time," Eve murmured, showing she'd gotten the drift.

"Yeah, I could. But like I told you, that's the usual. That's what I've had for years. That's my job. Like the old man is your job. But you're—" He had to stop as people began piling in.

Again they were quiet until the car emptied. As soon as the doors shut he grabbed her. "Is it tomorrow?" he asked. "It's either good-bye now, or it's the beginning of something we won't be able to say good-bye to." (He was pleased with that. It had come out just right. But he was also sweating blood. If she said it was good-bye, then he'd lose a day or two before he could try again. And that would mean only *eight* days left!) "It's up to you, Evie."

They stopped at fourteen and he let go. She walked out. He made himself stay where he was. As the doors began to close, she turned. "Friday after ten," she said, voice weak.

He shot his hand out, bouncing the doors back. It wasn't to-morrow, but neither was it next week. He made believe he was thinking it over. "All right. But why so late? Last night—"

"He'll be in deeper sleep."

He took his hand away; the doors closed. He lit a cigarette and inhaled deeply. He had another crack at the cherry; another crack at making his part of the plan work. *If* the plan could work. *If* Prager wanted the plan to work. *If* Ruthie wasn't right and he wasn't being played for a sucker.

If if if if!

He came out of the elevator fast, looking for the two stacked broads. He spotted them over at the mail desk, talking to the clerk, and was a few feet away when they turned. He said, "Did someone mention the Kennel Club? Isn't that where they have those crazy stuffed rabbits?"

4

WEDNESDAY, JANUARY 18
TO
THURSDAY, JANUARY 19, A.M.

Ellie was happy with him; he was sure of it. Yet there was ob-viously something *not* happy inside her, something he was de-termined to reach. It wasn't idle curiosity. This was the girl he wanted to marry; he was almost certain of that now. He tried a seemingly offhand question as he slowed the Jag behind a pon-derous tank truck.

"Oh," she muttered, looking out the window, "you know, everyone has his problems. Little problems and big problems, but they don't seem like problems to anyone else."

He swung around and past the truck. "Try me."

They were speeding along 41, the Tamiami Trail, through flat, swampy Everglades country, cutting the narrow neck of Florida on their way from east to west coast and Sanibel-Captiva.

"Just a dim view of the world," she said. "Through a glass darkly and all that. What are *your* problems?"

She'd sidestepped him, but he didn't press it. He had all day to grow close to her.

"Money, leisure."

"Obvious problems," she said. "The obvious problems are never the real problems."

He smiled. "Because you don't have them?"

"Maybe. But I never thought of them as problems. I always had enough money for what I wanted, even when I didn't have much. I always had enough leisure for what I wanted."

"Then you didn't want enough."

"I still don't."

"Then you have to be educated to want more."

Her smile lasted only a moment. "I was married, for a short time."

He hid his surprise. "Is it still a problem?"

"I don't know." And then, "It isn't, today."

He exulted. It was happening!

They drove. He told her about the accident and how his life had changed. The facts were the same as when he had told Lou, but he went further. He told her what he had told no one, not even himself in recent years. He spelled out exactly what he had lost when he lost his family.

". . . didn't get along too well toward the end. Dad was volatile, strained by his work, work he didn't like. Mother couldn't understand this. Her father and grandfather had held seats on the Exchange. She felt Dad should be supremely happy. They separated once . . ."

Traffic was light. The day grew brighter, warmer. The low-slung car seemed to glide along the highway, smooth and silent, with windows closed and air-conditioning on. They were isolated within its tight cabin. They were alone with each other and his past, which came crowding back into his mind.

". . . snowing, coming down heavily, a real blizzard so he couldn't get to the office the next day. I remember him running, pulling me along, the snow covering us, the world soft and padded, his laughter, my laughter . . ."

He told her about college and advertising and the decision seven months ago to leave New York for a place in the sun. He told her everything—or almost everything, not able to tell her how he was planning the good life for them both.

Later, she began to talk about her mother.

"I'm Jewish," she said.

"Funny," he cracked, "you don't look Jewish."

She smiled faintly. "My father isn't. My mother was. Her family came from Germany, and many were still there when the Nazis sealed the borders."

He knew about Hitler and the concentration camps and the ovens. Who didn't? But listening to her was almost like *being* there. She had absorbed tears and death from her mother as he had absorbed laughter and life from his father.

"She was a very pretty woman, before she began to drink. She drowned herself in vodka. By the case. She drank and read her books. Like *The Black Book*, a compilation of Nazi and Quisling atrocities against the Jews. Like *The Wall, Spark of Life, Letters from the Warsaw Ghetto, Last of the Just, Diary of Anne Frank*, every novel, every book she could find on the concentration camps, the mass murders. She had over a hundred of them, and the only time she left the house the last four years of her life was when there was a showing of concentration-camp films. She feared those films, hated them, but made herself go to them. She said she owed it to her dead relatives. She had other books too. Histories. Kublai Khan, Genghis Khan, the great conquerors who were the great butchers. The proof of what she called our green abattoir."

Her voice was ragged. He took her hand. She drew a deep breath. "I tried to read those books. I did read a few. But I couldn't read them all. They made . . . things too terrible. And besides, I was falling in love."

"There are other books. Books about falling in love. Books about kicks and games and—"

"Not histories."

"Yes, histories. Individual histories. People find each other and form armies of two against the bestiality, the idiocy, the death. That's what lovers are, Ellie. That's what families are."

She looked at him. Her hand gripped his. "Our family died," she said. "My mother couldn't hold on. She slipped deeper into her books, her horror. And one night she killed herself with vodka and tranquilizers and sleeping pills. My father was grieved, but he hadn't had a wife in four years and he was busy with a hotel—a smaller hotel, at first—and he soon recovered. And I was busy with a lover, a husband, and that helped me, for a while." Her head went down. "A short while."

He waited until she looked up. Then he said, "That's history too. Ancient history."

Sanibel was a tiny, banana-shaped island in the Gulf of Mexico, just off the mainland near Fort Myers. It was reached by a clean white bridge that charged an exorbitant three-dollar toll. Bruce muttered about that. Ellie said, "Helps keep the beaches empty. Helps preserve the birds and greenery. I'm a conservative in things like that."

Four hours later he was a conservative, too. Sanibel, and its smaller sister island, Captiva, were two green dots in the blue Gulf—two enclaves of relative purity in a state whose shoreline and islands were rapidly turning into one vast Miami Beach. Coming off that bridge was entering a simpler, more natural world, much of it set aside for wildlife. In park and sanctuary areas, trees lay where they had fallen, many half in the Gulf, providing roosting for water birds. And everywhere were shells, the most extensive selection in the continental U.S.A.

Ellie talked about it as they walked, swam, and walked some more. She said she'd been coming here since she was eighteen.

"It's the height of the season," she said as they stepped over a fallen trunk. "Look around."

There were two couples back toward the rustic little Trade Winds Motel, and one elderly woman walking up ahead, using a clamp-stick to pick up shells. They'd seen only one speedboat, but hundreds of pelicans, sandpipers, plovers, and herons. They hadn't heard a single transistor radio, but numerous gulls and the timorous splash of Gulf wavelets.

"The big-time developers obviously haven't found this place," he said. "Yet."

She picked up and then tossed away a flawed trumpet shell. "Bite your tongue when you mention developers. I own land here, but not as speculation. Some day . . ."

"Our honeymoon cottage," he said, head turned to the Gulf.

She didn't answer, and he wondered if he'd overplayed his hand. He finally glanced at her. She was looking straight ahead, smiling a little. She had a beautiful smile. Walking along in her silver-and-blue-striped bikini, she was an altogether beautiful thing. He drew her toward a sand dune and beyond it into a stand of pines. He placed both hands on her shoulders and looked into her face. "You'd better stop me now if you're going to stop me at all."

"Why? What are you going to do? Rape me?"

"Something much more serious for both of us."

He kissed her, a touching of lips that deepened only when she hugged him around the waist. "Tell me," she whispered.

"I don't have to."

She nodded. "An army of two, you said, against the bestiality, the ugliness."

"An army of privates."

"Can't you forget sex for even a minute?"

He laughed hard, and her grin was pleased.

"Well," he said, "one private and one general." He paused. "A poor private and a rich general."

"You're trying to tell me something."

"Nothing you don't know."

"Nothing I care about."

"Then we'll forget it."

"More to the point," she said, "a Gentile private and a Jewish general. You sure you want to serve under a Jewish general?"

"Now who's getting sexy?" He kissed her, and they remained busy kissing awhile.

"It's important," she murmured. "I'm very Jewish, Bruce."

"I'm already circumcised. And I'll learn Hebrew . . ."

"Not that way. Not attending temple and following ritual and observing holidays."

"How then? Eating lox and gefilte fish and pastrami? I'm good at all three. Chicken soup and knaydlach, on the other hand—"

"Don't joke. For almost two thousand years the definition of Jew has been *victim*."

"You're not a victim, are you?"

She began to walk, quickly.

He caught up with her. "Tell me what's wrong, Ellie. You were crying when I came to the suite this morning. It wasn't because of Jews and Christians and victims. It was because of something that happened to *you*. Let me help, Ellie."

She ran to the Gulf, flattening out in a shallow dive. He followed. The shock of cold water brought him blowing and snorting to the surface. They swam out, he passing her.

"The Gulf," she called, "has many fish. Among them . . . are sharks."

"Thanks . . . now I can . . . relax and enjoy . . . myself!"

She laughed and he swam toward her and she tried to flee. He caught her and held her and said, "I'm as Jewish as you are. You're as Christian as I am. We're not the orthodox kind."

"Do you believe in God?"

"God and little fishes."

"Do you?"

Her face was wet and solemn and he was falling in love with it. He said, "Yes, on occasion, and more a hope than a belief. Not that He's up there watching us. Not that He does us a bit of

210

good or bad. But—just so the Earth and the Universe and all the rest make some sort of sense."

"Yes, me too. Jonny . . ." She stopped.

"Your husband?"

"He believed in Heaven and Hell and angels and devils, and still he could be cruel, ruthless . . ."

When he realized she wasn't going to continue, he said, "Then we have the same religion. If you're Jewish, so am I."

She smiled. "I wouldn't have to worry about my name if it was Golden."

"I'm changing it to Wheeler."

The joke didn't go over. Her smile froze and she swam away. He couldn't figure it out. Why would a famous political name turn her off that way?

He hoped she didn't have hidden hatreds. He could love this girl, no matter what her secret fears, her secret agonies. But a *hater* . . .

They went back to the Trade Winds. The owner, a long-time friend of Ellie's, had given them a room in which to change, refusing to accept payment. When they'd first put on their suits, they'd taken turns in the room. Now Ellie said, "Come in with me—one of us can use the bathroom."

The room was small and clean, paneled in pine and smelling of sea and sand, the bed taking up most of the floor space, a kitchenette off in a little alcove. He got his clothes from the bed.

"Alone in a motel," she murmured.

"Now if I were the wrong type of man—"

"You'd let me alone."

He laughed and turned to the bathroom.

"No," she said. "I need it."

He waited while she gathered her things from the bed. When she bent over, he thought to himself he had never seen a lovelier behind.

She looked back at him. He grinned. "Feel the thought waves?"

"I think so." She stayed where she was a moment, but he made no move. She went into the bathroom, tossed him a towel, and closed the door. He rubbed himself down, flicking sand off his body, then drew off his bathing trunks. He was drying his legs when he heard the door open. Ellie was coming out of the bathroom, nude. "Let me do that," she said. She took the towel from him and bent and rubbed briskly, moving up his thighs. If it hadn't been for the arterial throbbing in her neck, he'd have thought her matter-of-factness authentic.

His own matter-of-factness was fast disappearing. Just looking at her, bending that way, her breasts swinging tautly, her buttocks bulging, her face so close . . .

And then there was the rubbing. He said, "I'm afraid you've gone and done it."

"I have, haven't I," she murmured, still bending over. She dropped the towel and took him in her hand. He moved his hips forward and she bent lower and he groaned and closed his eyes. She straightened in a moment. "That's all very well," she said, still holding him, "but what about me?"

He touched first one breast, then the other, circling her nipples with his index finger and causing her to bend over giggling. She pulled back, letting him go and looking at him. "You're loverly," she murmured. "You're bigger than—" She paused. "I could make a truly informative and shocking statement."

"Then make it."

She shook her head. She moved toward him, arms rising, but he said, "My turn to look."

"All right." She stepped back, placed her hands on her hips, and turned slowly for his inspection. That pulse in her neck throbbed on, but otherwise she looked cool, a model working for her fifty an hour.

She was even more beautiful without clothing than with it— which wasn't the usual, in his experience. He had once seen a photograph of Brigitte Bardot, nude, bending out a window, and Ellie DeWyant was very close to that. The rear was fantastically seductive, the breasts larger perhaps than Bardot's, but as saucily projecting. In face, there was the kittenish quality, but softer, rounder in cheeks and chin.

This time when she approached he didn't stop her. It wasn't in line with his plan—the slow growth to passion; the buildup that would have climaxed in his apartment, in his bed, and with his proposal. But she had made the move, not he, and there was no longer any way of stopping it.

They embraced. Now the matter-of-factness she'd assumed began to dissolve. He could feel the throbbing throughout her body. Her belly quivered against him, and he stroked her buttocks and began to feel violent. She put up her mouth. He bit the lips lightly and then the tongue that came into his mouth.

She was holding him again, moving her hand until he throbbed. The feeling of violence grew. He was ordinarily a subtle lover, accomplished and gentle. Having it happen this way and not being prepared for it and being somewhat worried about it made his hands rougher and his kisses stronger.

And wanting to excel with her. Wanting her to feel he was better than her ex-husband, better than any man she'd ever experienced. Wanting her to remember and hunger and keep hungering . . .

So the violence grew. He made it grow and used it to blur the importance of this sex. He forced her buttocks apart, then felt them contract violently around his exploring finger. She was shaking, sucking at his mouth, making high-pitched sounds in her throat. Her belly spasmed. She jerked her head to the side and gasped for air and he thought she would beg him to stop. Instead, she returned to his mouth, thrust her tongue in as far as she could, increased both grip and motion on his organ.

She surprised him. Not as Lou had, with male obscenities and total social equality in sex. But with her reciprocity of violence, with her total feminine involvement. She gasped, "I wish it were in *there!*" and she ground her hips into him, clutching at his buttocks, then drawing back to slide a hand between their straining bellies and grasped him.

They fell on the bed and she was all over him, clutching at him with her hands, taking him hungrily in her mouth, writhing around to clutch him between her thighs, flinging herself over on her belly and thrusting up those ripe buttocks and saying, "Just a little. Just for a minute. Please."

He turned her over and pinned both her hands to the bed. Her body thrashed. He kissed her breasts and navel. Her legs kicked. He kissed her thighs, buffeted by the thrashing, kicking movements. He put both her wrists in one hand and strained to hold them and moved the other hand down her body. He fingered her, and the thrashing lessened. He kissed and probed, and she began to squirm, arching up her chest and belly, sighing deeply. He let go of her wrists.

She lay quietly, looking at him through slitted eyes. He smiled at her. Her smile came, faintly, in reply. He bent and touched his tongue to the velvety skin of inner thigh. Her thighs parted. He was rarely moved to cunnilingus. He was moved to it now, by the same complex of motives as had moved him to violence.

His face pressed into her thighs. He was alone with her inner body, and made love to it. His mind said it was a good thing—not only because it would bring her closer to her peak, but because she would hunger for it later and know he could satisfy that hunger.

Her squirming resumed. He continued a while longer, and when her moans began to mount he withdrew.

Her arms welcomed him. Her hand took him and thrust him into her. They began the rocking, the grinding, the twisting. He should have been freed from thought, should have been swept up in that exquisite agony, that deliriously mounting need. And yet he continued to think.

He had to excel. He had to add to her future hunger.

His thrusts slowed. He varied them. He watched her, and himself, holding tight rein on the approaching crisis.

Her head began to turn from side to side. Her fingers dug into his shoulders, her nails paining him. She pulled him down and put her lips to his ear and whispered the ancient Anglo-Saxon word of lust, using it over and over, slowly, voluptuously, drawing it out and making it sound somehow beautiful.

He was finally freed from thought. He pounded her and the bed shook and he heard her cries and felt her spasms, and not until his own spasms had come and gone and he was sinking onto her did a really vital thought arrive.

"We didn't use anything. You'll have to—"

She touched his mouth with her fingers. "I said I *needed* the bathroom. You don't think I'd have come out the way I did without being safe?"

She napped on the way home, her head on his shoulder. She was restless in sleep, mumbling unintelligibly. At one point she said, "I'll *tell!*" and opened her eyes.

He said, "Yes, tell me."

"Soon, maybe," she murmured, and went back to sleep.

It seemed she had only just lain down and now the phone was ringing. She opened her eyes, expecting morning or perhaps afternoon to be filtering through the drawn blinds, and it was absolutely dark. Her father was taking his time answering. She finally reached for the phone, and as she raised it noticed the luminous dial of her alarm clock. One-thirty. She had been asleep only a few minutes.

"Ellie, listen carefully now."

It was the false, tinny voice of her tormentor.

"Your father is leaving the Platinum Room. He's talking to some people, but he'll probably be up in a few minutes. If he's the one who controls the purse strings, you should ask him for the money tonight. Tell him you've gambled heavily. Say your life has been threatened. But be sure to say the losses are legitimate and you *must* pay."

She was drugged with sleep and with the good day and she didn't want to hear him or to understand what he was saying.

"One hundred fifty thousand dollars, Ellie. Cash, small bills. No bill larger than a fifty. In one week. To hire people to help punish the Wheeler clan."

She made herself laugh.

"Or the newspapers, the radio, the television will be talking about your marriage to President Standers and your money will stop and you might be dead." He paused. "And if the Wheelers don't hurt you, Ellie, I might. I just might."

"All right," she said, remembering her plan to call his bluff and scare him off. "Where do I meet you?"

This time *he* laughed. "You never meet me, Ellie. You get the money and I tell you how to give it to me and you're sure of striking back at the Wheelers and your secret is safe."

"You think I'm going to mail out a hundred and fifty thousand dollars in cash?"

"If I say to mail it, you'll do exactly that. But I haven't said to mail it. I haven't said anything because there's no sense making such plans until you have the hundred fifty thousand in your possession."

She sat up, trying to think, trying to outsmart him, beginning to grow frightened again.

"It's Thursday morning now, Ellie. You have until next Thursday to get the money together."

"And if I say it's impossible and to do your worst?"

"Then I'll do just that, my worst. Remember Marjory Fine's party, Ellie? That was just a sample. A tiny sample."

She was really frightened now. She gripped the phone tightly and said, "Let's talk sensibly."

"Good-bye, Ellie. I won't call again until I'm ready to give you delivery instructions."

"You can't expect—" But she was speaking to a dead line.

When her father came in, she was in the living room, sipping a gin and tonic, and had just put three bankbooks into her bathrobe pocket. She had a total of seventy-seven thousand dollars in savings accounts, another four or five thousand in New York and Miami checking accounts. She was roughly seventy thousand dollars short, and while this was no real problem in terms of the Wheeler yearly payments, she knew her father was paying off his part of the Metropole's monstrous cost and felt sure he would question her needing that much.

But she had to ask. She wouldn't be able to sleep until she settled the question of whether she could meet her tormentor's demands.

"Daddy, I need seventy thousand dollars. I can't discuss why, but I assure you it's no whim, no foolishness."

He was at the bar, mixing a Bromo. "Of course," he said, and gulped the fizzy liquid. "I should never drink wine. Acidy stuff. Yet I can't resist a glass or two, especially a good Chambertin. You know how I like a Sixty-four Chambertin, Ellie." He belched. "Sorry. When would you want it?"

She stood up. "By next Wednesday."

He drank the rest of his Bromo. "All right. As long as it makes you happy, darling." She went to him and kissed him and told him how good he was to her. "Good to you? It's your money, darling. It's all yours, the hotel and everything we own. You've never asked for anything before. I've had to force a decent income on you. If you wanted a *million*, I'd raise it for you."

She was almost at her door. "Could you really raise that much?"

"It surprises you? We've got considerably more than that in the Metropole, and a cash sinking fund of almost half a million."

She shook her head in wonderment.

He smiled. "We've been receiving the payments for thirteen years, and our hotels have always made money. We might be paupers compared to the Wheelers, but we *are* legitimate millionaires."

So there was no problem about paying her tormentor. The problem was, of course, whether it would *solve* anything to pay him. What was to stop him from coming back with a new request next year? Or next week?

She wished she could talk to someone.

No, not to *someone*. To Bruce. To her Golden Boy.

He hoped Ruthie wasn't getting suspicious. He knew he wasn't covering himself too well, but he had so much going, so much to do, and he had to do it all himself.

He was sure the DeWyant girl would come through. She was a kook of sorts, but what choice did she have? She could figure it out easily enough. She was getting anywhere from a hundred to two hundred fifty grand a year from the Wheelers. She had to pay out a hundred fifty—one payment to keep up a lifetime of payments. It didn't figure she would risk losing what could amount to millions.

All right, say she brought some guy into it. Broads always thought some guy could perform miracles. Say she was even dumb enough to bring a private eye into it—though she couldn't tell him anything without putting another noose around her neck. No matter *who* she brought into it, she would have to pay. Because Max would never give her a chance to see him, to know who he was.

It was so sweet, so perfect, so *safe*. A million miles from that snatch. Let Leech and the others put their heads on the block. Not him. Why should he? Not only did he have the DeWyant girl, he was getting closer to Jorge's boss.

The silly Spic thought he'd put him out of business. As if Max would allow himself to be trapped that way if he'd *really* thought the tail could work. He'd realized it was a dead issue when Jorge failed to show until everyone else had left the drive-in. That's when he'd switched plans.

So now Jorge was relaxed and happy. And Max was driving a different rental car every day, tailing John McKensil each time he left the hotel. They were going to nail the manager with that little Cuban broad, weren't they? Someone besides the girl had to be in on the action, right? It figured to be Jorge or someone hired by Jorge's boss—so Max had located the Surfside house where McKensil had taken Violetta twice this week. He hadn't stuck around because McKensil hadn't either. But when McKensil went *in*, that's when Max would stick, because that's when the odds dictated he'd get his best chance at following someone important some*where* important.

He let himself into the room. Ruthie was in bed and the bathroom light was on. He walked softly, murmuring her name. She sighed, moved, moaned. He went into the bathroom, closed the door, and took off his jacket. He checked his gun, then continued undressing. Let her sleep. Let her dream of Jerry. The poor slobs would need their dreams when this thing blew up in their faces. The poor dumb slobs!

How could they believe a snatch like Jorge's could work? Just thinking of it made his guts go cold. You didn't play around with the Feds when you could help it, and you *never* played around with money and power like the Wheelers'. He'd considered working a tip-off with the old man, trying for some kind of pay day, but had dropped the idea fast. That family could command too much brain and muscle. The old man would be out for blood.

He reentered the bedroom in his shorts, went to the dresser, and took out his pajamas.

"Max?"

"Yeah. Sorry I woke you."

She got up on an elbow. "Where've you been?"

"Working. Keeping my eye on important people." Which was no lie. He came to the bed and sat down on the edge. He remembered how they used to get along, and felt sudden affection for her. He wished he could tell her to pull out before the Senator's speech. But he couldn't; it would tip his hand.

He touched her arm. She shifted position, drawing away. He said, "Y'know, this job is beginning to give me nightmares."

She sat all the way up. "How do you mean?"

He should have done this before. He'd been busy, but he should have made sure she was as relaxed as Jorge about him. "Look, I don't have to con you, Ruthie. This snatch is a mother. At first it looked like everything would open up easy. But no matter how I work it, I see it coming down to a *rough* Saturday night."

"So?"

"So I'm asking Jorge for more help. We've got to have at least two gunsels and him and Leech. That's the minimum. And that's if the manager gets us keys to everything and an elevator just for ourselves and covers our getaway."

"But—you'll go through with it?"

He stared as if puzzled. "I got a choice? They'll give me that hundred fifty for being a mastermind? You figure I'm letting the one big payoff of my life fly out the window?" He paused. "Or is it that *you* want out, Ruthie? I can tell you right now I want you in the Krasmer dame's suite. I can tell you right now I won't—"

"It's not that, Max. It's just . . . I was beginning to worry that you didn't see how crazy some of Jorge's ideas were. Like talking to a famous singer like Wally Jones. Like expecting outsiders, strangers, people we know nothing about to help because they hate Wheeler and his family. Like that, Max."

He laughed. "Ruthie, I never argue with the guy who pays the bills. But I never put my ass in the fire either. I do it the way I see it—the way it can be done."

"And it *can* be done, Max? You sure?"

"Pretty sure, Ruthie. Not that I won't sweat my share. But we can make it." He patted her shoulder and went to the bathroom. "Trust me. We can make it." He whistled as he began running the shower.

5

THURSDAY, JANUARY 19

He brought a carbon of the speech along with him to Sochall's office, telling himself he would work in case he had to wait. What he actually wanted was to hold onto something—his craft, his sense of values, the continuity of his life.

Sochall closed the door, sat down, and began to talk. He was a busy man, but he didn't hurry. He spoke for twenty minutes, apparently choosing each word with care. Before he finished, Dan had forgotten the speech in his lap.

"I expect you to ask questions, Mr. Berner."

"You're not sure, are you, that the cancer is confined to my prostate?" (He still didn't believe any of it. Or believed, and felt he was talking about something totally apart from his own body.)

"We won't be certain until we get inside and remove it."

Get inside and remove it. "And what happens to me then? I mean, if your hopes are realized and it *is* confined to the prostate?"

"You're speaking of sex, I presume?"

"Yes."

"There'll be time enough—"

"I want to talk of it now. To help me decide."

"There's nothing to decide. We have to get in there before it metastasizes to adjacent tissues and bones."

"I'd like an answer."

Sochall shrugged. "If you're thinking of those stories of gland transplants, not only aren't they legal in this country, I never heard of a truly successful one, and that includes Switzerland."

Which ended *that* frail hope. "And if it *isn't* confined to the prostate?"

"We'll cross that bridge when we come to it."

"You asked for questions. I'm asking for answers."

"I thought you'd want to know how soon I could operate. Tomorrow or Saturday. I thought you'd ask how long you'll be hospitalized. No more than ten or twelve days. I thought you'd want to know your chances of recovery. Excellent, if all is as I hope it is."

"You thought I'd be hungry for fairy tales, bedtime stories."

The doctor began to protest. Dan cut him short. "I want to know the *worst*, not the best. Now, if it *isn't* confined to the prostate?"

"Probably an orchiectomy."

"You used that word before, Doctor. And you know I don't understand it."

Sochall lit a cigarette and blew smoke. "Removal of the testicles."

Dan nodded slowly.

"Subsequent treatment includes use of female hormones."

"What happens to the libido?"

"It undergoes changes."

"It rolls over and dies, you mean."

"It's not as terrible as it sounds. You'll adjust."

"Yes, ask any eunuch."

Sochall made a helpless gesture. "You won't suffer. Once the sex drive ceases to function, that particular hunger is as if it never was."

"What other course is open besides surgery?"

"Oh, cobalt treatments are occasionally—"

"Let's try it."

"But in this case I insist on immediate surgery."

"You insist?"

"I won't be responsible for any delay. I won't involve myself in cobalt treatments or other palliations. My belief—my conviction—is that we must operate."

Dan stood up. "I'll let you know, Doctor."

Sochall also stood up. His voice quiet, he said, "I'll admit something. The chances are you'll end up with the orchiectomy. But there's so much more to life than sex. Save that life and explore what's left, Mr. Berner."

"Part of what's left will be the development of breasts, a disconcerting change of voice, a general feminizing effect." He walked to the door. "I know a bit about female hormones, Doctor, and you're not being quite honest with me."

"Face one thing at a time, Mr. Berner. First the prostate. Then, if we must, the orchiectomy. And then, probably years from now, some of the changes you fear."

"Fear is much too mild a word," Dan murmured, gripping the envelope, remembering the speech now. He would get back to work. He would forget Sochall and seek other opinions. He would gain some months, and then decide.

Was death as bad as taking out glands and removing testicles and losing the self he was?

Sochall answered that unspoken question. "You haven't considered the alternative."

"Yes, I know, death."

"But what *sort* of death? Do I have to describe the effects of cancer?"

Dan said no. Sochall said, "All right then. Go back to your hotel. Think it through. Call me tomorrow." He scribbled on a card and walked over and pressed it into Dan's hand. "My home number. Call me any time you have a question."

Dan nodded and went out.

He had driven here in sunshine, not noticing the overcast blowing in from the sea. Now it was gray, with a feeling of wetness closing in. He drove his rental Ford onto Biscayne Boulevard and back toward the causeway and the hotel. It began to drizzle.

No operations. No castrations. No feminizations.

The drizzle changed to rain, the rain to a tropical downpour. He turned onto Collins, slowing to a crawl. Up ahead red neon spelled out: *Tavern Choppe House.* On impulse he pulled into the parking area and took the check the young Cuban in the bright yellow slicker gave him. He sprinted the few feet to the doors, and felt the rising throb of pain.

He was shown to a red leather booth and handed a huge menu. He said, "Martini, dry, on the rocks, please." He had another before ordering, and two ales with his mutton chop. And finished with a large brandy. The alcohol coursed through his blood, warming his brain, making it possible for him to preach a litany of hope to himself. He would seek other medical opinions. Back in New York, another doctor (New York doctors were superior to Miami doctors—everyone knew that) would contest Sochall's diagnosis. Sochall's *opinion.* After all, what was a diagnosis but an opinion? And opinions were notoriously varied, linked to prejudice and personal whim. And even if the opinion was, basically, similar to Sochall's, a New York doctor might feel that cobalt offered real chance of success. Or he might suggest that there was still much time—years, perhaps—before serious decisions need be made.

And hadn't there been something in *Time* about new cancer treatments?

Treatments . . . not operations, castrations, feminizations.

On the strength of that he ordered a second brandy, and sat long with it, watching the sun emerge and turn the rain-spattered window to a tray of sparkling diamonds.

There was nothing Wally could hang a blue on. The manager himself—not an assistant—came around from behind the desk and shook his hand and checked him in. And called him Mr. Jones every single time. The bellhops—two of them to handle his stack of luggage—were impressed but silent, their faces right, their voices right when he tipped solid but not big, even their eyes right. The room was more than right, being a twelfth-floor two-bedroom suite with a baby grand. Traveling alone this time, he hadn't expected so lush a pad. And it was good to know, via his agent's cousin who worked small-time bookings in Fort Lauderdale, that Barker was staying at his Buena Vista home. The less he saw of that mother, the better.

With that he'd made his first mistake, let in his first blue, and he went to the phone and called the desk to find out whether there were any messages. There were an even dozen, but only two were important. Stan, his arranger and pianist, was settled in a small hotel down the beach with Dee and Ace, bass and drums; men he used whenever he wanted a combo behind him. And a Miss Bea Chan was "waiting to hear from him at his earliest convenience."

He called Stan, who mumbled, "Hey man, it's midnight," and cleared his throat.

"Ten o'clock, baby. We got rehearsals today and an opening tomorrow. See you at eleven-thirty."

He called Bea, and the sweet voice said, "Wally!" and he said, "Chink baby, I hoped you'd call."

"I hoped *you'd* call, for the past three months."

"Yeah, well, I been working Vegas, reading Broadway musicals, doing a special and two guest shots, finishing a featured in a Levine flick, and getting divorced."

"I read about the divorce. What happened?"

"I don't like niggers."

She laughed. "There's one *I* like. When do we make it?"

"Today is madness from now till who-knows. Can you call say early A.M.?"

"One?"

"One, and with luck we can have a champagne dinner."

"I'll keep my fingers crossed."

"I got a little something for one of those lucky fingers."

She was quiet, and he quickly added, "Not the cheap kind used in motels, but the kind with stones."

"A girl's best friend," she said, but without zing.

"Next to you-know-what." He hung up. He was glad Chink was here (playing some slit-eye girlie review) and he was glad she felt the way she did. Though who knew how she *really* felt? She wanted the whole showboat, but was it for love of a coon with educated tonsils, or for his considerable bread?

He showered and wondered whether to put on trunks. And dressed in green stovepipe slacks and matching velour shirt. Time enough to try the pool and ocean, and feel like the only black man on earth.

He turned on the idiot box. He found a news program. Winter was a good time to watch the news. Summer he tried to skip it, including the front pages of the papers. The cities burned and he felt everything he'd created was burning with them. He *hated* those crazy mothers, those black nuts! Couldn't they see they were burning *themselves*? How long before the honkies took over and played the Hitler bit?

Which made him go to the phone and try the Senator's suite. He was out. Wally left a message. Dick Christopher had good guts and a good head and a good track record with the soul folk, and his friendship with Benny Barker was something a politician *had* to do and completely apart from his feelings for blacks. That was Wally Jones's instinct more than his reasoned summary of Christopher's acts and speeches. And he had always won by instinct.

Besides, Christopher was the leading contender for the Democratic nomination, and where could a Negro go to except the Democrats?

He called room service, and while having eggs and coffee called the manager to get the Platinum Room for rehearsal.

On the way down in the elevator and walking through the crowded lobby he picked up a touch more blue. People looked. Lots recognized the small, deep-black man who moved like a nervous cat. And some didn't recognize him. But all looked.

Miami Beach was in Miami and Miami was in Florida and Florida was in the South. And the South hurt him. The North and East and West hurt him too, but when the cities weren't burning a Big Name could make almost any scene and feel half human. The South was changing, they said. He supposed it was. But it still hurt him and he never played the South, except sometimes Miami Beach. And then he always stayed right in his hotel —the Fontainebleau twice and Hilton Plaza once—with the musicians and hotel cats and took a few swims with friends, but still sort of held his breath until he was back on the jet heading home, which was little old New York.

He was halfway across the lobby when he saw Benny Barker stride out of a dining room, his manager and a red-headed chick with him. It was the first time in three years that he'd seen Barker: they'd last met at Carla's funeral, where friends had to stop them from trying to kill each other. The time before that had been nice, too—Barker and Myron Ballechek, Carla's producer and a top-grade maniac who thought he was back in the days of Goldwyn, breaking into Carla's Malibu cottage and rousting them out of bed. There hadn't been a chance to go for Barker that time. Two studio cops in plain clothes had been waving guns and Ballechek had taken Wally aside and given him the Dutch uncle bit: "I got nothing against colored myself, Wally, but Carla Waring isn't just another broad. I've put millions into her. Can you imagine what the public would say if they knew she was . . . Well, you understand, don't you?" Wally had understood all right. He had tried to explain that they were deeply in love and wanted to be married. Ballechek had said, "There must be some mistake. She's engaged to Benny. You saw the publicity releases . . ." And on and on, with Carla weeping across the room while Barker lectured her, with Carla not even looking at him when a few minutes before they had breathed their undying passion into each other's mouths.

But he hadn't given up. He had dressed and prepared to leave, thinking that no one could play watchdog twenty-four hours a day. He would see Carla again. They would find their way. And then Ballechek had walked with him into the damp evening and directed him over to a car near the driveway. "You see those two men? They're friends of mine from Vegas. Businessmen. I just gave them a contract. *Depending*, Wally, on what you do. *Farshteit?* Take a good look, Wally." He had. The two men had stared straight ahead. The two men with faces like dead meat. Ballechek had slapped him on the back and said things about a part in a new musical and walked back into the cottage. The two men had turned then and looked at him. One had said, his voice a hoarse whisper, "I'd do it for nothing when it comes to shines like this."

And Wally Jones had never seen his love again, until five years later, when she'd reached the end of her third marriage and the end of her rope and taken that good old way out, booze and pills and a hot bath. And Benny Barker said he, Wally, was the cause of it, having "degraded a basically simple girl," and Wally knew he, Barker, had destroyed what could have been one of the best marriages of all time, out of hatred for a black man daring to love a white girl, and out of simple jealousy since Benny had wanted that particular white girl himself. But he hadn't got her, ever.

Barker was yokking it up for his chick and his manager and hadn't yet seen Wally. But he soon would. They were on a collision course, and Wally began building his cool and planning his shot. The manager did a double take and tugged Barker's arm. Barker looked up and there they were, not five feet apart and coming on fast.

He was better prepared than Barker. He said, "You engaged to this one, too, Benny?" nodding and smiling at the chick and the manager. He heard the manager say, "Ben!' and kept walking, watching one face, a woman's, off to his right. By her expression he could tell Barker was coming up behind him. By the way her mouth opened and her eyes widened he knew the hand that came down on his left shoulder was Barker's.

He turned, his right hand clenching and rising, his lithe, muscular body an engine driving that right hand. He turned, and delivered the punch he'd been saving for eight years.

And then couldn't stop it when he saw it wasn't Barker but the chick. She was just beginning to say something when his punch caught her high on the head and sent her sprawling. She landed on her back, her skirt flying up to her waist, her mouth still moving, the words still coming out, but in a squeaky way like a machine knocked out of line. ". . . some nerve to say . . ." He shook his head and bent to her, and the blinding illumination of a flashbulb hit his eyes. He looked up. The first face he saw was Barker's, and Benny was very pleased. Oh yes, his eyes and mouth were pleased, even though he made himself look shocked. It was the manager who'd taken the picture, with one of those cheap plastic Polaroids hanging around his neck.

Again Wally bent to the girl. She was rubbing her head, and scrunched back and said, "Don't touch me you—you dirty . . ." She never quite said it. He said, "I'm sorry, miss. I thought you were Benny." She scrunched even further back and Barker was there, helping her up, and other people were there, mostly men, closing in around him, saying, "What sort of man . . ." and, "Did you see him *punch* that girl?" and he was still trying to say it was a mistake and going numb inside, not believing this was happening to Wally Jones who could make it anywhere with almost anyone—Wally Jones who had earned half a million dollars last year and a quarter of a million and better for eighteen of his forty-three years. And not for soul music, black music, but swinging stuff that the *white* world dug. Wally Jones who was as well-liked as any entertainer, white or black, in these United States. And now an elbow dug his ribs and a heavy face glared into his and at least five men looked ready to take him apart.

He was suddenly very frightened. These five men *hated* him! This was what a lynch mob was like!

The chick was leaning against Barker, crying. Barker looked at Wally and said, "Let's break it up. Her lawyer will handle it."

Their eyes met, and Wally saw the pleasure and satisfaction in Barker's and realized that it was Benny who had delivered the shot, Benny who had gotten in the long-deferred punch.

The hotel manager was there. He took Wally's arm and walked with him to the Platinum Room, where a uniformed guard opened the door. They went past the guard, who looked at Wally the same way those five men had, and into the big club. Wally sank down on a bench-couch near the bar. He got out cigarettes and lit up and inhaled deeply. "Could you tell me about it?" McKensil asked.

He told him about it. He thought Mr. Barker had been coming up behind him to attack him. Striking the girl had been a mistake, and he wanted to make it right. "A gift," he muttered, head down, drained of strength. "Whatever you suggest."

McKensil said he'd speak to the young lady. Then Stan and the boys arrived, looking back into the lobby and saying, "What gives?" and, "This place smells like Cracker!" and he wasn't the only black man in the world any more. He said, "Got myself a lawsuit," and led them to the stage.

While Ace set up his traps, delivered earlier that morning, Stan shot more questions. Wally answered, finishing with, "Guess I'm tagged for some loot, baby." And thought, *If only that was all.* But there was Barker's happy look. Barker had put him down. He would carry the memory of Barker's happy eyes like he carried the memory of Barker's hate-filled face that night in Malibu. Like he carried the worn picture of the delicate blonde girl with the careful, spidery writing across the bottom: "Love only you,

Carla." Like he carried his pain at being black when the truth was he wanted only to be part of things and that meant being white.

He bent over the piano and turned the music and tapped a sheet with his finger. He sang "Just One of Those Things," and Stan said, "Man, you're wailing, and you *never* wail that." He sang it again, belting instead of wailing, like morning exercises, waking up, shoving away the blues. He said, "One more time!" and they took off, balling like it was opening night.

He sang "Blue Bugaloo," doing a little soft-shoe, and Ace laughed and backed him with brushes and it went so nice, so easy, he decided he'd do it in the show. They tried it again and it lost something, and they changed it here and there and it came back to nice and easy.

He sang "Baby, It's Cold Outside," doing the second go-round with Stan's baby-it's-*hot*-outside lyrics and they were cute enough but somehow he didn't want them. He'd used them in Vegas and thought he'd use them here, but he shook his head and said, "Let's drop it. Let's not play Sambo for the plantation owners."

Dee, who was the original quiet man and rarely looked up from his bass, looked up now and said, "Like razor blades, baby, like razor blades."

"What you say, white man?"

They all laughed (Dee putting down his golden-brown head, like Belafonte gone bald) and went into "Impossible Dream." Wally sang it hard and straight, and they all knew it wasn't right. They dropped it without further discussion. They went to the fast and the furious. Just about everything musical was Wally Jones's bag, but not always at the same time. This time he felt the stuff that *bounced*.

He sang, "I Won't Dance," "From This Moment On," "Oh Look at Me Now," "Honeysuckle Rose." Stan said it felt good to him and let's try "Black Magic," "Tea for Two," and "Sunny Side of the Street." Wally slumped into a chair, muttering, "We know that stuff and each other backwards. Except for the three new numbers it's all re-re-*re*hearsed."

230

Which was the truth, sure, but it made no difference, because rehearsing was like eating. You knew how to do it inside out, but that didn't mean you could *stop* doing it. Not and stay alive. And to stay alive as a star performer you had to be on top of your material every split second you were in front of an audience, or a camera, or a recording mike. So you rehearsed.

He knew it and Stan and the boys knew it, but no one answered him and they took five and smoked and talked about the dog tracks and chicks and Ace talked about his newborn son. Then Wally stood up and walked to the lip of the stage, and snapped his fingers. Looking out at the empty club, he began "Why Was I Born?" Ace said, "Whoops," quietly, and they all fell in behind him. Next he sang "Gin for Christmas," and again there was no sheet music because he hadn't done those numbers in years. And then he got down to the nitty-gritty with a little pure shouting on "Every Bit of It" and "What's the Matter Now?"

Dee broke silence once again. "Baby, ole Bessie would've loved you. But can you see what'd happen if you gave the pickled-herring crowd a program like that?"

Wally nodded, and sang one more number, again for himself: "Black and Blue." Stan got up from the piano. "Let's break for lunch, huh?"

The reporters were waiting right outside, about eight of them. Wally said, "No comment," a dozen times and they went to the crazy snack-shack called the Bon Bouche. The reporters followed and drew up chairs around their table, and it wasn't bad because he was used to reporters and they made sort of an island of insiders so that Wally was able to kid the snooty blonde waitress without tension. But the questions kept coming, and one was, "Is it true this is a continuation of the bitterness shown by you and Barker at Carla Waring's funeral?" and he found it hard to smile while not answering. He ate a hamburger and bowl of chili, and another reporter said, "Astrid Kane says she'll sue for half a million. Will you try to settle out of court?" Wally said, "Half a million *what*?" But that's when he excused himself and went to a phone booth and called New York and his manager. Nat Weisman said, "You actually *hit* her?" and then, learning it was a friend of Benny Barker's, "I'll get the lawyer!" Wally muttered that here he was all alone in Miami when Barker traveled with his manager and a chick, and probably a few producers and directors waiting in the wings.

"So who is it says he can't stand a goddam *entourage* of ass-lickers and hangers-on like a certain fat shmuck has? Who is it says I should concentrate on goosing the agents into bookings and recording contracts and getting a few featured spots in movies? Who is it says I should earn my twenty percent by upping the take, not holding hands? Who is it—"

Wally said, "Yeah, yeah, and who is it sounds like a Yiddish momma?" and hung up.

Afterward, they worked on a few more numbers and set up their program, and it didn't include any of the blue-black stuff.

"Eunice?" May called for the third time, and walked into the bedroom. The woman wasn't there. She shrugged and went to the closet to get her long bathrobe. She was sweaty, drained, exhausted after two games of tennis with Al, yet exhilarated, too.

She showered and changed into her bikini. She ran a brush through her hair and grabbed her robe and hurried to the door. And noticed that the hall closet was open. She looked inside. Empty.

How could that be? Eunice kept her clothes and two suitcases there.

She checked the other closets and called the desk. They knew nothing about Mrs. Dean leaving. She went through the suite, looking for a note. There was none.

It made no sense. Why would Eunice leave a good job, and leave it in a way that threatened her references?

May gave up. And at the same time began to feel a vague sense of fear. She told herself she was being foolish, that she would hear from Eunice later today and everything would be explained.

She went down. The ocean was there and so was the sun and

232

so was Al. They walked away from the hotel and talked and held hands and swam and teased and played. She forgot Eunice. She remembered something she had seen as a child—two butterflies, orange and black, dancing over a meadow, playing in the sunlight, rising and falling and circling and, finally, disappearing into the summer haze. Now she felt they were back, and that she was one of them. She and Al danced together in the sunlight. She and Al shared lightness, purity, and joy.

It always changed, of course. As the day grew older, they began wondering if they would be able to see each other in the evening. Tonight they couldn't. His mother wanted to visit friends just arrived at the Americana. They had a daughter who had taken a week off from high school and Al didn't know how to refuse.

"You'll enjoy yourself." She walked ahead of him, starting up the steps to the deck of the Metropole. "The girl must be pretty."

He came up quickly behind her, and even though there were people everywhere he clutched her arms and his body pressed her backside and he said, his voice a high-pitched, raging whisper, "I wish I'd never met you! And I wish I'd never told you to buy that bikini! You don't know what I *do* to myself after—" He stopped then and drew away. They'd reached the top of the stairs, and he hurried toward the last row of lounges, to the one on which she'd left her robe, and sat down. She walked toward him, and he looked at her, his hunger so strong she felt the pain of it and wanted to ease it. And stopped in front of him, standing in such a way that a man would have known she was open to his hunger and hungry herself to the point of pain.

But he wasn't a man. Not quite.

"I didn't mean to talk . . . filthy, May. Please don't be angry."

"Don't be silly, Al. Tennis tomorrow morning?"

He said yes, and she was happy.

She smelled the heavy-sweet tobacco as soon as she opened the door. She knew what it meant even before entering the living room, and understood why Eunice had left. Harold rose from the armchair, tall and lean and remote, giving his condescending little bow. She was surprised at how handsome he looked; how much like an older Al Fortens he looked. Except for the remoteness.

He took the pipe from his mouth. "Your young swain's wearing you down, May. You look tired."

Just like that, the flight of the butterflies was over, the joyous dance of youth finished. She felt her face grow hot, her insides grow cold.

"Well, we'll talk about it later," he said, coming across the room to kiss her cheek.

She still couldn't speak, and he murmured, "I'm sorry if I shocked you. We needn't talk about it at all, if you prefer. Just as long as you understand . . ." He made a little gesture with his pipe.

She nodded, eyes falling. He said, "Why don't you help me unpack? Then you'll show me around the hotel. It's a little—well, shall we say *extreme,* but I'm sure we'll enjoy the next two weeks."

She managed a smile.

In the bedroom, he talked about the miserable winter weather he'd left behind in Chicago, described his flight, was warm and kind—and careful not to approach the subject of her "young swain" again. She knew he considered the matter closed. He was a civilized man, a considerate man, a gentle man. She began replying, telling him about Miami Beach, slipping into the same condescending style he used. He suggested she make a reservation "at that highly touted Vale Room" while he changed into a lightweight suit. When she turned to the night-table phone, he cleared his throat and nodded at the door.

A very reserved man.

She phoned from the living room. Her voice was the voice of May Krasmer, owner-manager of Jem-Boxes, Inc. It sounded strange to her ears—cool, aloof, almost without emotion. She hadn't heard that voice in two weeks.

But, of course, two weeks was bound to lose out to seven years.

They left the Bal Metropole and walked south along the beach, both wearing suits, shirts, ties—Max Prager chewing a dead cigar and staring straight ahead, Bert Cooper smoking his third cigarette of the past fifteen minutes and watching Prager from the corner of his eye. It was getting difficult to see the stout man's face, now that a cloudy night was closing in, but his expression didn't seem to have changed from the vaguely amused, vaguely puzzled one he'd worn when Bert first approached him on the deserted sun deck.

He was glad they were out here instead of in a room. You never knew how a man was going to react, and while he expected no physical nonsense from someone like Prager, the beach and the sea comforted him, were his natural elements, gave him room to handle whatever might come up. In addition, he had a six-inch switchblade in his trousers pocket. He felt a little foolish about that, however, and had stopped touching it ten minutes ago.

"What it amounts to," Prager said, "is your asking me for part of something that doesn't exist."

"If it doesn't exist, Mr. Prager, then you're taking chances for nothing. And I don't see you doing that. No. I'm sorry, I just don't see that, sir."

"Sir," Prager muttered, and chuckled. The wind whipped up and carried his laughter away. "Look, Cooper, I wasn't the one pushing that girl around. And even if I was, it would be for the usual reasons. Like wanting to feel her tits in the dark."

Bert snapped his cigarette into the sea, directly in front of Prager's face.

"I'm sorry you're disappointed, Cooper, but that's no reason to—"

"Then it won't bother you if I visit Miss DeWyant tonight and tell her what I saw?"

"Not at all."

"And what someone heard your wife and Jerry Leech discussing in Mrs. Fine's bedroom?"

Prager came to a sudden halt. "Now you're going too far, mister! You're saying my wife and that pool boy—"

"I'm saying they were talking, and that their talk worries you a lot more than anything else they might have been doing."

They stared at each other, and Prager shook his head. "You're a mixed-up guy, Cooper. A badly mixed-up guy."

Bert turned and began walking toward the hotel. He wasn't at all surprised to hear, "Mr. Cooper!" He went back through the sand, smiling to himself. "Are we finished with the preliminaries, Mr. Prager?"

"It's no use telling you I was just feeling the girl up a little, is it? That I'm embarrassed and would be willing to pay . . ." He shrugged. "Whatever it is that men pay not to be further embarrassed in matters like this. Say a hundred bucks? Make that two-fifty."

Cooper showed his smile.

"No, I didn't think so." Prager began to walk again. He looked toward the sea, which was rough tonight. Waves crashed with a deep, continuous thunder. Up ahead, their sound increased. Up ahead, the huge Venetian Hotel abutment stood out in deep water and took each wave at its crest.

"Actually, Cooper, you know nothing. Nothing at all."

"But you won't let me tell the nothing I know to Miss De-Wyant, will you?"

"No. Can't do that. But you still don't know why."

"If you tell me, I'll do my share."

"I'll have to ask permission of my partners. I can't go ahead on my own."

"That's reasonable. As long as you ask tonight, and get the answer to me by morning."

Prager threw his cigar away and put both hands in his jacket pockets. "Chilly," he muttered.

"Be sure to point out I'm a reliable, determined man, once I'm involved in a project. A Royal Navy man," he added.

Prager said, "Yes," voice quiet.

They were approaching the massive black shadow of the abutment. Behind it rose a curved tier of lighted glass—the hotel. Music sounded faintly, then faded under the hammer-blows of water on concrete. Bert smelled a return of this morning's rain.

Instinctively, he searched the black horizon for ships. There were none. No ships on the sea, no people on the beach.

Prager walked on in silence.

"Were you in service?" Bert asked, wanting to establish some degree of normal communication with this man. He had never done anything like this before. His life, hard as it had been in the past, had always run strictly according to the rules of law.

"What?" Prager asked.

The thundering crash enveloped them as they came to within ten feet of the abutment. Bert stopped and raised his voice. "Were you in service during the war?"

Prager shook his head. "No. Defense plant. Not the type, anyway. Couldn't kill people."

"Man can be trained to anything," Bert said, but he believed Prager. Definitely the wrong type.

Prager went on to the wall and turned to the sea. "Mr. Prager," Bert called. "You can't get by . . ." But Prager was stepping cautiously toward the water. Bert walked over to him, took his arm. "You can't get by," he shouted. "Several feet of water . . ."

Prager nodded, pointing. Bert didn't understand. Prager made a going-around-the-corner gesture, and moved right up to the edge of the sea, where the waves lapped out. Bert was still holding his arm, still trying to understand, when Prager suddenly turned to face him and said something and the pain tore into Bert's chest. He crumpled to his knees, clutching at the wall with his right hand, and looked up for an explanation.

". . . no choice," Prager was saying, bending to him. Bert still didn't understand. Didn't understand how the pain had come and why he was on his knees and why he couldn't get up. Didn't understand why Prager looked so sick. Didn't understand when the sea crashed in his ears as it had never crashed before, as nothing on earth had ever crashed before. . . .

6

FRIDAY, JANUARY 20

Eve wanted to contact Jerry Leech, but didn't know how she was going to manage it. She couldn't see him tonight, as she'd promised.

Mr. Wheeler had slept until six-forty, and immediately asked her to place a call to a Palm Beach number. When she'd said it was a little early to be waking people, he'd said, "Not people. Servants. Want to show you . . . my winter home. Probably move down there . . . after Dick's speech." He'd smiled at her, and it was no longer lopsided. "Feel better than . . . at any time since the stroke!"

And he *looked* it, too. Yesterday had been a particularly good day for him. He'd walked a great deal on the beach, using her to steady himself rather than leaning on her. And they had actually managed to get up the stairs to the deck without calling on Jerry (though Eve had been just about at the end of her strength when they reached the wheelchair). In the suite he'd insisted on having his first steak, and had eaten most of it with gusto and with only a little help in trimming the bone. In the evening he had asked her to call his son-in-law, and they'd entered the Senator's suite through the connecting door and spent an hour there. This time he'd been less sharp, not quite so impatient with everything the Senator said.

Now he had arranged for the car and chauffeur to take them to Palm Beach and then back tomorrow. Now she was preparing breakfast and trying to think of a way to reach Jerry. (Perhaps as they went by the desk, she could stop and leave a message without Mr. Wheeler hearing?)

He ate enormously—eggs and bacon and oatmeal and two large glasses of orange juice, finishing with coffee and marmalade-covered toast. And insisted she sit and talk to him. (She ate quite a bit herself, out of nervous frustration.) By the time she'd washed the dishes, their car was ready. The chauffeur, a light-skinned Negro in uniform, was waiting near the desk and stepped behind the chair to help her, so there was no opportunity to leave a message.

That's when Eve lost all nervous frustration. It was out of her hands now.

The street was wet, the sky slate gray, and even as they entered the limousine it began to rain. They pulled onto Collins Avenue, the huge car smooth and silent—windows closed, air-conditioning at a comfortably mild setting, the clean, rich smell of leather in their nostrils. "Bad weather, suh," the chauffeur murmured. Mr. Wheeler grunted, and asked him to close the glass panel sealing off the driver's section. Not very nice of him, Eve thought, looking out at the rain, thinking it a perfect day for a trip, feeling enveloped by luxury.

"People down here . . . always saying . . . *bad* weather."

She turned. "Well, isn't it bad weather when it rains?"

"Not unless . . . it's destructive. Not destructive . . . or unusual . . . to have rain in . . . coastal southern Florida. Plenty rain . . . plenty sun. All good weather."

She smiled, liking that.

"Smile more often . . . for me, Eve." He took her hand. "Need it . . . for therapy."

She smiled again, and he squeezed her fingers. He didn't let go, and she left her hand in his. Soon, he fell asleep.

She enjoyed the trip, looking out the window, seeing the rain end—or the limousine leave it behind—and the sun emerge, watching towns come and go and the country grow less crowded and built-up. And when they pulled into a driveway and stopped, she was surprised that two-and-a-half hours had passed and they had reached their destination.

They were off a quiet, private road with the muted roar of the sea a continuous background sound that soon lost distinction and seemed no sound at all. At first she didn't see the house, just a path leading from the half-moon driveway into a near-solid wall of trees, flowering bushes, and high hedging. Then, after the chauffeur had unfolded Mr. Wheeler's chair and they'd started up the path, she saw the second story and thought it ugly and told herself it would look different when connected to the rest of the house. The path seemed endless, but they finally came around a turn and she was able to see it all—and it wasn't different. It was a big, square, red-brick house that looked a little like a factory and seemed totally out of place in semitropical Florida.

"Grim looking, isn't it?" Mr. Wheeler said, and chuckled. "No pink stucco . . . or Mediterranean tile . . . or modern gimmicks. Had it built . . . thirty, no, thirty-one . . . years ago. And I mean *built*. The ocean's . . . right out back. But no hurricane . . . can do a thing . . . to this house. And inside . . . you'll see real . . . solid comfort."

He wasn't exaggerating. Half an hour later she'd been shown through fourteen spacious rooms, and felt there had never been a house laid out better for a large family and servants to *live* in. But still, there was a certain feeling—*gloom* was the word that moved into her mind, though most of the rooms had plenty of sunlight, and many looked out on the Atlantic and a private beach of gleaming white sand, and the front rooms had those massed trees and shrubs as their view, and one, an enormous combination sun porch and gymnasium complete with wall weights and electric horse and rowing machine, led to a small swimming pool. "The pool heater's been on since President Wheeler called," Mary, the housekeeper said. She was a strong, stocky woman with untouched gray-black hair and a mild Irish brogue. She went on to say that she had contacted the employment service and a maid was expected momentarily, but that of the "regular staff" there was only herself and "Rand, who's out getting a few of the things the President likes." Eve asked how large the regular staff was. "Six— but that was when the President had his government guard. Now it's five, when we can keep a decent cook for a decent time. You know what people have come to, don't you, expecting coffee breaks and short hours and long vacations." She made a sound of disgust. "The President now, he didn't have coffee breaks and short hours and long vacations when he was making his way and when he was making his family what it is."

Back in the sitting room, where Mr. Wheeler was on the phone, Mary looked at him as Eve might have looked at—well, the *Pope!* Mr. Wheeler held the phone in his left hand and spoke strongly, spacing his pauses in such a way as to make them sound almost natural. A door slammed somewhere and the housekeeper's mouth tightened. "Fool," she muttered.

A man entered the room. He was tall, about fifty, with lank gray hair and a lined, outdoor face that still managed to look boyish. "Mary," he said, smiling, "I got some—" He'd seen Eve and Mr. Wheeler as soon as he'd entered, couldn't have helped seeing them, but was obviously a slow reactor—the type that having once planned and started something was unable to make changes. "—real good steaks," he concluded, voice running down.

Mary continued to look at Mr. Wheeler and Mr. Wheeler looked at the man, and the man froze to stooped attention. Mr. Wheeler said, "I'll expect to hear . . . all about it soon. Yes, at the winter home. Next Saturday. Make it as of . . . Monday, the thirtieth. *All* reports." He listened and said, "Doctors run the show . . . only as long as you . . . have to let them. I no longer . . . have to let them." He hung up without a good-bye and turned the chair a bit, so he was facing Eve, Mary, and the man. The man muttered, "Mr. President, welcome."

"I told him you'd be here when he came back," Mary said, voice a monotone. "He didn't remember."

Mr. Wheeler took the heavy cane from the corner of his chair and thumped it on the floor, holding the head with both hands. "You'll remember . . . from now on, won't you . . . Rand?"

Rand nodded quickly. "Yes, that I will, sir."

Mr. Wheeler said, "Good. We want a . . . tight ship . . . an efficient crew."

Rand nodded again, and repeated softly, "Welcome."

Mr. Wheeler tucked his cane away. "How's the pool?" He didn't wait for an answer. "Eve, I'll get into . . . my swim shorts. Has Mary shown you . . . my room? Then take me . . . there now.

And Mary, I'll want . . . a light lunch . . . and a full dinner . . . for myself . . . and Miss Andrews. And I'll want . . . to talk to you . . . about a staff . . . to be ready . . . the thirtieth, this month."

He had wheeled up to Eve, and she stepped behind the chair, putting her hands on the aluminum bar. But the way he was acting now, she wasn't sure whether she was pushing, or being pulled.

He stopped at the door. Without turning, he said, "Miss Andrews will have . . . complete authority. She's to be treated . . . as mistress here. Understood?"

Mary and Rand murmured yessirs and Eve hoped she wasn't blushing as furiously as she felt she was. He shouldn't have said that—at least not that way!

But at the same time she was flattered, and the house began to seem just a little less gloomy to her.

Senator Christopher took a ball from the return rack, and with excellent form, spun it down the alley. The other bowlers had stopped to watch, and John McKensil led them in applause as Christopher registered a strike. "With luck like that," Christopher murmured, "I wish the convention were being held today!" He shook a few hands and signed a few scorecards, and they headed for the glass doors that led to the back of the cabana area. "All free for our guests," McKensil said, continuing the guided tour and explanation of the hotel's facilities.

"This too?" Dan Berner asked, stopping at the small bar.

"Generally not," McKensil replied. "But for our purposes . . ." He beckoned the bartender, though his feeling was that Berner had already exceeded his limit.

Christopher was watching Berner, and seemed puzzled. "Celebrating something, Dan?" Berner nodded and ordered a martini, very dry. Christopher and his bodyguard declined and McKensil said not while he was on duty. Berner said, "Alone then," and raised his glass. He looked through the doors at the concrete decking, still wet from this morning's showers. "To life, gentlemen. Our most precious possession." He swallowed half the martini. "A cliché, I'll admit, but a universal truth as well. So universal and so much a truth that—" he finished the drink— "that there's no topping it."

Christopher said, "Now that we've taken care of universal truths, shall we proceed with more mundane matters?" He nodded at McKensil, and they went out of the bowling alley.

They had been touring the hotel for the past two hours, starting at the rooftop solaria. Now they went into the Arcade Level and over to the elevators. Christopher asked about the body found on the beach this morning, and as they entered a car Berner murmured, "In the midst of life."

"More eternal truths?" Christopher asked, and he seemed annoyed. Berner didn't react. He stared down at the floor as they reached the lobby. Christopher and his guard got out, as did McKensil. Berner said, "I'll be at the suite in an hour," and stayed put. Christopher said, "Take a shower, Dan. Snap out of it—whatever it is." The doors closed, Berner still staring at the floor.

They went to the desk where McKensil thought they would part, but Christopher walked a step further with him, away from the guard, and lowered his voice. "About Wally Jones . . . did he actually strike that woman?"

McKensil told what he knew. Christopher looked grim. "It wouldn't have been so bad, except for that awful picture in the morning papers." He then shook McKensil's hand, thanked him for the tour, and walked away, his guard falling in half a step behind him.

McKensil checked the desk and went on down the hall to his office, thinking he was one of life's fortunates, having a position that not only paid well but brought him into contact with some of the most important people in the country. To place it in jeopardy for a momentary pleasure, an erotic spasm, something a man of his years should be outgrowing—*had* outgrown; he was sure of it—was unthinkable.

And then he entered his office and Violetta looked up from her typing table and it had no front panel and her legs were braced firmly apart and she smiled her beautiful smile and his breath

243

caught in his throat and his heart beat as it beat for no amount of money and no professional triumph and no important personality. And he remembered his niece Anita and the one true sexual satisfaction of his life. And he remembered Violetta in the car the day he'd told her she was hired and his hand on her warm thighs and his finger touching . . .

He went by her, nodding brusquely. She said, "I hope you don't mind the package."

He turned, beginning to ask what package, and saw it across the room in the corner behind Miss Bayleth's desk. He had to smile, thinking how the acidy old maid would have reacted to anything that enormously phallic. But Miss Bayleth had given notice last week and was using up her vacation time and would be in only once more, to pick up her personal belongings and final check. "What in the world *is* it?"

"A lamp," she murmured.

"Large enough, I'll say that for it."

"It is a gift from an uncle. He has money, and strange tastes. Do you know what teakwood is?"

"Of course." He went around the desk and tried to heft the tall cardboard container in one hand, grunted, and had to use both. "Must have a lead base."

"Metal, yes, because the top part swings out . . ." She shook her head. "It is an ugly thing, but my mother will be pleased— when she comes home next week. Though why he had it delivered here . . ."

"That's quite all right. How are you going to get it home?"

She crossed her legs. "A taxi, I suppose."

He sat down at the edge of Miss Bayleth's desk and reached for a cigarette and looked at her legs. "I can take it in my car." She began to thank him. He said, "Why don't we bring it over right now?"

She seemed startled, and he quickly added, "Unless you're loaded with work?"

"No. Just the last of the letters. It is very kind of you."

"Then it's settled."

"I—have to make a call. Someone who expects me to be here for lunch."

"A young man?"

She shook her head, eyes falling. He laughed and said, "Go ahead then," and lit the cigarette, aware that his hand was trembling. She hesitated. He knew she wanted him to leave, but he didn't leave. She raised the phone and dialed carefully. "*Jorge, por favor.*" A moment later she said, "Violetta. I will not be at the office for a while. I have to bring my lamp home. Yes, that is right. No, I am leaving now." She listened. "I will try. *Adiós.*" She stood up. "If you will excuse me a minute, Mr. McKensil?" She walked to the hall, and he turned his head and leaned forward to watch her as long as he could. Then he called the front desk—and then told himself he would do nothing to risk his wonderful life and sat and smoked and waited.

He waited longer than he'd expected to. The lamp was in his car and his car at the main doors by the time she returned. "I'm sorry. A girl's face must be made up."

She didn't appear to have any makeup on, besides her usual touch of pale lipstick and eye shadow.

In the lobby, she suddenly stopped and said, "Oh, I forgot my key. It is in the desk," and hurried back to the office.

Again he waited longer than he expected to. And began to feel irritated. She finally returned, saying, "There was a phone call. Someone asking foolish questions, but I could not be rude."

His irritation disappeared the moment they drove away from the Metropole. She turned to look into the back, where the long package was placed, her knees coming up on the seat, her green miniskirt riding to mid-thigh. "It is like a day off!"

He chuckled, eyes darting to her. "You've got a good boss, right?"

"Right!"

"He deserves a reward, right?"

Her "Right!" remained naïve and enthusiastic.

"What do you suggest?"

"I can make you a cup of strong, black, Cuban coffee. Or a whiskey—we have three kinds. Or something to eat."

"Or give me a kiss." He concentrated on his driving.

She remained silent, and he finally glanced at her. Her eyes were down. He said, "You'd be surprised what some bosses would expect."

Voice low, she replied, "I do not think a kiss from me is much of a reward. You must have the whiskey, too."

He laughed, and she covered her mouth and leaned toward him. He kissed her hair. She grew still. He turned west off Collins and then north onto Abbott. "Mr. McKensil, that did not count as your kiss, did it?"

"Do you want it to count as my kiss?"

They were pulling up before the green stucco house. She got out without answering and walked to the front door. He took the lamp from the back seat and lugged it up the path, promising himself that one kiss, and nothing more.

"Another drink?" she asked, and McKensil said no and lit a fresh cigarette. His voice and hands shook and his eyes went everywhere but to her. She rose from where she sat beside him on the couch and excused herself and walked through the arch and into the main bedroom. She closed the door and put her ear against the wall. She heard nothing, but Jorge must be in there; she had seen his car down the street. Yet she wanted to be *certain*.

Not just because of the pictures. Because she wanted Jorge to see her. Wanted to know he was watching. Wanted to feel his eyes burning through the camera as she did the things she yearned to do with him, and would make him *die* to do with her!

She went to one of the circular pictures. She tapped the wall near it with her finger. She did it again and again, until finally there was a tiny tapping in response. She smiled, drew off her underpants and returned to the living room.

McKensil stood up. "Well." He cleared his throat. "I've had my drink."

She nodded.

"I, uh . . . the rest of my reward?"

How nervous he was, this big bad lecher, this seducer of little girls! "All right," she whispered, and stood waiting. He came to her and laughed a little and said, "Now, now, why so serious about something you've done a thousand times before with your friends?" His hand came to her arm, hesitantly, and he bent to her. She whispered, "But you are a man, Mr. McKensil, and they were boys."

That must have been the right thing to say, because his arms went around her and his kiss was strong and open-mouthed. She gave him everything she could in return, and still he began to withdraw. She tried to hold on, impatient to do what had to be done and have Jorge hunger for her.

He stepped back, and again he laughed his untrue laugh. "Quite a reward."

She wanted to put her hand on him. She wanted to tell him to take her. But she couldn't. She had to remain the trembling little girl—when it was he who trembled—and make *him* do the seducing. That was his pleasure. He might lose interest if she revealed how easy it was.

She covered her face with her hands. "I do not think I can work for you any more, Mr. McKensil."

"What?"

She turned away. "Seeing you every day, and having certain thoughts . . ."

He still wasn't moving toward her, and she had to forget words and use her body. As if distraught and trying to find something to do, some way of changing the mood and subject, she went to where the packaged lamp stood near the door. She bent to it, as if to examine the printing on its base. She didn't flex her knees but bent straight over from the waist, something *never* to be done in a miniskirt. And heard his sharp intake of breath. She moved a little, turning her head to the side. And heard him come toward her. She murmured, "Fragile, this end down," and he stopped behind her. Voice high and weak, he said, "Violetta, dearest, don't be afraid," and his hands went to her bare bottom.

She stayed where she was, thinking of Jorge, until she felt something beside his hands and realized he was trying to do it right there. Then she straightened and turned and came into his arms, gasping, "No, Mr. McKensil, no . . ." and kissed him and touched him and led him, clutching and staggering, to the bedroom.

It was daylight. They hadn't counted on it happening in daylight. With the shades drawn, there was an uncertain light.

He didn't notice when she threw the wall switch and the ceiling lights went on. He didn't notice because he was intent on getting her to the bed; and then he was crouching over her, pulling off her clothes. He saw nothing but her, and he became more and more excited, and she realized it was not going to be a quick and simple thing that she might have to embellish for the cameras. He was kissing her body now, working up and down, and she gave herself to the pleasure of it. His mouth was everywhere. She turned her head to the wall with the round frames that no longer had pictures and formed "Jorge" with her lips and said, "Mr. McKensil, please."

He was a violent lover. He bit her, spanked her, made her cry out several times, and this too she enjoyed in the way of such things—and because she knew Jorge was watching. When he finally mounted her, he said so much about her youth and beauty and purity she had to hug him and kiss him and cry out with him, and this too was made more and made better because of Jorge.

He was a violent lover and a greedy lover. He stopped himself from orgasm three times, changing position: pressing her legs back over her head and plowing her body furiously; mounting her through the rear; bringing her mouth to him. During this last she experienced a kind of frenzy, never having done it before and knowing how it must affect Jorge and mumbling his name around the pulsing flesh. She wanted to bite and scream, and then he drew away from her and put her on her back again, head on the pillow, and with a strange and almost frightening gentleness—like the quiet before the hurricane, like the priest's voice before the firing squad—entered her and stretched out on her and enfolded her in his arms.

"Violetta," he said. "Violetta." Over and over. "Violetta," breathing quickly. "Violetta," breathing harshly. "Violetta," with the word beginning to blur.

She turned her head to the wall with the round picture frames and made Jorge's name with her lips and had her orgasm. McKensil went on, no longer violent but still greedy. Went on, stopping when he came close and then resuming. Went on with her name a rising and falling song, until suddenly he gripped her buttocks so hard she cried, "*Dios!*"

His grip relaxed. His body relaxed. His head fell past her shoulder and he seemed asleep.

"Mr. McKensil," she said, after a moment.

"My God," he whispered. "What can I say!" He got off her and sat slumped at the edge of the bed.

She glanced at the wall, and the pictures were again in their frames. "We have to get back," she said. She picked up her clothing and went to the bathroom. She washed, seeing all the red marks on her body, smiling and feeling wonderful. Because of the plan and because of Jorge. And yes, because of the love she had made with John McKensil.

Ay, when she and Jorge made such love! (Maybe tonight, because of what he had seen and because he must be dying for her.)

McKensil was dressed when she came back. He was looking at the lights over the bed. She said, "My mother's idea of beauty, like my uncle's idea of a lamp." She shut off the lights.

"Why did you put them on?"

"Habit. We must get back." She took his arm.

He looked at the lights and at her, and he almost seemed to know. Then he came along. At the street door he stopped. "What are we going to do?"

"Do?" She shrugged. "It is already done."

"Do you—know how to take care of yourself? I didn't protect you."

"It's all right. I took nurse's training in school. Come."

"I'm sorry. I know I shouldn't have—"

"It's already done," she repeated, hiding her impatience. Did he expect her to go back to being a trembling little girl after all that had happened?

But then again, a trembling little girl would have remained a trembling little girl, not become a woman who had succeeded in a plan. He was puzzled because she was becoming herself.

They went out to the car. He started the engine, but didn't drive away. "Before, in the living room, you said you didn't think you could work with me any more. Perhaps you're right."

She looked at him.

He quickly added, "It's up to you, of course. And I would want to help, financially."

"I don't want your help," she said, tired of the talk. "And I'm going to stay on at the Metropole."

He paled at her tone and drove off. Not until they were in sight of the hotel did he speak again. "Violetta," he said, voice begging, "please don't hate me."

She laughed then, and thought of how he was one of those who had stood by unknowing, uncaring, while her father and brother and uncle died at the Bay of Pigs. All this planning, all this playing at love, had robbed her of hatred. Now hatred was back and it cleansed her and she said, "Thanks for reminding me."

She opened the door and went into the hotel without waiting for him. More guests were checking in. More people rushing around. Rich Americans playing while Cubans sweated in the kitchens and changed the dirty linen and went home to poor lives. Rich Americans who fought in Asia for people who hated them, and failed to lift a finger for people who depended on them. *Rich Americans!*

She heard an increase in sound and turned to look. A man was coming from the elevators—a small black man followed by many white men with pads and cameras. Wally Jones, the singer. Wally Jones, hurrying toward the nightclub, his smile wrong and full of his trouble.

Lamas was right. They could get help from that one. He too must hate the rich Americans.

That he was rich himself made no difference, because he was poor dirt here with his black skin. And he had hit that American girl and now he couldn't deny the hate Americans felt for their blacks, the way blacks could when they were making money and everything seemed good.

She decided to call Lamas without waiting for Jorge's approval, and turned to the phone booths.

7

FRIDAY, JANUARY 20, P.M.

McKensil went into the green stucco house with the girl this time, but then again he had carried a package for her. Max parked far up the street near the corner, hoping the manager wouldn't come right out again. The pictures had to be taken before he could risk tailing Jorge a second time. The pictures had to be taken and Jorge had to rush to his boss, excited and less inclined than usual to keep a sharp eye out for persistent cars in his rear-view mirror. Max had a Mustang. A new car every day was his vacation "kick," he'd told the auto-rental people, and paid the extra tab. And he thought he saw Jorge's Plymouth about halfway between the Mustang and McKensil's Continental, though he wasn't close enough to read the license.

He wasn't going to get out and check it. He wasn't going to risk being seen. He'd taken too many risks already. Last night, for example.

He picked up the salesman-type ledger and busied himself making doodles . . . just in case anyone wondered why a stranger was sitting around doing nothing.

He missed his little Colt .25, which was lying out in the water off that concrete abutment, as far as he'd been able to throw it. (Even if they found it, it was a hot gun, and untraceable. He wouldn't carry another gun unless it, too, was untraceable, and he didn't have the proper contacts in Miami. Besides, after this job he wouldn't need a gun.)

He glanced up the street. McKensil had been in there fifteen minutes now. This might be it. He wondered what they were doing. He wouldn't mind banging that Cuban broad himself. Hot-looking piece. Made Ruthie look ninety.

What would Ruthie think if she knew he had killed a man in cold blood? Would she be disgusted? Afraid? Maybe respect him more?

He himself felt only fear. Fear of being found out.

He'd never killed before, though he'd had to put a bullet in a Canadian tough guy's leg seven years ago. He didn't consider himself a murderer, a strong-arm, a gunsel—just a man who'd had a few bad breaks and been pressured into an act of self-defense.

But still, Cooper's face as he'd fallen and looked up. Cooper's mouth moving, his eyes stupid with shock and approaching death . . .

His heart was pounding almost as wildly as it had when he'd turned from the body and begun walking back toward the Metropole. *That* had been the worst of it, because that was when he had been most vulnerable. No weapon, and if someone had appeared from the shadows, someone had shouted from atop the abutment, someone had been there to see and identify him . . .

He put his hand to his chest. *Easy*, he told himself. It's all over and the police talked to the Fine dame and no one knows anything. "Police Suspect Gangland Slaying," the papers had said. He was home free.

He waited, and suddenly McKensil and the girl were entering the Continental. He watched them drive away. They'd been inside the house about half an hour. It could have happened.

About ten minutes later Jorge came hurrying up the street toward the Plymouth, carrying a brown briefcase. Max dropped his ledger to the floor and bent after it. When he heard the engine cough into life, he counted five, and raised himself to see the Plymouth moving off. He followed.

Jorge drove quickly, like a man anxious to pass on exciting news. They went north on A1A, Max using moderate traffic as a shield, laying back as far as he could without losing the Plymouth. They reached Golden Beach and Jorge turned into a wide driveway. Max caught a glimpse of a rambling house amid palms and shrubbery, and slowed to read the number on a brick gatepost.

He drove on, passing a small shopping center, and came to a gas station. He stopped at the pumps and told the attendant to fill it up and stood beside the car chatting about Miami Beach and Golden Beach and how much nicer Golden Beach was. "Take the houses. Real quality." The attendant agreed and said that lots of important people lived here. "Like Sanford Blassington. Supposed to own half the stock in that big electronics company."

Max had the oil and water checked and said, "I've seen bigger houses, but none nicer than the ranch-type about three miles back along the highway. I even remember the number . . ."

The attendant asked if it had two burst-brick posts and a wide concrete driveway. Max said, "That's the one." The attendant closed the Mustang's hood. "I service their cars. An Imperial, a Maserati sport, and a Plymouth. Rich Cubans. Quiet people. Mr. Ivan Lamas . . ."

Max drove back to the shopping center. He entered a sidewalk phone booth and used the directory to find Ivan Cesar Lamas.

"Jorge, please."

"Who is it calling?" the woman asked, her accent heavily Spanish.

"Max Prager."

"Wait please."

He waited, his heart pounding. But not with fear. He was in control now.

"Who is this?" Jorge asked.

"Max Prager, Jorge. Didn't the woman tell you?"

There was silence.

Max laughed to himself, remembering how pleased Jorge had looked walking up to him in the hotel lobby.

"It's time for another meeting, Jorge, now that we've nailed McKensil."

Still silence.

"Listen, Jorge. I need some money. I was a little unlucky at cards. No, why should I lie? I was *damned* unlucky. If you could see your way clear to letting me have my hundred fifty thousand in advance . . ."

Jorge said, "That is impossible," his voice harsh.

Max was sweating in the phone booth. If Lamas decided to drop the whole plan, Max would have no leverage. But he was sure Lamas wouldn't do that, wouldn't stop now that things were beginning to roll. He wondered if Jorge's boss was listening in on the conversation.

Max said, "Yeah, I know our agreement, but what difference does it make *when* I get paid? I'll still do the same job, won't I? If you explain it to Mr. Lamas, I'm sure he'll be willing. A big man like that, it won't bother him to pay out a few bucks a little sooner."

Silence.

"Maybe he'd like to come along for the meet? You and me and Lamas, we could talk things over. Ask him, Jorge."

He waited out the silence this time, and was rewarded with, "I'll call you."

"Could you make it tonight, Jorge? Honest, I'm being squeezed for that money. You wouldn't want your top man knocked off for a few grand in gambling debts, would you?"

"Tonight."

Max drove back to the Metropole. He didn't kid himself that Jorge, or Lamas, would believe his gambling-debt story. He'd used it to give them a way of saving face. He hoped they accepted it. But he missed his little Colt more than ever. Not having it made some extra precautions necessary.

No more meets in drive-in movies or in anyone's car. No more meets at night. No meets in rooms, or on dark beaches, or anywhere else he could suddenly find himself alone with "unfriendly" characters.

From now on he would see Jorge only in broad daylight, out in the open, with plenty of people around. From now on he would stay out of dark, empty places *all* the time.

May and Harold walked along the beach. They had almost an hour before Wally Jones's opening, at the Platinum Room. It was a mild evening, the sky bright and the sea quiet. Harold talked about the small legal firm in which he was junior partner to his two brothers' senior partnerships. He would always be the junior partner, because he wasn't very good at anything besides detail, research, background. Eli and Henry went into court; Harold stayed in the office and dug through books. He made it sound as if he preferred it that way, and perhaps he did, now. But at one time he had resented it, thought it unfair, vowed to change it. He'd had several chances, and failed, and now he talked of "intellectual legal battles" as opposed to "performances" in front of judge and jury.

He had also resented May's success in Jem-Boxes, Inc., and tried to get her to give it up just before she opened her third branch. He'd been clever about it, finding her a buyer, and at the same time hinting at the possibility of cunnilingus as a solution to their sex problem. She had been willing to accept oral lovemaking, but not as a condition to selling her business. Besides, she had felt he was incapable of so great an intimacy without the spur of overriding passion. She'd been right. He had never gone beyond talking. And, in time, he had rationalized her business success into something rather humorous. "May has this talent for junk jewelry. It's amazing how much money vulgarity will bring."

He had attempted to get that money into a joint account, not because he wanted it for himself, she felt, but because he was afraid of having her become too independent. And his fears were justified; she had asked him for a divorce soon after her corporation was formed. Which led to his suicide attempt, and to her entrapment. Which led to Miami Beach and Dan and Al and

Eunice. And back to Harold. And so she walked along the beach where she had walked with Al only two nights before, and talked to her husband, as she had talked to him for seven years, and the moon shone and she tried not to remember the driving youth and intensity and lust for life that was Al Fortens. . . .

She saw him as they lined up behind a dozen or more people waiting to enter the Platinum Room. He was at the head of the line, with his mother and a large man who looked like his father. Also with him was an animated girl, cute rather than pretty, whose voice clearly reached May.

". . . Mr. Baxter, you remember him, don't you, Al? You had him for History."

Al nodded and said something May couldn't hear, and the girl put back her head and laughed. "Yes, that's the one. All you have to do to pass is be a girl!" She had a superb body, full enough where it counted, yet lithe and quick of movement, and it was enticingly packaged in a pink minishift. (May suddenly felt eighty in her high-necked, low-hemmed black gown, a gown Harold found pleasing.)

"See someone you know?" Harold asked.

May realized she had stepped out of line the better to see the girl. She moved back in, shaking her head. "Just glancing inside. It's quite a place."

At that moment Al turned to his mother, saw May, and smiled. Harold caught it. May glanced off to the side, trying to keep her expression bland. "So *that's* your young Lothario?" Harold murmured.

She said nothing. Al couldn't understand her situation, and when she straightened her gaze he waved (defying his mother, she supposed). She looked at him, and through him. His hand dropped, his smile died, his eyes went to Harold.

"You're ignoring the boy, May. No use being rude. I'll answer for you."

The blood seemed to still in her veins as he waved and smiled. Al responded automatically, stiffly, and turned away.

"Want to go over and chat?" Harold murmured.

That didn't deserve an answer. She got a cigarette from her bag and used her lighter. She smoked and wondered at the extent of her pain.

The management had cleared all newsmen except for the official hotel photographer from the backstage area when Senator Christopher made his appearance. Wally was talking to Marjory Fine, who seemed to have put away more than her quota of sauce and was a little too gay, a little too excited and talky. He didn't get it. This wasn't her bag. Still, she was a real friend, an affectionate old broad, and he loved her dearly. She hadn't worried about being seen with him or photographed with him— not that the reporters were interested in *her*. She'd wasted no time calling him yesterday after hearing about the mess in the lobby with Barker's chick. She'd said exactly what he'd wanted to hear, and hadn't heard from anyone *but* Marjory, and hoped he would eventually hear from Dick Christopher: "You couldn't do what they're hinting you did. You could hit a woman, of course, but not for any reprehensible reason." He'd cracked about not understanding ten-buck words, and she'd said, "Wally honey, you understand so much more than most people that I believe you rate *million*-dollar words." But he wasn't understanding *her* too well at the moment. She just wasn't the cool, cool lady he knew.

When Dick walked into the dressing room, Marjory got up and said, "I'll leave you two old friends alone." Wally had a few sharp cracks at the tip of his tongue, but didn't use them. This was the first he'd seen *or* heard from the Senator, and he'd left word at his suite as soon as he'd arrived yesterday morning. And lookee here, all the reporters and photographers except that hotel shill were gone.

"Wally," Christopher said, and grabbed his hand and sat down on the chair beside the makeup table. The wide Tonto character leaned against the closed door like a heavy in an old movie. "Good to see you again."

"I was hoping to see you last night, Senator." He turned to the mirror. "Excuse me while I put on some blackface."

Christopher chuckled.

"Gotta look *real* black to match those pictures. You seen the papers today?"

Christopher nodded. "I'm sorry about that, Wally. But it's only a temporary discomfort."

"Yeah, it'll blow over. But meanwhile there's a million pictures —make that fifty million, since other cities must've picked it up and I hear they even flashed it on some of the independent TV newscasts. Huntley-Brinkley and Cronkite didn't touch it—but still, fifty million pictures of a very black boy bending over that lily-white chick with what looks like a bad grin on his face and her dress up over her belly button. And did you dig some of those captions? "Singer Slugs Sweetie Silly." Makes it sound like she was *my* sweetie, which'll really help me professionally. And how careful they tiptoed through the story, making sure not to say I was hot for her but making just as sure to mention that Barker and a room full of white boys rushed to her defense and that I was, quote, '*escorted* into a nearby room by the hotel manager.' " He stopped, realizing that he wasn't being funny any more but was crying on the Senator's shoulder.

"Unhappy business," Christopher muttered.

Wally waited for something else.

"But tonight you'll be doing what you and you alone do best —what no one else in the world can do—singing those Wally Jones songs in that Wally Jones manner."

Oy vay, as Nat would say. The kiss of death. Dick had nothing to offer. Dick was dancing swiftly backward. Wally turned to the mirror.

"You know, Wally, I'm in an awkward position here."

Okay, so now he'd get down to cases.

"I'm your friend and Ben's friend, and it's impossible to discuss this matter objectively with either of you. Ben called me, and if I were to believe what he said I'd have to consider you psychotic and dangerous." He laughed.

Wally smiled a little. This *was* the next President of the United

258

States, as he saw it, and *was* the best hope for Negroes, as he saw it, and you didn't piss on such a man and his friendship.

"Of course, I don't accept Ben's evaluation. You obviously made some sort of mistake."

Wally told him the whole thing, quickly. He didn't tell him *why* he and Barker hated each other's guts, but Christopher, it seemed, already knew.

"I'll always believe Ben made a terrible mistake in Hollywood, Wally. He's not to be forgiven that kind of act."

Wally leaped up and talked into his fist as if it were a microphone. "Now would you say that for the record, Senator? That Benny Barker is a bigot and you hate his guts? That you dig miscegenation and high-yallers? That you personally want to tell everyone who disagrees with the NAACP—make that the Non-Student Violent Committee—that anyone who disagrees with Black Power can take his vote and shove it?"

Christopher nodded slowly, smiling, saying, "That's about the position I'm in, Wally. So forgive what you obviously can't forgive right now, and remember that I want your help and want to repay your help."

"I'll take three Astrids in miniskirts—"

"Repay with a resumption of *positive* action on the problems of the ghetto."

That was politicians' talk, but how else could you say you wanted to work at solving what so many people (including maybe Wally Jones) felt were insoluble problems?

Christopher rose and squeezed his hand and said, "Keep the faith, baby."

"We still using that line?"

Christopher smiled and walked to the door. Tonto opened it and Christopher went out. Tonto looked back and said, "The Senator forgot to mention it, but we're at a ringside table, left of center, and if there's any problem . . ."

"Left of center is my politics, too, Chief."

Tonto smiled. "Any trouble, I'm your man. And that includes the rest of our stay here." The door closed.

Wally hadn't thought in terms of *real* trouble. Maybe a redneck or two making with wisecracks. But muscle? In the Bal Metropole?

He felt like a drink. But he didn't drink this close to a performance. He peeled a stick of gum and chewed like crazy.

Marjory Fine finished her second highball. The liquor wasn't working tonight. She tried to find their waiter in the crush and bustle of the Platinum Room.

"We live in a racist culture," Marco was saying. "All this nonsense about Wally Jones." He looked squarely at Benny Barker and Astrid Kane. Benny didn't seem to hear him; he stared off into the crowd. Astrid flushed darkly.

There was Marco (drinking heavily, which explained his bravado), Benny, his manager and Astrid, Bruce Golden and Ellie DeWyant (holding hands under the table), Mr. and Mrs. Lorsh of the real-estate Lorshes, and Marjory. It was the nucleus of the party that would take place in Marjory's suite after the show.

Astrid said, "You can talk fancy, but no *white* man ever punched me."

"I know at least one who's wanted to," Benny muttered.

Marjory beckoned to a waiter, but it was Benny who said, "Drinks, drinks, drinks," waving his arm at the table.

Astrid stared at him. "What's the matter with you, anyway? You're the one got me a lawyer and said—"

Barker's manager patted her shoulder. "You should know him by now, Astrid. He's off before an opening. I mean *his*, tomorrow night. We could be going to war, but he'll be thinking about his material, his timing, his props. The only thing that counts with Ben, starting about twenty-four hours before a show, is doing his thing."

"Oh, I'm King of the Twilight Zone," Barker muttered. He wasn't funny tonight. He wasn't even here. But Marjory wasn't too interested in his preoccupation. She had one of her own.

Bert was dead. Why, she didn't know. But he was dead and

there was a two-way mirror in the bathroom and how could she change it without him?

That was one of several obvious problems. There was also something far from obvious, a problem she hadn't allowed herself to face as yet: How was she going to *live* without him?

She'd had to answer questions (mainly with "I don't know") and identify his body this morning. They'd driven her to the Dade County Morgue where, along with his employer from the motel, she'd shrunk from the bloodied, waxen figure and nodded numbly and been driven back to the hotel. And remembered him as he'd been Wednesday night, working on her and for her, and succeeding because of what she had seen Mrs. Prager and Jerry Leech doing through the two-way mirror. And afterward, holding her hand as she talked about the party and what Mrs. Prager had said to Leech and how Leech had immediately begun chasing Michael Wheeler's nurse and how he must be a veritable bull in sexual matters.

Bert had smiled. "When a man likes a women he can be quite strong that way." She had closed her eyes, satisfied for the first time in almost a year, and drifted toward sleep. And heard him murmer, "I could be a bull myself, if you were the woman."

She excused herself. She went to the washroom and took a fifty-milligram tranquilizer and sat in front of the mirror, touching her hair.

"I could be a bull myself, if you were the woman."

Now that it was too late, she wanted to try.

She reentered the Platinum Room just as the houselights were going down, the spotlight coming up. It was five to twelve. The star was about to make his appearance.

8

SATURDAY, JANUARY 21, A.M.

There were little night lights in plug-in fixtures between the rooms, and Eve made her way quietly along the hall toward the living room. There, too, a night light burned, and she remembered how Sister Innocenta would scold the girls for leaving a light on and "wasting precious electricity, precious money."

She walked to the door on the opposite side of the living room, wondering if she was going in the right direction. She couldn't sleep; was disturbed by what had happened three hours earlier. Not that she hadn't handled it correctly. But it was bound to happen again, if Mr. Wheeler continued to improve.

She chided herself for being foolish. It wasn't anything personal—just an ordinary physiological reaction.

He had swum in his heated pool for an incredible forty minutes, gaining considerable mobility toward the end. It had exhausted him and he'd gone directly to bed and slept until seven, at which time he'd eaten a large dinner and again grown sleepy. But he'd needed a sponge bath; the chlorine could irritate his skin if left on overnight.

She had bathed him, and as soon as she'd reached his genitals he'd gained a partial erection. He hadn't said anything, closing his eyes—after one intense look—and she had walked away, to change the water, she'd said. By the time she came back, he had returned to a limp stage.

So it was nothing to be disturbed about. (Forget that look! He's a sick old man!)

He had asked her to sit with him, and held her hand, and had spoken briefly before falling asleep. "You can have . . . a home . . . all the luxuries . . . here with me, Eve. For as long . . . as I live. And much money . . . after I die. Agree . . . and I'll consult . . . my attorneys . . . next week."

She had said he would soon be well enough to dispense with her services. He'd smiled. He wasn't the type to fool himself. He would always need some sort of help.

She was at the kitchen and saw light under the swinging door. She thought it was another of the night lights, but when she entered the entire room was lighted and Rand looked up from the table. On reflex, she drew her robe close about her. He stood up. "I'll be going," he said, standing in that stooped way of his.

"Please go on with your meal, Rand. I just wanted a glass of milk." She smiled, and he sat down slowly and looked at his plate. She went to the refrigerator behind him and got the milk and found a glass on the drainboard and filled it. She wanted to sip it standing, but he sat in such an uncomfortable manner that she came to the table and took a chair.

"Strange how we get thirsty and hungry at night, isn't it?"

"I'm always hungry," he said, voice a mild rumble, "when I can't drink. I'm not allowed to when President Wheeler's here."

She was startled.

"I mean whiskey, miss. He'll tell you. You're going to run the house—"

"You don't have to—"

But he had started, and he couldn't stop until he'd finished his thought.

"—and you'll know I'm not supposed to touch a drop while he's here. Otherwise, Mary lets me have some and I go out to a place where they give me credit and Mary sends over a check once a month."

She was embarrassed, and decided to take the professional approach. "Is it a real problem?"

"Sometimes. But I don't drink more than I can pay for. I pay for my own, you know. Or I stop." He picked up his fork and put what looked like chicken salad into his mouth. "But President Wheeler, he don't care about that. He says no blood of his will be talked about."

"You mean you're a *relative?*"

"First cousin. That's why I can't go to the dog tracks any more.

He says no blood of his can hang around tracks and lose money and get talked about." He ate. "But it's my own money. I get fifty dollars a week plus room and board. I never spend more than that."

She felt upset. "I'm sorry."

He looked at her, puzzled. "What for, miss?"

"That you can't . . . do what you want with your own money."

"Well, I don't have any now. Spent it all. But when President Wheeler's here for a while, I save some."

"Do you call him 'President' all the time?"

"President Wheeler? What else should I call him, miss?"

"He's your cousin, Rand."

He stared at her, his lips moving as he tried to understand what she meant.

"Didn't you call him Michael, or Mike, when you were younger?"

He shook his head. "It's not allowed, miss. Not Mary nor the cook nor the maids. I'm the gardener and handyman and it's not allowed for me, either. Maybe for you, like for Miss Ellis, but not for me."

She drank half the milk, wanting to get back to her room.

"Miss Ellis wasn't a nurse," Rand said, picking at his salad, "but she was pretty." He smiled. "She would give me a drink sometimes and say I was better looking than any man in the house. She was a girl for play, that one. She had her room—your room now, miss—she had it all fixed up in pink things. When President Wheeler got sick, Mary took out all the pink things and had it painted like it is now. I liked it the other way, too. Mary didn't. She said President Wheeler was risking his immortal soul."

"Why?" Eve asked, and then flushed, thinking of how her room had no door but an arch leading into Mr. Wheeler's room.

"I don't know. Maybe because Miss Ellis was so young. Mary said she was just a child, but she didn't look like a child to me. Mary told the cook—the one we used to have—that Miss Ellis was seventeen and what sort of mother would let her child live in sin?"

"Miss Ellis's mother knew about it?"

"She would come to visit once a month and get an envelope. Mary said it was money. Miss Ellis got money, too. Sometimes when President Wheeler was away she'd drive me to the track and lend me money when I lost." He smiled his sweet smile. "I don't think she was that other word Mary called her. No, just one for play. So pretty." He shook his head, smiling, looking down at the plate.

Eve rose.

"Should I go to bed, miss?"

"You go to bed when you want to," she answered, angry somehow.

He heard the anger, and stood up. "Did I say something wrong, miss?"

She said no, of course not, and put her hand on his arm. "Good night, Rand."

"Good night, miss. I hope you'll be happy here. Miss Ellis was always happy."

Eve went to the sink and rinsed the glass. "Where did Miss Ellis go, Rand?"

"I don't know, miss. But I heard Mary say she had plenty to live on the rest of her days."

"It must have been different when *Mrs.* Wheeler was alive. Were you here then, Rand?"

"Different? I don't remember it being different, miss." He frowned. "But maybe it was. Mary says I don't remember things like they were."

"I mean with Miss Ellis not being here."

He frowned again. "If you say so, miss."

"You mean she was here at the same time as Mrs. Wheeler?"

"Not Miss Ellis, no. But that other one who worked as a maid a while and then moved into the pink room. She was pretty, too. Big and pretty."

"You must be mistaken, Rand."

He made his frowning, thinking face. "If you say so, miss."

She walked past him. "I say so."

"But Mrs. Wheeler and the girls wouldn't come here after a while because of that other one."

She stopped with her hand on the door.

"What did Mary think of *that?*"

"Mary?" He shrugged. "She always says things about President Wheeler risking his immortal soul."

"And she's right, isn't she?"

He shrugged again. "But she also says he's a special man, and special men—kings and presidents—have special rules, get special dispensation. She says I have to treat him like a special man."

Eve opened the door.

"And I *will*, miss. You can be sure of it. I always do."

She hurried toward her room, where the "girl for play" had lived and before her the "big and pretty one." And thought, suddenly, of how it would be to live here with Mr. Wheeler for years and years. How it would be to serve him, and be served by others in return—and what her service might entail, now that he could no longer get the girls for play, the big and pretty ones.

Ridiculous! That deathly sick old man!

But those were only words to comfort her. Inside she no longer thought of him as quite that sick and quite that old. Inside he was becoming someone different—frightening and exciting and distasteful and promising.

She entered Mr. Wheeler's room and paused at his bed. He lay on his back, lips slightly parted. Even in deep repose, his face now held strength. Yes, he was changing . . .

The sponge-bathing scene flashed through her mind, and so did an imaginary continuation of that scene.

She turned away, flushing, and went to her room and lay down.

Her father had looked something like Mr. Wheeler. Not as big and not as sure, but still . . .

She was dozing. Awake, she would have turned from thoughts of her father. Half asleep she didn't turn, began to face what she had avoided since Caspar Andrews had died and she had fled to Philadelphia. Half asleep she began to exorcise, by reliving, the deepest hurt of a life that had known far too much hurt.

There had been a slip of paper in her carriage, and on it was printed: "Eve Breen, four weeks old, please love my child." Love was the one thing the St. Theresa Home for Foundlings had not been able to provide—at least not in proportion to a child's needs. At age seven, when she was obviously outclassed in the adoption derby, the sisters had begun preparing her for something less than her dream of Mommy and Daddy miraculously appearing to claim her. By her thirteenth birthday she had experienced an even half-dozen foster homes, some good, some not so good, all destructive to her personality because they were temporary. She'd had temporary mothers, temporary fathers, temporary sisters and brothers and dogs. Then, with puberty upon her and the need for close relationships greater than it had ever been, Heaven had seemed suddenly intent upon making up for the long years of unanswered prayers. Mr. and Mrs. Caspar Andrews surprised everyone at St. Theresa by adopting her after only two visits— that gangly, plain-faced, mumbling girl—when several cute little cherubs had been available.

How good it had been! How happy she had been—though Father was never well, or never thought he was well, and pushed her toward a career in nursing when she had wanted to be a teacher. She'd had a good home. She'd had what she'd felt was love. She'd had decent clothing and gone to Bannesville High and then Rensburgh Nursing and felt she'd escaped forever the emptiness, the loneliness, the impermanence of institutional and foster-home life. Not that she'd changed into a gay and popular thing, but warmth had entered her life, and joy of a quiet variety. Many good days, many good evenings, many wonderful hours. She would cherish these people, she'd felt, until the day she died.

She was out of nursing school and working in Bannesville General when Father underwent exploratory surgery for two polyps of the intestines. She wept when Dr. Avedon told her the prognosis was terminal, and returned to Caspar Andrews' semiprivate room. He was awake, and the first thing he said, his voice a raging whisper, was, "I've been thirsty. I've wanted a drink. Why weren't you here?"

She began to explain that the doctor had summoned her, but he went on, red tinging the cheekbones of his otherwise pale face—his fleshy, handsome face that was already beginning to deteriorate. "Is this the way you repay my giving you a home, my giving you a profession?"

That was the theme of four months of tirade, four months of abuse (unopposed by a constantly weeping mother), terminating on the night she sat slumped at his bedside, exhausted both physically and emotionally, and heard him whisper:

"You don't care whether I live or die, do you?"

She said yes, she did, and to please, please not think of those things any more.

"You say you care but you don't. And you have to, you hear? You have to! I took you from that orphanage for one thing. I gave you a home and fed and clothed . . ." He paused to gulp air, and she didn't have the strength to tell herself it was the sickness—couldn't stop him and couldn't run from him. "Fed and clothed and spent thousands, *thousands,* on someone no one else wanted. For one reason. To have you trained to care for me. I knew I was sick. Alice kept saying my imagination, but I knew I would need help some day. So I gave you everything and now you're not here when I want you and now I get sicker and sicker and you don't do anything . . ."

She began to cry. The man in the next bed said, "My God! You've practically been *living* here!"

He took a decided turn for the worse that night. He survived eleven more days, and at three A.M. of the last day mumbled: "Dying, and you . . . no one wanted you . . . not even Alice. She begged for younger child. Good money . . . you . . ."

He died at four-ten A.M. She went to the desk and informed the nurse on duty and went home. She didn't wake Alice, who looked almost as bad at this stage as her departed husband, but before leaving (with one suitcase and a hundred sixteen dollars) she paused in the bedroom doorway. She wanted to ask how such tricks could be played on people. She wanted to say, "You called me daughter. How could it all be a plan, a lie?"

She wrote a brief note saying she was going to Philadelphia. And then she walked three miles to the diner where the bus stopped. . . .

She was awake. She heard sounds. For a moment she thought she was sitting beside the bed in Bannesville General, steeling herself for the next flood of invective.

It was Mr. Wheeler. He was clearing his throat. Light stood in the windows. She lay quietly, not wanting to face living just yet.

"Eve. You awake, Eve?"

She wouldn't answer. He would let her sleep a while longer. "*Eve!*"

A special kind of man. Not soft, not considerate. But never a whiner, never a complainer. A man who frightened her in certain ways. But one who never asked for a free ride, who always paid for what he got. *And he would pay a lot more if she agreed to his spoken, and unspoken, terms.*

She sat up. "Yes?"

"Feel like another . . . swim. This time, you swim . . . with me. Got bikini?"

She said no. He said she should go to the shopping center and buy one. She said her suit was good enough.

"Tell Mary . . . your size. That's an order!"

He was smiling as she came to the bed. He held out his hand, and his spirit, his growing joy, was infectious. She took the hand. "All right, Mr. President."

He looked at her, and then shook his head. "No . . . not Mr. President. Not with you. A private . . . person with you."

"All right, Mr. Wheeler."

Again he shook his head. "Time for . . . Mike."

She smiled, but she couldn't make herself say it. A "special man," and you didn't call a special man "Mike." At least not yet.

She dressed him and he asked her to get a hat from the row of five on his closet shelf. He put it on, the big, gray western hat she remembered from pictures in the Philadelphia home, from vague memory-pictures of the President when she was a child of six or seven. He looked at himself in the mirror, and he sighed and took the hat off and told her to put it away. She said she thought he'd looked fine. He said no, not the way he wanted to look.

She put the hat back in the closet, and returned to him. He was still looking into the mirror. She put her hand on his shoulder. At that his face changed, grew hopeful again. "We'll make it," he said, voice strong. "You just . . . stick around . . . and see, Eve."

She thought she might at that.

9

SATURDAY, JANUARY 21, A.M.

He finished "Honeysuckle Rose," his fifth number, and did his little ducking, bobbing bow right and left and center, and realized for the first time that the audience wasn't his. He'd expected some initial resistance—he'd had plenty during the last three years when playing cities hit by riots—but there'd been good applause after the opener and solid laughs for his patter, and the little "Blue Bugaloo" dance had brought heavier applause and a few whistles.

But this was an opening night, and there was a certain electricity that ran between him and his audience on opening nights and big-event nights, building from that first number and growing and hitting its peak around the fifth or sixth.

It wasn't here.

No boos. No hecklers. No one making faces. Few nonapplauders that he could see. So Christopher was dead wrong to worry about strong-arm, and Tonto wasn't needed.

But no electricity.

God damn! This was his opening night and he could see

Benny Barker with Marjory Fine's party in the first tier. Benny smiling his fat-cat smile, the mother! Benny laughing inside because he knew what was happening, could feel the audience slipping away, was enjoying it . . .

He turned to Stan. "Ladies and gentlemen, this fair-haired lad . . ."

Stan touched his head and frowned. The audience chuckled. It was the first colored gag Wally had allowed himself, and he knew he was beginning to press. But maybe a little opening up of the white-black situation was called for.

". . . is known for his fast fingers, and matching temper. So will the first three rows . . . tiers? . . . half-bagels? . . ."

The laughter increased.

". . . please look out, 'cause I'm about to change the program he rehearsed."

Stan rose, monster-like, eyes bulging, arms stiffly outstretched. Ace and Dee rushed to restrain him. The laughter was building when Wally said, "Looks like that picture in this morning's papers, doesn't it?" then knew with sinking heart he'd made one hell of an error in judgment. The laughter rose in spots, where the never-die liberals whooped for him, but dipped everywhere else. It was as if he'd said shit-piss-corruption into that mike.

"Sooo, as the creative consultant for a hotel down the street would put it . . . And *awaaay* we go!" He turned to Stan, who was shaking his head just enough so that Wally could see. Stan was warning him not to do the blue-black songs. And he hadn't intended to. The next scheduled number was "Baby, It's Cold Outside," and that's just what he'd been about to do. The change-of-program line was nothing but a reaction to the lack of electricity, an attempt to build a little laughter. But Stan's being *that* worried made Wally's hackles rise.

He turned back to the audience. "You see that bird fightin' me?"

Those in the audience hip to the term "bird" laughed. No, they *snickered*, and Wally realized he was getting down too low, he was beginning to fight on the wrong level.

He looked out over the rising tiers, the near-thousand people, the opening night crowd that should have been in his pocket by now, loving him and rooting in each song, each gag, and his entertainer's heart reached out for them and he fought the germ of anger, of resentment of them as individuals that threatened his cool, his magic, his control. He stood quietly, waiting for the laughter and the talk to die away. It didn't die as quickly as it should have. They weren't hungry enough for that next song.

He said, "We can make it, people! We can *fly* tonight!" and snapped his head at Stan and murmured, "I've Got It Bad," which he'd been saving as a show-closer, his third encore, but which he needed now—the song he did so well it had sparked a recent album to golden-disc status.

It was a slow number, but one with a beat, especially in his arrangement. He laced into the opening all alone, his strong, slightly acid voice cutting through the continuing murmurs. He fixed his eyes a little above the top tier so as not to see *this* audience, so as to sing to all the audiences who had ever loved him, and whom he had loved for their bringing him fame and riches and what had been a reality until recently, partial freedom from being black.

> Never treats me,
> Sweet and gentle,
> The way she should . . .

Ace came in with three dynamic, booming beats of the big drum, Wally whipping his right arm with each beat.

"I got it *baaad*" (the whole trio swinging in solidly), "and that ain't good!"

The crowd reacted, stirring.

> My poor heart is *sen*timental,
> Not made of *wood!*
> I got it bad, and that ain't no-how good!

The trio played with that extra touch of drive, and he sang it as if it had been written this morning, for him alone. He used his entire body, reaching, reaching for the heart of the song and the heart of the audience, reaching for what was unique and perfect in himself and that he could find only when he sang, and most often when he sang this song.

> . . . and Monday *rolls* around,
> I end up like I *start* out,
> Just crying . . . my heart out!

He was sweating the good sweat, fighting the good fight, and all his tightness was gone and he lowered his eyes to those front tiers where he could distinguish faces, and he sang to them, and he saw Barker, and even that dirty mother was listening, looking away but listening. Even that dirty mother knew that this song sung this way was the truth. And Wally felt he had them, at last he had them, all of them!

He sang, God, he sang! He wanted a worldwide mike, he sang so well. He was willing to make *this* song *this* minute the criterion of judging Wally Jones forever.

He drew into a crouch, putting his guts into his throat and his throat into the mike. And finished with an explosive uncoiling of voice and body—"*Yeah!*"—leaping up and trying to embrace them all.

They applauded. For a weekday evening in Chicago, okay. For an opening in Miami Beach, not okay.

He said, "Thank you, thank you. I've been noticing that others in the audience are *also* wearing formal attire. Yes, *I'm* in formal dress. Lenox Avenoo formal."

He turned completely around as the laughs came—laughing-at-the-nigger laughs, but he was asking for them, wasn't he? He showed them his pale green tunic, no lapels, eight buttons down the front; his tight white ribbed trousers with wide cuffs; his boot-type black shoes. He pointed at everything, describing the outfit as if it were tails. He milked the laughs, mocking himself and beginning to hate them for making him do this. He'd done it before—but never with this much anger.

". . . cost three thousand dollars."

The audience paused, puzzled by the figure, not knowing where the laugh lay.

"Honest. Three thousand. Of course, that's after credit charges, carrying charges, and one hell of an alteration charge."

The laughter trickled in, and he said, "*You* can get it for thirty-two dollars."

The laugh rose to respectable proportions.

"Just don't buy it in Harlem," he said, which wasn't part of the joke and blurred its outlines and cut the laughter.

But what the hell, he'd lost them anyhow. He could go on singing and gagging and tomorrow's local papers would give him decent reviews, but short in comparison to the rehash of the Astrid Kane story. He could sing his guts out and they would applaud politely and never know what it was he could have given them, what it was they could have given each other, what it was—as much as money—that he worked for.

He turned to Stan. "Gin for Christmas."

Stan nodded, and there was death in that nod.

He sang it. And "Every Bit of It." And "What's the Matter Now?"

. . . haven't seen ya baby since a way las' spring,
Tell me pretty momma have you *broke* that thing?

He sang "Why Was I Born?" He sang "My Daddy's Blues."

My brother took the Santa Fe,
My momma took in wash,
My sister took the easy way,
And that is how the soul folk play
The game . . . the game of life, my child.
The game . . . the game you'll play, my child.

He sang eight blue-black numbers, and finished with a comic rendition of "Cal'donia," but it was too late to make out it was a great big joke. The applause was polite, perhaps a little less polite than it might otherwise have been, but there were enough shouts and whistles from the scattered rooters to justify his one encore—which he would have done even if they'd been coming at him with tar and feathers.

He sang "Black and Blue," and walked off and went to his dressing room and locked the door—not just closed it but turned the bolt and didn't open when the knocking came and the well-wishers came. Stan and the boys called to him. He said, "See ya tomorrow, cats, and we'll start all over."

"Well, it was fine," Dee said. "It was *art*, baby."

He shook his head in the mirror. Anger was what it was. Pain was what it was.

And now that it was over, he began to be afraid. He didn't want to be a so-called "artist," singing for a few thousand fans. He wanted to stay what he was—Wally Jones, who sang for *millions*, and almost all of them white, and no piss-poor hippies, druggies, or dropouts need apply.

That was what he had and that was what he wanted.

But tonight he felt it beginning to change. Tonight he felt a shifting in the solid structure of his success. Like those slag heaps that stay solid as mountains for twenty, fifty, a hundred years—and then one day begin to quiver and then one day begin to slide and then become lousy piles of mud.

He sat where he was. He closed his eyes and sat just where he was.

She didn't plan it. They went to Marjory Fine's suite after the show and Dick Christopher was there and she wanted to leave. Bruce asked why—and she found herself telling him, right there on the couch with her father chatting at the bar and Dick near the windows glancing her way and people all around them talking about Wally Jones's performance and whether it was good or not so good and why he wasn't here. When she reached the part about marrying Jonathan Everett Standers, Bruce looked quickly around and said, "Wait." But she didn't. He was her man and he had to know. And it felt so *good* telling him that she just couldn't wait.

He drew her close, drew her head to his shoulder and her mouth to his ear. She held his hand with both of hers, spilling out all the fear and confusion of the past few weeks. She felt that hand tighten several times, and told him about her tormentor's last call and how her father had the cash ready in the hotel safe.

With that she had nothing more to say. She knew she should be anxiously awaiting his first comment, but she wasn't. She stroked his arm.

"You've *lived* for your years, haven't you?"

"Yes. And more years than you figured." But still she wasn't anxious. He was hers, if she wanted him. Being a few years older wouldn't make any difference, she knew that now.

But *how* did she know? Had he demonstrated love over so long a period of time that she could be sure of him in all circumstances? Obviously not, and so it was a matter of her knowing she had more than herself to offer, and that he was aware of it, intensely interested in it . . .

She straightened, the thoughts bothering her. He said, "Let's go somewhere. I have opinions, and they may not be the same as yours."

"Opinions? I see only facts."

"Facts are the past. I mean what you're going to do about that voice, that blackmailer."

She shook her head a little. "I don't want to do anything but what he said I should do. . . ."

They were walking past the spotlighted pool, toward the beach. It was mild now, and she said tomorrow's forecast was for a really hot day. She'd interrupted Bruce. He'd been saying there was no point in paying such a huge sum without first testing the blackmailer's "starch."

"I'm speaking of a small fortune, Ellie, and you bring up the weather."

It was the first time she'd heard sharpness in his voice. They reached the railing and she looked out at the sea. "It's my small fortune, darling."

He didn't answer. She tried to resist the quick feeling of remorse, of fear that she might have hurt him. (She also tried to fight the feeling that no matter *what* she said, he wouldn't allow himself to be hurt.) She waited, and finally glanced at him.

"That's not exactly true, Ellie. At least it won't be, soon. It'll be *our* small fortune."

She laughed, the sound torn from her by shock.

"That voice isn't the only possible blackmailer. *I* also know everything."

She looked up into his face, and nodded. He said, "We have a covenant now, you and I. Your trust, your future well-being, is in my hands. You placed it there. You brought me into your life at Sanibel. You *locked* me into it tonight. You can't make me leave, and I can't get out. You have to accept that. You can't expect that I'll stand on ceremony in anything concerning your life any more."

Again she nodded.

"I'm not saying I should *dictate* what you'll do. Never that. Just as I'll never let you dictate what I should do. An exchange of opinions, Ellie. This is the first serious exchange."

"Yes," she whispered, and the good feeling was back. She had a partner now. Not just a lover but a full partner. In her problems. In her possessions. The last was what made the first possible. It was payment of sorts, but it didn't bother her now. Nothing bothered her now.

"If I don't pay," she said, "he could make the marriage public. If he does that, I lose the payments. And—if the Wheelers suspect that I had a part in it, they could be ruthless. You know what they say about absolute power corrupting absolutely? The Wheeler fortune and political position equal absolute power."

"Why should they suspect you had a part in it, when you stand to lose so much and gain so little?"

"I already have much. The Metropole will keep me and my father more than comfortable the rest of our lives." She hesitated. "And I've never forgiven the Wheelers for what they did—forcing Jonny's hand that way. Of course, I realize he must have had second thoughts on his own—that he could have refused . . ." She suddenly hugged him around the middle. "For the first time I don't really mind!"

He stroked her head. "About the blackmailer. You said that if you didn't pay, he could make the marriage public. What would he gain if he did that?"

"What does any blackmailer gain when he makes good a threat? The satisfaction of hurting the person who thwarted his plans. Anyway, the threat is enough for me."

"It shouldn't be. I think that whether you pay a hundred fifty thousand, or twenty-five thousand, he'll still be back for more, next month or next year. As long as we pay *something*, something substantial, he won't throw away his chance of a continuing income. And we'll gain time to discover his identity."

She held him closer. She wanted his help, yes, but she wanted something else even more. Her cheek pressed his chin. "Golden Boy . . ."

"Ellie, don't pay it all."

"I'm afraid."

"Let me handle it. Refer him to me."

"If he refuses to deal with you?"

"Then whatever he tells you to do, I'll be the one to do it."

"How can you be sure?"

"I'm not sure of anything. Maybe I'll end up paying it all, and maybe I won't, but I don't want you dealing with him."

"And I don't want to deal with him. I don't want to think of it any more. I want to forget it and concentrate on you."

He kissed her, but it was a brief thing, preempted by thoughts of small fortunes and blackmailers. "I'm going to be available to you from now on," he said.

"Goody. Are you available right this moment?"

"Yes. But first—"

"No, *second*. First . . ." Her kiss held him; her body movement strengthened the hold; his hand slid over her bottom.

"We have to plan . . ."

"Squeeze it," she whispered, her voice shaking. "I loved the way you did it Wednesday."

He looked around, then kissed her and squeezed her bottom and pressed a finger between the cheeks, making her remember and making her shake with longing. Longing to have it all again. Longing to forget everything but having it all again.

When he lifted up his head, she said, "It's such a beautiful night, I wish we could do it right here, up against the railing, hearing the waves and seeing the sky."

"You romantic, you," he said, and it broke her up. They laughed a long time, holding to each other, and then went to the car park and his Jaguar.

He couldn't have known he would feel this way, and denied to himself that he actually did. What did *pity* have to do with his feelings for Ellie DeWyant? Especially now that she was so happy with him, so open in her expressions of love. Especially now that he had a role to play beyond that of lover—now that he could serve her, absorb her problems, stand between her and the ugliness of that blackmailer.

Their lovemaking, from his point of view, was much better than it had been on Sanibel. He was sure of her, free of doubt, able to enjoy that marvelous body without obstructive thoughts. (Except that once he had to push away the image of President Standers doing what he was doing, of Ellie crying out, "Oh, Mr. *President!*" which was ridiculous on the face of it and nothing but camp pornography, and what was pornography of any sort doing in his mind while he was making love to the girl he would marry?)

Afterward, she sat lotus fashion, legs tucked into each other and arms crossed over her breast, talking to him as he lay on

279

his back. She stopped him from drawing up the blanket. "I want to look at you."

"And you all covered by arms and legs?"

She glanced down at herself. "Not quite *all* covered."

Passion revived and he pulled her down beside him. And insisted he did *not* feel pity, sadness for her, anything but lust and love . . .

Pity because she was getting him and not the man who would think of nothing beyond Ellie DeWyant? Pity because she had lost that man and suffered despite payoffs and hotels and all the things that he, the man she was getting, valued above men and women and anything on earth?

She said, "When will it happen?"

He knew what she meant. "Whenever you say."

"I'll tell my father tomorrow—I mean today, as soon as he gets up—or as soon as I get up." She laughed, snuggling into his body. "I can't think now. I can only feel. And I feel *alive*, after so long not feeling alive. And it's all because of you, Mr. Golden Boy. Thank you, thank you—" she was covering his face with little kisses— "thank you, thank you, thank you . . ."

It hurt him, and he insisted there was no reason for the hurt and he stopped her voice with his mouth.

"Wally Jones," the fat woman said, nudging her husband and Wally waved and went past them and past the other people beginning to turn and look. Always before this had been the kick, being recognized, but now he wondered when the hell people went to sleep out here and what was the sense of having sat in his dressing room two hours when they were still standing around the lobby and doing whatever the hell it is these vacation types did. He didn't want to go to his suite and he didn't want to go to Marjory Fine's party and he couldn't stay here. So he broke his Miami rule.

He went out the revolving door to the car-park booth. "Hey, man, where're the cabs?" The blond kid looked up and blinked.

"On the street, Mr. Jones, but I'll get one." Wally nodded and turned away.

What was it like to be a blond kid in Miami? What was it like to be a blond kid anywhere in the States? Wally Jones was the biggest, and he couldn't buy what it was like to be a blond kid in Miami.

Shit! He peeled a five off his roll, and when the kid opened the door of the cab he tucked it in the pocket of his shirt. "Toward your next orgy," he said, and hopped in. The kid checked the bill and smiled.

A cool smile. No flip. No snap, crackle, pop. It would take a century to do that. And Wally Jones saved his century tips for the chicks.

But this was the South. He had to remember that. Not that he advertised all the white ass he got anywhere else, either. The public wouldn't approve. It was Aunt Jemima for Wally Jones— like Lisa, whom he'd married a year ago and left six months ago, bored to death with the very same sweetness that had first hooked him. As he'd been bored, eventually, by every chick since Carla, white or black.

Wouldn't all those red-neck bastards, those square honky mothers *plotz* if they knew . . .

The cabby was asking where to, and he said, "Down Collins, baby," and asked himself what the hell was getting into him. Those square honky mothers were his *public!* Those square honky mothers had taken him out of Harlem and given him the world!

All right, tonight was an off night. He'd take a ride and look around and maybe have a quiet drink in a quiet bar.

Make that a quiet *hotel* bar. No use asking for trouble. They'd recognize him in any of the big hotels. He'd get in, if not get cheers. If that Astrid Kane nonsense hadn't happened, he might even have gotten cheers.

An off night. An off gig. A bad scene. All he had to do was stay cool and play it out and he'd be back in New York and back with friends and back to the cheers.

"That place there," he said. It was big and white like all Miami Beach hotels, and just a few blocks away was the Americana's huge electric sign. He gave the driver a ten, said, "Fun," and turned away.

"Mr. Jones," the cabby said. Wally reached for his pen, anticipating an autograph. "You going right inside?"

He dropped his hand, nodding.

"You're not going to do any walking, are you?"

"It's a nice night."

"This is Surfside."

"So?"

The driver's smile was strained. "They're careful here. Strangers on the streets at night . . ."

"Okay, gotcha, *gut nacht*."

"Along Collins to the Americana, no sweat. But otherwise . . ."

So he'd said okay. So what did the man want, a shuffle and a yassah-boss? He strode to the hotel entrance. The doorman stayed put. He walked right up to the center doors, and at the last minute the flunky recognized him and jumped to it. Wally found a buck and passed it on. "Heavy work, baby."

The Melody Bar was almost empty, and close to closing. The bartender moved slowly in the dimness, and Wally said, "Hey, friend, you purvey that great American booze, Scotch?" The bartender recognized the voice, and then the face, "How do you like it, Mr. Jones?" Wally said with water, a double.

A flashy, big-tit chick looked his way. She was alone and spelled *whore*, and still she seemed to be hesitating. Yeah, she was willing, but this was Miami, and if word got around she might end up across the bay in the Central Negro District where the pickings were not only black but lean.

Besides, he rarely used pay dirt. Not with all the chorus lines from coast to coast.

The chick decided to take a chance. She smiled. He smiled back. She waited to see if he would come to her. He lit a cigarette and his drink came and he sipped. The bartender glanced at the chick and then turned his back and worked on bottles. He didn't raise his eyes in the mirror. The chick came over, carrying her glass. "You're Wally Jones." She had a touch of Southern accent.

He said, "Yep."

"You're staying at the Metropole, aren't you?"

"Yep."

"You opened there tonight, didn't you?"

"Yep."

"How'd it go?"

"Nope."

Her eyes blinked vacantly. He said, "Now I get on my horse and ride into the Fontainebleau."

She finally dug and laughed and looked at his cigarette. He brought one out for her and lit it. She took the stool beside his. Sitting at the end of the bar was a big guy with a big woman, both with big, outdoor faces. They got up noisily and the guy slammed some money on the bar and they went out, looking daggers at him all the way.

"Say, I think I know those cats," Wally said.

"Not *those*," the chick said, patting her black wig.

"Sure, I'll remember in a minute." He made a thinking face, then snapped his fingers. "Converts of Elijah Muhammad's!"

Again she laughed. "I don't believe what I read about you and that girl, that friend of Benny Barker's. Everyone knows you and Barker have a feud going."

"Feud. That's a good word."

"What really happened?"

He leaned over and whispered, "She wanted to change her luck. She hounded me and hounded me. Finally, I asked Ben to get her off my back. She went wild—a woman scorned—and tried to slug me in the lobby. I ducked. She hit herself, *blam,* right on the head. I tried to help her and they took that picture."

"Oh, come on now!" She glanced at the bartender, still tending his bottles, and lowered her voice. "What room are you in?"

He really boomed it out. "*What room am I in?*"

The bartender's eyes came up in the mirror. The chick colored to quadroon, minimum. Wally put a five on the bar and a twenty in the chick's hand. "Not tonight," he said, and walked out.

He didn't want to go to another hotel. It was too late anyway. He wanted to walk and think. He wanted to walk where people lived and kids grew up. Those kids would make it different. He believed that. Christ, he *had* to believe that!

Two blocks west and he was among houses. Another block and the lights and traffic of Collins were gone. He turned left, walking in the gutter because there were no sidewalks. The smell of ocean was replaced by green smells, tree and grass and flower smells. A dog barked as he passed a house. The air was soft, sweet. He thought of Carla. He thought of their plans to have a house on a street like this, in Hollywood where the barriers had seemed to be coming down. He remembered their talking together, dreaming together, feeling that love would find a way . . .

The light stabbed him like a needle stabs a butterfly. He froze, caught in the piercing white beam, blinded, hearing the car pull up—and remembered what the cabbie had said.

A door opened and someone got out.

"Listen, I'm Wally—"

"Just stand quiet," the voice from the car said. A pleasant enough voice, with no more than a touch of the South, like that whore's. "Police."

"Okay. Just wanted—"

"He said *quiet*," another voice said. It was behind him, and the shove caught him unprepared. He staggered forward and slammed into the side of the car. He bounced off it, and was shoved again, hard.

"Hands on the roof, legs apart . . ."

He was pulled and pushed into the position they wanted. He was out of that beam of light, but his eyes were still blinded. He leaned forward, knees trembling, and felt himself being searched. Damned thorough. A faggot would have a ball playing cops and robbers here.

He closed his eyes, trying to bring back sight more quickly. The voice behind him said, "Turn around."

He pushed himself away from the car and turned. The spotlight was off. A tall cop was using a flashlight to examine a wallet. *His* wallet, Wally realized.

"Jones, Wallace," the cop read, and looked up. "What're you doing on the streets at three-thirty, Jones?"

"A walk," he said, trying to smile. He would explain, politely, and they would apologize, politely, and that would be that.

But he couldn't find the proper spirit in him for politeness. He knew it was necessary with cops—for whites as well as blacks—but everything worked against it and all he could say was, "A little walk."

The cop waited. Wally reached into his pocket for cigarettes. He was stiff-armed in the chest and slammed backward, and the next thing he knew he was facing a gun. "Just wanted a cigarette."

The cop in the car got out, older and heavier than the first one. He took the wallet. "You Wally Jones, the singer?"

"Yes." His voice was tight and dry.

"What're you doing away from your hotel?"

Away from his hotel. Away from his cage. "I told you. Taking a walk."

"What's wrong with Collins?"

Wally shrugged. That damned gun was still out and pointing at him. But he wouldn't talk up a storm! He wouldn't give them smiles and chatter and the satisfaction of hearing him *plead!*

"Get in."

The gun was returned to its holster. The older cop walked around the car and got back behind the wheel. The younger cop motioned at the open door. Wally got in and the younger cop followed and the door slammed. He was sandwiched between them. They U-turned and really moved. The younger cop said, "Your wallet."

He took it and held it, not wanting to touch them while putting it away.

"Not much money for a star," the younger cop said.

Wally didn't answer.

"We could book you for vagrancy," the older cop said.

Wally felt like a creaky piece of machinery. He didn't want to, but he had to begin functioning. "I carry my money in a roll in my pocket."

"Better for the crap games, right?" the older cop said, and chuckled.

Wally glanced at the younger cop, and was sure he looked embarrassed. "No," the younger cop said. "Better for those brown babes. A roll. You know what they say about being *rich*, Ed?"

Wally knew. *Nigger rich.* A few big bills on the outside and all the rest ones. He could have shown them they were wrong. He could have shown them almost a grand.

"You taking me in?" he asked, his voice not the way he wanted it.

They didn't answer. They turned and drove and turned again, and he recognized Collins Avenue. They were approaching the Bal Metropole. He was so relieved he couldn't help himself. "You boys drop by Monday night with your wives and see the show."

"That's white of you," the older cop said.

Wally looked at him. No reaction at all.

"Martin and Faller," the younger cop said. "I'll bring my girl."

"Just take your walks before three A.M.," the older cop said.

"We'll call the club tomorrow," the younger one said. "Martin and Faller."

"Better let you off here," the older cop said, and pulled over on the opposite side of Collins from the hotel. "They'll think you were pinched for hitting that girl."

The younger cop got out. Wally got out. The younger cop put his hand on Wally's shoulder. He was a nice-looking young guy with a nice smile. "Thanks again. Don't forget—"

"I know," Wally said. "Martin and Faller."

The younger cop said, "Right," and got back in and the patrol car pulled away.

Wally walked across Collins, not being careful, and a car

286

blasted its horn at him. He put his head down, cursing steadily.

He kept telling himself to take it easy, nothing had happened, they'd have done the same to a white guy found wandering their streets at night, that was what a community paid its cops for, too bad they weren't as sharp in Harlem, he'd been rougher to them than they'd been to him, they'd saved him cab fare . . .

Why had he played Tom and asked them to the show!

He hated himself for that. He should have let them book him. He hated himself for not having the guts of a teen-age slum kid— the guts and the pride!

Cool it, he told himself. *You're a star.* He walked through the lobby and the night manager called, "Good night, Mr. Jones."

In the elevator, a couple nodded at him and the woman asked if he would give her his autograph and he signed an envelope.

Cool it, baby.

He got to the suite and let himself in, and there was Chink. He'd forgotten. He'd given her a key and asked her to be here at three, figuring he'd cut out from Marjory Fine's party around then.

She said, "If it was possible, I'd say you were pale." She wanted to know if he was all right, and he said, "Yeah, let me make a call." He phoned Marjory Fine and apologized, saying he'd been so beat he'd fallen asleep and please let's stay friends. She said, "Of course, Wally," and he sent her a kiss and she returned it.

He called room service and Chink went to take a shower. They had steak and chicken and two bottles of champagne. Chink didn't ask about the show and he figured she'd heard. He didn't need talk anyway, not with anyone like her around. She was about his height and built like a solid gold shit-house. She had jet-black hair, silky-rich and long, and creamy white skin, and lips like pale rose petals. Her green eyes had a touch of slant, yeah, but she was about as Chinese as he was. Her great-grandmother had been Oriental—no one was sure just what—and the rest of her family white. She billed herself as Bea Chan, but her real name was Bea Arnold. She was just good enough a hoofer for the China reviews, so that was where she did her thing.

In bed he went wild, really took off. Afterward she turned on her side, away from him, and he remembered some of the things he'd said. "Hump it you white cunt," and similar sweet lyrics.

"I didn't mean it," he said, touching her shoulder.

"I think you did."

"Aw, Bea, you know I dig you as a person. You *know* that."

"Maybe. But, still, you meant it when you said it."

"It was the opening, baby."

"Whatever it was—" her voice was thickening— "I don't want any part of it. I don't want to be hated while I'm loving."

She cried, and he brought her the last of the champagne and talked about a trip to Europe in the summer and how he wanted her to come along as part of a new show he was heading up. She drank the champagne and nodded, but he knew something even if she didn't. He'd turned her off. He'd made her white and him black, and it had never been that way with them, not inside where it counted.

She left. There was a sheaf of telegrams under the door. Congrats from Nat and the agents and two dozen others, most from New York and some from L.A. And three from Miami: Claude DeWyant, Marjory Fine, and Bea Chan. More would come tomorrow; he was sure of it. The Senator's would be among them.

But it should have been here *tonight!* The main reason he was playing Miami was to honor that ofay . . .

He went to bed and had nightmares. In them he was black. He *was* black, but he never dreamed about it—not with the rest of the cast-of-thousands glaringly, fluorescently white.

He was awake in two hours, knowing he wouldn't be able to sleep again.

Dan Berner was up at six-thirty, in the Bon Bouche for breakfast at seven, out on the deck at seven-thirty. It was cool and he buttoned his red cardigan as he walked toward the beach, passing two couples in evening dress leaning wearily against the dew-damp railing.

He walked along the shore close to the sea. It was quiet, incredibly quiet for Miami Beach in season. It was as if the near-solid line of hotels and motels didn't exist, as if the thousands of tourists were thousands of miles away.

Christopher had made him an offer. Get on the ball and operate the way he'd been operating, and when the Presidency was his there would be a government position. No name for it yet, but a big one.

Eunuchs had risen to great heights in Eastern civilizations. He could start a trend in the U.S.A.

He laughed, and without thinking began to run. Pain stabbed deep—the stern finger of the schoolmaster. *Now, Daniel, let's have your answer.*

He gave it by phoning Dr. Sochall's office as soon as he entered his room. A recording reminded him that it was still too early, and he called the home number. The doctor answered.

"Did I wake you?"

"No, I was shaving."

"Will you operate on me yourself?"

"Unless you have someone else in mind."

"The fun is all yours, Doctor. I'm available any time after next Saturday."

"I'd like it to be sooner."

"Sorry."

"The following Monday, then."

"Your office?"

"No. I'll make arrangements to have you admitted to the hospital Sunday afternoon. We'll operate Monday morning."

"Can't wait, eh?"

"I want to give you the benefit of every possible moment."

"I know." He switched the phone to his right hand, his left going numb from gripping so hard. "I appreciate it."

"That's a doctor's satisfaction, Dan."

"That and his fee."

Sochall laughed. Dan said, "Well, you'll want to get back to your shaving. You don't cut yourself very often, do you?"

Sochall laughed again. "Nothing but a local anesthetic for you, Dan. I can use a few laughs while operating."

Dan chuckled. Sochall said, "Is there anything you want to ask me? Anything that will help you through the next week?"

"Sleeping pills will help me through the next week."

"I'll phone the hotel pharmacy—"

"Another joke, Doctor. Whiskey will do." He paused. "Will I be . . . lethargic? After the orchiectomy, I mean."

"It's not certain we'll do the orchiectomy Monday. It may be—"

"I know. But will I?"

"Less energetic. But all the organs, all the muscles that determine energy will be there, so it'll be up to you to restore *motive* for energy."

"I'll have motive, Doctor. I have a stimulating career now, and might have a really exciting one in the future."

"Then you're a lucky man."

Dan laughed, and choked on it, and was suddenly crying. "Poetry," he said. "Women and song. The beauty projected by desire."

"There's no answer to that, Dan. But to live long is to grow weary of poetry, women, song, the beauty projected by desire. To live long is to lose the libido. You're no boy. It would have begun to dip sharply anyway. It probably has already, if you'll compare your capacity, your enthusiasms, with what they were ten years ago, twenty years ago."

"Yes. I noticed changes. But that could have been because of my condition—" He stopped himself. "It goes in circles, doesn't it? Questions and answers and why hast Thou forsaken me. It'll all come out on the operating table, won't it, Doctor?"

"I hope that's not another joke."

On that last laugh they said good-bye.

At nine he called the Senator's suite and was told to come up. Christopher met him at the door, wearing a truly baronial black silk dressing gown, heavily figured and sweeping the floor. "Shades of Alexander Hamilton," Dan murmured. "Don't let the electorate see you in *that*."

Christopher grinned. Bryan Whitelock poured coffee and they sat down and began to talk. After a while Christopher said, "Glad to have you aboard again, Dan. I was beginning to worry. Want a sympathetic ear, now that whatever was bothering you no longer is?"

"Just a matter of making a difficult decision, Senator. I made it. End of eternal truths and all that sort of jazz."

"Good. Now the last draft still leaves much, *too* much, to be desired. . . ."

10

SATURDAY, JANUARY 21, P.M.
TO
SUNDAY, JANUARY 22, A.M.

He didn't turn directly toward the right and Ellie's suite as he came out of the elevator. He was in tux, and they were going to dinner and then to Benny Barker's opening in the Platinum Room, but it wasn't eight yet and there was something he wanted to do. He walked left along the blue-carpeted corridor and left again, around the corner to the three adjoining suites that took up the entire ocean-frontage on the fourteenth floor. He walked slowly, glancing at each of the gold-colored doors, remembering that McKensil had said the Senator had the center suite and his father-in-law the first, or southernmost. The last was May Krasmer's, who had seemed like a prospect until Ellie had appeared at that party.

He turned back, wondering what the Wheeler clan would feel, what they would *do*, if they ever found out Bruce Golden was privy to the best-kept secret in American politics. They might suspect, after Ellie was married, that she had confided in her

291

husband, but by then he would be a concerned party in the payoff and so quite safe.

Ellie was wearing a short silver sheath, so simple, so perfect for her that he felt an immediate physical response. She read the look on his face and shook her head, smiling. Looking him over, she said, "No one will mistake you for one of our waiters in that, Bruce."

"I should hope not." He had on a ruffled lace shirt, black string tie, short, tight, double-breasted white jacket, and lean black trousers. He reached for her and she held him at arm's length, bending forward to offer her cheek. He was puzzled, until Claude DeWyant appeared, wearing smoking jacket and casual slacks.

They shook hands. DeWyant seemed more reserved than usual, and Bruce guessed at the cause.

DeWyant said, "I'll join you at the Platinum Room, if you don't mind."

"Since when can anyone tell the boss—"

"Or his father-in-law."

Bruce smiled. Ellie took her father's arm. DeWyant said, "I don't usually intrude on my daughter's evenings, but her engagement is a special occasion, wouldn't you say?" His smile was thin.

Ellie murmured, "Nothing so official, Daddy."

"You *will* be getting married, or did I misunderstand?"

Bruce answered before she could, trying to inject some warmth into the conversation. "We will, sir. At a time and place to be determined by Ellie. If she says tomorrow—"

"I think you should allow me to make some arrangements first. I'd like you to hold back on an announcement until I—"

"We may never announce it," Ellie said, her tone brittle. A reaction, perhaps, to something that had occurred before Bruce arrived. "We're not engaged. We're *seeing* each other." She turned, taking a cigarette from a china box on the coffee table. DeWyant held his lighter for her. She inhaled deeply, and tried to smile. "If we decide to get married, we may do it the very day we decide."

"You'll need a license . . ."

She laughed, naturally, and took his arm again. He gave her a look that touched Bruce, and said, "I'm sorry. I'm playing father of the bride." His pause was barely perceptible. "It's a once-in-a-lifetime thrill for me."

So Ellie hadn't told him she'd confided her first marriage in Bruce. Her quick, warning glance confirmed that. Bruce nodded. "We're both in the hands of your daughter."

"An admirable suspension of the male prerogative," DeWyant murmured, his lack of warmth quite clear.

Bruce busied himself lighting a cigarette. He wasn't totally unprepared for resistance. DeWyant knew how little he earned. DeWyant couldn't help but suspect the poor-boy–rich-girl marriage.

Prepared or not, he still felt a tightening of the stomach.

Ellie said, "Maybe you *shouldn't* join us, Daddy," voice brittle again.

Bruce said, "I'd feel very badly about that, Ellie." And then, jumping into it, "We'll have to grow used to each other, unless you expect to avoid your father the rest of your life."

It shocked them both. They'd flashed their little daggers, but it had only been a game. These two were basically devoted to each other.

"I'd prefer to have everything out in the open, Mr. DeWyant. I'd prefer to have any problems settled now. I can understand that you might have fears for your daughter—"

"Not *fears*," DeWyant murmured.

Bruce said, "Then join us. I haven't *totally* relinquished my male prerogatives. I insist on it."

Ellie said, "Forgive me, Daddy."

DeWyant put his arm around her, then turned to the bar. He poured Cognac and brought it to them in fragile crystal stemware. "To your happiness," he said, looking at his daughter. Bruce repeated it, also to Ellie. Ellie said, "You *are* joining me in this marriage, aren't you, darling?" They all laughed, but Bruce felt something other than pleasure. He tossed down his drink, along with DeWyant. Ellie sipped slowly, pausing to smoke. DeWyant said, "I hear Barker's primed with new material—material he held out from his last three television shows so as to have a smash opening."

"I'm looking forward to it," Bruce said. "He's a client, you know."

"How long do you expect to stay on with Andy?"

"Not very long."

"I've asked him to give notice Monday, Daddy."

DeWyant nodded, looking at his empty glass.

"I don't want him doing anything but concentrating on me. At least for a while. It's important."

Again DeWyant nodded, and raised his eyes. Now it was Bruce who looked at his glass.

"There's no problem," DeWyant murmured. "I can put him—Bruce—on the payroll . . ."

"That won't be necessary," Bruce said, though damn it, it *was*. He had no more than a month's living left in the bank, and Ellie *had* asked him to be available to her from now on.

All right, in a month they'd be married, and whether or not DeWyant had him on the payroll would be academic.

"We'll talk about it later, Daddy. All three of us," she added quickly.

DeWyant collected their glasses and they stood chatting—about everything but what was on their minds.

Bruce felt perspiration trickling down his sides. He'd suspected there would be some problems, but nothing like this—nothing that came from inside himself.

Ellie said, "We'd better go." Gratefully, Bruce led her to the door. She looked back. "See you about eleven?"

DeWyant nodded.

They went out, Bruce controlling the exhalation of breath. She said, "What happened? How did it get so unpleasant?"

"Unpleasant?"

"*Don't*, Bruce. When I told him about it, he seemed quite pleased. Or maybe I didn't really see what he felt, just what I

294

expected him to feel. We didn't get much chance to talk about it. I told him only half an hour ago."

"I think he reacted exactly as he should have."

"Do you really?"

"Fathers aren't expected to like poor sons-in-law."

They were approaching the elevators. She hugged his arm. "You're not poor, darling. You're as wealthy as he is. *Exactly.*"

She was laughing, and he was looking into her face, beginning to loosen up and feel something like he should have felt, when her eyes shifted and her laugh froze, literally froze on her lips and in her throat. He looked up. An elevator was open. The old man in the wheelchair was coming out, his nurse behind him.

"Miss DeWyant," the old man said, stopping. He smiled. "It's been . . . a long time. You're even . . . more lovely . . . than . . ." He stopped, then resumed. "More lovely . . . than ever."

"Thank you." Her voice was level—icy cold and level. The nurse looked at her curiously.

"Would you . . . and your companion . . . care to join . . . me in a . . . drink?"

The nurse murmured, "Just briefly, please. He's had a long day."

"My master's . . . voice." He smiled. He looked a lot better to Bruce than the day he'd checked in. He was tanned, and his head no longer sagged to the side. With his western hat and boots, people might soon begin to recognize him again.

"No thank you," Ellie said, stepping around him toward the elevator which waited with doors open. The doors chose to shut at that very moment.

The old man turned in his chair. "Fate dictates . . ."

Bruce would have loved to have a drink with the old tyrant. He would have loved to talk to the man who had been one of the nation's strongest, if not best-loved, Presidents; the man who had used his daughters, and their willingness to accept his choice of their suitors, as a means of building a political dynasty, the Wheeler clan. The man he would ask for help if and when he identified that blackmailer. But he said, "I'm afraid we're already late."

"Some other . . . time," the old man said, his eyes moving over Ellie, his admiration clear. Yet he had booted her out of Jonathan Standers' life like so much excess baggage, bought her compliance and silence with money and threats—an unbeatable combination, Bruce had to admit—because he'd had a goal and Ellie stood in the way of his achieving it.

And now she was being booted into *a life, Bruce Golden's, because Bruce had a goal* . . .

All this thinking, sweating, moralizing! Was it part of the proverbial jitters that hit men when they approached marriage?

An elevator arrived. Bruce said, "Good evening," and followed Ellie into it. The doors closed. Ellie looked down.

"It's not all *that* bad." He smiled and took her hand. "Forgive and forget. He made restitution, and is still making it."

She looked at him, and his smile died. "A joke, Ellie. I can't dislike him as you do, because he made me and you possible."

She said, "Yes," and the elevator stopped and a couple got on. It stopped three times, filling with laughing, talking, excited people. This was Saturday night, another big opening night, and the hotel was jumping. People were primed for food, drink, entertainment, and action. This was what Miami Beach was famous for, and he and Ellie owned a piece of it.

But her eyes were down, her face was pale, her hand lay still and dead in his.

In the lobby she began to come out of it. He talked steadily, joking, stopping to say hello to Marjory Fine, who stood surrounded by her usual group of soon-to-be-guests. Ellie answered Marjory's greeting, then looked past her and said, "I'm really *starved*, Bruce." They walked away, and he realized she was gripping his hand so hard it actually hurt.

"That short man and woman. Prager, I think their name is. They came to my table my first day here. They talked to me—the man did. He said things . . ."

They entered the Vale Room and were shown to a ringside

table. Ellie wanted a martini and he ordered two. She talked about the Pragers. It didn't sound like much, and she hadn't thought much of it when it actually happened, but now she felt there might be a connection between Mr. Prager and that voice at the party and on the phone. "Looking at him, I suddenly felt—*afraid*, Bruce."

"It's meeting Wheeler. It's the excitement and pressure of everything that's happened. I'm feeling it myself. But I'll talk to Mr. Prager first chance I get. Find out what he does for a living—"

"Manufactures clothing, I think."

"I'll check on him. And he'll turn out to be just what he says he is."

She sighed. "I suppose so."

"Our blackmailer is more likely to be someone who works in or near the hotel. A cabana-boy type who's seen you several seasons and heard a rumor and made a very lucky guess. Like the man found shot on the beach."

"You don't think *that's* part of it?"

"No, I was just drawing a parallel. That type is usually mixed up in underworld projects. Out for the easy buck . . ." He paused then, finding it difficult to gather his thoughts, and dropped it when the waiter brought their drinks.

She felt better after the martini, and so did he. They had a leisurely dinner, and later they danced. He held her close against him and her gown was a second skin and he reacted strongly. She whispered, "If my father didn't expect us at the opening . . ."

"It's a long night, Ellie. We'll find time for everything."

"*Everything?*"

He tightened his hold.

Mr. Wheeler admitted he was tired, but he wanted a drink—bourbon—and a sponge bath. Eve said she would be speaking to Dr. Cormond Monday morning and would bring up the question of hard liquor. As for the bath, it wasn't necessary. He'd had one before leaving Palm Beach.

He didn't argue, but his eyes tried to catch hers.

She busied herself getting him onto the bed, a task that became easier each time because of his growing strength. She began undressing him, still avoiding his eyes, but there was no avoiding the tumescence that appeared when she drew off his undershorts.

She went to the dresser for pajamas and paused there, giving him time to return to normal. When she came back, his eyes were closed, for which she was grateful. The tumescence, however, had increased, and as she began drawing the pajama bottoms up over his knees he sighed and raised his hips in a manner that made her face flame.

She stopped short of the genital area. He was attaining an erection, and it was either strike it or run, and she couldn't do either. The erection was a sign of his continuing recovery, his growing strength, and to treat it as anything else would be cruel. As for leaving the room, that was senseless. She would only have to face the same situation tomorrow and every day afterward.

And then there was their talk—or his talk—of staying on with him and being more than just a nurse and running his house and being in his will. . . .

She stepped to the lamp and put it out.

"Eve."

She neither answered nor looked at him. She grasped the pajama bottoms and worked them up. He wasn't helping her now. He made her struggle. The living room door was open, but she told herself she could see nothing. She felt the pajamas meet resistance, and was rough in overcoming it, yanking hard and dragging them over his hips.

He moaned, but not in pain. "Eve, please . . . help me . . ."

She should have left the room. She was a nurse, not one of his girls.

But she didn't leave, because that would mean leaving his employ. If she decided never to touch him, never to help him, there was no way of staying on. And she wanted to stay on.

So she *was* one of his girls. The last of the line.

Surprisingly, the concept wasn't painful. It took hold as she stood there, and when he repeated the plea she answered, "It's ridiculous. What do you expect me to do?"

"Nothing . . . Eve . . . just touch . . ."

She took his pajama top and worked him into it, continuing to avoid his gaze.

"Eve . . . I have so little . . . to enjoy. So little . . . time . . ."

She was buttoning the last button when she looked and saw the bulge. He was maintaining his erection. The problem wasn't going to disappear this time. She had to make a decision this time.

She sat down at the edge of the bed. His hand grasped her arm. "Act of . . . mercy," he said.

"But it's ridiculous," she whispered. "Ridiculous." She put her hand on him and then into the fly opening. His fingers tightened on her arm. She freed him, held him lightly, noted that he was larger than Jerry. *An act of mercy*, she repeated to herself, and began to stroke him.

He moaned. She said, "It's also dangerous."

"Don't stop! I'll tell you . . . if I feel . . . bad."

She felt his other hand move over her hip. She increased the pressure, and the speed. His hand stroked her bottom, tried to reach around but couldn't.

An act of mercy. But she wasn't sure who was breathing the heaviest.

It went on and on. She grew tired, and shifted position, bending a little closer.

"Yes . . . *that!*"

She said, "Faster?" to prove that she didn't know what he meant.

He didn't answer. She felt he was afraid to. Good thing, too!

She looked at it. The penis didn't show age and sickness as other parts of the body did. And his thighs were still strong, and his belly was heaving. And suddenly she wanted to help him, to have it culminate and not leave him wanting, not after all this.

She didn't know she was going to do it. And when she did, it seemed a minor thing, like stroking him. She moved her mouth over it, and immediately afterward felt the spasm and received a very minute ejaculation. She maintained the pressure of her lips until his gasps quieted and the spasm ended. Then she went to the bathroom.

He was half asleep when she returned. She covered him and he muttered, "I didn't think . . . ever again . . ." His hand found hers. "Now we . . . will stay . . . together . . ."

"Yes." She felt strangely gentle, and sure of herself. "Do you feel all right?"

"Tired. But . . . happy. You're going . . . to be happy . . . too, Eve."

A moment later he was asleep.

She came into the kitchen. She was prepared for a feeling of sin and degradation . . . but instead felt hungry. She had coffee and biscuits and felt fine.

She was still breathing more quickly than usual, and she *wanted* something—but still, fine.

She thought of Jerry then. She should call him. She owed him a call.

She went to the phone, and just as she hadn't known she was going to help Mr. Wheeler, she didn't know she was going to call her mother.

The soft, hesitant voice said, "Hello, who is it?" and she clenched the phone tightly and asked herself why she had done this thing.

"It's me, Eve."

"*Evie!* I've been so worried . . . your note said Philadelphia, but it didn't say where! Thank God you're all right!"

She sounded so concerned, so truly, legitimately concerned. A very good act—or was it self-delusion?

"I'm fine. I'm in Miami Beach, with a patient."

"When are you coming home? I've been so lonely . . ." The soft voice broke.

Tears. Alice Andrews was good at tears.

300

"I'm sorry. I'm not coming home. The job is permanent. I'll be moving to Palm Beach from here."

"Not coming home? But—but when will I see you?"

"I don't know. I just wanted to let you know about me, and to find out how you are."

Alice Andrews began to speak again, but Eve didn't want to hear. She'd phoned. She'd ended Alice's worries. It was over.

"My patient is calling. I really have to go now."

"But will I hear from you again?"

"Maybe. Good-bye . . ." She couldn't call her "Mother," and again said good-bye and hung up.

She took a deep breath and sat there, looking at the phone. Then she called the number Jerry had given her—his home. There was no answer. She called the desk and asked if there were any messages for Mr. Wheeler's suite. There were several, and among them was Jerry's. He wanted her to call him at the Burgundy Room. She got him there.

"Eve? You in the hotel?"

"Yes."

"I'm coming up!"

"All right. Don't shout."

"I mean right now."

"I know. I'll leave the door open, so don't knock."

"Well . . . okay."

She smiled at his surprise, and then surprised him even more.

"Would you stop at the Arcade Pharmacy for me? There are a few items I've been meaning to get. . . ."

She went into the bedroom and past Mr. Wheeler, walking softly but without fear. She got a towel and folded it neatly and brought it to the couch. She hung her bathrobe over a chair, washed her face in the kitchen, and put on some makeup.

Jerry kept her in the foyer a while, and during that while she was set on fire. Then he led her to the couch and removed her clothing. She spread out the towel and lay down on it.

He looked at her. "You sure?"

She said yes. She was sure and she was ready. She was a woman in all other ways now, and this was only the last, most beautiful way.

It didn't seem too beautiful at first. She had a fully formed hymen, and it took some breaking. When it happened, she asked him to stop, and he seemed grateful for the respite. She put on her bathrobe, took the package he'd brought and went to the bathroom. In a moment she was fresh, comfortable, and relatively safe.

They began again. He struggled. She drew up her knees to help him. With that, he went deep into her, clutching her rear with both hands. "My God," he gasped. "So tight!"

It was something men valued, she gathered. Then he was moving, and she began to feel pleasure. The pleasure mounted, and she began to move with him, began to cause friction at the part of her that demanded friction.

He stopped. "Wait, please, Evie . . ."

She waited. She didn't understand why they should stop when it felt so marvelous, but he knew more about these things than she did.

He said, "All right." He didn't move much, clenching his teeth and looking as if he was trying to forget something. *She* moved. She rocked and squirmed and jiggled. She felt it getting better and better—and then he said, "Evie, I can't hold out! Evie . . . I'm—"

She wasn't able to pay much attention to him. Something was ripping loose inside her, and it was so much better than anything she'd ever felt, it took an act of will not to cry out.

He was sitting on the couch, head hanging. "I'm sorry, Evie. Next time will be different."

"I hope not."

He looked up.

"It couldn't be better. It just couldn't. If it was, I'd die."

"Did you? . . ."

She nodded. "I'll bet you thought you were premature."

He bent to kiss her mouth. "Virgins aren't supposed to be this good. Virgins are supposed to be a mess and cry and raise general hell. No one's supposed to have much fun."

"I guess I'm a failure as a virgin."

He laughed, and looked at her, and his surprise was another compliment. He told her to roll over. She was going to ask why, but then didn't. He had said things about her bottom while making love. He liked her bottom.

She rolled over and he touched her and kissed her and murmured, "In a little while . . ."

She excused herself and went to the bathroom again. Then she returned to him. Then they played and he bent her forward, over the arm of the couch, and stood behind her. It was good that way, too. He was very long in finishing, and she had more than enough time to reach her climax. Once, she caught herself thinking of Mr. Wheeler.

They sat on the couch. He smoked and kept his arm around her. It was ten o'clock and she was sleepy and happy. He talked to her. He was better at loving than talking, but he said he wanted to keep seeing her, wanted to come to the suite this way every night. She nodded, thinking they had a week and wouldn't waste it. Afterward, if he decided to continue seeing her, he could come to Palm Beach on her days off. And if anything more developed, if he began to get serious about her, as he hinted he might, and she began to get serious about him, which she wasn't sure she could, then she would rethink her future.

But the present was fine. She supposed she was a fallen woman. Father Garrity would certainly think so. She was Mr. Wheeler's woman and she was Jerry Leech's woman. But she didn't *feel* fallen. She felt . . . complete, and just couldn't believe anything bad could come of it.

They'd had dinner in the suite, Harold wanting to relax and watch television after a full day's swimming, tennis, and sightseeing. Besides, there was no rush tonight. They weren't going to the Barker opening, but to the Fontainebleau's Boom Boom Room for a trio Harold appreciated and some of the Latin dancing at which he excelled.

May was dressed and ready at ten, but he was just entering the shower. As he closed the bathroom door, she said, "I'll wait in the lobby," and almost ran to the foyer and the door. She wasn't sure whether he'd heard, or if he'd called to her. She was already out in the hall and hurrying to the elevators.

A pool boy she'd noticed because of his massive physique was entering a car, and held the doors for her. She thanked him. He nodded, and yawned. She was wearing another of Harold's favorite gowns—a pink thing in three layers that effectively removed her body from contention. She didn't blame Mr. Muscles for yawning.

In the lobby she told herself she was *not* looking for anyone in particular. What good would it do even if she *were* to see Al? What could she say to him?

Still, she walked completely around the lobby, then went onto the deck and strolled to the pool, telling herself the night air was *marvelous*. Dan Berner, Senator Christopher, and a third man came around the high-dive pylon. May quickly looked away, but Dan stepped over to her and murmured, "I've wanted to apologize to you." She made a smile and nodded and kept walking. He went with her. "I was sick, May." She nodded again. He said, "I should have explained—" She said, "Yes, well, it's not that important," and hurried back to the lobby. She was upset, and told herself she shouldn't be now that he had explained, and was even more upset because she didn't believe him and he had reminded her of something that still hurt, hurt like hell!

She was fumbling in her bag for cigarettes and lowering herself onto the couch when Al said, "This was where we first met." She looked up. He was standing there, big and tan and relaxed-looking in a snug-fitting gray suit.

"Hello," she said, and got the cigarettes and went through the taking-out and tapping and lighting routine.

He sat down. "I don't like your dress."

"I don't either."

"Then why wear it?"

She shrugged.

"Does *he* like it?"

"Yes."

"And you wear what he likes, do what he likes?"

She dragged on her cigarette.

His voice lost its edge. "I know I'm out of line. He's your husband, isn't he?"

"Yes."

"Why didn't you tell me he was coming?"

"I didn't know."

"And now you're ashamed of having bothered with a kid."

She turned to him, shaking her head. "Don't ever think that, Al. I'd rather be with you . . ."

He leaned forward, his hand reaching for hers. She let him take it.

"He'll be down soon," she said softly.

"You said you'd rather be with me!"

He seemed about to come all the way to her and kiss her, and she felt a weakening of the senses, a wanting so intense she couldn't have stopped him.

"May, we're leaving Sunday morning."

"We, too."

"Isn't there any way? . . ."

She stood up. "How can there be? And what good would it do?"

"Plenty good!" He was standing with her. "I feel like a boiler about to burst! At least—at least *once!*"

"It's impossible." She was shaking. He was a man at last—now that it was too late. "There's just no way."

"There must be. Quarrel with him. Walk out on him. Say you're going to spend the day by yourself. Next Saturday would be perfect. My parents will be busy with convention affairs, and at night there's that speech. We can rent a car. We can drive down the coast . . ."

She was shaking her head.

"Just try, May. That's all. And if you can, leave a message for me at the desk."

"How could I? Your parents might get it."

"I used to have a friend they didn't want me to play with. So we had a code. He would phone, changing his voice a little, and leave a message under another name. It's simple. You say, 'Miss James called. She'll be in the lobby at ten.' But no matter where you *say* to meet Miss James, we'll meet in the Arcade Level, near the artist's shop."

"You seem to have thought it all out."

"I've thought of nothing *but*, since seeing you last night. I realized then I'd thrown away the chance, the one chance . . ."

She walked away, back to the elevators. Her head was splitting. There was no way. No possible way!

Or was there, and she was unwilling to take the chance, to risk having Al grow cold in the act as had the other two men who'd experienced her body?

An elevator arrived. She stepped forward, then stopped. Harold came out, his face stiff. "I called to you," he said, and took her arm and walked her toward the street doors. "Why didn't you wait?"

"I didn't hear you."

"I think you did."

She laughed. "You're really too much."

"You act as if I didn't have good reason for suspicion."

"Don't be silly. I walked around outside . . ."

He was staring past her. She knew even before she looked what she would see. Al was just turning away.

"You were with that—teen-ager!"

Again she laughed. "You're here, Harold. Nothing can happen. So please drop it."

His face was pale. His eyes darted from Al to her and back to Al. His hand dug clawlike into her arm. "Don't make the mistake . . ." he began, and shook his head at her. "I won't be degraded, humiliated—especially by that *boy!* Don't ever make the mistake of thinking I will!"

She looked away from him, acting amused but feeling frightened. Cool, urbane, sophisticated Harold, but when it came to something like this . . .

"If you want to kill me," he said, "you can. No one will know it's murder. But *you'll* know. It'll hang on your conscience and drag you down to hell!"

"Please," she whispered. "We've *been* through all that."

"Yes, we have. Remember it. My instinct for self-preservation is tenuous at best. You can free yourself easily enough, May. But this time there's an added risk. Eunice. This time everyone will know why—"

She walked quickly ahead of him and out the doors.

"What time is it?"

Lou Degano rolled over and looked across the room at the clock. "Ten-thirty."

"You're kidding!" He groaned. "It was seven-thirty when we finished dinner, and that was only a few minutes ago!"

"We don't have to leave," she said. He was a sweet man, a generous man, a satisfying lover. She liked him. She'd liked him last Wednesday when he'd taken her home from that hotel party and made love to her for the first time, and she liked him now. "I'm not that wild about Benny Barker."

"But it's a crime to waste reservations for an opening booked solid a month ago! If I'd known—"

She sat up. "Then we'll go. And make whoopee. And spend your money."

"You dress first."

"You scoundrel you."

He flushed. "I didn't mean . . . I like to watch you, yes, but if you—"

"Lesson number three. Enjoy your kicks when you can and screw the explanations. Besides, I enjoy admiration."

"And I admire you," he murmured. "I really do, Lou."

She got up and walked to the dresser.

"What were lessons one and two?" he asked.

"What were you doing these past few hours that seemed like a few minutes?"

He smiled. He watched her. "I never realized how beautiful you are, Lou."

"Go on, boss." She opened drawers and took out clothing. "And on and on and on."

"I mean it. You're not an ordinary girl."

She looked down at herself. "No? The last time I counted I had two of those and one of these."

"I wish I'd met you years ago."

She said *oops* to herself and began to dress.

"I think . . . I really think I *could* forget certain people, Lou, if we spent enough time together."

"Then perhaps we shouldn't spend time together."

"Perhaps, but I don't want to stop. If it's all right with you?"

"Everything's all right with me, boss. You should know that after *this* session."

"And how wonderful you made it all. I've been married twenty-nine years—"

"Like wow."

"You won't believe this, but in all twenty-nine years I never had a night like this."

"Sure, boss. I was too young for nights like this most of those twenty-nine years."

He laughed, but he wasn't about to stop. And maybe she didn't want him to stop. She was alone, despite boys and dates and kicks. She was alone and needed someone to talk to her like this.

"I want to see you on some sort of regular basis, Lou."

"Like five times a week and sometimes Saturdays? That's the present arrangement in the office."

"I wish it was the present arrangement at home—your home, I mean."

"I figured you didn't want me moving in with Janice and the girls."

She thought that might cool it, but he murmured, "How is it no boy ever grabbed you, Lou? If I were single—"

308

"You'd run like a thief, and come back only for goodies. Remember? That's how boys are."

"Maybe. But the real goodies can't be grabbed by thieves. The real goodies require cultivation. They come from being with a girl like you day after day."

"You'd better start dressing."

"I'm sorry," he muttered. "I said things I have no right to say."

She turned, wearing panties and hooking up her brassiere. "You have every right to say things like that, Andy. It's the *hating* things we have no right to say."

He nodded. "At your age I wouldn't have known that. At your age I was an absolute fool, shackled by convention, talking morality while mentally undressing every woman I met. I think your most exciting quality . . ."

She wanted to stop him now. He was reaching her now, and she didn't want to be reached. She liked him, and she could go on with him, but he wasn't the man to say such things to her.

"You mean the two of those or the one of these?"

"I mean your freedom. You're *free*, Lou, and so few of us are."

She went to the bathroom and turned on the water. She scrubbed her face and began applying makeup. She stopped and stared into the mirror and stuck out her tongue. *Free.* Sure, like Prometheus, with that goddam Golden Boy tearing away at her liver.

"Oh come on now, Lou Degano, wise and free child of our century!"

Andy called, "Did you say something?"

"Yes, boss. The bathroom is all yours."

At three A.M., the party was two hours old and a roaring success. Marjory stood at the bar with Benny Barker, Senator Christopher, and both their groups, and laughed as Barker went on with his bravura performance. He was drinking steadily, but wasn't drunk. He was exhilarated, but in full control of his material. He had scored the greatest opening-night success of his career, and had drawn so many guests and guests-of-guests that there was barely room to move in the suite. And here came Vincent, the hotel guard, to inquire again about new arrivals not on the list.

". . . people named Cohen, Joyce and Murray. And people named Irving . . ."

She said to tell them sorry, there just wasn't any more room, but she would be glad to meet them some other time. Vincent nodded, his eyes flickering over her, and she smiled and turned away. He'd obviously heard rumors. He wondered whether he might work himself into something interesting.

She'd wondered, too, but not any more. She couldn't approach Vincent, or any of the other guards she'd interviewed. She couldn't approach *anyone*, period.

She stepped back, and someone moved into her place to be closer to Barker, and she walked, or squeezed, through the crowd. The music was loud, but the voices and laughter were louder. She smiled and nodded and exchanged greetings with dozens of people, and suddenly felt stifled.

Too noisy! Too crowded! Too much!

She made her way to the bathroom and actually had to push a woman, a stranger, aside to get at the door. She used her key and the woman said, "And here I fought my way clear across to the other . . ."

She stepped inside, closed the door and leaned against it a moment. Nausea tickled her throat. She put on the light and went to the sink and washed with cold water, drinking some from the palm of her hand. Then she lifted her head to find a towel, and saw movement in the two-way mirror. She shut off the light. Marco Renier sat on the bed. He was alone. He was smoking a cigarette and looking at the door.

She dried her face and waited. She waited at least ten minutes before Marco stood up, stubbing out his second cigarette in the bedside ashtray. He went out, looking disappointed. She waited another ten minutes, but he didn't return. She left.

He was in the Barker-Christopher crowd, smiling at Barker's

antics, adding his voice and applause to the general hubbub. He stood directly behind the Senator.

Marjory began to feel a little better. The nausea lifted, and so did the emptiness. She joined the group and had a drink.

The Senator looked around and said he saw someone he knew and pushed through the crowd. His guard began to follow, but Christopher shook his head. The guard turned back to Barker. Barker made a joke about Indians, punching the guard's arm. The guard smiled.

Marco moved off. Marjory followed him with her eyes until he was almost lost, then moved after him. She didn't go all the way to where he was standing. She stopped and spoke to Mr. and Mrs. Lorsh, and looked beyond them to the table of hors d'oeuvres. The Senator was taking a plate. Marco was beside him. They looked at the table, but spoke to each other.

Marjory chatted with the Lorshes. The wife asked for Wally Jones. Marjory said he'd called to say he had an emergency rehearsal in his suite. "He needs it," the husband said. "I was never so disappointed . . ."

Marjory decided on one more party, next Saturday. It would run from noon until just before the Senator's ten o'clock speech. It would have fewer people than this one, but enough so that a couple could feel secure, and lost, in the crowd.

Any kind of couple.

The girl called at four, at which time Wally and Stan were arguing over the last two numbers for tomorrow's show. Stan wanted old favorites, as usual. "It's changing things that fouled us up." Wally wanted new tunes from an off-Broadway show. His instincts told him the usual way was not going to work this scene. "And who's massah here?" Stan did a Stepin Fetchit shuffle to the phone. "For you, massah."

The voice was cute. "I'm dancing at the Harlequin-Nights Club just down the Beach a ways, Wally. I did a specialty in Vegas last year when you were there. Dianne Marmon, remember?"

He said, "Sure, lady, you're the pretty one."

"You busy?"

"I won't be in a while."

"I'm hungry. Got anything to eat up there?"

"Just happen to have the chef from 21 whipping up all sorts of goodies. What'd you have in mind?"

"Oh, pastrami and potato salad and rye bread and cream soda. All that kosher deli jazz."

"You sure you got the right Negro? The Jewish one isn't due in till February."

She laughed. "I got the right one, Wally. Remember?"

"How could I forget? Let's say fivish."

"I can be there in fifteen minutes. I want to talk about your friend Greg Beiler. Y'know, for bookings in Vegas."

"Save it for after the pastrami. *Fivish*, baby. 'Bye."

Stan was already putting on his jacket. "Anyone I know?"

"Maybe. *I* sure as hell don't."

Stan got his music together. Wally went to the bar. "Time for one last cup of tea."

"Please, massah, don't mention tea. Getting busted here might mean the chain gang."

Wally mixed their drinks and called room service and said he didn't care where they got it but he wanted pastrami sandwiches and potato salad and cream soda. Then he kept Stan talking and drinking until the waiter brought in the cart. Stan tried to make it to the door, but Wally insisted he have a sandwich and cream soda.

"Massah, that cream soda'll rot your brain away!"

So they had another round of the hard stuff. Stan finally said, "Listen, I'm dead on my feet."

"You're not on your feet."

"I'm still dead." He paused. "What about you, Wally? I don't think you've had any sleep since the opening."

Wally opened a sandwich and nibbled pastrami. "Had a few hours last night."

"You've gotta relax, man. This ain't like you."

"I'll relax when the chick gets here. She'll rock baby to sleep."

Stan made another break for the door.

"One for the road, Stanley."

Stan shook his head, but took the drink.

Wally nibbled some more. "What d'you hear about the Barker opening?"

"You're *really* tired, baby. I've been in here with you since ten-thirty. How would *I* know?"

"Yeah, forgot. Hey, let's try 'Impossible Dream.' I got a feeling that might be *it* for the closer."

"Can I say one thing first?"

"Sure."

"*Help!*"

Wally grinned and checked his watch. "You want to leave me alone when I'm down, the porthole's over there. Just follow the other rodents."

"But baby, you ain't nowhere *near* sinking."

He let him go. The chick would be here in ten minutes.

In fact, she arrived before he could mix a fresh drink—a small broad with black hair piled too high to be her own. "Saw your piano-player," she said, sweeping up to him in a pale brown mink and kissing his cheek. She looked around. "You always go first class, don't you, baby?"

"What'd you expect? A room near the elevators?"

She laughed, and took off the coat. The impression of small-ness disappeared. "Hope you don't mind. We have a late show on Saturdays and I didn't bother changing." She walked to the windows and looked out. "*Fabulous!*"

"Yeah." He hadn't recognized her when she'd first come in, but he did now. The ass was familiar. Like a big pale peach. She'd worked in that Fleshpots of Paris thing that opened his show in Vegas, and had turned up in his bed one night after a party.

"Come get your drink."

She jiggled toward him. She wore a bitty silver thing over her top and a bitty silver thing around her hips with teardrop gim-micks tinkling front and rear. They didn't tinkle low enough.

313

"That legal?"

She took the drink. "To you, Wally. And to your friend Greg Beiler. I need a break. I lost my specialty." She sipped. "Legal? Oh, I wear one thing more when I go on. Sort of a G-string, but it's uncomfortable. Anyway, I'm with a friend."

He drank and enjoyed the view, then murmured offhandedly, "You hear how Benny Barker went over tonight?"

"Some people who made our place afterward said he was a smash."

He nodded, and drained his glass.

"They had it in for you this time, didn't they, Wally?"

He shrugged. "I'm reopening tomorrow."

She saw the food cart. "Pastrami!" She ran over, strong white legs flashing, and bent to pick up a sandwich. "Better hurry," he said. "I feel faint."

She turned, biting into the bread and meat. She smiled as she chewed, and licked her lips. "Dr. Marmon will be with you in a minute, baby." She took another bite, and put down the sandwich.

It was that big pale peach he wanted. It was that big pale peach he got . . . until he simply fell away.

She was gone when he awoke. So were the sandwiches. He stumbled around, groaning. He was hung over, and he hadn't even been drunk.

He called down for a pot of coffee and all the Sunday papers. The man said it was still too early for some papers, and it was then he realized it was only eight o'clock. No wonder he felt hung over. He'd finished with that big pale peach at six-thirty! A lousy hour and a half of sleep. He had to do better than that!

He went back to bed and pulled the blankets over his head. The doorbell rang. It was, of course, his coffee and newspapers.

He had a sip of java, opened the *Herald* to the entertainment section, and saw Barker's picture grinning out over half a page. The review was, like the chick had said, a smash. But a *smasheroo*.

. . . in fifteen years has this reporter witnessed an opening-night triumph like Benny Barker's at the Platinum Room of the Bal Metropole Hotel. It was as if he were determined to make up for the disappointment of the previous night . . .

Wally threw the paper across the room and stamped into the shower. He took it hot, as hot as he could bear it, to drain away the tensions and bring on the sleepy feeling. He got into fresh pajamas and flung himself into bed and pulled the covers back over his head. He was there for what seemed like hours, wide awake and hating this motherin' town and all its motherin' tourists and reporters. And its cops. *Think of those two bastards coming to your show free of charge!* He was reliving Thursday afternoon and Friday night and suffering the pangs of self-hatred when that doorbell went off again and he leaped up and shouted, "Dammit! How's a man supposed to sleep!"

The bellboy looked worried. "They said you'd called for breakfast and it was all right to bring up the mail and . . ."

"Sure, baby, just throwing my usual morning fit." He grinned and tipped a ten and the boy left convinced that all was well in the glorious sepia world of Wallace Edward Jones.

The mail was from New York and agents and ex-wives and ex-wives' lawyers. And then there were three from local fans.

Dear Jigaboo:
You'll never leave Florida alive. The hand that struck a white woman will be chopped off and stuffed down your dirty black throat . . .

The other two were *really* rough. He dropped them in the wastebasket. He'd had them before, and was prepared for a real shit-storm this time.

There was a telegram from Senator Christopher. An honest-to-God telegram saying better-late-than-never congratulations on his opening. He looked at it and said, "Oh baby, the timing. The *timing!*" He laughed and shook his head and dropped it into the same basket with the hate shit.

He checked the clock. It was nine-ten. This day was going to be a thousand hours long!

He remembered the Do Not Disturb sign and hung it out and returned to bed. He was under the blankets trying to think good thoughts, big-pale-peach thoughts (but how much of *that* could a man want in any three-hour period?), when the phone rang. He lifted the covers and glared at it, but it wouldn't stop ringing. He lifted it and said, "Gestapo Headquarters. This is the victim speaking." (See? He was a smash, too.)

There was a moment's silence. "I wanted Mr. Jones's room." It was a real sweet voice, with a touch of South of the Border.

"You got it."

"Mr. Jones?"

He rubbed his eyes. They felt like two dying hunks of charcoal. "Jones here. Who dere?"

"My name is not important."

"If you say so, Miss Blank. Or is it *Mrs.* Blank?"

Another moment's silence. "Vi."

"What's your pleasure, honey?"

"Revenge is my pleasure. I'm Cuban. I hate white Americans, just as you do."

"Now that's what I call a subtle opening."

"If I am wrong, Mr. Jones, please stop me."

"You're stopped." But he didn't hang up.

"I don't think so. I see what they've done to you. If it was a white man, do you think the newspapers—"

"I dig, Vi. I've dug since Day One. They did it to me, and they've done a lot more you know nothing about. So I'm supposed to blow up the Statue of Liberty?"

"You can humiliate one of their leaders."

"What's that supposed to mean?"

"You can humiliate Senator Christopher and show them that we nonwhites—"

"You a *negrita*, Vi?"

"No. But I am not a white. Not in *their* eyes. So I am of your world."

"You mean you're in show business?"

Silence.

He did a Senator Claghorn. "That is a joke—a *joke*, ah say!"

"I know, Mr. Jones. I just don't believe you are laughing very hard today."

"You're right, Vi. But I'm not going out and throw eggs at a friend."

"He is *not* your friend. No white American is. Even if they try."

Amen, sister. It made sense, this morning. "I can't do anything to the Senator. And I warn you, I'll call him—"

"That's all right, Mr. Jones. You won't have anything to tell him, even if you decide to help us."

"That I don't get."

"We don't want to hurt him. We just want to shame him. To show how foolish these superior people really are. These leaders of the world. These masters who, we will prove, can't take care of themselves, not to say other countries. We will make people laugh at him. We will give him a failure in public relations."

Like mine, Thursday and Friday. "I don't see how I can help."

"All you have to do is call him."

"What do I say?"

"Will you do it?"

"First tell me what I say."

"I will telephone you again, next Saturday between eleven and eleven-thirty at night. Will you be in your room?"

"In this town, that's the only safe place for me to be."

"You'll expect my call?"

"I can't stop the phone from ringing, can I?"

"No matter what he says in his speech, you can be sure it will be lies. His brother-in-law said things, too, and has anything changed?"

"You bet! We burned a few more cities! That's *progress!*"

She laughed.

"Hey, why don't you come up for breakfast, Vi?"

"I would like to. But I can't trust you yet, Mr. Jones. Not

317

until you help us. Then I would be glad to come up for breakfast, or any other time."

He didn't want to be alone. He would call Chink.

Or he would phone New York and speak to Nat . . .

No, it was Sunday.

He'd sleep, then get Ace and Dee for a hot poker session.

"Mr. Jones?"

"I didn't catch that, baby."

"Please help us. It will be helping yourself. Your *inside* self."

"I doubt it. My inside self is beyond help."

"I know what I'm saying, Mr. Jones. I haven't felt this good in all my life."

A kook. A sweet-voiced kook who was trying to rope him into something rough.

But all she wanted from him was a phone call, she said.

Yeah, *today*. Saturday she'd ask him to throw knives!

"Good-bye, Vi. You sound too nice to serve time."

"You sound too honest to fool yourself. I will call again Saturday night." The line clicked.

He stretched out and said, voice high and veddy British, "Mr. Bond, your assignment is to humiliate the Senator and bring the government of the United States down in ruins."

He should call Christopher right now. But what would he tell him? That a sweet-sounding kook was calling back next Saturday?

He switched to the Kingfish. "Oh yeah, we takes him down to de lodge and paints him all over black. Den we sells him to de Arabians fo' a harem slave. Ummmmm! I think he be worth ten dollah!"

His heart was slamming away and he couldn't help wondering what that kook had in mind. And Jesus Christ, he didn't owe Christopher a thing! Not a damn thing, the way he'd been acting!

He pulled the blankets over his head for the skeighty-eighth time. He told himself to forget it. He was a star, not a black militant! He had the world by the *petzle!*

"What we do after we sells him, Kingfish?"

318

"Why Andy, den we in business! We get another one, and another one, and soon we runnin' dem in wholesale!"

"Ain't dat against de law?"

"Naw! You thinkin' of the 'Mancipation Prolication, ain't you?"

"Somethin' like dat, yeah."

"Ah'm *ashamed* of you, Andy! Have you fo'got *every*thin' you learned in de fo'th grade? Don't you remember who Lincoln freed with dat paper?"

"Well . . . it was *us*, wasn't it, Kingfish?"

"And we is *what*, Andy?"

"People?"

"No, no! Sapphire's momma must've been yo' teacher! We is *blacks!*"

"Ah still don't see—"

"We goan be runnin' *whites*, Andy! Ain't no 'Mancipation Prolication for whites!"

He clamped his eyes shut against all the kooks and the fair-weather senators and the Benny Barkers and he fought his way toward sleep.

11

MONDAY, JANUARY 23, P.M.

Jorge was sitting in a booth when Max arrived. Max slid in on the other side and said, "Mr. Lamas joining us later?"

Jorge was grim. "Mr. Lamas knows nothing about this. He knows nothing about anything. My working for him is . . . a mask."

"A cover?"

"Yes. A cover."

Max smiled. "I get it. You chauffeur him around so no one will find out you're a multimillionaire."

In the adjoining booth, a three-year-old boy stood up, looking past Jorge's head at Max. Max waved. Overcome by shyness, the boy dropped straight down. A woman's voice said, "Sonny, you stay in your seat!"

Jorge said, "Why did we have to meet here? How can we discuss? . . ."

The boy rose up again, using Jorge's head for support. Jorge looked pained, but didn't turn or move. The woman slapped the boy's bottom and pulled him down. "Sorry. He's at that age."

The waitress came. Max ordered a Scotch. Jorge said nothing for him.

"Don't you like Howard Johnson's, Jorge? It's where the Miami racket boys hold their meets."

The chauffeur looked disgusted.

"No kidding, Jorge. It's neutral territory. The demilitarized zone. A safe place to talk turkey."

Jorge lit one of his little cigars and spat tobacco.

Max's drink came. He sipped. "Did you bring the hundred fifty grand?"

"No."

Max put down his glass. "I told you, Jorge, I'm desperate for that money. It's all right with me if Lamas wants to stay out of the limelight, but I've got to pay my debts . . ."

"I'll have it for you at the end of the week."

"*When* at the end of the week?"

"Friday night."

"No nights. And Friday is cutting it too close. If you have any trouble, we're into Saturday, and Saturday is not only C-Day but the morning I pay my debts. I've got to have it Thursday, Jorge. In the morning."

Jorge nodded slowly. "You are not an honorable man, Mr. Prager."

Max picked up his drink. "There are worse things."

"Not for me." He rose.

"Hold it, Jorge. You don't know where to meet me Thursday."

"I thought you liked Howard Johnson's?"

"Not twice in a row."

Jorge sat down again. "I don't understand you. I don't follow your thinking, Mr. Prager."

Which was good, Max thought. He looked out the window. Two men were parked at the curb in a Buick convertible. They looked Cuban. Across the street, a man walked slowly, staring at the Howard Johnson's. He looked like a gunsel. And any one or two or three of them could belong to Lamas.

"What are you worried about, Mr. Prager? As you said on the phone, I will not be losing money, just paying it a few days earlier. You will still do your job and I will still get what I paid for."

"That's right. But I can't be certain you accept that, can I?"

Jorge spread his hands. "What then will make you happy? To meet in a schoolyard during recess? Or at Convention Hall during a television show? Or at—at the Seaquarium with screaming children and mothers and noise and foolishness? Or maybe Pirates World . . ."

"The Seaquarium," Max murmured. "That's not bad, Jorge. Not bad at all."

"You joke too much, Mr. Prager. Some day you will be sorry."

"No joke, Jorge. I like fish. I like kids and mothers. You might not believe it, Jorge, but I once had a mother myself."

Jorge's face was stiff.

"The Seaquarium it is, Jorge."

"I will *not* drive all that way so you can enjoy a private joke! There are a dozen places nearby that—"

"I mean it," Max interrupted. "The Seaquarium."

Jorge looked down at the table. Voice choked with rage, he said, "If I had my way—"

"But you *do*, Jorge. You're the millionaire chauffeur who runs the whole show. Who could possibly stop you from having your way? Certainly not Lamas, your *cover*?"

Jorge kept his eyes on the table. He seemed to be having trouble breathing. Max picked up his drink. He was almost finished before Jorge spoke again. "All right, Mr. Prager. One o'clock, at the main entrance."

Max thought a moment. Thursday would be very busy. He would arrange the DeWyant payoff for the afternoon. He had to allow for minor delays, had to give himself some leeway in between.

"No, eleven o'clock. And inside, at the main exhibit."

"Have you ever been there, Mr. Prager? The Main Tank is always crowded. We'd better meet somewhere else."

"I like crowds, Jorge."

"But how will we find each other? With all those people—"

"We'll look, Jorge. We'll stroll around and keep looking. And sooner or later, there we'll be."

Jorge got up and walked away. A moment later he came by the window, head down, stalking toward the parking area. Max smiled. Everything was meshing. Everything was working. Copasetic, as they used to say. Thursday night he would be flying to the West Coast. Friday he would be on his way to Buenos Aires. Then he would write Chuckie . . .

"Will you be ordering now, sir?"

He nodded. He was hungry.

When the waitress left, he turned to the window. The two men who looked like Cubans met two women who looked like wives and they all drove away. Across the street, the man who'd looked like a gunsel was gone. The sun shone brightly and it would shine the same way Thursday, and even if it didn't there'd be kids and parents and tourists at the Seaquarium and they'd annoy the hell out of Jorge but make Max happy. Daylight and thousands of people—just what the doctor ordered for a long, happy life.

At five-thirty Violetta knocked and went into McKensil's office. He'd been out most of the day, returning an hour ago to meet with Mr. DeWyant, then staying behind his closed door. In fact, she'd barely seen him since they'd returned last Friday from her place.

"Are you busy?" she asked.

He looked as if he hadn't slept all weekend.

"Yes, actually I am," he said, smiling nervously. "I've wanted to speak to you, of course. I mean—" he cleared his throat— "about Friday."

She sat down in his guest chair and crossed her legs. His eyes did all their little tricks, and he smiled again, and she smiled back at him.

"If I took advantage . . ." he began. She kept smiling. "I mean, you seemed perfectly willing . . ." She nodded. "Then there really isn't any problem, is there?" She shook her head.

He still looked sick with fear.

"No problem at all, Mr. McKensil. In fact, I want you to take me home again."

"You? . . ."

She smiled.

"Uh, no, I don't think I can, tonight. Not that I wouldn't want to, but the press of business—"

"Don't you want to make love to me any more?"

He stared and swallowed. "But Friday, you seemed so . . . Do you resent me, Violetta?"

"If I did, would I ask you to take me home?"

He hesitated. "I want you to know I really care. I want you to know—"

"Tell me at home."

In his car, she found a station that specialized in Cuban music and hummed and shook her shoulders.

"Do you like to dance?" he asked.

"Yes. But I don't get much chance." She smiled. "I'm a very serious person."

"Would you like to go dancing some night?"

"Yes." She thought of Jorge dancing with her. She thought of Jorge holding her in his arms. "Yes, I would."

323

The moment they entered the house, she was up against him. "Kiss me, please."

"Beautiful child," he murmured, but he was still worried, still cautious, and she didn't have more than a few seconds. She kissed him and opened his fly. He sighed deeply, his hands pressing her bottom. "I was so worried, my dear. I imagined all sorts—"

Jorge's voice was thin and tight. "I am no longer taking pictures."

She stepped back, laughing, and gave it an extra tug.

The manager stared at them, horrified, then twisted away, fumbling with his zipper. Violetta walked by Jorge. He glared at her. She was laughing so hard she could barely gasp out, "*Amor! Amor!*" and stumble into the bedroom.

She changed into the clothes Jorge had laid out, and returned to the living room. McKensil was sitting on the couch, face chalk white, holding a thick sheaf of photographs. Jorge stood nearby, smoking a *cigarro*. Violetta said, "Oh the pictures! Can I see them?" McKensil looked up, glassy-eyed—then reacted to her new outfit. "Do you like it?" she asked, and put her thumb in her mouth.

"Let's not be foolish," McKensil muttered, and began to rise.

Jorge said, "Sit down." McKensil sat down. Jorge said, "Look at her." McKensil was looking at her. She wore a blue dress that a backward thirteen-year-old might like, and white stockings and white shoes. It wasn't baby-doll style, which was little-girl sexy—just a very plain, very young dress. "Her hair will be different," Jorge said, "and no makeup, of course. What do you think a jury will do to you, taking advantage of such a child? And what do you think your wife and children will think? And your employer?"

McKensil moved his lips. At first nothing came out. Then he said, "No one will believe it."

Jorge smiled. "Do you think we might have to bring your niece from California?" McKensil was silent. "Violetta is fifteen years old. Statutory rape, Mr. McKensil. And these pictures show what you did to the morals of a minor. And she will explain how you tried to get her to sell her favors to hotel guests . . ."

McKensil put down the pictures. "How much do you want?" Now that he'd learned the worst, he actually seemed to regain his composure. Violetta sat down beside him. He didn't look at her. She picked up the pictures. Jorge said, in Spanish, "What is the matter with you! First the filthy joke, and now you look at those—those things!"

She answered in English, "I think I came out well. You must have enjoyed developing them, Jorge. Ai, this one!" She turned it so he could see. He jerked his eyes away. She wondered why he hadn't visited her Friday night. She had expected him. And Saturday and Sunday. What was holding him back, now that he'd seen her in action?

"Well?" McKensil asked. "How much?"

"You don't have to pay a thing."

Violetta said, "Oh, this one, Jorge! Look!"

"If you can't be quiet, leave the room!"

She murmured, "Sí, padre," and turned to the next photograph. Seeing herself that way was terribly exciting. She wouldn't interrupt them any more. The sooner the manager left, the sooner Jorge could admit he had to have her. She looked at the pictures and listened to them talk.

"For you," Jorge said, "there is no payment."

"Get to the point."

"Friends of mine are going to rob the suites on the Metropole's fourteenth floor. They want keys to all doors and connecting doors."

"You can't be serious! Senator Christopher, the President's brother-in-law, is up there!"

"And his father-in-law, Michael Wheeler. And a wealthy businesswoman, and the hotel owner and his daughter. Exactly why we picked that floor."

"I won't do it!"

"They will also need help in leaving the hotel without being stopped. That means setting aside one elevator for their use—"

"Didn't you understand what I said?" He jumped to his feet. "I won't do it!"

"Violetta will give you full instructions in a day or two."

McKensil strode toward the front door. Jorge said, "Mr. Mc-Kensil," his voice mild.

The manager turned. "I've a few thousand dollars put away. You can have that. But nothing else!"

Jorge smiled. "I was just going to say you had better do it to-night."

"Do what?"

"Kill yourself. Your life will be a terrible thing tomorrow. The photographs will be delivered into the hands of the district attorney, your wife, Mr. DeWyant, the newspapers. And a sworn statement—"

McKensil shouted, "You're bluffing! It won't do you any good to destroy me!"

Jorge looked at Violetta. "You're mistaken. I would enjoy it."

Violetta looked at McKensil. "So would I."

McKensil came back across the room. Violetta smiled. *He* was the one who'd been bluffing. Then her smile ended. Jorge had grabbed the manager by the throat and struck him two open-handed blows across the face. The sounds were like pistol shots. McKensil cried out. Jorge flung him backward onto the couch. Violetta shifted away. "Animal!" Jorge said. McKensil's eyes filled with tears. Jorge looked down at him with loathing. "You will receive instructions from Violetta in plenty of time to do what you have to do. The keys are to be given her as soon as possible—in the next day or two."

McKensil nodded, using a handkerchief.

Jorge went on, explaining when the "robbery" would occur and that a temporary hostage might have to be taken. McKensil stiffened. "A hostage?"

"The wealthy woman, or whoever is there. Just until we get out of the city. Nothing to worry about. But that is why an elevator must be set aside for our use. And why arrangements must be made for our car to be waiting in the basement garage with clear exit to the street."

McKensil nodded again, but weakly.

Violetta finished with the photographs. "I feel we are related!" she said to McKensil, and laughed.

He finally looked at her. He said, "It was not unpleasant, was it? Nothing like a rape, nothing like a crime?"

She shook her head.

"You didn't suffer or anything like that, did you?"

"No."

He turned to Jorge. "You see? Your revulsion is unjustified." He paused. "And you're making me do something that can just as easily destroy me as those photographs." Jorge began to deny that, but McKensil said, "Please let me finish. You've struck me, humiliated me, but you can't stop me from seeing the truth. I *could* be implicated, after making those arrangements. And so I feel entitled to get something for myself."

"You want part of what we will steal?"

"No." He wet his lips, and took the pictures from Violetta. He looked at one and then another.

"After the robbery," Jorge said, "you will get the negatives and three sets of prints. Also, a reel of motion pictures. When you destroy them, not one picture will remain—I give you my word."

McKensil said, "That was understood. I meant . . ." He seemed afraid to go on. Jorge looked puzzled. Violetta laughed delightedly. She said, "If Jorge says all right, I will agree."

Jorge looked at her, and slowly understanding came to him. McKensil said, "I might as well be hung for a wolf as for a sheep. Once more with her."

Jorge stepped forward. Violetta stood up between them. Mockingly, she asked, "Now what difference does it make to you, Jorge?"

"None. But I have my instructions, and that isn't in my instructions."

Violetta said, "Sorry, Mr. McKensil."

Jorge said, "You can leave now."

McKensil got up slowly and began to speak.

Violetta said, "I wouldn't say any more."

The manager looked at Jorge, and went to the door.

"One last thing," Jorge said.

McKensil turned.

Jorge stepped to a rattan armchair and reached under the seat cushion. He took out a revolver with a heavy metal extension—a silencer. He raised it, pulling back the hammer. He aimed it at the manager's chest, sighting carefully. McKensil stumbled back against the door, one hand rising. Jorge tightened his finger on the trigger. Violetta said, "*Jorge!*" Jorge pulled the trigger as McKensil made a small crying sound. The hammer clicked on an empty chamber.

"In case the pictures didn't convince you," Jorge said, "remember this."

McKensil was gasping for breath as he left.

Jorge looked at Violetta. "And the bloodthirsty one was frightened," he said in Spanish. "The vengeful one was frightened."

"Yes, frightened that you would throw away everything because you hate him."

"I hate him?" He put the gun down on the coffee table. "Why should I hate him? It was all to make him do what we want. I pity him."

"And seeing what he did to me—"

"*With* you, not *to* you."

She shrugged. "Let's not worry about him any more. Let's have something to eat and something to drink and relax."

He checked his watch. "I will eat with you. But the *patrón* expects me by seven."

"That is time enough. Come into the kitchen while I make dinner. We will talk."

"In a moment." He turned to his bedroom.

His moment stretched into fifteen. She finally left the kitchen and went looking for him. He was lying on the bed, reading the "Latino America" column in the *Reporter*. She didn't say anything. There was nothing to say. It was time to *do*. She went back to the kitchen.

Later, she called to him, "Jorge, it is ready." He came into the kitchen and sat down at the table, still holding his paper. He sighed and began to say something, and only then looked at her. She was carrying a plate from the stove. He dropped the paper. She said, "Nice and hot," and put down the plate. She turned back to the stove and filled her own plate. "Looks good, huh?" she asked.

"*Madre*," he muttered.

She looked back at him. His eyes were on her. She smiled and filled her plate. She took her time, letting him enjoy his view of a girl in a little black apron and nothing else. Then she came to the table and took the seat near his. "Aren't you going to eat?"

He put down his head and picked up his fork.

"Like the topless places, Jorge, to relax you."

He took a long time chewing and swallowing, as if his mouth were dry. She said, "Oh, I forgot," and ran to the refrigerator. She bent to the lower shelf, and glanced quickly back at him. He was looking. When she turned, he was again staring into his plate.

She opened and poured the beer and sat down. She leaned forward over the table, holding out his glass. "Here, Jorge."

He had to look up. Her apron covered her middle and nothing else. She knew what she was offering him along with the beer.

He looked long this time. He took the beer and drank it slowly, and with his free hand he cupped a breast and rubbed it. Her eyes closed and she whispered, "Jorge." His hand left her. He was standing up, turning away.

"You're not going to leave me?"

"I am."

She laughed, full of sudden rage. "Look at yourself! Look and tell me what you'll do with *that!*"

He was aroused, bulging plainly through his trousers. He said, "Come, I'll show you," and went into the living room. He picked up the pictures from the couch and moved toward the bathroom. She stepped directly into his path. With his free hand he drew her in and flexed his knees and rubbed against her and felt her body, then shoved her away so that she struck the wall. He went into the bathroom. She ran to the door and shook it. When she stopped, she heard him panting. She screamed, "Pig! Dirty pig!"

and began to cry. The toilet flushed; the water ran; he came out and went back to the kitchen. He sat down at the table and began to eat. She came up to him, still crying. "For God's sake, why that and not me?"

He didn't answer until he'd taken another mouthful and murmured his appreciation of her cooking. "Because that is one thing I will not do unless I *wish* to do it—with my mind as well as my body. And after seeing your *joke* with McKensil, and the pictures, my mind does not wish to do it."

She went to the bedroom and put on a dress. His plate was empty and he was drinking another beer when she returned. She said, "Something else your mind does not wish to do—admit that I am becoming as important to Lamas as you."

He leaned back, lighting a *cigarro*.

"You didn't like my getting permission to call Jones, did you?"

"It's dangerous, and unnecessary."

She sat down. "It will turn out to be the most important part of the plan, wait and see! It will get rid of the most dangerous man on that floor, the Senator's guard! You're jealous of me. Your wonderful *patrón* trusts me, wants me along the night of the kidnapping, goes against your wishes! If you were a real man you would admire me, but no, your *love* for your *patrón* has turned you into a . . . a . . ."

He laughed. "How you burn, little whore."

She slapped him, sending the *cigarro* flying from his lips. Calmly, he picked it up and said, "When you learn that I am not interested in whores, when you understand it is necessary for *me* to come to *you*, when you realize I feel more . . ." He stopped then, and relighted the dead *cigarro*.

Her rage melted away. Timidly, she touched his hand. He didn't withdraw it. She took it in both of hers—a big, smooth, hard hand—and raised it and kissed it. He said, "Violetta, no." She turned it over and kissed the palm. He leaned forward and murmured, "When you realize I feel more for you than I want to feel, than I will allow myself to feel until all is finished, then you will become what I want and you will have me forever." He leaned back, smiling grimly. "Which you might regret."

She was looking at him, her passion stilled—wanting him, yes, but tasting a new and overpowering pleasure that turned her insides not to fire but to jelly. "Say more."

"There is nothing more to say."

"Sit with me, then."

"The *patrón* expects me at seven."

She let go of his hand, nodding.

He stood up, hesitated, then sat down again. "A few more minutes," he said.

It felt so good it hurt.

"Five guns," Lamas said. "Three large ones with silencers, two small ones for Violetta and Mrs. Prager."

Jorge took the wooden box. Lamas went back to his chair and sat down. Jorge stood near the desk, trying to find words to express his doubts without seeming to doubt the *patrón*.

"The girl bothers you, Jorge?"

Jorge nodded. "She is too young for such responsibility. Believe me, she will grow frightened. She is just a child."

"You're wrong. And you're wrong about the Negro singer. He will either help us, or he will not. But he will never hinder us."

"I accept your judgment, *patrón*. You know more than I do. But why is it necessary to have her there when we take Christopher? Why is it necessary to have her carry a gun and risk her life—"

"Then it is not her ability but her *safety* that concerns you."

Jorge began to deny it, and fell silent.

"It is necessary because we need even more help than we have. It is necessary because she is a employee of the hotel and as such will add to the security of the plan. She can speak to bellboys and others. She can explain certain things—like having an elevator reserved for the Senator, or a man with a bandaged face and head being helped into it, or whatever else might develop. She can make such things seem normal, when otherwise they might create suspicion."

As usual, the *patrón* had the power to convince him.

"Ramon Pedras is expecting you tonight. You will bring him into the plan. Vidal Morales will also be there. Is it necessary to remind you that my name is not to be mentioned?"

"They will guess the truth, *patrón*."

"Of course they will. But guesses aren't proof."

"I am concerned about Pedras, *patrón*. He hates too much."

"So am I. But with Prager being phased out . . ." He shrugged. "Ramon is a fanatic, yes, but the only man of proven ability we can trust on such short notice. I had intended to use Morales as the extra man, but now he takes Prager's place and Ramon is the extra man."

"Could we not do with one man less?"

Lamas shook his head. "Not the way I've made the final plan. Of course, when you speak to Prager, if he has any new ideas . . ."

"I doubt if he has any ideas at all, *patrón*."

"Still, you must question him. He is clever and will think hard to convince you he is invaluable." He smiled. "You were very expert with Prager, Jorge. I commend you. We would have handled him no matter what meeting place he chose, but to maneuver him into choosing the Seaquarium . . ." He shook his head admiringly.

To cover his intense pleasure, Jorge changed the subject. "Nothing further about Miss DeWyant, *patrón*?"

"Not enough. She definitely had some connection with the Wheeler family, but just what it was . . ." He shrugged.

"I think Prager is interested in her," Jorge said. "He acts as if he isn't, and that is why I think he is. And he might have learned much more than he's told us."

Lamas smiled thinly. "What difference does it make what Prager knows or thinks or does any more, Jorge?"

Jorge was silent.

"Besides, it is now too late to bring her into it. And too dangerous. She is a very unstable woman, Jorge. She was hospitalized twice for suicidal tendencies, and has been under psychiatric care for years. No, I would not want to be involved with her in any way, even if she were *anxious* to help. One can never trust such a person."

"I've been wondering about Mrs. Prager, *patrón*. Will we be able to trust *her* if Prager isn't there for the kidnapping?"

"She prefers Leech, and he will be there."

Jorge said good night and went to the door.

"One more thing, Jorge. Do you have any doubts about what you must do Thursday?"

"No doubts, *patrón*. A little distaste, yes . . ."

"Remember it is necessary. Remember he menaces the plan."

Jorge nodded.

"We are going to succeed, Jorge. I'll admit I wasn't sure before, I was worried before. But now—" He leaned forward, his smile sudden and strong. "Now I can almost *feel* Havana!"

BOOK 3

Checkout

1

THURSDAY, JANUARY 26, A.M.

She was approaching her cubicle and heard his laugh and saw him step out of Andy's office, looking back. It wasn't quite a quarter to nine and he hadn't been in early for weeks and she just wasn't prepared to meet him. And lately, she *needed* preparation.

". . . inaccurate to say I'm marrying the boss's daughter. That would mean your Cindy, and she's a little old for me at seventeen."

"Anything you say, Bruce. Have to keep the client happy."

Bruce grinned and waved, and turned to see her. She knew now that the rumors about him and Ellie DeWyant were true, that he'd put together his winning combination and wasn't going to be around much longer. She said, "Morning, Golden Baby," and went into the cubicle.

He followed. She took time hanging up her groovy striped jacket.

"Just wanted to say good-bye, Lou. And to wish you all the best."

No longer. Nevermore. Smile you dumb bitch smile.

"Hey, crazy. Andy promised I could have your office if and when. You won't renege now, will you?"

He smiled. "Word of honor."

She started for the door. "You'll forgive my unseemly haste. Have to make sure the boss man remembers."

He stopped her as she was going past him. "Kiss good-bye?"

"Sure. Here or at a secluded rendezvous?"

He leaned forward and touched her lips with his.

"Okay," she said. "You've sold me. You get a farewell fuck."

He flinched. "C'mon, Lou. You're someone special—"

He wasn't finished, but she didn't want to hear his motherin' lecture and interrupted with, "So all the boys tell me."

He nodded slowly. He said, "Well, see you."

She was going to let him walk out. She was going to stand there laughing at him and his dumb look, but all sorts of things began eating at her. Lecture her, would he!

"That lucky hotel broad. And to think the only difference between us is her looks and a few million dollars."

He smiled, but he was white around the lips. "Find someone," he said, voice quiet. "It's important, Lou. Find someone before it's too late."

"Hey, like the late-late show, Golden Baby. I always cry."

He turned away.

"You found someone, huh? Or is it correct to call a hotel *someone*, Golden Digger?"

He stopped. She thought he was going to muscle her, his neck got so white. But he said, "Peace," his voice a ragged whisper, and went out.

She was glad! The furies ripped at her guts and she was glad she'd said it!

She went quickly up the hall past Andy's closed door and Bruce's open one to the stock room. Manny, the combination mail, delivery, and office boy, was just unplugging the electric percolator. Patricia Delehanty was lecturing him about the reality of the Devil. "Just because the Ecumenical Council wants to put nuns in minihabits doesn't mean that the dangers of eternal damnation are reduced."

Manny sighed and looked at Lou. "Hey, will you please tell her I'm Jewish and we don't worry about those things?"

The aging, heavyset redhead muttered, "She can't tell me anything. She's rejected all faith."

Usually, Lou treated Pat the Mick as she would her own mother —with understanding, good humor, and caution. Now she said, "Pat's got a right to worry. If they ever do away with the concept of Hell, what would she have to look forward to?"

The Mick glared. Lou poured herself a cup of coffee. Voice trembling, the Mick said, "You've just compounded your damnation!" She left without filling her cup.

Manny said, "Why is it she can hand it out so good but when anyone *gives* her a little, on goes the faucet? She spends half her mornings crying."

"You know what she needs, don't you, Manny?"

His thin face split in a wide grin. He moved closer. "I think it's the same thing *I* need."

"Really? I've got just the man for you."

He laughed, and came to within an inch of her. "Hey, Lou . . ." He touched her arm.

She added a drop of milk to her cup.

His eyes slid to the door and he stepped past her and closed it. "You're the kickiest," he said, coming back to her. His arm went around her waist, buddy-buddy casual, except that he was trembling. "I really dig you, Lou. I mean, you're the greatest ever."

She took a long swallow of coffee. "You say that with all the experience of your seventeen years, do you?"

"Listen, I get around!" He made the laugh sound almost natural. "No, honest, Lou, why can't we—" He suddenly grabbed her and kissed her, hitting the side of her mouth.

"Watch the coffee."

"Then put it down." His voice was high with excitement. "*Please*, Lou."

She wondered when Andy would come for his coffee. She wondered if Jackie had come for hers yet. She put down the cup.

He kissed her and moved his hands over her body. Light touches. Frightened touches. She opened her mouth. His touches strengthened. He raised her miniskirt and felt her thighs and slid one hand inside her pants and over her buttocks. It was time to stop him. She didn't stop him.

A moment later he tried to break away. She held him. He mumbled, 'The door. Lemme lock—" She said, "Uh-uh." He had her pants down around her knees and was ready to go for broke. "But what if someone—" She shrugged. "I'm the greatest, right, Manny? What will you risk for the greatest?"

The boy surprised her. He risked everything.

And Andy walked in.

It took a second for him to see, another second for him to accept what he saw, and then he went out. Manny's face was white. "Cheeze, we'll lose our jobs!" He began buckling his trousers.

"I'm sorry, honey. I'll say it was my fault."

"No . . . hell, so I'll get another job. I mean, he said he was going to teach me copy-writing, but all I've been doing . . . No, it was *my* fault."

She stepped out of her pants, went to the door, and turned the lock. She came to him. He said, "We can't—"

She drew him to the wall.

He whispered, "Sure, why the hell not? What can he do to us, right?"

She nodded.

He was a good kid, but only a kid. He was through before she'd begun. She told him he was marvelous and that they'd get together again and he was so full of pride he was ready to walk into Andy's office and say he'd been raping her. She told him to sort the mail and not worry about anything.

Andy's door was closed. She walked in without knocking. He was sitting at his desk, all the hurt in the world on his face.

She suddenly knew why she'd done it. She said, "I'm leaving, but I want you to promise Manny will stay on. It's important to him. He's got no other way than with a good boss, a good job."

He moved his lips a moment, then: "Now wait. I want to understand—"

"Nothing to understand, Andy. I'm going home. I've been thinking of it for a while now. I was saying good-bye to him."

"Like *that?*"

"Picking flowers, singing songs, eating hors d'oeuvres. Remember?"

He nodded. "Yet I kept thinking it was something special, you and me."

She shrugged. "I've had it with this sun-filled isolation ward.

I'm going into the real world again. There might be risks involved, but at least I'll feel *alive*."

"This is as much the real world as any other place. I've lived in three northern cities—"

"You're right." He wasn't, but there was no use trying to make him see it. You either knew or you didn't. "I'm just making excuses. Miami's not my town any more."

"But why? If you're anticipating my letting you go . . ."

She had to end it. He was getting ready to forgive her everything.

"Got your pecker up, did it, boss?"

He blinked hard. She leered delicately. Voice choked, he said, "You needn't finish the day. I'll mail you your check."

She cleaned out her desk and got the Volks from the car park and drove home. She took her suitcases from the closet, thought about it a moment, then put them back. It was Thursday, the twenty-sixth of January. Her rent was paid until the end of the month, which meant six days, counting this slightly used and much abused one, to enjoy the sun and ocean.

Why not? What was she rushing back to New York for? Just another beginning. And beginnings were a dime a dozen in her life.

She would take a six-day vacation. She would read and sleep and hunt on the beach. She would bring home a different boy every night. She would get a few joints and do some flying . . .

Which reminded her. She had the remains of four roaches in the cupboard.

She found the dish and rolled a joint and struck a match. But then she remembered the roaches were from the night with Bruce, and she blew out the match and took everything to the bathroom and flung it in the toilet and kept flushing until there wasn't anything left. That's what she wanted to do with *him!* Flush him down the toilet! The mother! The builder of the dream and killer of the dream! The Golden-Digging mother!

She was trembling with rage, or what she insisted was rage.

To hell with Golden. And to hell with marijuana. She needed something stronger. A little acid. A little trip into her own insides. There was that Miami U character. So she'd let him play his weirdo bed games. Who was she to quibble over sex hang-ups?

She decided to call him right now.

He wasn't in, but a friend took the message.

She also called the Metropole, the thing she named "rage" building by the second. "Miss DeWyant, please."

The voice was weak, sleepy. "Yes?"

"This is the society editor of the AP, Miss DeWyant. We've received word that you're engaged to a Mr.—let me see now—to a Mr. Bruce Goldman?"

"Golden. But I don't understand how—"

"Golden, thank you. And the wedding will take place when?"

"There's no . . . Who did you say this was?"

"No definite plans, yes, got it. But the engagement *is* definite and you will be marrying Mr. Golden at some future date."

Ellie DeWyant tried to speak, but Lou went briskly on, the rage continuing to build. "Now we have everything, except a rather important point. You are, of course, well known in Miami circles. But Mr. Golden—is he in the hotel business, too?"

"Advertising. But we don't want any publicity—"

"Advertising? Madison Avenue then. His firm and position, please?"

"I—I'm afraid I'm going to have to hang up now."

"Oh," Lou said, dropping the brisk tone for a surprised one. "Oh, I see. Then one more question, Miss DeWyant. Do you think Mr. Golden would be your fiancé if it wasn't for your money?"

There was a moment of complete silence, not even the sound of breathing, and Lou put her lips right up against the phone and laughed and said, "You stupid, stupid . . ." The line clicked. Lou said, "So nice to speak to you, Miss DeWyant. We'll have to do it again, and again, and again."

She waited for the rotten feeling to come, the guilty feeling to come, because hurting people had never been Lou Degano's bag.

But then again, *being* hurt had never been Lou Degano's bag either, and she was badly hurt now and the rotten feeling, the guilty feeling, didn't come. She put a bikini on under a shift and left for the beach and the boys.

The Skytop Salon was one of the Bal Metropole's two beauty parlors, much smaller than the one in the Arcade Level and much more expensive. May had just completed a shampoo, color rinse, and set and had been placed under the dryer. To her right was a woman in her middle to late sixties, her high-piled silver hair undergoing drying while she chattered to the dark little girl manicuring her nails.

At first May kept her eyes closed and her mind a comfortable blank, savoring this time away from Harold and the endless round of pointless activities. Then the gravelly voice, a feminine whiskey tenor, began to get through to her.

". . . can't cry about my figure, but you can see what's happened to my face."

"You have a *nice* face, Mrs. Eden."

The laugh was gay as buckshot. "Sure. *Gorgeous!* C'mon, honey, we both know I need a face-lift."

The manicurist protested that Mrs. Eden was among the best-looking women her age. "Ask any of the girls, go on."

May moved her head a little and her eyes the rest of the way. Mrs. Eden was right. Her face was the result of too many years and too much sun—brown and wrinkled like a gnome's.

"The customer's always wrong," Mrs. Eden said, "when she's telling the truth about herself. Let's not have any more foolishness. I'm *dying* to get a face-lift. There's this plastic surgeon in Larchmont. He'll tighten the lines under my eyes, stretch the skin over my cheeks, fix my neck, freshen my upper lip. And it won't cost more than a thousand dollars. But I'm *scared!* Honey, I'm so scared of anything with a knife . . ." She shuddered.

The girl switched tactics. She now began assuring Mrs. Eden there was nothing to be scared of. "I had another customer. She had the job done here in Miami. Said it was less than having a

filling at the dentist's, and she was *really* in bad shape. Not just
. . . a few lines, like you."

"So what happened?"

"She came in here after the lift, and I *swear* I didn't recognize
her. She looked eighty before she had it and fifty afterward.
And she didn't have your figure, either."

"So what's the good? I mean, if a man sees your arms and legs
are old, what good is a cutesy face?"

"*Your* arms and legs—"

"My legs are varicose. My arms are sagging. Only the torso's
held up. I could get a husband with my torso, if he'd forget
the rest." She sprayed her buckshot laughter and suddenly turned
to May. "Now if I looked like you, honey . . ."

May smiled and murmured a disclaimer.

"In fact, I *did* look like you at thirty-five and forty. I have a
picture here . . ." She turned to the manicurist. "Get my bag,
Celia."

The manicurist picked a brown purse up off the floor. Mrs.
Eden searched around in it and pulled out a plastic flip-fold.
"Here we are. Take a look at me in a bathing suit twenty-five
years ago. The guy in back is my Arnold, may he rest in peace."

The manicurist handed it to May. May was startled. The
woman *had* looked something like her! Shorter, perhaps, and
slightly thinner, but still . . .

She handed it back and turned away. The restful lethargy was
gone. In its place was an inner choking, a sense of suffocation,
a need to *do* something.

She met Harold in the waiting room. He rose, dapper in blue
and white yachting outfit complete with captain's cap. "You
look lovely," he murmured. She noticed a young woman eyeing
him as they walked out. She took his arm, hugged it a little. He
glanced at her surprised. She murmured, "Let's go back to the
suite." He asked why. She said she wanted to change. Again he
asked why, since they were going for a motor-launch trip along
Miami's inland waterways and her white culottes were perfect
for that. She tightened her grip on his arm, looking into his eyes.

He finally understood, and smiled his thinnest smile. "You know very well it's impossible."

"*How* do I know? It's been years since we even tried. How can you be sure—"

"We'll discuss it some other time."

"I want to try," she whispered, as he began to ease away. "Please, Harold, it's so important."

"Well it's not important to me! I've told you that the very idea . . ." They reached the elevators. A young couple was waiting there and he lowered his voice. "We've just got time to make the boat. I don't want to talk about this any more, *ever*."

She nodded. They rode to the lobby. She excused herself, went to the ladies' room and used the phone to call the desk. She left a message for Mr. Al Fortens—or rather "Miss James" did. When she hung up, she was weak with excitement and trepidation. But the choking, suffocating feeling was gone.

2

THURSDAY, JANUARY 26
TO
FRIDAY, JANUARY 27, A.M.

By ten-forty-five, Max had covered a goodly portion of the Seaquarium's fifty-odd acres, ending with a second visit to the shark channel, more to smile at how the women shuddered than to watch the ravenous fish. He hadn't seen Jorge, or anything that might have caused him to worry. But his feet hurt and he was beginning to perspire heavily as he made his way to the Main Tank.

He mopped his face and entered the circular building. He went up on the lower-level ramp and looked through curved glass walls at giant sea turtles, porpoises, groupers. At exactly eleven he walked through a tunnel-like exit into the sunlight and leaned against the wall, touching the plastic gun in his pocket. Within five minutes he saw Jorge approaching, carrying a large brown suitcase.

"So you see, Jorge, we had no trouble meeting."

Jorge said, "Walk with me. Before I pay, I have things to tell you."

"I'll walk, Jorge, but not outside the gates."

Jorge turned back the way he had come. Max looked around and fell in beside him. "Open the case while we walk, Jorge."

"What, *here*, with all the people?"

"That's the only place you and I are going to be together— here, with all the people."

Jorge lifted the case in his arms and fumbled with the snaps. Max said, "Let me." He got the snaps open, raised the lid a crack, and looked inside. Greenbacks. Solidly packed with greenbacks.

"How will you count it?" Jorge asked.

Max closed the case. "When I get back to the hotel, I'll count it." (But he wasn't going back to the hotel. He was going to the airport for the DeWyant payoff, then onto a three-o'clock jet.)

"We have to have a meeting about the plan, Mr. Prager. To-morrow night, at your room."

"Sure," Max muttered, trying to decide how best to leave. He put his hand in his pocket, gripping the toy automatic. "Look at me, Jorge. I'm prepared for any sort of double cross. You understand that, don't you?"

Jorge kept walking. "There will be no double cross, Mr. Prager. Not on my part. But if you think to leave Miami before the kidnapping, we will hunt you down wherever you go."

"Don't be foolish, Jorge." He wasn't worried about Jorge or Lamas or their threats. Just let him get on that jet to Los Angeles with his two bags of money and he'd forget this whole shmear.

Jorge said, "Then we are through with our business. Will you take the case now?"

"No hurry." There were people everywhere, and nothing could

happen to him, and he concentrated on how to instruct Jorge. Better have him stay right here, under strict injunction not to leave for half an hour, and get away as fast as he could. Then kill time driving around, making sure no tail was on him, and at the last minute head for the airport.

That way the risks would be minimal. No one could tail Leo Skein for *hours* without giving himself away.

They were approaching a small wooden building, Jorge a step ahead of him. Max was suddenly aware that the crowd had thinned, but before he could react, Jorge said, "I am tired of this, Mr. Prager. I have important work to do, as do you."

"All right."

Jorge turned. Max reached for the extended case. "You stay—"

Jorge's knee caught him in the pit of the stomach, his big, soft stomach. He doubled over and began to retch. Jorge was saying, ". . . sick, Mr. Prager? What is it?" Two other men were there. Max managed to say, "Help me," while choking on sour vomit. One of the men used his knee exactly as Jorge had. Max jack-knifed, but they had him under the arms. All three were close around him, shutting him away from the noise and laughter, shutting him away from his long, happy life. He was almost unconscious now, being moved out of the sunshine in a choking, pain-filled nightmare with whispered Spanish words flitting about him.

He heard a door close, and it was dark. His mind cleared a little. He was on his hands and knees on a dusty wooden floor. He heard Jorge speak in Spanish. The answer came from far away . . . no, from outside the door. He gasped for breath with which to shout, and something smashed into his mouth. He flattened out on the floor. He still wasn't unconscious, but lay as if he were.

They couldn't get away with this—not among all the kids and mothers and tourists! He had planned too well! No dumb Spic messenger . . .

He saw, or sensed, someone standing over him, and forced himself to remain still. Jorge murmured, "Are you conscious, Mr.

Prager?" He breathed as shallowly as he could. "If you are, I just want you to know I am going to kick you again." At that he couldn't help flinching, and the back of his head exploded into brilliant fireworks. Something else went off in his chest, but before he had time to worry about it he was asleep.

Bruce phoned the suite at noon, wanting to give himself at least an hour to get to the airport. Ellie came to the lobby with the blue suitcase. She was obviously upset. He murmured, "Take it easy now. Nothing to worry about."

She nodded, but didn't seem to see him. He took the case, and keeping his voice a murmur, asked, "Is the entire hundred fifty thousand in here?"

She nodded.

"Good. Have a big lunch. Lie in the sun. Relax."

She finally looked at him. "Give it all to him, Bruce, please. I'm afraid."

"We agreed I was to handle it."

"But—it doesn't mean that much to me."

He smiled. "Do you ever need a business manager. Or a husband."

She drew a deep breath, and went back toward the elevators.

Bruce was almost at the doors when he saw Claude DeWyant sitting in a high-backed armchair. Their eyes met. Bruce hesitated, then continued out to the car park. DeWyant had been spying. DeWyant would require explanations.

But one thing at a time. He had to put the money—or the twenty-five thousand he'd decided to pay—in a rental locker at Miami International Airport, then tape the key that opened it behind the phone in the first booth of six near the Eastern Airlines desk—all as Ellie's caller had instructed. Afterward, he would do a little spying of his own, hoping to catch the blackmailer in the act.

He should have been concentrating on his plan, on where to position himself, but all the way across the Julia Tuttle he kept thinking of Ellie's drawn face, her remote eyes.

She needed him. God, yes! She needed him more than he needed her. The sooner they were married the better—for *her!*

He turned the radio up high, trying to blot out thoughts, doubts, worries—that never-to-be-admitted touch of shame.

Before-the-wedding blues.

Long Distance Information found Maximilian Originals for him without any trouble. Bruce asked the operator to connect him with that number.

He was in his apartment. He'd watched that airport phone booth almost an hour. Now it was three o'clock and Ellie was waiting for him at the Metropole. She hadn't asked how much he had left for the blackmailer when he'd called her from Miami International. She'd refused to discuss the money, period, and he'd recognized that grayness, that dullness of voice that worried him. So he'd come here to put the suitcase away and change into beach clothes and run this basic check on Max Prager.

The line clicked and began to ring. A woman's voice said, "Maximilian Originals."

"Max Prager, please."

There was a pause. "Mr. Prager senior passed away more than a year ago. Mr. *Ralph* Prager is now . . ."

Bruce thanked her. He dialed the Metropole and asked for Max Prager's room. The phone rang without answer.

He went to the bedroom. While changing, he checked the closet and the blue suitcase. He hated to leave so much money here, but it was only until tomorrow, when Ellie would be more reasonable.

He turned away, then gave in to an impulse and opened the bag on the bed and looked at one hundred twenty-five thousand dollars. It represented only a portion of what he would soon own, and sent him out with his little beach bag and a little smile.

He had just entered the hotel lobby when Bob Lewin called to him from the desk. "Mr. DeWyant would like to see you, Bruce. In his office."

He hesitated. He had no desire to talk to DeWyant now. Ellie was waiting. Besides, it was time he established himself as a perfect equal, a son-in-law and not a toadying employee. In reality, everything belonged to Ellie—and Ellie belonged to him.

He went to the desk. "Tell him I'm with his daughter. I'll see him tonight, or tomorrow."

Lewin stared. Bruce said, "Put the eyes back in the sockets, Bob. You might lose them."

Lewin flushed, seemed about to answer sharply, then thought better of it. He managed a smile. "You and Miss DeWyant? . . ."

"Yes?"

"I mean—well, you're hitting it off, right?"

"Right." He walked away.

Poor boy, rich girl. Employee and boss's daughter. He'd be stuck with that, and with a host of unspoken comments, for a while yet.

He kissed Ellie when they met near the pool, knowing that Jerry Leech and others were watching. "Let me admit something," she said. "Up to now it's been a *terrible* day. Change it for me, Bruce."

"Okay." He put his arm around her shoulders and they began to walk. "How about going to Sanibel next week?"

"Yes!"

"On our honeymoon."

She looked up at him. "If you think it's a good time," she murmured.

"I'm not sure whether Jupiter is in the house of Venus, or whether Mars is in conjunction . . ."

She smiled—a small smile, but it transformed her face. And it clutched at his heart. *Pity? Pity for the girl getting short-changed? . . .*

"Then it's settled," he said, more loudly than he'd intended. "No announcement. No engagements. We get the license next Monday and get married as soon as the law allows. Thursday, I believe."

"Yes, Bruce." Her voice was hushed.

"Hey, you act like it was something *important*."

350

She smiled again—a strong smile this time, a happy smile—and put her arm around his waist and hugged him.

They went down to the beach. Men turned to look at her. Now that she was happy, she actually *radiated* beauty.

He touched her cheek with his lips. Next week they would be married. Next week doubt and confusion would end. Next week everything would change.

Jorge would have killed him before he regained consciousness. He'd had his moment of revenge, his payment for the ridicule Prager had heaped upon him, and would have preferred to end it painlessly—a simple matter of squeezing that fat throat. But the *patrón* had said to talk to him, to find out what he had planned for the kidnapping, and even though Jorge was sure it was a waste of time, he would obey.

Except that it began to look as if the fat man would *never* wake up. Jorge sat on an upended wheelbarrow, half dozing, Prager lying at his feet. When Prager finally stirred, Jorge picked up his gun.

Prager groaned and tried to sit up. Jorge bent and put the revolver against his forehead. "Can you understand what I'm saying, Mr. Prager? This is a gun with a silencer. One loud sound, one sudden move, and you are dead."

It took some moments before Prager was able to respond. His lips were split and puffy, his chin covered with dried blood, his clothes stank of vomit. He touched his head and groaned.

Jorge helped him into a sitting position. Prager cleared his throat and spat to the side. "Where? . . ."

"In a tool shed."

Prager turned his head slowly, looking around the small, shadowy room. "Still . . . in the Seaquarium?"

"Yes."

Prager belched, began to speak, then pressed his chest. "Hurts," he said.

"You tried to cheat us, Mr. Prager."

"My heart. I need a doctor."

351

Jorge didn't answer. He was through worrying about Prager's lies, Prager's tricks. He lit a *cigarro* and inhaled deeply. Prager licked his lips. "What are you going to do?"

"Wait."

"How long?"

"Until everyone goes home."

"What if someone comes here? A worker, to get a tool?"

"No one will come here. The door is padlocked. A new padlock. Only my friends have the key."

"They'll break it open."

"Maybe tomorrow, when they find out no employee has the key. But not today. Today we are safe. Tomorrow we'll be gone."

"Where will we be gone to?"

Jorge blew smoke and looked away.

"You're crazy! How will you pull off the snatch—"

"Much quieter, Mr. Prager. I don't want to have to hurt you again."

Prager's voice dropped. "So I squeezed you for advance payment. So I didn't get away with it. So you'll hold my money until after the snatch."

"I don't think you plan to go through with the kidnap, Mr. Prager."

"Of course I do!"

Jorge leaned forward. Prager said, "Okay, okay, I'll keep it down." He pressed his chest again. "Listen, I feel real sick. I think I'm having some sort of attack. When your friend opens the door, take me to a doctor."

"How could I do that, Mr. Prager? How could I trust you after the way you've acted?"

"Well—" He was gasping. "Well, I *swear*. My word of honor."

Jorge smiled. "Remember what I said in Howard Johnson's? I said you are not an honorable man, Mr. Prager. And you said there are worse things. Now there are no worse things, because now you have no word of honor to trade on."

"You'll never work the snatch without my plan." His hands

were no longer at his chest but clenched at his sides. "You'll never figure out how I was going to do it."

"You have no plan. You weren't going to be in the hotel Saturday night."

"Of course I was! You're just guessing, and you're wrong!"

"Shhhh." He struck Prager lightly across the face. The man started, and put his hand to his chest.

"Please don't hit me. I told you, I'm feeling sick. If we can talk quietly—"

"Plenty of time for talk, Mr. Prager. Hours. But as you said, *quietly*."

Prager spoke in a whisper. "How are you going to get Christopher? Tell me that? Have you got a plan?"

"Yes. A very good one."

"You're amateurs, Jorge. All of you. I'm the only professional you have. Without my plan—"

Jorge waved his gun impatiently. "Lies, Mr. Prager. From the beginning, all you did was lie. You have no plan."

"If you think I'm going to tell it to you without a guarantee . . ." He was staring up, swollen lips trembling. "Make me a deal, Jorge. C'mon, any sort of reasonable deal. Put up or shut up, Jorge."

"I'll shut up. And so will you, Mr. Prager. I've been fooled by you for the last time."

"Then you're finished," Prager whispered, and slumped down. "You'll all be dead or in prison by midnight Saturday."

"Which gives us a full day more of life than you."

Prager kept his head down. Jorge finished his *cigarro* and lit another. Prager's breathing was loud and harsh. Jorge settled himself more comfortably.

"Another thing," Prager said. "How do you expect to get me out of here? Or do you think you can leave me in this shed and not have witnesses turn up who saw you and your friends drag me in?"

"If there were witnesses, they would already have made themselves known."

"No, that's not the way it works. Only when they read about me being found here, only then they'll go to the cops. You're risking everything just to get back at me for the squeeze."

Jorge smiled with genuine satisfaction. "They won't find you here, Mr. Prager. They won't find you anywhere."

"Oh, sure. Dump me in the bay or ocean. It never works, Jorge."

"As a professional, Mr. Prager, you know it works more times than the public is told. And besides, we've got something better than that."

Prager looked up at him. "Tell me."

Jorge smoked.

"Go on, see if you can convince me it'll work. What have you got to lose? I can't get out of here. I can't do a thing and you know it."

Jorge said, "You will be dropped into the Shark Channel," and immediately leveled his gun to cut off any possible scream.

Prager laughed, but Jorge caught the momentary pause, the split-second flash of shock and horror.

"Would you like a *cigarro*, Mr. Prager? Very good. Pure Havana. A friend brings them in."

Prager's breathing was louder, harsher. Jorge waited. Prager said, "All right, I'll prove that you're making a mistake. I'll tell you my plan, but I'll leave out a few key—" He swallowed and pressed his chest. "I'll protect myself. That's fair, isn't it?"

Jorge nodded, feeling it would be so much easier on both of them to finish him off right now.

"Okay. First Jerry goes into old man Wheeler's suite, gets Eve to help him, and opens the connecting door to the Senator's suite."

"*How* does he get the nurse to help him?"

"What do you mean? He's been sleeping with her almost a week. She'll—"

"Yes? She'll what, Mr. Prager?"

Prager was moving his lips without speaking. He'd realized Jorge wasn't going to let him gloss over the details, and that

354

there was no assuming the nurse would do anything for Leech outside of bed. "I have an angle," he finally said. "Don't ask me what. A strong angle. I mean, why did we bother with the nurse in the first place, right? We had a purpose, right?"

"Our purpose was to get into Wheeler's suite in case the manager resisted Violetta. Our purpose was to have another approach. Just as we have with the Krasmer woman. And with the speechwriter. And with everyone we can think of. Approaches, Mr. Prager, many of them, adding up to a strong plan. But you're not even aware of much of that plan. You resigned some time ago, and we went ahead on our own."

"That's what *you* think," Prager replied, and waved his hand to cut off any interruptions. "Amateurs. I'm the professional. The nurse will help Jerry because she won't know what he's up to. He'll con her as I'll instruct him."

"*How* will you instruct him?"

"That's one of my little secrets. God's truth, Jorge."

Jorge said, "Yes. And you are a truthful man, aren't you?" He reached behind him, picked up Prager's toy pistol and played with it. "Go on with your God's truth, Mr. Prager."

"Two," Prager said, voice trembling. "Ruthie goes into May Krasmer's suit, immobilizes anyone there—"

"By herself?"

"She can do it with a gun. Or you give her an assistant."

"Very clever. Very complex. Something we could never have figured out for ourselves."

Prager pushed on desperately. "Three. Jerry lets you into the Senator's suite and you give the Senator a shot of something strong, something to knock him out. Sodium pentothol, say. Then you put him in the old man's wheelchair—"

"And the bodyguard? He is applauding while I do this?"

"You're not giving me a chance!"

Jorge put his fingers to his lips.

"Sorry. But listen—the bodyguard isn't there. Because I'm with Dan Berner, see, and Berner has called the guard to help him." He was growing frantic now, his words running into each other.

"It's this way. I cultivated Berner. We've talked and become friends. I'm in his room, see—"

"And how can you be sure *he* is in his room?"

"Because . . . I'll go there with him after the speech. I'll make him call the Senator and ask him to send the guard down with some papers."

"Won't Berner be with the Senator after the speech? Won't he be part of the close group—"

"Give me a chance to think!" Prager whispered hoarsely. "I have an angle . . ." He thought a moment. "But it's another one of my guarantees, and I'll tell it to you when we get back to the hotel."

Jorge said nothing.

Prager's voice was rising along with his panic, his desperation. "Now what if Jerry fails with the old man and the nurse? Ever thought of that? What if he can't even get into the Senator's suite?"

"With the keys McKensil has given us—"

"I don't care about that! I mean if something goes wrong, *wrong!*" He pressed his chest again. "I'm trying to explain how I've got the saver, the clincher. Ruthie will be with May Krasmer, remember? She'll say she's a private eye hired by the husband and knows about her carrying on with Berner. She'll make Krasmer knock at the Senator's door, and you can get in that way." He was panting, sweating. He was pitiful.

"Where will *you* be all this time, Mr. Prager, if Berner doesn't go to his room?"

"Me? Moving. Operating. Running the show. If I have to, I'll be in the Senator's suite. Or the old man's. Or wherever the action is. That's why you hired me, right? And I'll do a job for you, I swear I will!"

Jorge smoked. Prager said, "Listen, I have more. Little angles. Safety measures. Tricks. Things I learned and used all my life. Just get me to a doctor, Jorge! Please, I feel . . . my heart . . ." He began to cry.

Jorge had never seen a man fall apart like this, and turned his eyes away. Prager had always been so cool, so cynical, so sure of himself. Now he was babbling. His "plan" was nothing but what they'd discussed at their first meeting—the skeleton, not the flesh. He hadn't progressed into meaningful details—as Lamas had, once he'd decided he might have to do without Prager. He hadn't anything to offer, except perhaps the idea of drugging the Senator. But even there, Lamas felt the risks of putting the Senator in a wheelchair and trying to pass him off as his father-in-law were too great. If he could be made to walk into the elevator . . .

Prager was scrambling across the floor on all fours. Jorge leaped after him. Prager smashed into the door, shouting. He managed to get out, "Save—" before Jorge clamped a hand over his mouth. With his other hand, he hooked savagely to the kidneys. Prager jerked a few times, and went limp. Jorge held him, straining to hear what was happening outside. At first there was nothing beyond the muted blend of a thousand voices. Then a child said, "In there, Daddy. In *there!*" A man said, "Will you come on?" sounding tired, irritable. The child said something Jorge couldn't make out. The man said, "If you won't walk . . ." The child began to cry, and the crying disappeared rapidly in the distance.

Had the child been speaking of the shed with his "in *there*"? Would he convince his father to return, with a Seaquarium employee?

Prager made a gargling sound, jerked weakly, rolled his head. Jorge dragged him back to the wheelbarrow. He considered the possibilities, and decided to wait before killing him. Far better to be found with a beaten man than with a corpse, if the worst happened.

The shed seemed hotter now. Jorge wiped his face, his neck, rubbed his hands on his trousers. He hunched over Prager and listened to sounds from outside. Time passed. He dozed, wakened, checked his watch. Four-thirty.

More time passed. The muted roar lessened. The Seaquarium was emptying.

He suddenly realized Prager was looking up at him, and raised his fist. Prager said nothing, did nothing. His mouth gaped open.

Jorge kept his fist up. "Do you pray, Mr. Prager?"

Prager's lips moved. His chest heaved strangely. When he spoke, his voice was so low, so confused with gasps and grunts, that Jorge had to bend closer.

"Name . . . Leo."

"You'd better pray now, Mr. Prager."

"Leo . . . Skein. Call me . . ."

Jorge understood. The lies were over. Prager wanted the truth now. He wanted to die as himself, with a little *machismo*.

"All right, Mr. Skein." He put his hands on the thick throat, felt the heaving, the convulsing, and withdrew.

Prager hadn't been lying about his heart. He was going through some sort of seizure.

Jorge knelt beside him, undecided what to do.

Prager suddenly rolled over and curled up, knees to his chest. "Chuck . . . see . . ." Then he cried out, and Jorge had to cover his mouth.

Jorge felt the breath pounding against his palm and muttered a Hail Mary. It went on a while. When it ended, he checked the pulse, breath, and heartbeat. Nothing. He stood up and went to the door and listened. He returned to the wheelbarrow and sat down.

Later he heard someone at the door. He sprang up, drawing the gun from his jacket. Metal rasped against metal, and the some-one went away. Ramon Pedras. Jorge relaxed and smoked a *cigarro*. Light faded from around the door. He got the suitcase from behind the barrow and opened it. In a lower compartment, under the single layer of money, were sandwiches and a Thermos of coffee. He ate. He drank. He smoked another *cigarro*, and bent to Prager.

He undressed him completely—shoes, clothes, jewelry—and put everything in the suitcase. Then he settled down for another long wait.

At a few minutes after twelve, he went to the door. He opened it slowly and looked out. Not too bright a night, and no one around. But he knew about the watchmen, and there was no way of being sure he wouldn't run into one.

He drew his revolver, returned to Prager, and picked him up, the gun in his right hand. He went out of the shed, kicking the door closed behind him, and turned directly toward the snaking Shark Channel. It wasn't a long walk, not more than three minutes, and the overcast held. But the naked body was two hundred pounds of stiffening dead weight in his arms, and it seemed to gleam with a light of its own.

He went into a stumbling trot the last few feet, coming up to the metal railing that ran along both banks of the channel. A sign warned of the dangers of going under the railing. He didn't go under it. He raised the body up and, straining mightily, threw it over. The sound it made seemed more explosion than splash, and he crouched low.

The grounds were empty, the buildings dark blotches against the lesser dark of night. He saw nothing, heard nothing.

He heard nothing at all, and wondered at that. Sharks made noise, didn't they? Many of them, thrashing in the water?

He stood up, looking over the railing. The water was dark and oily-placid. He began to worry. Was it possible these sharks wouldn't eat human flesh? Could they be so well fed . . .

He heard a *swishing* sound. He saw a shadow under the water, a fin cutting the surface, another shadow darting in—and then so many that the water sprang alive, boiling beneath him.

Just before he turned away, he saw something he wished he hadn't seen: the luminescent white shape bobbing upward, dancing left and right as the shadows struck from both sides, staining the water with a heavy black pall.

He returned to the shed. He found the padlock against the wall, took it inside, and closed the door. He went behind the wheelbarrow and used a match to find the stack of canvas covers. He made a pallet, lay down, and was asleep instantly.

He awoke several times, and the last time saw daylight around the edge of the door. He finished the Thermos of coffee, took out his safety razor, and began scraping his cheeks, wincing at the dry shave but continuing until his face and neck felt smooth to the touch. He walked completely around the shed, making sure he had left nothing behind of his or Prager's. Suitcase in hand, he went to the door and waited.

The first voice he heard brought a smile to his lips: a child asking for a souvenir. He cracked the door and saw the young mother and little boy moving away. He stepped out, replaced the padlock, and began to walk.

He visited a rest room, then sat in the picnic area enjoying the morning sun. He had to let a few hours go by. He had to allow enough people to enter so that his leaving wouldn't be noticed.

He lit a *cigarro*, trying not to remember that luminescent white shape. He had far more important matters to think of. It was Friday. Tomorrow . . .

Ai, mañana!

3

FRIDAY, JANUARY 27

Friday morning, still in his pajamas, yawning and rubbing his head, Bruce called Max Prager. He'd tried three times yesterday, the last at eleven-thirty, and had finally got Mrs. Prager, who said she didn't know when Max would be in. A night out with the boys, you understand. Every man should be allowed it once in a while. And chuckle and see-you and good night. It was now eight o'clock, far too early for a social call, but he was determined to catch Prager in.

The operator said, "One moment, please," and then, "Mr. and Mrs. Prager are no longer in the hotel."

"Are you sure?"

"I'll connect you with the desk, sir."

He recognized Bob Lewin's "Good morning, may I help you?"

"Bruce Golden, Bob. Have Mr. and Mrs. Max Prager checked out?"

"Prager . . . yes, that's right."

"Mind telling me when?"

"I wasn't on the desk. Let's see. Twelve-thirty last night. Or this morning, if you're a stickler for accuracy."

"That's strange. We had a golf date."

"Teddy's still around. Let me ask him."

Bruce drained his glass of orange juice.

"Bruce? Teddy says it was some sort of emergency. Mrs. Prager did the checking out. Mr. Prager had already left. Business crisis, as close as Teddy could gather."

Bruce dressed and took the suitcase of money from the closet. He put it in the trunk of his car and drove out of the sub-garage. He had to go to the airport and make sure that the money was gone. It would just about pinpoint Prager as the blackmailer—his checking out at this time being too right for coincidence. Then professional detection would uncover the man's true identity. . . .

He was stunned to find the key behind the phone box. He went to the locker, took out the airline bag, and opened it in the Jag. The money was there—all of it.

He put it in the trunk with the suitcase and drove to the Metropole. He used a house phone in the lobby to order breakfast from room service, and was kissing Ellie good morning when the cart arrived. Poppa, she explained, was in his office, seeing to some business.

He told her all that had happened. They were at the kitchen table, and she put down her fork. Her face, a moment ago gay and lovely, grew drawn and gray. She huddled inside her lime silk peignoir. "I begged you," she whispered. "I knew something would happen if we didn't pay what he asked. You didn't hear him. You don't know—"

"Now stop it," he interrupted sharply.

Her eyes blinked.

"You can't allow yourself to fall apart this way. If he's dissatisfied, he'll be in touch again."

"I don't want him to be in touch again. I never want him to be in touch again." She rose and walked into the living room.

He followed, catching up with her and turning her to face him. "We'll be married next week. I'll be taking the calls then. He'll be in touch with *me*, not with you."

She looked at him, and some of the grayness left her face.

"But I doubt that he'll call. He seems to have been frightened off."

"That's wishful thinking, Bruce."

"It's a hunch. Let's wait before we label it wrong."

She said she wanted to dress now. He kissed her. She was very still in his arms. He moved his hands over her body. She began to warm. He said he would watch her dress. They went into the bedroom and he sat at her vanity. She took off the peignoir and a shortie nightgown. It was his turn to warm. She was at the dresser, taking out underthings, and looked into the mirror as he came up behind her. She turned slowly, then surprised him with sudden passion, quick violence. She sucked at his mouth and tore at his clothing and said, "Yes, God yes! Take me *hard*, Bruce! Wipe it all out and start the world over again!" And on the bed, as they writhed together, she cried out, "Rebirth!" and bit his shoulder so that he felt sharp pain, which was forgotten in his own climax.

He touched the shoulder and discovered blood. She lay on her side, eyes closed. He went into the bathroom and washed and used a Band-Aid. He came out and she hadn't moved. He said, "Hey newly born."

Voice muffled by bedding, she said, "When I open my eyes the world will be one day old. Adam and Ellie. Garden of Eden."

He laughed and stroked her hip, but was made uncomfortable by her intensity. "Look out for snakes, baby. I'll meet you at the pool in an hour."

She turned her head. "Must you leave me?"

He nodded. "Some business."

"*I'm* your only business. You said so yourself."

"Next week, yes. This week, a few loose ends still to be snipped."

"It's not that you're angry, is it? Because I bit you?" Before he could laugh at that, she said, "I didn't mean it. Or I meant it . . . Yes, I must have, but I don't know why . . ." She put her face back in the bedding.

He turned to the chair and his clothing.

"No snakes in our garden," she said. "We've driven them out. See you at the pool."

He tried to make her laugh. "I'll be the one with the fig leaf."

She didn't laugh. "I'll be the one with the new-born eyes. No snakes, ever."

He dressed. She seemed to doze. He went to the hall door, and the phone rang. He heard her say hello, and waited in case it was the blackmailer. She said, "You again. How you must hate him, or love him, to say those things." He felt he was eavesdropping, but didn't leave. "If *I* don't mind," she said, voice shaking, "why should you?" She hung up, and began to cry.

He hesitated, then left quietly. Next week he would find out everything. Next week he would begin changing everything.

DeWyant was just leaving his office. Bruce said, "I can catch you later, if you're busy."

"I wasn't busy yesterday," DeWyant said, and reentered the cypress-paneled room.

"Sorry about that. Ellie—"

"I'm concerned about Ellie—too." He went behind the thin black desk. "Close the door, will you?"

Bruce did, and sat down in an armchair across the desk. "I know you must be puzzled about my having the suitcase yesterday."

"I'm puzzled about far more important things than that. The money is Ellie's business. I told her I wouldn't ask questions, and I won't. If she wants to give it to you . . ." He shrugged.

Bruce laughed. "I always ask my fiancées for a few hundred thousand in advance."

DeWyant took a cigar from his breast pocket, looked at it, and put it down on the desk. Bruce said, "The money is safe. If I have anything to say about it, it will remain safe."

"I wish you joy with it."

Bruce flushed and began to answer. DeWyant overrode him. "If that's all you want, take it with easy conscience."

Bruce didn't bother replying to *that*. He filled the long silence by lighting a cigarette.

"If it's Ellie you want, take *her* with easy conscience."

Bruce looked up. "Then we're agreed."

"*All* of Ellie. Ellie as you've known her, and Ellie as you may only have glimpsed her. Ellie as you're certainly going to see her in the months to come. Ellie who needs love so constant in a husband that I would be frightened no matter *who* the man was."

"I understand. I assure you—"

"You don't understand, and you could never assure me." He was sitting stiffly, eyes piercing. Bruce met the gaze, keeping himself under tight control. It was the last hurdle—the father putting the prospective son-in-law through his paces. "I *know* you, Golden."

Bruce smoked. "What is it you know, or think you know, Claude?"

DeWyant's mouth twitched in distaste. Bruce smiled. "You were a different man in the suite last Saturday night."

"Ellie was there. When Ellie is there, games are played. Only a man who loves her in a way I'm not sure any man can love her can stop playing games and be himself. One thing is certain —you're not that man."

"I think I am. She thinks I am."

"You *know* you're not. She . . ." He suddenly seemed uncertain. "I think she's fooling herself. She's at a particularly low point, and she's using you to make things better. But when you shatter her delusion . . ."

"You underestimate me," Bruce said, deciding to talk a little fact. "Even if I wasn't in love with her that way—how did you put it?—a way you're not sure *any* man can be in love. Even so, I'd still make her happy. I'm in this thing for life, for good, forever, Claude. Please understand that."

"You're in this thing for money."

"For Ellie."

"For money and for Ellie."

"Would that necessarily mean I'd fail her?"

"Yes."

"Come on now. Haven't there been successful marriages where one partner is influenced by the other partner's money?"

"Many, but not with a *partner* like Ellie."

"You're a father. Fathers tend to think their daughters unique."

DeWyant leaned forward. "For three years she's been no more than a step away from death."

Bruce froze.

"Not heart trouble. Not an incurable disease. The death I'm talking about wouldn't come from anything but Ellie herself. She tried suicide twice, the last time only eight months ago. I don't know the reason—the specific reason that specific time. But the time before—three years ago—it was a man who swept her off her feet. A man who talked marriage. A man who eased himself out of the picture when they grew close and he found things in her he didn't like."

"Psychiatric care—" Bruce began.

"Eight years of that. Hospitalization for two long periods, and for several week-long rests. And intensive analysis the last three years. Maybe it's congenital . . . from her mother. Dr. Iglesias doesn't rule that out. But whatever it is, and despite all the care and help, she still walks a tightrope over a black pit. Forgive my purple prose. You always disapproved of it in our ads, didn't you? Maybe you were right. But this is my daughter's life I'm talking about, and you haven't got the love for her—*you just haven't got it, Golden*—to assure me that she won't end up taking a jar of sleeping pills again. You're not in love, Golden."

The last hurdle, Bruce thought. *The last complication.* She was a depressive, but so were a million other women. DeWyant was exaggerating. He was pushing the thing to its utmost limits. He was making a sensitive girl into a psychopath in order to scare the fortune hunter away.

"I *am* in love. And I'll be more in love as time goes by."

"Yes, with Ellie and her money. You as much as admitted it before. But only a *little* with Ellie, and a lot with her money."

Bruce shook his head, and used the ashstand to crush out his cigarette. "I hope to disprove—"

"Not *hope*. No qualifications allowed. Only absolutes. This is her *life* we're talking about."

Bruce sighed and rose. "I don't think there's anything further to be gained—"

"Sit down."

"No, I don't think I will." He went to the door. "We'll talk again, when you're more rational."

"Golden!"

Bruce turned.

"I hold you responsible!" Then he sank back in his chair, suddenly old. "I could stop you, but it would mean using methods that would shock Ellie and throw her over the edge as surely . . ." He shook his head, kept shaking it as he said, "If anything happens to her . . . if she does anything to herself while you're in her life . . ." His head stopped shaking. He stared at Bruce. He was old, he was beaten, but for a moment he was also frightening. "What happens to her happens to you. Understand, I don't talk through my hat. I have partners. I don't want them, but in order to build the Metropole I had to take them. They'll do as I ask."

The moment ended, and Bruce's fear ended with it. "So the rumors are true," he murmured, not believing it in the slightest, embarrassed for the old man forced to bring in tales of Mafia and Syndicate to gain some bargaining power.

"In Miami, the rumors are always true. Besides, who else has enough money to build fifty-million-dollar hotels?"

Bruce smiled, reading a withdrawal from threat, hoping it indicated an end to the melodrama. "I'll make her happy, Claude."

366

"I hope so. I doubt it, but I hope so. I don't want to hurt you. I don't like you, I don't trust you, but I don't want to hurt you." He looked down at his hands, his eyes blinking rapidly.

Bruce felt he should say something final and convincing. He couldn't find the thought or the words. He opened the door.

DeWyant's voice was a tired mutter, utterly lacking strength or conviction. "Remember, I hold you responsible."

"I'll remember, Claude. We'll laugh about it in a few months."

DeWyant finally lifted his head. He nodded a little. Bruce smiled and left. That was the very last hurdle. A beaut, he had to admit! But definitely behind him.

Jerry was earlier than usual. Eve let him in and they kissed near the door, his strong hands moving over her. He'd come to her every night since last Saturday, seven consecutive nights, and it got better each time. She was learning much about being a woman. And not only with Jerry. She had served Mr. Wheeler twice more, Tuesday and Thursday. The other nights, including tonight, he'd been unable to respond. She'd been glad in one way, sorry in another . . . sorry for him. His gratitude was clear. There had been fresh flowers each day beside the sleeper couch, and she wore a beautiful diamond pendant he'd bought on the Arcade Level. More important, he was seeing his lawyer about changing his will the day they moved into the Palm Beach house.

Jerry began moving her toward the living room. "He fell asleep only ten minutes ago," she whispered.

"Ten minutes, ten hours, what's the difference?"

She could have explained that a person asleep minutes is generally much closer to consciousness than one asleep an hour or more, that sleep has levels, depths, strengths. But he said, "He hasn't bothered us before and he won't now," and she forgot to worry.

It was a mistake. They were on the couch, still dressed but touching each other, when she heard a sound from the bedroom. Her head jerked around. Jerry began to say something. She stood up, finger to lips. The sound came again, louder this time. Jerry rose and put his mouth to her ear. "He's only turning over or something."

She shook her head, and pointed at the foyer.

He kept his mouth to her ear. "He can't get out of bed by himself, so why worry?"

Again she pointed at the foyer. She didn't have time to explain how far Mr. Wheeler had come since the day they'd arrived. He *might* be trying to make it to his wheelchair.

She pushed Jerry a little, and he finally nodded. "All right. Tomorrow then."

She shook her head violently. He knew very well that tomorrow was the Senator's speech!

"The old man's not *really* staying up for the speech, is he?"

She nodded. The sound from the bedroom seemed closer to the door. She stabbed her finger at the foyer.

The thump was loud, and *quite* close to the door. Jerry turned, surprised, then ran to the foyer. Eve brushed at her skirt, patted her hair, and heard the hall door closing softly. She stared at the bedroom door, not quite believing what she saw. The knob was turning.

The door opened. Mr. Wheeler stood there, leaning on his cane with both hands. He looked at her, then past her and around the room.

"I heard something," he said, breathing hard.

The television was off, but she had a transistor radio on the flower-laden table beside the couch.

"Why didn't you tell me you could walk!"

"I didn't know myself . . . until just now." He came forward, the left leg taking a step, the cane jumping out and thumping down, the right leg dragging up, the process starting over again. She backed away from him, frightened, and at the same time full of admiration. What a man he was! What a fantastic man he must have been!

He went to the television set, anticipating what her excuse might be. He put one hand on the top, moved half a step, put the hand on the back. "I heard a man," he said, and turned his head to her.

She wondered what would happen if she admitted it. It might be the best way—bring out once and for all that she was going to see men, men her own age, even if she stayed with him the rest of his life.

But she couldn't. He might be only a small part of her awakening womanhood, but she was *all* of his failing manhood. She said, "You wouldn't mean my radio, would you?"

He began to move toward the table. She said, "If you expect a transistor radio to be warm after it's off a moment or two . . ."

He stopped. He stared at her, and she smiled and came toward him. She was still a little afraid, but she was also proud of him, proud of her part in his remarkable improvement. "That's enough exercise," she said. "At least for today. And you need your sleep if you're going to stay up late tomorrow."

When she reached him, he suddenly sagged against her and she had to grab him about the waist. "Eve, tell me. Is there . . . a man in your life?"

"After seeing this, I'd say there was."

He flushed, and smiled, and allowed her to lead him back to bed.

Jorge finished explaining the plan and they sat on the couch in Leech's apartment, looking across the little coffee table at him. Mrs. Prager had moved in only last night, but they already had a domesticated look. "It is dangerous," he said. "Of course. Anything like this *must* be dangerous. But only *very* bad luck can make it go wrong."

"Better than I thought," Mrs. Prager muttered. "Especially if the singer comes through."

"We're going to make it," Leech said. He rubbed his hands together and looked at the woman for confirmation. "We're going to make it, Ruthie!"

She nodded. "I think Max figured wrong."

Jorge reached down for the suitcase on the floor beside his chair. "To show you how sure I am that we *are* going to make it, I've decided . . ." He paused, feeling his way toward their complete confidence. "I and some very important people behind me, that is . . . we've decided on another advance." He opened the case and brought out two canvas zipper bags. He leaned forward, giving one to Mrs. Prager and the other to Leech.

"Christ!" Leech said, looking inside.

The woman tried to conceal her surprise and pleasure. "How much?"

"Half, exactly. Twenty-five thousand for you, Mrs. Prager. Fifty thousand for Mr. Leech." And now that they were at their happiest, he brought out the two weapons. Leech took the large one; Mrs. Prager hesitated a moment before accepting the small one. "Only for show," Jorge said. "However, you should know how to handle it."

Mrs. Prager released the clip expertly, looked at the full load of bullets, snapped the clip back in. She checked the safety and put the gun in her purse.

Leech was brandishing and aiming his loaded revolver. "What about extra rounds?" he said.

The woman answered before Jorge could. "Honey, if you have to fire that thing even once, we're in trouble."

Jorge went to him and pointed out the safety and explained how to crack open and spin the chambers in case of jamming. Leech said, "Does it make much noise with the silencer?"

Jorge snapped his fingers. "About like that."

Leech grinned, hefting the weapon like a child with a toy. Jorge returned to his chair and took two rings of keys from the suitcase, each key tagged and labeled. "Complete sets to every door on the fourteenth floor."

"Why do we need *all* of them?" Leech asked. "I mean, I won't be using the ones to Krasmer's suite and Ruthie won't be using the ones to the old man's suite, and none of us are going into DeWyant's suite."

"A precaution," Jorge said. "Every member of our group will

have a set, in case we have to improvise. No matter what happens, we can go anywhere on the floor."

"If that elevator will be waiting," Mrs. Prager murmured, "we'll be in."

"It will." He closed the suitcase. "I believe that does it. I'm meeting the manager for a final review of his role."

"A lot depends on him," Mrs. Prager said.

"A lot depends on every one of us," Jorge said, and turned to go.

"Mind telling me what happened to Max?" she asked.

"He'll be kept quiet until after the abduction, then released."

She didn't answer, and he didn't try to convince her. As he reached the door, she said, "Just for kicks, what's to stop me and Jerry from taking our half shares and cutting out right now?"

Jorge turned, smiling. "The same thing that stopped Mr. Prager."

She nodded slowly, and he left.

4

SATURDAY, JANUARY 28

They'd worked late last night and given the speech to a typist and Dan had fallen into bed at two A.M. Now here he was again, seven hours later, in the Senator's suite, ready for the final run-through. But the Senator wasn't present.

Bryan Whitelock poured coffee and brought it to where Dan sat on the couch. The guard took an armchair and sipped from his own cup.

"What made him change his mind?" Dan asked. "He wasn't going to let Wheeler see the speech, wasn't going to let him know anything about it."

There was a stentorian bellow next door, followed by thumping and loud voices. Dan murmured, "And that's *why* he wasn't."

Whitelock shrugged. Dan said, "You must have *some* idea?"

More shouting. Dan recognized Michael Wheeler's voice. He grinned wryly. "Doesn't sound like a sick old man to me."

"I think that's why the Senator changed his mind."

Dan questioned him with a look.

"President Wheeler's come a long way in the last few weeks. He's been in touch with his political friends, and he's been asking to see the speech. The Senator thought about it, and early this morning he made his decision. Things have changed, he said. A month ago it looked different. Now . . ." He drank coffee.

"I see. Do you think he'll allow his father-in-law to influence him?"

"That I wouldn't know." He paused. "But he always did before. And so did President Standers."

Dan began to worry. The speech was everything he and Dick had wanted. A few phrases, a question of semantics here and there, a decision on how far to go in one matter or another—these still remained. But anything major had appeared to be over and done with. The speech was now a fighting declaration of liberal, rational, humanitarian independence.

He comforted himself by remembering how Dick had planned to shock his father-in-law and brother-in-law.

The connecting door in the foyer opened and the Senator entered. He wore white tennis slacks and shirt, with complexion to match. He went directly to the bar, poured coffee from the electric percolator, and added a stiff shot of Wild Turkey.

"Rough, was it?" Dan murmured.

"No, not really." He drank half the cup at one swallow, walked to the couch, and sat down. "He likes to shout, but we . . . reached an agreement." He handed Dan the speech.

Dan turned the pages. At first it looked all right. A line here and there, but nothing drastic. The Southeast Asia section was practically untouched, and he smiled and said, "You must have fought the good fight for this."

Dick nodded, "I fought where I had to fight."

Dan turned two more pages, and stopped. He looked up. Dan said, "And where I had secret doubts, I gave in. That was the one section—"

"But it's *all* gone," Dan interrupted. "You have no statement whatsoever on the black ghetto now."

"This speech is only the opening gun in the war. I'll have time later to promulgate an approach to the ghettos."

"Promulgate an approach? Our approach was hammered out . . ."

Dick got up and returned to the bar. He made himself a second Irish coffee and drank it standing there. Dan turned the remaining pages, and found little changed. He went back to the section excised by penciled slashes and began to read, aloud:

" 'What we must do is expand our understanding in terms of history and also in terms of the human heart, sadly deficient when dealing with our Negro compatriots. These people who were kidnapped from their homes, packed into the bowels of ships like no intelligent cattle shipper would pack his stock, sold like any domestic animal, and bred the same way. Now, overnight as it were, we expect the recent descendants of these tormented people to accept all middle-class virtues at face value, even when they have no part in middle-class benefits. We expect them to leap into the mainstream of American life, and we speak of our poor-folks' childhoods to show it can be done easily enough. But our grandparents were not black and were not slaves, and we are not black and are not saddled with the malaise of recent slavery.

" 'Answers, you say, not questions are what we need. Answers, I'm afraid, are not easily come by. And when offered, are not easily accepted. Germany has dug into its pocket to indemnify, massively, the remnants and descendants of those killed in the Nazi holocaust. Not all Germans were Nazis. Not all Germans are, strictly speaking, responsible for what happened to the Jews. Yet all are paying.

" 'Not all Americans are responsible for what happened to the

Negro people. Yet all Americans must dig into their pockets, and then into their minds and hearts. First for massive indemnification—' "

"An impossible approach in the present climate of opinion," Christopher said. "I knew it when we wrote it. I knew it when my father-in-law said it would destroy any chance of my getting the nomination."

"And what happened to that I-don't-have-to-be-elected stance?"

It was tough talk, and the Senator had obviously had more than enough tough talk for one day. But Dan wanted to know. He was a free man—freed by what would happen to him Monday. There was nothing to be afraid of beyond the fear of what would happen Monday.

Christopher flushed. "I *didn't* say I had to commit political suicide."

"Didn't we discuss that? Wasn't it I who warned you, and then was convinced when you said the time had come to *lead* and not follow the people?"

"Political suicide doesn't come only from bucking the people."

"I don't understand."

"Delegates aren't always controlled by the voters. Mike Wheeler is a grand master in the moving and capturing of delegate strength."

And that was that.

"One paragraph," Dan said, as Dick sat down again. "Let's include one simple paragraph—"

"Not even a word. Because that would be worse than nothing. This way, I'll have time to work out a new approach. And perhaps later . . ." He moved his hands.

Later there would be references to crime in the streets, when the platform committee decided not to allow the Republicans to capture *all* the backlash votes. Later there would be a meaningless repetition of Democratic Party mumbo-jumbo, and the loss of a golden opportunity to lead the nation to awareness of the debt owed the Negro.

374

"One more paragraph," Dan said, turning the page, "before we kiss it good-bye." He didn't hide his disapproval.

Christopher said, "Read on. If I could read it to the nation, and survive, I would. But I had all I could do to save the Asian approach." He put his hand on Dan's arm. "It was a triumph, believe me. The greatest of my life."

Dan read the paragraph anyway—read the simple truth that might have swayed some American minds and saved some American lives.

" 'The wonder is not that so many Negroes have flung our ideals in our faces, but that so many more have not, that so many more have chosen to continue to work, to educate themselves, to struggle for security in our dualistic society. That is why the time has come to end a deception we all practice in our hearts. Equality under law is now a fact. Equality in the sight of God has always been a fact. But equality in the eyes of man, *that's* where the battle lies. Your eyes and mine. Your heart and mine. For when we—' "

"All right," Dick said. "I'm hungry, and we have to work on the transition between the Asian section and the closing, now that two pages are eliminated."

Dan closed the speech. "Simple enough. Five minutes' work. I'll do it in my room." He stood up. "Well, until tonight."

He was at the foyer when the Senator stopped him. "What about Marjory Fine's party?"

"I think I'll skip it. Haven't been too well lately. Some sun on the deck is what I need."

Again Christopher stopped him. "Stay and have breakfast with us."

"I'm not—"

"Think, Dan. Think of the opportunity you'll have to do what you want to do, help people learn what you want them to learn —and what I too want them to learn—*if* I become President and you a member of my personal staff."

Dan thought, and went into the kitchen with Dick and Whitelock. He sat at the table and ate eggs and bacon and chuckled at a joke and told one of his own. After all, he was a realist if he was anything. He was going to prove that as few men could on Monday morning.

They finished eating and began to revise for smooth transition. Somewhere along the way, he realized that Senator Richard Bernard Christopher was a most unhappy man. It gave him hope. The Senator was suffering from what he'd had to do. The Senator would remember, and bring back those deleted concepts, those vital statements, at some future time.

When Dan left, the Senator was mixing a very large bourbon.

Jorge was in the Metropole at eleven-thirty, walking through the lobby, stopping at the entrance to the Main Dining Room where, along with a large group of people, he watched television crews from the three major networks and a local independent station setting up their equipment on and in front of the dais. Other newsmen were in evidence, and many foreign tongues were heard. The Senator was big news. Jorge smiled to himself. By midnight, he would be even bigger news!

He went to the Bon Bouche, where Violetta was already waiting. They sat at the counter together, and the counterman gave them a curious if not unfriendly glance. Not many *Cubanos* were guests here.

"I picked up the car this morning," he said. "It is now parked in the Metropole garage. Here is the ticket. The description and license number are on the back, in case of confusion."

She took the ticket, read it, nodded. "The manager will see that it is waiting near the elevators tonight for our passenger. A surprise visit to a Cuban patriotic club will be his given reason."

"What is the elevator number?"

"Three. It usually goes no lower than the Arcade Level, as do all the passenger elevators, but it can be programmed to go all the way to the subbasement parking area. At ten tonight it will carry us to the fourteenth floor, and then wait there."

"What if others enter it?"

376

"They can ride up, if they wish, but then I will hang an out-of-order sign on the door and it will not descend again unless I use a certain key." She reached into her purse. "This key. I have two of them." She gave him one. "Why did you not wish all of us to have them, as we have the other keys?"

Jorge put the key on his ring. "Because it is our escape route. The *patrón* has decided to trust only the two of us with control of it. If someone—Leech for example, or even Pedras or Morales —should panic, he might use the elevator and leave us with no way to get our guest to the basement. So only you and I can work the elevator. An honor."

She smiled. "You finally agree I'm to be trusted?"

"I always trusted you—your will, your honesty. It is your ability that remains in doubt."

"Then you'll just have to wait until tonight to test it."

Their food arrived. "Aren't you afraid?" he murmured.

"No," she said. "Except for you."

She was eating her sandwich, eyes down.

"And I for you."

She looked at him then. Their eyes met. She said, "There is still time for us. We can spend an hour . . ."

He shook his head. "Afterward, like a celebration. Afterward, when it will mean much."

She nodded slowly.

He spoke as he ate, going over her role, reminding her of details, lecturing her on what to do if the unexpected happened. "The call to the singer is of the utmost importance, now that we have included it in the plan. You'll use a phone in the Krasmer suite, then go back to the elevators. You'll see whether the guard leaves. You'll be standing outside, ringing for one of the other elevators. If the guard enters Elevator Three, you say, 'It doesn't work.' If another elevator comes, you step aside and let him use it himself, as if afraid of his excitement, his hurry. But he will probably run for the emergency stairs. It is only one flight down to Jones's suite, since there is no thirteenth floor."

She sipped her Coke. "I know all that, Jorge."

He continued as if she hadn't spoken. "You will then tap at the father's door, where I will be with Leech, and let me know. If the guard does not come out, we will call the manager and have him try and get the guard down. You have told McKensil what to say?"

"Of course."

"He will say they have received a package for the Senator and it makes ticking sounds and will the guard come down and examine it. You have prepared the alarm clock?"

She nodded. "Why must you keep going over things we both know?"

"To make sure we both *do* know. And that we both do not forget." He sipped his coffee. "Does McKensil act . . . responsible?"

"He acts miserable. But he will do as he is told. He is afraid of you."

"Naturally. The pictures . . ."

"Not just the pictures."

She tilted back her glass, catching ice in her mouth. "What did you do with Prager, Jorge?"

Jorge lit a *cigarro* and looked around. "In Havana, the hotels were nicer than this. Not so full of glass and shiny metal, but nicer, finer. More respectable, you might say."

Her voice dropped to a whisper. "Did you kill him?"

"I never stayed in those hotels, as a guest. But I was with the *patrón* several times. Now, when we return, I will be a guest. An honored guest."

"Did you feel sorry for him when you killed him?"

"I will have a home near the water. Of course, I will still serve the *patrón*, but in a different position. He will lead the nation, and I will be his right-hand man."

"Does it hurt to think of killing him? Is that why you will not talk of it?"

He beckoned the counterman and got their checks. He paid and placed a coin before each of their settings and stood up.

378

"When will you tell me about it, Jorge?" Her large eyes sparkled. "I want to hear. I want to know what it is like."

"I will *never* tell you," he said, face hard. "Perhaps you will tell *me* what it is like to kill a man, after tonight."

"Perhaps I will," she said, and nodded. "Yes, that might be."

He leaned toward her. "Just you remember what the *patrón* said. No one is to be hurt. *No one.*"

"That's if everything goes well. If it fails . . ." She shrugged. "Then we are on our own, aren't we?"

"Then we are finished. But you can get away. It is what I have told you over and over again. You will not be directly involved. You can just walk away. Go to the *patrón*. He will tell you what to do."

"Or I can shoot that rich American senator and show them all—"

He gripped her arm. "It is not that easy to end a life!"

She glanced around. He let her go, remembering where he was. She said, "Tell me how it is not easy to end a life, Jorge. Tell me." They started out; her hand and hip brushed his. This *niña* was excited by the idea of killing! "I'll bet you've done it more than once, Jorge. I'll bet you've done it for Lamas . . ."

He said, "Speak to McKensil. Make sure he knows *exactly* what to do." And he walked away.

Later, he worried that she might use that little gun and ruin her life. Later, he was sorry all over again that the *patrón* had allowed her an active role in the abduction.

At two-thirty, Marjory was ready to concede that her third party was a dud. There was an air of anticlimax about it—or perhaps pre-climax was more to the point. The evening's events foreshadowed the afternoon's festivities. It was the Senator's speech her guests wanted, not cocktails and small talk. Also, her guest list had turned out disappointingly lightweight. The Senator had come, yes, and so had his father-in-law (in wheelchair with nurse), but Dick was doing much drinking and little talking,

Michael Wheeler much frowning and little talking, the body-guard much watching and absolutely no talking. Benny Barker could have livened things up, but he wasn't here. His manager had called to say he was out on his boat, soaking up peace and rest and so on. Wally Jones had failed her again, but she wasn't surprised that he was withdrawing, the way he continued to disappoint audiences in the Platinum Room. Even her old standbys, Leech and Mrs. Prager, hadn't shown.

She moved about, smiling and chatting, trying to bring people together. Bruce Golden and Ellie DeWyant were handsome silhouettes against the sun-bright window, and then they were saying good-bye. May Krasmer introduced her husband, and after a drink they too were gone. At three o'clock Michael Wheeler peremptorily turned his chair to the door and, nurse in tow, departed. Marjory expected the Senator would follow, and that the other guests would then begin to drain away, leaving her with the wearisome handful of never-go-homes. She was wrong.

Within minutes after his father-in-law had left, Dick began to show signs of life. He lectured the real-estate Lorshes on the responsibilities of the moneyed, bringing grim silence to the husband and delighted agreement from the wife. He then danced with the wife, holding her close and with one hand definitely low. Marjory looked around and found Marco standing with two business-type men. She wondered that the little decorator had sold her (well, *almost*) such a bill of goods!

Christopher danced with three women in a row, the last young and *zaftig* and very obviously willing. Mopping his brow, he approached Marjory. She threw up her hands in mock horror. "I can't follow *that* one!" His speech a trifle blurred, he said, "Steer me to the men's locker room." She did, holding his hand. They passed Marco. The decorator said, "When you have a minute, Senator . . ." Christopher never even glanced his way.

So much for that.

At three-thirty, Dick was with the *zaftig* one, doing a very animated bugaloo. He could really move, for a presidential hopeful.

At three-thirty-five, a businessman she didn't know asked to be introduced to the Senator. She turned, looking, and after a while went to the couch where the guard, Bryan Something, sat with a nervous little cardboard-container tycoon. She passed by, however, asking no questions, and went to her bathroom and the magic mirror.

Marco sat at the edge of the bed. Christopher stood before him, partially blocking the decorator from Marjory's view. She turned up the sound.

". . . wanted to see me?" the Senator was saying, voice unusually thick.

Marco laughed. He put out his hand, touching the Senator. "Wait a minute," Dick said, and the thickness had grown, was swallowing his words. "Wait just a minute."

Marco's hand moved; he leaned forward. Christopher lurched to the side. His fly was open, his penis stiffly emerging. "Just what do you think—" he began. Marco leaned further, and took him in his mouth. Christopher exhaled, a deep rushing sound. His eyes closed.

Quite suddenly, Marco stopped, leaned back on his elbows, smiled up at the big man. "You asked me to wait a minute? You wanted to know what I was doing?"

Christopher stood hunched over, breathing like a steam engine. His eyes opened.

Marco stretched out full length.

Marjory had never realized how very feminine he could be— his delicate, almost pretty features, his flirtatious, sensuous, mocking ways. With the big-framed Christopher, it was hard to see Marco as anything *but* a woman.

However, one thing about him was decidedly *un*feminine, and he brought it into view by casually kicking off his trousers and slipping down his tight-fitting Jockey shorts. "Man to man," he said, that smile of his wet and mocking, "what do you *think* I was doing?"

Christopher sank to the edge of the bed, staring. Marco was something to stare at. He was the eighth wonder of the world. He was big—bigger that way than Bert or Melvin or any man Marjory had ever seen. Bigger than Christopher.

"Tell you what," Marco said. "You try it and then I'll tell you exactly—"

Christopher slapped the little man. A mild slap, but it changed Marco. He lost the smile, and the mockery. He moaned. "Don't be mad, baby. I was just teasing."

Christopher grabbed him by his thick black hair and hauled him across the bed to his lap. "You *hurt*," Marco whimpered, and again took the Senator in his mouth.

Marjory told herself it was the most exciting thing she'd ever seen. But something stopped her from enjoying it fully. Something bothered her. The Senator's face. It wasn't as much gripped by passion as twisted by pain. There was something *frightening* about it.

Again Marco withdrew before giving satisfaction. "A meaningful exchange of ideas," he said, regaining some of his playfulness. He stretched out, crooked his finger, and murmured, "Come on now, serve the public with more than words."

Dick seemed much drunker than he'd been a few minutes ago. He swayed, leaned forward, put down his head. Marco's face lit up with an unholy glee. He was enjoying a combination of sensations, the smaller part of which, Marjory guessed, was physical. She could almost read his thoughts.

"Gently," Marco said, his smile dripping triumph. "Like at Mommy's breast."

Nothing appeared to have changed, but Marco suddenly cried out, his knees jerking up. "That was *beastly!*" He tried to pull Christopher's head away, but the Senator grasped both delicate wrists in one large hand and with the other hand reached between and under Marco's legs, clutching his scrotum.

Marco shrieked. Marjory shrank back in terror, and wondered if anyone outside might have heard over the talk, laughter, and music.

Marco tried to sit up. Christopher released his wrists and struck him, a heavy slap to the face. Marco fell back, stunned. Christopher lowered his head, moving wildly now. Marco was mumbling, stammering, "Oh no no I don't want—" Christopher put his free hand over Marco's mouth. A second later, Marco jerked and his muffled shriek just did reach Marjory's ears. Christopher brought up his right hand and struck Marco in the face, again and again.

The right hand moved back down. The left hand stayed over Marco's mouth. Christopher's head went up and back, almost a blur of movement. Marco's body began to arch, and then his belly heaved. Christopher sat up, took his hand away from Marco's mouth, and spat more than saliva into Marco's face.

"Why did you? . . ." Marco began, tears mixing with semen on his cheeks. He didn't finish, because Christopher had grabbed his wilting penis and begun to pull at it. Marco said, "Be reasonable! Give me some consid—" Christopher struck him, so hard a slap that blood showed at the corners of Marco's mouth.

Marco shouted, "You're insane! I won't—" Christopher's free hand went back over his mouth. Christopher jerked at him, violently, brutally. Marjory had backed another step from the mirror, shaking her head, wanting to run from this and yet afraid to. Christopher kept on, kept on, and at some signal from Marco's body bent his head again.

The arching came; the belly heaved; Christopher spat in Marco's face.

"It's over now," Marjory whispered. "Over now."

Marco seemed half unconscious. Christopher rolled him over and put an arm under his haunches. He elevated the buttocks and began to hunch and thrust at them, his back to the mirror. Marco began to sob, to wail. Christopher used his free hand to shove Marco's face into the bedding.

Marjory was backing further and further away. She could see that Marco was struggling. She could see that Christopher's hand was still grasping and jerking at Marco, that Marco was being hurt, terribly hurt. She could see that Christopher wasn't going to stop.

The Senator spoke for the first time since he'd turned wild—

hoarse, panting speech. "This what you wanted? This what you got me for? This what you'll brag about? *This? This?*" Words gave way to a creaking groan. He spasmed and fell away from Marco's streaming buttocks.

At last, Marjory told herself, but it was more prayer than statement. She saw that Christopher still moved his hand under Marco's body. She saw that Marco still struggled to get free.

Christopher struck him across the side of the head, three, four times. He pulled Marco's haunches back up and jammed his face into the bedding and yanked wildly, cruelly at his genitals.

She suddenly understood it. He was castrating Marco. He had been made to reveal himself and he hated the man who had forced him to do it and he was going to castrate him. He might even kill him in the process, if not stopped.

But how could she stop him? How could she bring other people into it? How, when it was Richard Bernard Christopher?

Marco got his head up briefly, screeching, *"Please! God—"* and then he was smothered in bedding. Really smothered, it seemed, from his desperate, choking sounds.

Marjory left the bathroom, sick and shaking. She went across the room and someone spoke to her and she smiled automatically and someone else tried to stop her and she pulled away and at last she reached the bodyguard, Bryan Something. He was still with the cardboard-container tycoon. He looked up, and said, "Excuse me now," and followed her to the bedroom door. He kept looking at her. She said, "Hurry. In there. Stop him."

He tried the door. She shook her head. "I haven't got the key."

"Any key to any inside door?"

She began to shake her head, then remembered the bathroom key. "But it won't fit."

He took it. "Stand in front of me. Talk to me. Smile." He bent to the door.

Someone came over—that damned cardboard-container maker. She said, "Mr. Clyme, your wife has been waving at you."

He turned. "Where?"

"Near the bar, see? Go on now, or we'll have a battle royal on our hands."

"I still don't—"

She shoved him, smiling. He looked at her, startled, and moved away.

Bryan used his knee under the knob. The door clicked open. "Stand here," he said. He went inside and closed the door. She stood there. Mrs. Lorsh came over and asked what had happened to the Senator. Marjory said the only thing she could, with the knowledge that Christopher had to come out of that bedroom and be seen.

"A little too much to drink."

Mrs. Lorsh chuckled. "Happens to the best of us. Makes him that much more human, doesn't it? A *charming* man."

She said more. Marjory answered as best she could. She wanted to throw up, but made conversation.

Ugly! Ugly!

Bryan opened the door a crack. "Could I see you a minute, Mrs. Fine?"

Mrs. Lorsh said, "Can I help?" smiling oh so brightly.

Marjory said, "Yes, make sure we have a full bucket of ice cubes."

Mrs. Lorsh hurried away, delighted with her top-secret mission.

Marjory came inside. Bryan closed the door, leaning against it. The Senator was sitting on a chair near the dresser, bent over, head in hands. Marco was lying in the bed, under the covers, rolling his head from side to side. He had some very livid facial bruises, and his lips were beginning to puff.

"He needs a doctor," Bryan said. "Can you stay with him while I take the Senator back to his suite?"

She couldn't think. Bryan said, "Don't worry. I'll be right back. The lock doesn't work now, but you can push that armchair up against the door."

She nodded, and stepped toward the bedside phone.

"Mrs. Fine."

She turned her head.

"You'd better stay near the door. The moment I leave—"

"Yes, but first I'll call the hotel doctor."

"That's not necessary. The Wheelers have a family doctor in Palm Beach."

"Palm Beach? It'll take hours. You don't know what he *did* to Marco!"

"You do?"

She realized what she'd said. "I mean, I was near the door and heard cries . . ."

Bryan moved the armchair over to block the door and walked to the mirror. He leaned forward, looked closely, then looked at Marjory.

She wet her lips. "I heard him," she said.

He nodded slowly. Her face flaming, she said, "I would never say anything. I came for you because I didn't want—"

"I understand that, Mrs. Fine. And *I* would never say anything." His eyes flicked to the mirror. "But let me solve something for both of us."

He went to the Senator and helped him out of the straight-backed chair. He took the chair and swung it into the mirror. It shattered all the way through both thicknesses, leaving a hole between bedroom and bathroom.

"I'll see that someone repairs it," he said. "Today. Or did you want your own people to do it?"

She shook her head, not able to look at him. Her "own people" were dead. She was sick with what she had seen and sick with shame and sick of everything she was.

Bryan went to Christopher, who was staring dully at the smashed mirror. He said, "Senator, we're going to leave now. You've been drinking too much. Can you walk by yourself?"

Christopher went to the door, shambling, head down. Bryan followed, "Not like that, Senator. *Straight.*"

Christopher took a deep shuddering breath, and straightened.

Bryan moved the armchair and opened the door. He and Christopher walked out. Mrs. Lorsh was waiting. "I've got the ice—"

Christopher walked past her, ramrod stiff. Bryan smiled and said, "Not necessary, thanks," and caught up with his charge. Marjory closed the door, shoved the armchair in front of it, and sat down.

There was knocking. Mrs. Lorsh said, "Marjory, what in the world? . . . Marjory?"

The knob rattled. Marjory looked at Marco, who rolled his head and moaned in semiconsciousness. Tears trickled down her cheeks. How terribly ugly it all was—Marco and Christopher, and most of all herself. How terribly ugly what she had become these past few years. How lost and low and ugly.

It was over. She could never watch people doing such things again—not without remembering this ugliness. It was over, and she feared the emptiness that would come.

Bryan returned. He said he would stay with Marco until Dr. Visner arrived. "He's coming by helicopter. It won't be more than an hour."

She went out. She saw the Lorshes in a corner, others around them, Mrs. Lorsh talking and waving her hands. She steeled herself, and walked over. "He wasn't as high as I'd thought," she said, by way of openers, then went on to carefully destroy any air of mystery Mrs. Lorsh might have been building.

The party folded quickly after that. She wasn't too gentle with the never-go-homes, saying, "Fun-fun's over." But before she could clear the room, in walked Wally Jones. He was with an Oriental-looking girl and came to Marjory with hands outstretched, smiling, saying, "So I'm late. So at least I made it."

She tried hard to be her old self, but her old self had already died. "You didn't make it, I'm afraid."

"Well, so I'll sing 'Auld Lang Syne' and tell a few jokes. Just for us." He started for the bar. She put her hand on his arm. "I'm sorry, honey, I'm just falling apart with a migraine."

He nodded quickly. "Sure. The next one. We'll make it big." He went out the door without waiting for his girl, who murmured, "Drop, please," and followed.

Marjory didn't blame her. Wally was a sensitive soul to begin with, and after all that had happened to him . . .

She just couldn't worry about Wally now. She heaved the rest of the never-go-homes with the help of her doorman, tipped him fifty dollars, and nodded at his thanks. Now *he* became a problem. He looked her over and murmured he sure could use a drink and seemed ready to take a chance and find out what she was all about.

She said, "I really do have a terrific headache, Vince."

He said sure, they'd have that drink after her next party, and went out with a little swagger.

He'd have a long wait. She didn't know what her life would be, but it wouldn't be in Miami. She would stay just long enough to see that the wall and mirrors were repaired, then fly home. Not that home would hold her for long. She wasn't the clubwoman, ladies'-aid, hospital-visitor type.

Friends had talked about Acapulco. It was supposed to really jump this time of year. Why not Acapulco? Or maybe San Juan? Or Grand Bahama? Or any other sun spot? One place was as good as another when you were on the run . . . from yourself.

5

SATURDAY, JANUARY 28, P.M.

May was to meet Al in the Arcade Level at ten, the time Senator Christopher would begin his speech and just about everyone would be in the Grand Ballroom, so she began her argument with Harold shortly after nine. They were watching television, having returned to the suite because she'd complained of feeling slightly ill after dinner. He was engaged in his usual sport, mockery. Mocking the show they were watching. Mocking the story and sets and characters—especially the characters and most especially the female characters.

"Did you know," she said, "you never just watch a show? You have to make fun of it."

He finished his Canadian and put down the glass. "Not surprising, with what they give us to watch."

"Regardless of quality, you have to mock it."

"An indication of taste, I'd say."

"An indication of total insecurity, Freud would say."

He presented her with the opening she'd been seeking. "And what would Freud say about trying to make an eighteen-year-old boy?"

"He'd ask what the husband in the case was doing, or *not* doing, to set up such a situation." And as his face tightened, "Would you have been any happier if I'd tried for an older man?"

"You certainly *are* feeling ill," he muttered.

"Because before the boy there *was* a man. An old friend from New York who's staying—"

He was on his feet. "What sort of woman are you, to talk this way!"

She was on her feet, marveling that it was so easy, that she was actually pulling it off. And at the same time she realized it wasn't a trick, wasn't an act. She was only speaking the truth. "A normal woman with normal appetites."

"And an utter disregard of a husband's feelings, a husband's capacity for pain!"

"You're not a husband, Harold."

His fists were clenched, his face whitening. "*That* again! I'm a husband in every way but one, and you take that stinking, smelly one—that *toilet habit*—and try to make it seem all of life!"

"It's a very big part of life. I don't want to live without it any longer."

"Is it a divorce you're asking for?" White, white face and trembling lips and shaking hands, something she had always backed away from. "Is it scandal in court with Eunice talking about you and the boy?"

"Nothing to talk about," she answered calmly. "No consummation."

"But she'll testify and they'll laugh—" He interrupted himself. "And I'll repeat what you said about your friend from New York."

She went to the bedroom and got her mink wrap and purse. He followed, stopping in the doorway.

"Where are you going?"

"Out. At least for a few hours. To think things through."

"You think I'm that stupid? You think I don't know you're going to meet that boy? You think I'll stand for the humiliation—"

She walked toward him, facing the whiteness and trembling and growing darkness of eye. "You have no choice, Harold." She came right up against him. "Please let me by."

He didn't move. His mouth was quivering, his eyes wide and hollow. "Once before . . . you remember, May? I won't live with such a thing."

She became frightened, and hoped it didn't show. "That's *your* choice."

"Push me aside and it's *your* choice."

She put her hand on his chest. He moved back. She walked past him, and heard him entering the bedroom. She told herself to keep going, not to engage in another exercise in futility. He wouldn't kill himself. The last time had been a fluke, a freak of timing. He'd been in conflict with his brothers, failing in a final attempt at courtroom work, and she had picked just that time to pressure him. It was different now . . .

She turned. He was going into the bathroom. He left the door open, and she heard the water running. She moved after him.

He was at the sink, swallowing a sleeping pill. He took another from what looked like a full jar, and another, and she said, "You can't be so stupid. You can't!"

He took a fourth, fifth, sixth. She grabbed his hand. He shoved her away. He took a seventh, an eighth. She stood there, counting: *Eleven, twelve, thirteen* . . .

She said, "Not this time," fighting back the tears, the hysteria.

"No, it's *your* decision and I won't be part of it! I'm going to walk out and spend an evening just as I want to and you're not going to stop me!"

. . . fifteen, sixteen, seventeen . . .

She turned and ran. She heard his voice, quiet now: "Good-bye, May."

She ran from the suite. He had about ten more pills in that jar, and he knew where her twenty-five-milligram tranquilizers were. The pills alone were enough, and between pills and tranquilizers he would be dead in an hour and she couldn't let him die; she had to turn back and call a doctor and stay with him, had to surrender and forget, forever, any man but Harold.

Why couldn't she let him die?

An elevator came and she stepped inside, not seeing the people there, staring at the doors and into her own heart.

Why couldn't she allow him to free her without courtrooms and humiliations?

She got off at the lobby and went to a chair and sat down. She smoked and tried to think further and couldn't think further.

She checked the time. Nine-thirty. He had taken all the pills by now. She simply sat.

She lit another cigarette. There was a stirring of sound around her, and then a scattering of applause. She saw a group of people moving toward the Grand Ballroom, among them Senator Christopher. She looked at her watch again. A quarter to ten.

The group entered the ballroom. Sound swelled, then exploded into shocking uproar—shocking to May Krasmer because it brought her out of her self-imposed stupor and made her know what she was doing.

She was allowing Harold to commit suicide. She was, as he had said, killing him.

Murder! her conscience shrieked, along with the thousand-tongued shout from the ballroom. She rose. She knew she was going to back away from freedom.

Something else she knew. She was afraid of Al as much as she was desirous of him. She was running from him now as she had run from the thought that she was killing Harold. If he, too, found her unexciting in bed . . .

She had to find out!

She stood there, torn by indecision—seeing Harold lying down and drifting toward death, seeing Al waiting in the Arcade Level, then leaving with anger. Seeing herself forever fearful, forever doubting her ability as a woman.

The solution was so simple she couldn't believe it when it came to her. She went to the phones near the desk and asked the operator for the house doctor. There was ringing and then a recording that said: "Dr. Bennet is out of his office but in the hotel. Please leave word with the operator and she will contact him."

She spoke to the operator. "Please get the doctor to Suite Fourteen-C. It's terribly urgent! A man has taken sleeping pills and tranquilizers. A suicide attempt. He needs help *quickly!*" As the operator tried to ask who she was, she repeated, "Fourteen-C, Mrs. Krasmer's suite. *Fourteen-C*." And hung up. And went down to the Arcade Level to face the other fear.

Harold spat a pill from his mouth as soon as he was certain May had left. He dumped the rest into the toilet and did the same with the tranquilizers and flushed them all down. But he'd taken eighteen sleeping pills, by his own careful count, and while he had a little time before calling the doctor he couldn't allow himself to grow careless.

Not that he was really worried. He went into the living room and packed his pipe and stood watching television. As long as he didn't sit or lie down, he would know just when to get help. And he was willing to bet his life—he chuckled at that—on May's being unable to stay away more than half an hour. Either that, or she would send a doctor to him.

So there was no danger, just as there'd been no danger the last time she'd tried to leave him. He'd had the situation under control then as now. Exactly as now. He had May, and would always have her. He didn't have to ask himself why he *wanted* to have her. A man needed a wife to accompany him to the theater, concerts, restaurants, and friends' homes. And if she left him, Eli and Henry might begin to wonder at his general disinterest in women. Having May, he was able to act the unusually devoted husband. Without May, they'd have something else to sneer at—in private, of course, where they did all their sneering at the kid brother who was not too good at anything.

He'd never allow that to happen! Even if she decided to let him die, he would find another way to keep her with him. If threats of taking his own life weren't sufficient, threats of taking *hers* might be. And if everything failed, threats would become reality. He would *not* allow her to survive to talk about him, laugh at him, bring down the contempt of his brothers . . .

He staggered a little, and braced himself on the back of the armchair. Almost time to call for a doctor. He'd researched his "suicides" thoroughly, and knew he had another five minutes, ten at the most. He hated to give in this way. He was sure she'd return. The amount of pills he'd taken wasn't a *massive* overdose. It was just that once a person fell asleep, the damage to the central nervous system progressed rapidly, and he wouldn't be able to summon the simple help—stomach pump and stimulants—needed for survival.

He began to walk. Movement would add a few minutes to his stay-awake time.

The doorbell rang. He smiled. She'd sent someone.

He went across the foyer, feeling numbness moving into his hands, his feet, his nose and lips. The extremities first, and then the rest of the body. But the process would be reversed as soon as he admitted the doctor.

He opened the door, and the woman said, "Mr. Krasmer?" There was a man behind her—dark, stocky, wearing a tight blue suit—and Harold wondered where May had found *this* doctor and nurse. He nodded, and the man and woman and hall beyond swung violently up and down. Yes, it was time for treatment.

He began to ask them in when the man stepped forward and shoved him with his shoulder. In his rapidly weakening condition, he fell to the floor. They stepped over and past him, shutting the door. They obviously expected resistance—which was natural enough from a potential suicide.

"No need to get . . ." He couldn't enunciate the word "physical," the numbness having reached his tongue. "No need for that. I won't make trouble."

The man hauled him up, saying, "Good, you stay alive then," in a mild but identifiably Spanish accent.

They brought him into the bedroom. The man drew back the covers, and Harold wanted to ask where was the little black bag doctors carried. The woman was walking around, looking into doors. The man threw him down on the bed, rather roughly, and he wanted to ask whether it wasn't best to keep him moving even while administering a stimulant. And what about the stomach pump?

The man put his hands together on his chest and tied them with brown electrical wire. Harold again tried to say there was no need to anticipate resistance, but he mumbled badly—and he was also beginning to wonder at these two. If only he could clear his head for a moment.

"You shouldn't be here," the woman said to him. "You should be downstairs with the others, for the Senator's speech. Is your wife coming back, too?"

Harold shook his head, trying to clear it, and mumbled, "What difference . . ." and stopped as the man tied his ankles together.

"If she does come back," the woman said, "we'll have to do the same to her. But don't worry. You won't be hurt."

The man pushed a balled-up handkerchief into Harold's mouth and took a thick roll of white tape from his pocket. When a long strip was pressed over his lips, Harold knew, finally, May hadn't sent these people and they weren't here to treat him.

It was a robbery! He had to stop them . . . tell them about the pills!

He rolled his head, and as he did everything spun and he lost the sense of urgency, and fear became a dull thing drowning in waves of numbness.

The man covered him with blanket and spread, looked around, and said, "That must be the connecting door." He walked to Harold's left and out of sight. The woman said, "Don't touch it. What if someone's still in there and hears?" The man said, "Who could be in there? And even so, I can handle anyone—" The woman said, "Remember the instructions! The Senator's suite stays empty, untouched, until he's back up there and the guard leaves." The man said, "Foolishness. I have experience in these matters. I was in the Cuban underground until four years ago. It would be better to be waiting, hidden, when they come in, and so not have to count on the guard leaving." The woman said, "Maybe, but the guard always walks into rooms first, and if he sees anything wrong he'll shoot and the Senator can run . . ."

She said more and the man said more, but Harold didn't care. His eyes were closed. Sleep was the only reality.

Was there anything wrong with falling asleep?

"Are you sure they said Fourteen-C?" Ruthie asked the neat-looking man with gray hair and thick gray mustache.

"That was the message. A suicide attempt."

Ramon Pedras stood behind her in the foyer, smiling affably. Ruthie said, "My husband and I are alone here. It sounds like the kind of joke some friends of ours might pull." She turned to Ramon. "The Baileys, right, dear?"

He nodded, shaking his head and chuckling.

The doctor flushed angrily. He stalked back toward the elevators, passing the Senator's door and Michael Wheeler's door, muttering furiously.

Ruthie looked at Ramon. "I *thought* he was acting funny!"

The squat man returned her look impassively. "That is none of our affair."

"But if he's dying!"

"Impossible. He came to the door and talked to us. He'd been drinking, yes, but that's all."

She hurried to the bedroom and shook Krasmer's shoulders. He didn't stir. "Ramon, he's—"

He pulled her away from the bed. "He is drunk," he repeated. "Anyway, what can we do for him? Can we call doctors, ambulances?"

Slowly, she shook her head. They could do nothing at all for him. Besides, she *had* smelled liquor on his breath. And he had let them in and smiled and acted perfectly calm and rational. Would a suicide act like that?

She listened to Krasmer's steady breathing, and relaxed a little.

"Even if he *was* committing suicide, why should we stop him from an act of free will? I believe in the right of every individual to do exactly as he wishes with his life—even to end it. If it was up to me, there would be no traffic lights. People would drive at their own risk, with full freedom of will. At every corner individuals would make choices, accepting the risks and consequences of freedom . . ."

She stared, thinking the man insane. She just hoped he wouldn't try to put any of his wild theories into practice *tonight!*

He finally stopped, took out a tiny transistor radio and tuned in the Senator's speech. "Not that I care what the fool says, but to know when he is finished."

She checked her watch. Ten after ten. In less than an hour, Christopher would enter the next suite. Shortly afterward, they would take him down to that limousine in the basement. Then she and Jerry would drive off in his T-Bird and buy a new car in South Carolina and go on to Canada.

Remembering how it had been last night after Jorge had left, she wet her lips, forgetting Krasmer and Ramon and everything but her wish that the next hour pass swiftly.

"She shouldn't be here," Jerry said, puffing furiously at a cigarette. "She should be in the Krasmer place, where you decided she'd make the call."

Jorge nodded, but said nothing to the little Cuban broad who sat beside him on the couch, the same couch where Jerry had bounced Eve. She wore the shortest damned dress Jerry'd ever seen, and he thought he'd glimpsed something when she'd crossed her legs a minute ago.

What the hell did she think this was, a ball or something?

She and Jorge held hands. Jerry sat facing them, smoking and glancing at his watch and feeling itchy around the neck. He took out the gun for the fourth or fifth time and checked it and put it back in his waistband under his jacket.

The broad crossed her legs the other way, and this time he *knew* he'd seen hair. He jumped up, outraged somehow. This wasn't the time for stuff like that! This wasn't the time for anything but *concentration!*

"Are you nervous?" she murmured.

"Listen, what the hell is it with not wearing pants? I mean, tonight when we—"

Jorge interrupted sharply, "Do not talk to her that way."

"But it's true! I'm sitting here sweating blood . . ."

Jorge turned to the girl. She nodded calmly. "I discussed it with our partner. He thought it a good idea. Another possibility, in case we need to distract someone. If a bellboy comes up unexpectedly, one of the desk men, anyone who could be troublesome." She shrugged and smiled. "Do you know a man who would not pause for a few moments? . . ." Again the little smile.

Jorge looked upset. "It is foolishness," he muttered.

"Such foolishness has won wars," she said.

"What the hell have wars got to do with what *we're* doing?" Jerry snapped. "Why doesn't she get out of here?"

Jorge said, "She will leave in a few minutes. She wanted to stay here awhile." He paused. "With me."

She said, "And I could make the call from here as well as the other suite."

"But you won't," Jorge said. "Mrs. Prager and Ramon know you're to be kept from being seen there. Here it might not be possible. Here it could be dangerous."

"What difference does it make if I'm seen or not? We're all leaving as soon as it's over, aren't we?"

"Another precaution. Only useful in case things don't go well. Then you won't be connected . . ."

Jerry began pacing the room, muttering to himself. "The hell she won't be connected! We've all put our necks on the block! Holding hands and no pants and changing plans . . ."

The chick laughed and Jorge joined her. Jerry whirled, glaring at them, then smiled sheepishly. He went back to his chair and lit another cigarette. If she wanted to show her snatch, he'd enjoy it. Why not? He could play it as cool as they could, any day in the week. It was just that he was pitched fine, tuned for the job and nothing else.

She crossed her legs again. He didn't even look. He was busy checking his gun.

He had begun the speech in a daze, reading the first page, not speaking it. There was no charisma, no Christopher magic left, and he was doomed to failure. What had happened this afternoon at the party was the end of him. Oh, everything had been hushed up by payment and threat, his family's surefire solution to every problem, but it made no difference. Because this audience, and all the millions watching on television, and all the millions more who would see it on replays tomorrow, were sure to sense he was an empty man, a false man, no man at all . . .

The sudden roar, the pounding of hands, stopped his voice and his thoughts. He raised his head, startled, and looked out at the massed rows of folding chairs, the thousands in evening dress, the cameras above and left and right. The applause continued for a full ten seconds, and as it did he found his father-in-law and Dan and Benny Barker in the first row, along with other celebrities. They looked pleased, not worried. They were clapping. Father was nodding and clapping.

"What *is* this thing we have feared for so many years, this humiliation one administration after another has been unable to face in the name of the people—in the name of all of you? Is it a defeat of arms to shame us before the nations of the world?"

The roared "*No!*" that Berner had predicted came.

"Is it a betrayal of governments of patriots supported by the blood and will of their citizens?"

Again the roared "No!," and he marveled, thinking that if stockbrokers and other moneyed types responded this way, the rest of the nation certainly would.

"Is it a *true* retreat from our aims and aspirations as Americans, a retreat from interests vital to our survival? Before you answer," he said quickly, "think whether those aims include forcing governments of elite on nations ill-suited to support even a moderate middle class. Think if those aims include Americans becoming the new Romans, policing an entire world in the mistaken belief that we can make foreign nations over in our own image. Think if those aims include spilling the blood of our youth in one senseless war after another. Is *this* retreat?"

"No!"

He didn't pause now. He went on quickly, to bring back the image of an all-powerful America, feeling his timing returning, feeling his magic returning, feeling the charisma springing up full grown, a phoenix from the foul ashes of this afternoon.

"Let no nation mistake our purpose. Where . . . we . . . are . . . threatened, legitimately threatened, we . . . will . . . *fight!* And without confusion, dissension, the half-heartedness that has marked our agony these past years. We are still the same nation that survived revolution and civil war and two world wars and the successful holding actions in Europe and Asia. Or we will *become* that nation, once the indecision is gone, once the hand upon the wheel of state steadies. Once *you* put *your* hands back with the government's, give *your* full strength and will to the government, return *your* moral purpose to the government."

Applause was rising, but he lifted his voice over it to make the point, to end the foreign policy segment, to complete his break with all but splinter groups of the Democratic Party.

"Once *you* make known what you're willing and not willing to spend your blood and treasure for! And make it known you will, with your voices, your votes—"

There was no continuing. It was bedlam. It was more than he

had hoped for. The audience seethed, shouted, rose in sections. He looked at his father-in-law, and the old man was proud. Michael Wheeler had hated—and probably still did—this speech for its opposition to the President and the Party. But it worked, and that was Master Mike's true religion: Whatever worked.

The transition to the next stage was smooth, incorporating a safety valve of humor.

"If my brother-in-law is listening tonight, he's probably saying, 'The man comes from a good family, but who in the world formed his opinions?'" Laughter. "I would answer that *you* did. You formed his, and you formed mine. The change in opinions indicates a change in the times. And those among us wise enough, and compassionate enough, to be in the *forefront* of this change are going to make our country again what it was and should always be. First among nations." The applause was strong.

He entered the second phase of his program—what used to be called "fiscal responsibility," and which he termed "an end to the wasted-treasure madness." From a liberal he became a near-conservative. But it was a type of conservatism, he was assured, that both reason and the electorate demanded.

"The plains of history are dotted with the skeletons of nations that forgot their wealth had a limit and an end. Charity begins at home, the old saw goes. So does sanity. And sanity has been sadly missing from our handling of the federal purse strings since World War Two. I do not mean to say that the Marshall Plan was anything but a tremendous success, nor that many of the other aid programs didn't have positive results. But more and more often in the recent past the people have asked themselves, 'What has our money, our massive outpourings of aid, earned for us in this particular nation or that besides an equally massive enmity?'"

Roars of approval. A shout of "Egypt! Egypt!" which, in Miami, was not totally unexpected.

"From the 'thirties, when we were locked in the web of traditional isolationist suspicion, we have gone through a period of effective world participation—and beyond it. Beyond it to where

400

we now stand at the opposite extreme from naïve isolationism. And that is naïve expansionism. Not the healthy expansion of a profitable business, but the profligate expansion of a spendthrift Uncle Sam who hopes to buy his nephews' love and loyalty with endless gifts.

"My fellow citizens, the time has come to call a halt to the endless gifts. The time has come to turn our eyes toward our own underdeveloped areas, our own hungers and needs."

Heavy applause. Father tapping his cane on the floor. Berner looking wan, looking sad now. For this was the point at which they would have launched into the black ghetto section. "We'll surprise them, take them with honesty," he had told the writer. "We'll conquer with that rarest of political qualities, a wide-open approach to *everything!*"

He'd amended that to exclude the black ghettos. He'd been sorry to do so, mainly because Mike Wheeler had dictated the change. But now, standing here, playing this crowd as Heifetz would a violin, he knew the old man had been right. If he'd had those two pages in front of him, his instincts would have forced him to skip most of what they said. For this audience, this nation, was turning *away* from crusades, both foreign and domestic.

He went on to the third section of his speech, education and urban affairs. He explained his avoidance of the most pressing of urban affairs, the ghetto, with a brief statement:

"To make hasty prognoses and offer hasty solutions to what has been called the problem of crime in the streets would not only be an insult to your intelligence, but a disservice to those who *live* amidst this continuing malignancy of the American spirit. Yet solutions are on the way. Believe me when I say this. For I have met with the foremost leaders of the social sciences. For I have sat with them—these men of all races and religious persuasions—and I will sit with them again. And together—but not in haste and not for gain of publicity—we are going to hammer out approaches that will at least *begin* to heal these wounds that have scarred our land."

401

Solid applause. Their consciences had been appeased, without their fears, their prejudices being aroused.

He went on. He held them. He played them. The charisma was alive as never before.

He raised both arms outward, making an appeal for hearts and minds, and in the pause amidst the roar felt himself tingling and sweating. Felt himself pulsating. And wondered that he had ever been willing to risk losing *this* eroticism for Marco Renier's brand.

She barely had time to be afraid. It all happened so quickly. Al was waiting near the Arcade Level artist's shop, a rental sedan was at the front doors, and he had a reservation at a small motel in Golden Beach. As soon as they entered the room, he pulled her to the bed. His hands shook but he undressed her completely, and then leaned back to look. She closed her eyes. He said, "May . . . oh, May!" and his mouth went to her breasts.

She reached down, opened his trousers, put her hand inside. His head snapped up. "No . . . *wait* . . . I . . ." She felt the pulsations, and after a moment's shock she stroked so as to give him full satisfaction. He sank onto his back, an arm over his eyes, gasping her name.

She went to the bathroom for a washcloth and towel. She paused there, not knowing what to feel. Triumph? Disappointment? Laughter? (Oh God, not laughter! Not after all she'd done to get here!)

She came back and he hadn't moved. She bent to clean him, and realized he was still stiff. She used the washcloth, opening his clothing further, and felt his hand on her breast. She raised herself and they kissed. He whispered, "Don't be angry," and she said no, of course not, and began to undress him. When he was nude, she took him in her hand again and they began to play. He removed her hand a short while later, but continued his own play.

They made love. It was brief, but she was so thrilled at his frantic response that it was enough.

He went to the bathroom. She lay back on the bed, smoking

a cigarette, smiling, smiling all the way through. How he'd wanted her! A young man, a handsome man, and how he'd wanted her!

She stretched luxuriously, and realized he was watching from the bathroom doorway, and writhed sensuously for him. He came toward her, and by the time he sank down beside her he was ready. She praised his virility. He said, "With you, I don't think I'll *ever* stop!" He hurt her with a biting kiss and his hands rushed over her as if unable to decide where to pause, where to play.

How happy she was, how grateful! He had erased all her fears in these few moments. Stupid fears, they now seemed, but how they had ridden her!

She bent to him, full of the need to make him know her feelings. She sucked him, and his cries were beautiful, more beautiful than any song.

He stopped her. She said there was no need to—she *wanted* to finish. He said yes, he understood, but he too wanted to give. They gave to each other. He climaxed before her, but only by seconds.

She asked if he wanted to go now.

"Do you, May?"

"No." She had her head on his chest. "But your parents—"

"I'm all right until very late. Morning, even. They're going to be partying at a private home on Indian Creek. What about you?"

"As late as you want, dear."

He crushed her in a bear hug. "I'd better drop dead tonight because life's all downhill from here!"

They laughed together, but her laughter was quieter, briefer than his. He was joking, while she couldn't be sure whether his joke wasn't her literal, terrible truth.

Still, nothing could diminish her joy for long. Tonight was far from over, and it had already surpassed everything she'd dreamed of.

Tomorrow? . . .

Tomorrow she would remember tonight.

Wally Jones sat in an aisle seat a few rows from the back of the Grand Ballroom, a seat he'd taken instead of the one reserved for him with the other celebrities. As Senator Christopher approached the end of his speech, heralded not only by the time but by rising rhetoric, Wally rose and slipped out the nearest door. He'd hoped to feel foolish giving up his first-row seat—but now he felt justified, and anguished.

Not one word about Harlem, Southside, Watts, the hundred hell holes of black poverty! Not a single offering of hope to twenty million Afro-Americans! It was as if the Negro had finally disappeared in this land where he and his problems had always been camouflaged, hidden. *Invisible Man* was right!

He thought he'd go to the Burgundy Room and have a drink, but as he entered the lobby he found he was looking for other black faces—and there were no other black faces. "Move directly to suite," he murmured. "Do not pass bar. Do not collect nirvana."

The phone was ringing as he opened his door. By the time he reached it, it had stopped. He made himself a drink and said, "Let's add it all up. First there's the Astrid Kane bit, a fun thing if there ever was one." He had received a summons to appear in Dade County Court at ten A.M. next Thursday morning. He'd called New York and been referred to a Miami attorney and the attorney had assured him he could go on to his Las Vegas engagement. There would be postponements, and then a settlement. Nothing to worry about. Except the bite, of course.

"Next there's the beautiful gig with the happy audience sitting on their hands and the columnists wondering if ole Wally shouldn't try to work up an act with three other guys, a guitar, and a long wig. And the *loverly* cracker cops sitting in the Platinum Room last Monday with their *loverly* cracker broads, chuckling at the jigaboo who stood them treat after they'd humiliated him all over Surfside. And how 'bout ole Marjory Fine there, the liberal sister of mercy who couldn't wait to stomp the star who faw down? I mean, like she could have used her *fists* to make me leave that party, right?"

The phone rang. He looked at it with distaste. "And finally, the white hope of the East, Senator Dickie-boy Christopher, who emptied his bladder over the soul folk tonight and washed them *all* away."

The phone kept ringing.

"Stop the world," Wally sang softly, "I want to get off." He picked up the phone and said, "What is it?" without trying to hide anything.

"It is your chance to strike back," the Cuban chick said.

"You again, Bloody Maria?"

"Call the Senator's suite in five minutes. If no one answers, call again—every five minutes until they are there. Then say you are being threatened by a man with a gun because of that trouble with the white girl. Ask for help."

"Sure. And when Tonto gets here I say, April Fool, baby!"

"You will not have to say anything. The man who is threatening you will take care of that."

"You're forgetting that we made up that man who's threatening me."

"I did not make up anything. He will be there. He will not hurt the guard, just as we will not hurt the Senator. We will merely make him look like a fool to all those newspapermen downstairs. Tomorrow, at the press conference, they will ask how he can expect to take care of the country when he can't take care of himself."

That really clinched it. A chance to make white turn red. A chance to piss back, and without killing people. But he said, "Forget it. C'mon up for a drink and we'll talk *señores* and *señoritas*."

The line was dead.

Five minutes later he'd finished another drink—and called the Senator's suite. No answer. He had his third drink and sang, "Happy Days Are Here Again," and went back to the phone. This time Tonto answered. There was laughter in the background—the ofays celebrating their cop-out. Wally said, "Listen,

I don't know what it's all about, but there's a Bilbo-type in the hall with a gun . . ."

Tonto said, "Stay away from your door. If he gets in, lock yourself in the bathroom. I'm coming."

Wally went to the door and looked through the peephole. Not a soul. He sang, "All the darkies am a-weepin', Wally's in the cole, cole ground." He went back to the bar and had that prince among drinks, the Black Beauty, better known as belting from the bottle.

Ivan Lamas sat in the lobby of the Bal Metropole, smoking a cigar and turning the pages of a *Miami Herald*. He hadn't told Jorge he would be here. He hadn't actually known himself he would come here, until an hour ago. Then his need to be close to what would happen, his curiosity, had overwhelmed him. And why resist it? There was no danger. He wouldn't even see any part of the abduction, since they would go directly from the fourteenth floor to the basement garage. He would merely fill the long hours of waiting. He would get a little of the atmosphere.

But he was getting more than he'd bargained for. That atmosphere was . . . disturbing. Seeing the Senator and his group move into the ballroom, seeing the crush of people through the open doors, hearing the speech over the lobby loudspeakers and the roars of approval, tasting the atmosphere of the hotel itself— all this had made the plan terribly real. What had been figures on a chessboard became human beings, people who could easily leave their allotted squares, make unexpected moves, throw the game into confusion. What had been an exercise in planning became life, became flesh and blood, fraught with the essence of life—error and death.

Of course, he had known all this before, had been aware of the element of danger and the unexpected. But knowing and *feeling* were worlds apart, and his heart beat as it hadn't when making plans and listening to tapes; his mouth dried as it hadn't when giving orders to Jorge and flattering him so as to build his confidence. Now his own confidence needed building.

He was uncomfortable. It had been a mistake to come here. He would leave.

The speech ended. The lobby flooded with people. The Senator and his group emerged, and amidst much surging and seething, made their way to the elevators.

The noise was abominable! He put his head down, trying to lose himself in the printed word. Printed words were manageable, safe. He felt very unsafe at the moment.

The noise began to lessen. People went quickly to bars and clubs and lined up outside for automobiles. The lobby remained crowded, but more normally so. He began to lose some of his discomfort. He lifted his head and looked at the elevator area. People were still waiting there. The "up-down" light above one car was out—something as solid in reality as it had been in his mind.

He took out a cigar. No reason to hurry. He wasn't needed at home. All the orders were given, all elements of the plan set in motion.

He would stay awhile.

They listened to the speech while driving back from dinner at Juanito's Centro Vasco. Ellie had said she wanted Cuban food for a change, but she'd been tense all day and Bruce knew that what she really wanted was to put some distance between herself and the Bal Metropole, this night when it belonged to the Wheeler clan.

"Turn it off, will you, Bruce?"

He wanted to hear the end, but did as she asked. She sighed, looking out the window. It was overcast, windy, quite cold. "It'll be over soon," she said. "By tomorrow they'll be gone."

"Feeling better?"

"I felt fine all—" She stopped. She looked at him and nodded.

He drove off the causeway, the big Caddy convertible soft and unresponsive to his touch. "I hate to bring it up again," he said, "but you have to make a decision. That suitcase is still in my

407

Jaguar. I can't leave it in the hotel garage forever, and I won't drive around with a hundred fifty thousand dollars."

She looked away again, as if it were somehow unpleasant to be in possession of a small fortune she'd believed lost.

"Can't you just—put it away?"

"Where? It's your money, Ellie, so tell me."

She waved her hand. "A bank. A vault. Anywhere. We'll only have to get it out again when he calls."

He didn't bother arguing that the blackmailer might *not* call. She seemed obsessed by the idea that the money was already lost. He didn't want to disturb her; he wanted to get through the next week with a minimum of trouble, wanted to become her husband, after which he would handle the money and everything else.

"The banks are closed until Monday."

"Leave it in the Jag then."

"A hundred fifty thousand dollars? I've had clothing taken out of cars. If someone opens that trunk . . ."

"Well, what is it you want? Should I bring it up to the suite?"

"Put it in the hotel vault."

"Why can't *you* do it?"

"I'm not a guest."

"Oh, all *right!*"

His own anger flared. He swallowed it. She was justified, in a way. He *could* take care of it, if he went to a little trouble. The desk wouldn't stand on the letter of the rule, for Ellie DeWyant's fiancé.

But they would check with Claude DeWyant, and that talk with Claude had had its effect. He wanted Claude to know *Ellie* had the money, and that she had it in her own name. He wanted to prove things to Claude.

"We'll go to the garage," he said, "and pick it up."

"Why can't one of the boys—"

"I'm sorry," he interrupted sharply. "You probably consider it gauche, but I just can't be casual about that much money."

She didn't answer for a moment, then said, "I know," voice dull.

He was shocked at the insult. He drove more quickly, turning onto Collins toward the Metropole.

6

SATURDAY, JANUARY 28, P.M.
TO
SUNDAY, JANUARY 29, A.M.

Michael Wheeler sat in his chair, all sharped up in tux, and reached for the cane stuck in the corner. "Let it alone," Jerry said. Not that he expected the old wreck to try anything, but just to show him he couldn't make Move One without asking permission.

The old man said, "Idiots! Get out now . . . while you have chance!"

Eve stood behind the wheelchair, staring at Jorge's gun, not looking at Jerry. He had to get her to look at him, and to believe him. His own gun was out of sight, under his jacket. He said, "Listen, Eve, they forced me. My mother—if I don't help them, and if you don't help me, they'll kill her."

She finally looked at him. She seemed embarrassed.

"*Honest!* And what's the big deal? They'll take some money, some jewelry. Just open the connecting door to the Senator's suite when we tell you. Just walk in first and say something so they'll—"

"*Not* a robbery!" Wheeler interrupted. "Haven't looked for money, jewels, *here.* I have more than Dick. Political assassination, like the Kennedys!"

Eve gasped and went white.

"That's crazy!" Jerry said.

Jorge stepped forward. "We must all be a little more quiet. There is not going to be any assassination, any bloodshed. No one will be hurt. It is a simple abduction, for profit." He looked at the old man. "You will determine what will or will not happen, by your future actions. You will control the entire situation. So there is certainly no danger to your son-in-law."

"And tell her about my mother," Jerry urged.

"He must help. It is our only hold over him. Either he helps or we must harm the mother."

Jerry nodded at Eve. From her expression, he understood she still didn't believe it. Or was she just so scared? . . .

He walked around the chair and touched her arm. "Honey."

She didn't move, but she looked at him and the look made him drop his hand. "It's not true," she said. "And even if it was, you used me. All the time, you—"

A tapping at the hall door. Jerry pulled his gun and saw Eve's lips tighten. To hell with her. From now on it was a straight muscle play. Should have been that way from the beginning. Waste of time with all the other angles—at least once they had the manager.

Jorge was at the door. He listened and whispered something and turned to the living room. He was smiling. "The guard just left."

The old man slumped back. Jerry grinned, and jerked his gun. "We're all going to the connecting door."

"It's locked," Eve said.

Jerry shoved her. She moved the wheelchair. They went down the foyer to the connecting door, where Jorge was using his key.

"Don't help them," the old man said, voice loud.

Jerry slapped him lightly across the back of the head.

Eve said, "Please, he's sick!"

Jorge said, "Knock at the door, miss. Say the President wishes to enter."

She hesitated. Jorge reversed his gun and raised the butt over the old man's head. Eve came around the chair and knocked at the second door. A voice, not the Senator's, answered. She said, "Mr. Wheeler would like to see the Senator, Mr. Berner."

There were voices and footsteps; the door clicked and opened. The Senator and Berner stood there, the Senator smiling. "Changed your mind? . . ." he began, and then he saw the guns. He stepped back. Jerry said, "That's right, back up, both of you. Very slow. These are silencers. We can kill all four of you without a sound."

Jorge went first, murmuring, "No need to talk of killing. There is no danger for anyone."

They had reached the living room, the Senator and Berner backing all the way, when there was a distant tapping sound. Jorge nodded at Jerry. Jerry ran across the living room and into the second bedroom, and couldn't find the connecting door. The tapping came again. It took a minute for him to figure out that the dresser had been moved, and another minute to shove it away from the door. And the one thing they didn't have was minutes to spare.

Ramon Pedras entered from a bedroom, Ruthie standing behind him. Ramon said, "The woman hasn't returned," and hurried to the living room. Jerry began to close the door. Ruthie said, "Leave it open in case you need help, or I do."

"The plan is to keep each suite sealed. The plan goes. You have to wait for the woman."

She said, "All right. Just wanted to be able to see you, hear you." She smiled. "It's working. Soon . . ."

He nodded and closed the door. Most of his fear was gone now. He knew plenty remained to be done, but the guard was taken care of and the elevator was fixed and what could go wrong? What had he been so worried about?

He returned to the living room. Eve was sitting on the couch. Ramon Pedras was tying her feet with electrical wire from a roll in his pocket. He snipped it with a single-edge razor and straightened to tape her mouth. She shifted her eyes to Jerry once, briefly. "Lemme help," he said, moving to where the Senator and Berner stood beside Michael Wheeler's chair.

Jorge said, "No, that is not the plan. Ramon does the tying, you guard the hall door, I guard the prisoners until they are tied."

"Then we leave," Jerry said, walking down the foyer.

"If all is clear," Jorge said. "We leave only when all is clear."

"Yeah, yeah," Jerry muttered, rubbing his hands together, touching the gun in his belt, thinking of the hundred fifty grand he and Ruthie owned—half in his Thunderbird, half to be handed them when they put the Senator in that limousine down in the garage. And he'd never have to see another lousy basement again, never have to worry about cold concrete floors and sweaty, crummy jobs again!

There was a knock at the door. Wally put down the bottle and ran over. As he opened it, he saw two things simultaneously. Tonto looking at him, hunched like a fullback ready to plunge. And a door opening up in the hall behind him, a linen closet, with a skinny little guy coming out holding what looked like a small cannon. Wally said, "Christ!" The skinny little guy said, "Mister, your hands—" Tonto never hesitated. He turned, digging at his hip under his jacket. The skinny little guy was still talking. ". . . up in the . . ." Then his mouth opened wide and he stuck the cannon out straighter. There was a popping sound and wood splintered high on the door. A split second later there was a series of explosions, maybe three of them, and the skinny little guy did a funny thing. He jumped up, his arms and legs moving like Jackie Gleason's in an *away-we-go!* At the same time he snapped back, as if blown by one hell of a wind, and ended up sitting in the closet, propped against the shelves, his shirt front a bloody mess. Not that he knew it.

Tonto turned back to Wally. Wally said, "Bet I'm whiter than you, Chief." Tonto smiled tightly. "That seems to take care—" He stopped; his smile died; he muttered, "The broken elevator," and began to run. Wally watched him go through a door marked *Emergency Exit*.

He went back to the bar and took a good belt of Scotch.

Nausea rippled his guts. He wanted to throw up, but didn't have time just now. He picked up the phone and asked for Security.

Violetta heard the pounding of feet, and quickly went from the elevators to the bend in the hall. She flattened against the wall and looked around the corner. The guard, coming from the emergency stairs beyond the Krasmer suite!

She fumbled with the snap of her bag as the guard slowed and went by the Senator's door very carefully, very quietly. She found the little gun and drew it and held it in her right hand. The guard stopped at Wheeler's door and put his hand on the knob. She got the slide safety off and remembered to check the grip safety and magazine disconnector, as Jorge had taught her. So many things to do . . .

The guard opened the door. A mistake had been made! The door was supposed to be locked with the chain so no one could enter!

No time to think of that. The guard had gone inside and closed the door. She kicked off her shoes and ran. She went by Wheeler's door and reached the Senator's door and tapped lightly. Leech's voice was close on the other side. "Yes?"

"The guard," she whispered. "Coming through the connecting door from—"

She heard movement, a grunt, something falling. She got her keys out and dropped her bag and found the right one. The sounds on the other side stopped. She opened the door, finger tightening on the trigger of the little gun.

Leech smiled at her. The guard had his back to her, hands on his head. His automatic lay on the floor beside the open connecting door. "Nice," Leech said. "You got me turned around just in time. All I did was clip that gun hand."

Jorge was at the end of the foyer, blocking the living room, and anyone in it, from seeing her. He said, "Get back to the elevators." But then he nodded. "Excellent." She stepped into the hall, closing the door. She picked up her bag and put the

413

gun and keys back inside. She went past Wheeler's suite to the turn in the hall and put on her shoes. She returned to the elevators.

She felt warm from that "Excellent." She felt they had handled the *worst* that could happen. In a matter of minutes they would bring the Senator . . .

She heard the car before the "up" light flashed green. The middle one. Its doors opened and a waiter wheeled out a serving cart covered with a white cloth. She smiled, her mind whirling with plans and discarded plans. He nodded, and wheeled his cart left, toward the three suites. He was bald and looked about sixty. What could she do with such a man?

She walked briskly after him. "Is that the Senator's champagne?"

"Champagne and dinner, yes."

"It's about time. I was going down to check on it."

"He ordered for eleven-thirty, didn't he? It's not—"

"Yes, well, let me get the door for you." She went around him and walked as fast as she could. She reached the door and knocked and said, "The Senator's dinner is here," and stepped aside. Leech opened up, his right hand hidden behind his back. "Come in," he said to the waiter. The man wheeled the cart inside. The door closed. One more set of hands and feet for Pedras to tie, one more mouth to tape. Otherwise, all still went smoothly.

Of course, she had been seen.

She shrugged. Lamas would protect her as he was protecting the others. Jorge and Leech and Mrs. Prager and Pedras and Morales, all had been seen by one or another of the Americans. And all expected to be safe. So now she was completely equal with them.

She returned to the elevators.

"What is taking you so long?" Jorge snapped.

Ramon was at the couch where the nurse, already bound and gagged, Berner, gagged and with hands tied, and the waiter, so frightened they had decided to bind and gag him immediately, sat side by side. The Senator sat in a red armchair, facing them. He was pale and still, but otherwise controlled. He had spoken only once, saying, "Just don't hurt my father-in-law." The guard, standing some five feet behind him, hands stretched high above his head, had looked at him, surprised. The Senator had seemed somewhat surprised himself. "We won't give any trouble," he'd said, "but remember, President Wheeler's very sick."

Michael Wheeler appeared to bear out that statement. His strength seemed gone. He sat to the left of the Senator, slumped in his wheelchair. The nurse kept shifting her eyes to him and making crying sounds. He was having trouble breathing, and Jorge worried what would happen when they gagged him. It was important that he stay alive, because the Senator would allow no resistance as long as he did.

Ramon pressed a long strip of tape over the waiter's mouth, and turned his head. "I am being careful," he said coldly to Jorge. "You have your job, I have mine. If you do yours as well—"

"Move faster," Jorge interrupted.

From the foyer, Leech said, "I told you I should help him."

Jorge shifted the gun to his left hand, wiped the right on his jacket, felt the guard's heavy automatic bulging his pocket. He took his revolver back in his right hand, and felt wetness trickling down his sides. He hadn't counted on the tying taking so long. He hadn't expected the guard would escape Morales and that there would be a waiter. He was worried about Violetta being seen by the waiter. "And if I'd let you," he answered Leech, "who would have been in the foyer to handle the guard?"

"Okay, but *now?*"

Ramon moved back to Berner to finish the job interrupted by the waiter's arrival. He murmured in Spanish, "Feeling a little frightened, Jorge? If you had been in the Resistance instead of chauffeuring—"

Jorge said, "Finish with the writer and get to the guard. Later, I will give you a chance to eat those words!"

Ramon whirled. "You can die right now if you wish!"

Jorge took tight hold of himself. Leech called, "Hey, Ramon, cut that shit!" Ramon glared, a tightness of expression, a glitter of eyes, showing his madness. Jorge said, voice very even, "Finish the tying."

Ramon glared one more second, and bent to Berner's feet.

Jorge said, "Leech, tie the old man."

The nurse made a sound. Jorge muttered, "He will be all right."

Ramon said, "We could leave immediately, if you listen to me. Knock the rest unconscious—"

Jorge said, "It is *you* I will knock unconscious if you don't follow the plan!"

Ramon turned again, still in a crouch, and began to answer.

At that moment, with Leech crossing in front of Jorge to the old man, Berner leaped up. Jorge couldn't believe it. The writer's hands were tied, his mouth was taped, but he was lunging forward, kicking at Ramon. Ramon fell back in a sitting position. Berner kept coming. The fool! The crazy fool!

Dan felt he was moving slowly, very slowly, as if the air had turned to water and he were swimming his way off the couch. He hadn't thought much about what he was doing. There had been no buildup, no progression of thoughts leading to action. He had suddenly decided it was necessary to save the next President of the United States from whatever danger threatened him.

He wondered at himself. He was totally free of fear. But perhaps fear would come in a second or two when that hard-faced Cuban with the gun, the leader of these men, began to shoot.

He felt his foot connect with the man they called Ramon. His head, he hoped. He floated over him. Yes, floated, danced, no sensation at all of frantic movement. But he knew it was impossible that he was actually moving that way. His nervous system had done something to protect him from fear, to stop him from understanding what he was really doing.

He was over Ramon, and with head down, coming at the leader. To his right, he saw other movement. The old man was rising up out of his chair. He too was floating, dancing, moving in water, his left arm holding that wicked black cane high over his head. He was going for the cabana boy, Leech.

Leech the Beach, the boy had said that first day leading to this last day.

Oh yes, he knew that, too. This *last* day.

He was reaching out for the leader's gun, and the leader was going backward, mouthing things.

"Back!" Dan heard. "Back or—"

"Or *else*," they used to say in the movies when he was a boy and beginning to form tastes that would eventually eliminate most of those movies from his life. Now he was eliminating life itself, and it was still a matter of taste.

Pain! Oh God such pain in his stomach and the sensation of floating-in-water gone and the world with him yes too much with him because he couldn't even scream there was so much pain. Yet he kept to his feet, reaching out, and managed to strike the end of the silenced revolver and it took another second for the leader to re-aim. And in that second he began to fall. And in that second he understood what he had done. And in that second he said, or thought he said, "Sorry, Dr. Sochall," his feeling one of satisfaction.

The gun jerked and snapped a second time. He was looking right at it and saw it and heard it, but this time he didn't feel it. At least not as pain. A soft, dull fist punching his chest, that was all. *Tap*, that was all. Afterward there was no afterward.

Jerry turned, wondering what the hell was happening. That damned fool Berner couldn't be jumping Jorge, could he? Not with his hands tied and Jorge holding a gun right on him?

He started to say something, to reason with the man, when he caught movement from the corner of his eye. He threw up his arm, but the cane caught him a real good lick at the side of the head. He stumbled backward, sat down, saw someone hurtling by him, tried to warn Jorge that the guard was coming. But Michael Wheeler was standing over him, his cane whipping down again. Jerry squirmed to the side, catching the blow on his left

417

forearm. It still hurt like hell! The old man had been playing possum. He had plenty of fight left in him.

But Jerry's head had cleared, and he reached around and grabbed the end of the cane before it could rise for a third blow. He yanked, and Wheeler came tumbling down. He punched him once, in the temple, and the old man groaned like he was giving his death rattle—and maybe he was.

Jerry got up. Jorge and the guard were rolling all over the place. Ramon was just sitting up, rubbing his neck and coughing and choking. Jerry reached for his gun, and didn't have it. He looked around, and saw it on the floor. As he picked it up, the guard let out a kind of war whoop and scrambled around behind the bar.

Jerry ran toward Jorge. Jorge was rolling to the side, shouting, "Gun! He has his gun!"

Jerry didn't even think. He put both his hands over his head, his revolver in one, and yelled, "I'm quitting! I'm quitting!" He went right by the bar, and heard the blast of the guard's automatic. But he didn't feel anything, and was in the foyer before he turned for a quick look back. He saw Jorge falling. He saw Ramon running and shooting, and then the Cuban was with him at the door and they were both running into the hall.

Jorge felt the pain and fell, unbelieving, wondering who was to blame for having it end like this. Pedras? No, Pedras could not be blamed for *everything* falling apart. The *patrón?* How could that be? The plan had been good; the *patrón* had figured brilliantly.

He fired at the bar, and heard answering fire and felt cloth and wood strike his face. He couldn't move. Something had struck his side and he was weak and growing weaker.

He had killed the writer. It was wrong. Killing Prager had been right, had been honorable. But not the writer, hands tied and helpless. He had shot him twice, the second time in the heart, and he was ashamed. He should have struck him, knocked him

418

unconscious, but he'd seen that set face, those blank, fearless eyes, and he'd panicked and killed.

The guard fired again, one shot, and Jorge was flung over as his right hip shattered. He twisted back onto his stomach, groaning, but not with pain. It was as if he had drunk a quart of good Cuban rum, the cane liquor reaching every nerve, dulling all feeling. He groaned with shame, with remorse—with guilt.

It was *he* who was to blame. *He* who had caused the plan to fail.

The guard wasn't firing. Jorge hadn't counted, but he reasoned the guard had used up his ammunition, perhaps several rounds when facing Vidal Morales. If only he could stand up now, go to that bar . . .

He tried. He didn't even make it to his knees. He slumped back to his stomach, and leveled his revolver, and fired into the bar, hoping to penetrate the thick wood and reach the guard. Hoping, but not believing. And not really caring any more, because the carpet around him was turning soggy with his blood. Because he knew death was approaching, and felt that even if he lived there would be no honor, no point to living.

He had failed the *patrón*. He had killed the writer and been unable to kill the guard and that had led to Leech and Ramon fleeing. He had failed Violetta.

He prayed she would escape. If only the *patrón* hadn't insisted . . .

He tried to clear his mind. The *patrón* had chosen Pedras and the *patrón* had insisted on Violetta being here and the *patrón* had made the plan.

But the *patrón* couldn't be so wrong! All his life Jorge had obeyed him. All his life he had considered him more a god than a man. All his life he had loved . . .

The guard raised himself over the bar. Jorge cursed him for bringing him to this evil moment, these evil thoughts, and tried to aim his gun. The guard ducked down. Jorge wept and did the only thing he could. Shot himself in the head.

419

Christ, it had fallen apart! They'd had it made and that writer had gone crazy and then the old man . . .

They were at the elevators. Violetta said, "Where—"

"C'mon!" Leech gasped. "Get us down! It's finished!"

She stepped back from them.

Ramon said, "The elevator key! Are you deaf? The guard—he'll call for help!"

"Jorge," she said, and she had her little gun aimed into the elevator where they stood, Ramon futilely punching the buttons.

"*La llave—dámelo!*" Ramon shouted. "*Jorge está muerto!*"

Violetta turned and walked away. Ramon said, "*Perra!*" and leveled the gun. Jerry knocked his hand aside. "Wait. It's better that we use the stairs anyway. This elevator only goes to the basement." He began to run, turning right so as not to pass the three suites. "Stairs near the owner's place," he panted to Ramon, who ran just behind him.

They reached the DeWyant suite. Jerry put out an arm, slowing and making Ramon slow, too. They walked by, and to the end of the hall and the emergency exit. He opened the door, and they entered the dimness of a metal stairway lighted by one small bulb per landing.

"Where now?" Ramon panted. He didn't look nearly so tough any more. He'd been ready to fight Jorge in the suite, the jerk, but now he was scared.

Jerry was scared too. Plenty. But he kept reminding himself of that seventy-five grand in the T-Bird. If he could get to the car-check booth before anyone knew to look for him. If he could only drive away from here . . .

"The lobby," he said, and started down the stairs. "People there. Can't get trapped like in the basement, in case cops are around."

He stopped at the eleventh-floor landing. "We'll take the elevator now." He reached back and stuck his gun in his waistband, lined up with his spine. "Check my jacket."

He did the same for Ramon; they lit cigarettes; he opened the door a crack. "All right." They came out, walking quickly to get away from the exit, then sauntering, chatting casually when they saw people waiting at the elevators. No one looked their way. No one seemed excited, except about the Senator's speech.

An elevator came down from Twelve. Two women were inside. *They* were excited.

". . . in the linen closet, bleeding!"

"My God, I'll never forget . . ."

They lowered their voices as Jerry, Ramon, and two couples entered. Jerry put his back against the rear wall; Ramon put his back to Jerry. The two women murmured. The others glanced their way and tried to overhear. The elevator stopped and more people got on. A chubby redhead, whose husband was a sunken-faced recent coronary, caught Jerry's eye. She smiled, forming, "Hi," with her lips. He answered the smile. She glanced at her husband, who stared glumly at the doors, then back at Jerry.

Someone else would have to oblige her. But her smiles and glances made things seem more normal.

They stopped at Three. A couple got on. They passed Two, and Jerry took a deep breath. Next stop, the lobby.

He began to feel hopeful.

Ruthie had heard the voices, the thumps, a scream or yell, and opened the connecting doors and come halfway across the bedroom. Just in time to hear shots and see Jerry running for the foyer. Just in time to see Jorge crumple. Then Ramon was running and shooting and the Senator was throwing himself on top of his father-in-law, and Ruthie returned to the Krasmer suite, closing both doors and locking hers.

She waited, holding her breath and listening. There were more shots, then silence. She strained to hear what was happening, and suddenly realized that the man in the bed was quiet; much too quiet.

On the way to the front door, she threw her little automatic behind the bar. She stepped into the hall, and saw Violetta approaching the Senator's door, eyes fixed wide and gun in hand. She ran to her, grabbed her by the arms, pushed her back, whispering, "No good! It's over!"

"Jorge," Violetta said, and blinked her eyes and came awake. "He's not—"

"He's had it. I saw, honey."

"Americans," Violetta whispered, eyes filled with hate. "They did it. Americans . . ." She tried to shake Ruthie off, tried to get to the Senator's door.

"Stop it!" Ruthie said, still pushing. "*We* did it, all of us, by thinking Jorge's plan could work. Jorge did it to himself."

Violetta looked at her. "No, not Jorge's plan. No . . ." Suddenly, the hate and fight went out of her. She dropped her head and allowed Ruthie to walk her to the elevators. Ruthie took the gun, dug it deep into a cigarette sand-urn, and entered Elevator Three. "The keys, honey. Unless you want to commit suicide?"

Violetta came in and gave Ruthie the bunch. Ruthie found the tag marked "El" and began to insert the key in the slot under the floor buttons, then stopped. "It'll only go to the basement garage—or was that a story to keep us straight?"

"Not a story," Violetta said dully. "It is programmed."

"I'm not sure we should go to the garage. We'll stick out like sore thumbs down there. The lobby would be better. The lobby, where we'll blend in with the guests."

She took Violetta's arm and they walked out of the elevator. She pressed the down button and said, "Snap out of it, sweetie. You're too young to rot in federal pen the rest of your life. Do you understand what I'm saying?"

Violetta's eyes filled with tears. "He was always so *right*. Everything had to wait for later. Now I can wait forever."

Ruthie got tissues from her bag and gave them to the girl. "No crying. People will notice."

"It hurts." She wiped at her eyes. "Can you understand how it hurts?"

Ruthie thought of Jerry. He was lost to her, but then again she had never really believed he'd belong to her. She shrugged. "I'm an old broad, honey. I've got scar tissue on top of scar tissue. Live long enough and you'll outgrow that kind of hurt."

Violetta asked for a cigarette. "Do you think we will get away from here?"

"Sure. It's only been a few minutes since the shooting. We'll just ride down . . ."

An elevator came. Ruthie held the door while Violetta looked in her compact mirror and composed herself. "Thank you, Mrs. Prager."

Ruthie smiled. Mrs. Prager. Twice a widow in two days? It was a lot better than being a corpse.

Ivan Lamas saw the two men walking from the elevators, stopping as five police officers appeared at the front doors, then turning much too casually toward the back. One was Ramon Pedras; the big one fit Jorge's description of Jerry Leech. They hurried while trying to seem not to, and went out the rear doors. Through the curved glass wall, Lamas watched them pass the spotlighted pool. He rose and strolled to the wall. The two men went through a wooden door leading to some sort of service area.

He went back to his chair and sat down, glancing with proper curiosity at the four Miami Beach policemen joining a hotel security officer at the elevators. One policeman and one security officer now blocked the front doors.

He lit a fresh cigar and turned the pages of his newspaper, his hands steady. Quite obviously there had been trouble. But no matter what happened, no matter who was captured and questioned, he was safe. Some didn't know him, and those who did understood who would provide money for legal counsel, who would support their families if death or jail claimed them. Ivan Cesar Lamas had to remain free if they were to receive help.

He relaxed, looking around and wondering what had happened to Jorge and the others. It wasn't long before he saw Violetta and a woman who could only be Mrs. Prager walk from the elevators. When they saw the police, Violetta tried to change direction, but Mrs. Prager laughed and said something into her ear and they continued on to the front doors.

The officers stopped them. Violetta showed them a card—probably identifying her as a hotel employee. Mrs. Prager talked and smiled pleasantly and the security officer said something to the policeman and the policeman stepped aside. The women left.

Lamas approved. If Leech and Pedras had been as professional as Mrs. Prager, they too might have walked out free. As for Jorge—well, whether he survived or not, he certainly wouldn't be driving the car tomorrow.

Maria had a nephew who was looking for such work. Mateo, the man's name was. Young, and probably without proper regard for the position of chauffeur-bodyguard to Ivan Cesar Lamas. But there was little choice, really. What would an employment agency say about his requirements of deference and loyalty? And what would they *send* him!

As a logical man, Lamas had already ceased worrying about a lost cause and turned to more important matters.

Bruce took the suitcase from the Jaguar's trunk. Ellie stood beside him, looking around the car-filled basement garage. Bruce slammed the trunk lid, the sound echoing hollowly in the huge concrete and steel cavern. No one seemed to be here. No cars coming in, none departing—and this last was particularly surprising since the Senator's speech had ended and nonguests should have been lined up three-deep at the car-check for at least an hour.

They began to walk toward the freight elevators, the only ones that came to the garage. They hadn't spoken since her remark in the car; they didn't speak now.

They went by the row of passenger elevators. Drawn up directly in front of them, blocking what was usually kept an open area, was a black Lincoln limousine. Bruce glanced at the sign propped against the windshield: "Special—do not move."

They both heard something a moment later, and looked back—

sounds of running, of gasping voices. A figure . . . no, two figures were weaving through the cars, coming from the basement area. One was Jerry Leech.

Leech saw them and stopped, in among the cars to their right. He laughed and shook his head. "Boy," he said, and shook his head again. "I mean, did you ever have a date and the guys can't find your car? I mean, just because I work here—" He laughed again, and jerked a thumb at the second man, who had just reached him and was smiling and nodding unconvincingly. Bruce wondered what the hell was going on.

"My friend, Pete. Listen, you seen my heap around? You know, the T-Bird with wire wheels?"

An elevator hummed around the corner where freight was loaded. Bruce said no and see-you and began to walk quickly, wanting to make that car. Leech and his friend began rushing around again, looking for the T-Bird. Ellie murmured, "Something's wrong."

As if in proof, two Miami policemen appeared around the corner. One quickly put his hand on his gun. "What're you doing down here?" The other was moving by them, looking off to where Leech and his friend were still scurrying through the rows of cars. "Hey! You two! Over here!"

Bruce said, "Had to get something from my car."

Ellie said, "I'm Miss DeWyant."

The cop said, "Oh, yes, I recognize you, miss." He took his hand off his gun. "I was at that presentation dinner last year and you were with your father."

Ellie nodded. Bruce said, "We'd like to get upstairs . . ."

The cop was no longer looking at or listening to him. He was watching Leech and his friend, who had stopped but not approached the second officer.

"I work here," Leech called.

The cop looked at Ellie. "That right, Miss DeWyant? He work in the garage?"

"No, at the pool."

"C'mon over!" the first cop called. "There's been trouble upstairs and we've got to see that no one leaves the hotel without identifying himself."

Leech still hesitated. Bruce began to wonder. Leech then said, "Sure," and came over. His friend came close behind him.

"What happened?" Ellie asked the first cop.

"Don't know yet. Something to do with Senator Christopher. Shooting up there—"

And without warning there was shooting down here, Leech bringing a revolver from behind him and the popping sound it made explaining why it was so big—a silencer extension over the barrel—and the first cop, the one they'd been talking to, sitting down and holding his chin, or his neck just under his chin, and the other cop throwing himself toward the cars, hitting the concrete while Leech's friend, also drawing a big revolver, sent bits and pieces of concrete flying about him.

Bruce did two things without having to think. He shoved Ellie left, toward the wall, hard enough to send her to the floor; and he threw the suitcase high and far over the first row of cars. Only then did he drop and flatten out beside the sitting officer, who slowly toppled backward.

Leech and his friend were running back toward the basement area. The cop behind the cars fired three times, the sound deafening in this vast echo chamber. Metal screamed, ricocheting, but the two men were low among the cars and continued running.

Bruce remained down, and glanced at Ellie. "Stay there," he said. The second cop came over, crouching. He bent to his comrade. "Van. Where'd they get—"

He didn't finish. The first cop dropped his hands and they saw the blood gushing from where neck and chin joined. He tried to speak, choked, rolled his head. Ellie made a little crying sound.

The second cop looked off to where Jerry and his friend had disappeared. "Where's that lead to?"

"The basement. And also the service entrance to pool and deck areas. He'll probably try for the beach."

"Show me." He drew the fallen officer's gun from its holster and slapped it into Bruce's hand. "You know how to fire? Any-

426

way, it'll make them think—" He was moving off. "Miss, call a doctor, fast!"

Bruce said, "Ellie, the suitcase."

The cop was shouting to hurry and he ran. He hated to leave. He hated risking his neck, but it wasn't just that. It was Ellie's face, Ellie's eyes.

She got up. The officer was looking at her, trying to speak, the hole bubbling red in his throat. She looked away from him, her reason trembling. A phone. There were house phones all over the hotel. They should be down here, too. On the walls. Look at the walls and you won't have to look at the hole bubbling red. And you won't have to think of Bruce and the money, always the money.

She went to the wall and along it—and there was a phone. She picked up the handset and said, "Hello? Hello!"

The operator answered. She identified herself and said an officer was badly hurt and to please get the doctor down. The operator said, "Oh God, not another one. The doctor's on Fourteen and he's—I'll have to call an ambulance."

Ellie said yes, do that, and the line went dead and she couldn't stand there holding the phone, had no reason to stand there holding the phone, had to turn to the man on the floor, had to help him.

She walked back, slowly, not wanting to reach him because what could she do for him? And because she felt her mind shaking. And not just because of him, poor human dying as all poor humans must die in a way that so many poor humans died with the red horror bubbling out of them. No, not only because of that did her mind shake but because of a more subtle horror.

Don't call it a *horror*, silly! Dr. Iglesias would laugh. Not a horror, just a meaningless—progression of events. That's all. He hadn't been thinking. He'd just acted.

The guns had been fired and death had begun flying around them and Bruce had been very brave, thinking not of himself but . . . *of the money*.

Of her, too, she told herself. Certainly! Of her, too!

But she was standing over the fallen officer and the red hole bubbled and the destruction that thought—*of the money*—had wrought was irreversible and compounded by those calls—first the blackmailer, ripping off the scabs and causing the thirteen-year-old wounds to flow again, and then the girl, mocking her . . .

Remembering the girl brought her back to *the money*. And then she remembered and accepted everything she had tried to forget and reject. His proficiency at planning things she felt should *not* be planned. His ability at lovemaking, satisfying her so well, so clinically, professionally well. His constant concern for that suitcase . . .

And so back to *the money*. And so the recognition of her own aloneness. And so the falling apart of the edifice of love, the structure crumbling to ruin in seconds, leaving her defenseless against the workings of her mind, her enemy mind.

The officer's eyes were on her. He moved his mouth, trying to speak. She knelt because she had to; the appeal in his eyes forced her to. She knelt to the irrefutable proof of what her mother had called, "this jungle world, this green abattoir." No reason, no love, nothing but tooth, claw, redness . . .

The officer said, "Wife . . . *urdle* . . . me . . ."

She covered her ears. "No, I'm sorry, I can't, I'm not able, forgive me, I can't listen, someone else will have to tell her, no, please . . ."

She turned to where Bruce and the officer had run, had disappeared. She screamed, "Us! Stay with us! We need you!"

After a moment she took her hands from her ears. The officer was making soft, sucking sounds like Grandma, centuries ago, drinking hot tea and *zupping* as Momma called it.

Suuuuuckkk. Suuuuuuckkkk.

She scrambled erect. "Wait," she whispered. "I'll get help." She stepped back, praying he wouldn't see the lie. She had already called for help and now she should wait with him and listen to the bubbling and the sucking and show her compassion for this dying bit of humanity.

428

But it wasn't humanity she was seeing. It was red horror, jungle horror, the ravening beast called man, the bleeding prey called man.

"Wait," she said. "I'll bring—"

He suddenly heaved himself into a sitting position, bloody vomit bursting from his mouth. She screamed, but mostly inside; most of it rising into her skull and expanding and exploding there. He said, "No . . . you . . . *urdle* . . ." And fell back, his head thunking on the concrete floor.

She backed another step. He didn't move, didn't choke and bubble. Yet his open, staring eyes seemed to follow her. She ran, and looked back, and in the gloom she thought his head turned smoothly and his eyes gleamed after her, pale searchlights staying with her every frantic step of the way.

All the dead heads turned that way for Ellie DeWyant. All the martyred eyes sought her out. All the victims said, "No . . . you . . . *urdle.*"

She heard a voice. The martyred? She heard it again, and it was a real voice, from outside her enemy mind. One of the blue-jacketed car-park boys was there, and she pointed at the martyred. The boy went to him and knelt and came back, face pale. "He's dead! What—"

"A car," she said.

"Well, sure, Miss DeWyant, but what happened? Should I call—"

"A car, now, please."

He stared at her and said, "Well . . . you want a Continental or Caddy?"

"Either. Please."

He went away, looking back at her. She leaned against the wall, avoiding the martyred, knowing he, too, was looking at her, his searchlight eyes accusing, accusing, asking how she could live when he was red prey, when so many were red prey.

The Cadillac sedan pulled up. "This okay, Miss DeWyant?"

She got in. The boy drove. He tried to make conversation, watching her from the corners of his eyes. "They say it started in the Senator's suite . . ." He turned into a curving, climbing ramp, the scream of tires blending with the screams of all the martyred. He stopped at the front doors and got out and went to the rental booth. She slid behind the wheel and drove away, seeing him turn and wave his arms, hearing him call something about papers and check-out.

She was on Collins, driving much too fast. Saturday night and heavy traffic and shrieking horns and screaming tires blending with all the shrieks and screams of the martyred. People shouting at her blending with the shouts of the martyred.

Running. Foot to the floor and running from the jungle world and through the jungle world . . .

To the jungle world?

Where else was there to run?

To death? To peace?

The truck loomed up ahead.

She made her choice.

The Miami-U character was asleep, his trip ended. Lou sat on the floor, wrapped in a blanket, arms and legs crossed, drawing into herself. She had eaten her acid sugarcube and looked at a lamp and seen a universe of whirling, blinding suns. She had stared at a new penny and seen rivers of flowing fire, mountains of flashing gold. She had sipped a glass of water and plunged into the deepest sea, seen the strangest fish. But all the time she had seen something else—herself. And all the time she had felt a bad trip coming on. Now it was almost here. Now she was fighting, terrified of the nightmare about to enfold her.

The Miami-U character had used her breasts, and she had looked up at him, listened to his grunts and then his cries, felt so far from him as to wonder whether he too wasn't a figment of the LSD trip. Back and forth he'd rubbed, and in the background the radio played, the Senator's voice rising and falling in its own pattern of peak and valley, climax and anticlimax.

The Miami-U character used her armpits. She sat with her back to him, jolting forward every time he hit her with his middle, hearing the difference in grunts as he struggled for his second orgasm, hearing the difference in the Senator's voice as he approached his own orgasm—the termination, the conclusion, the explosive ejaculation of words. And it was all part of her trip, with the nightmare lurking not too far away.

She'd had no climax of her own, but it was coming, she knew that, now that the Miami-U character lay mumbling in sleep and the radio played music and she sat rocking back and forth in her blanket. The climax to this trip, to all her trips.

It was coming, the emptiness of boys without end and love without heart. Of swallowing her life whole without time to taste, to celebrate. Of countless beginnings, and only one of them important—and that one lost to her.

It was coming, the bad trip that sent acidheads screaming through windows. It was coming . . .

She looked up. She wouldn't wait for it! Not Lou Degano!

Still in her blanket, she stumbled to the table and found her keys and went out the door. Night on Pine Tree Drive. Deep night and no one to see the girl wearing a blanket and nothing else. Black night and the bad trip closing fast.

She got in the Volks and fumbled and started and drove. She tried to remember to be careful, driving fast, running from the bad trip. She went toward lights, toward people, toward help against the bad trip. She went to Collins Avenue.

The Metropole ahead. Someone cursing at her, and the blanket slipping as she leaned toward the opposite window and laughed and said, "Whatsa matter baby?" The man's face going from rage to shock and then to the look she knew so well when men saw Lou Degano—or what they took to be Lou Degano. As men saw her legs and breasts. As men saw what they wanted, what she had always given without qualm.

She drove and the Metropole went away and the blanket fell to her waist and the man in the yellow car was following and grinning the way men grinned when they saw what they thought was Lou Degano.

But only Bruce Golden had seen Lou Degano, and only for a moment.

She drove faster, whipping the little bug in and out of traffic, losing the man in the yellow car. But there were other men, other faces grinning out of other cars at what they thought was Lou Degano.

She tore the blanket from around her waist and told herself to slow down, take it easy, the bad trip was far behind and she'd lose it. No sweat Lou baby and remember Golden's family and fucking-cars-they'll-wipe-us-out.

Horns blowing. A kid on a cycle pulling up even with her and looking in and grinning and talking to what he thought was Lou Degano.

She was about to grin back—when she realized *this* was the bad trip.

She looked around, all around. Cars and faces and grinning and calling and this was the bad trip. It had caught her! It was at her throat!

She sobbed in terror. The grinning. The calling. And would the real Lou Degano stand up please. *Please!*

There was no real Lou Degano—not any more.

It was the acid. It was the drug. It would pass. She had to remember it would pass.

She kept driving and kept sobbing.

"*Please . . .*"

"They're behind us," Pedras panted. "Listen, you can hear them."

Jerry stopped near the huge, square machines, still rumbling away, busy making ice for the dining rooms and bars and thousands of drinking guests. He tried to hear and heard nothing but machinery.

Fuckin' machinery working away in the basement. The steel and concrete that had haunted him all his life. The drabness, the ugliness of a workingman's existence that he feared as much as death.

And wasn't prison with its concrete and steel and workshops and bars and wire fixtures one big basement? One super basement?

He began to run again. Pedras was behind him, gasping, "We've got to stop them! Just a few shots . . . they won't be able to follow . . . next corner . . ."

The Cuban made sense for a change. If anyone was following, and it figured that the remaining cop would, a few shots back would slow him down.

They went past the kitchen that supplied the Bon Bouche and the employees' dining room, and people were moving around there, people on the night shift working away in the steam and the stink, and he ran harder to get to that turn past the TV repair shop where it was dead and quiet. He ran and he saw the rough plaster walls and the glossy green paint over everything and the wire fixtures and he was stronger in his resolve than he had ever been—stronger than when the stakes had been money because now the stakes were escape from hell.

They reached the turn. Jerry flattened against the wall and waited. Ramon moved up beside him. Jerry said, "Back! Let's surprise him."

Now he heard footsteps, more than one pair. Around the far turn and into the ghostly fluorescent shine from the kitchen came two men. The cop and Bruce Golden.

He didn't hesitate. He aimed at Joe College, at the one he had hated all his life. As he pulled the trigger, they left the light. He knew he'd missed when the ricocheting sound came and the two men threw themselves down and began firing back.

"That'll hold them," Ramon said, and began to run and then stopped when he remembered he didn't know the way. Jerry took one more shot, and prayed he'd hit the bastard. They couldn't do any more to him than what they'd do if that cop died.

They ran and reached the staircase. On the other side was the small locker room used by the deck help. Jerry realized he would never see it again, and somehow this frightened him because somehow this was real as nothing that had happened tonight was real. Not even shooting that cop was real. *Pop, pop* instead of *bang, bang*. Cap pistols and cops and robbers.

He laughed as he went up the stairs to the alley and around the turn to the high wooden door. Ramon said something in Spanish; it sounded like a quick prayer. They went through the door and Jerry said, "Walk! We can be seen!"

They walked past the pool, not too quickly, glancing first through the glass wall into the lobby and then around the deck. It was windy, chilly, and Jerry didn't see anyone. Yes, off to the side near the cabanas, two figures clutched together. Teen-agers. Kids. Only kids would be out here tonight.

They left the lighted pool area and began to run again. Jerry wished, fervently, he was a kid and out here with a girl. He wished he wasn't running from hell. He wished, he wished . . .

They were at the steps leading to the beach. "Where . . . how much longer?" Ramon gasped.

"Little bit," Jerry said, and remembered how he used to be able to outrun every kid on the road. But that was before he began smoking, and now he too was feeling the strain, unable to suck in quite enough air.

Still, he could outrun and outfight Joe College!

They reached the sand. Jerry threw his gun away and kicked off his shoes and went into the water, tearing off his jacket.

"This?" Ramon screamed. "*Idiota* . . . I can't swim!"

Jerry had to laugh. He was plunging in, cutting under good-sized waves, the chill penetrating to his vitals, but he had to laugh. He came up, turning toward shore, and the laughter froze in his throat. They were on the beach, the cop and Golden, and Ramon's hands were just going up.

He began to swim furiously, heading straight out. Later, he would cut right, go parallel to the beach until he was sure he'd lost them. Then he would come in and walk away from the whole mess.

He stopped a few moments later, out about a hundred feet now, and treaded water and looked toward the shore. They were still there. No . . . wait, there were *four* now. Another cop had joined . . .

He heard the sound. Right here in the water. Not far from him and coming from shore. He thought of sharks and told himself not this time of year and still couldn't help kicking out and taking eight or ten panicked strokes.

"Leech!"

He stopped and looked hard and saw the head in the water.

"Leech . . . go back in. Can't get away."

He looked at shore again and yes, there were four, and one had his hands way up so that was Ramon, and another was walking him up the steps so that was a cop, and two were spreading out along the edge of the water and they were also cops.

And in the water with him was Bruce Golden. In the water with him was Joe College. He said, "Okay. You're right. Let's go." And swam toward him.

Golden swam toward shore.

Jerry stopped. "Listen . . . I'm pooped . . . need help!"

Golden treaded water.

"Help me!" Jerry said, and made strangling sounds and went down. He stayed under as long as he could, and when he came up he reached out, sweeping his arms wide, and grabbed something. He had Golden's arm! Joe College had been suckered! He had him now. He'd pull him under.

He was struck twice in the face and the arm wrenched from his grasp with shocking speed and strength. He lunged after the receding head and flailing arms, and then didn't see them any more.

Golden had gone under. Jerry waited, unable to do anything else.

"Leech! You can't get away. Go in!"

Jerry swam toward the voice, giving it everything he had. And when he got to where Golden should have been, Golden wasn't there and he was much too close to shore and he could see the cops . . .

He was punched in the back of the head and went under and came up coughing and turned and Golden wasn't there, but the voice called to him again.

"Don't be a fool—go in."

Jerry called him everything he could think of, and began to swim out again. When he paused, the voice was behind him.

"No use."

"No use for *you*," Jerry panted. "Never bring me in. C'mon, try. Just try!"

"Not me. Just going to stick . . . with you. All the way."

"Damn it . . . why? What's it . . . to you? Get out and let . . ."

He told himself to stop wasting breath. He began to swim. He didn't stop until shore was far enough away to make spotting him, even if they used beach-patrol Jeeps and spotlights, just about impossible. Then he rested, moving arms and legs slowly, easily.

The voice was nearby, toward shore. It said, "Shot officer . . . shot at me . . . you're finished . . . better at *everything* than you."

At that the fear sprang up and he fought it with a loud braying laugh. Pacing himself he swam steadily, swam south. And then, as he had fired to slow pursuit, he turned abruptly and made a grab behind him. Golden wasn't near enough, but he went back a ways. Jerry gave him that braying laugh again. Golden answered with a high, piercing yell: "*Heyeyeyeyey!*"

Jerry swam. The cold was gone now. His clothing seemed to weigh more, but it wasn't too bad. He could keep going forever. He could outswim Golden. *He had to!*

No panic! No increase of pace!

He slowed, paced himself, went on and on. Life became a matter of stroke and stroke-breath, stroke and stroke-breath.

Golden yelled again. Jerry told himself not to break rhythm, that no one on shore could hear over the sound of the waves— and paused to look. The cops were some distance behind them, but moving in the right direction.

Jerry swam. He kept telling himself he'd make it. But he was swimming too fast for distance, increasing his pace every few minutes without knowing it, then realizing it and slowing, then swimming too fast again. Finally, he felt a need for air, lots of it, and stopped and took in huge shuddering breaths and heard himself shout, "A deal! Golden . . . fifty grand! Golden . . ."

The voice was so calm, so normal in spite of heavy breathing, that it terrified him. "Go in . . . or you'll drown." The voice was the voice of the Joe Colleges who had always defeated him, who had made him know himself as never quite good *enough*, who had spelled out his failure by their very existence.

He swam like a madman for about a minute, and then couldn't breathe, and went under. He came up strangling and begging for help. He went under a second time, and broke surface, and got some air, and located shore. He struck out for it. He swam and regained some strength and regained some courage. The longer he swam, the closer he got to shore. The closer he got to shore, the stronger he became. And when he saw that the cops were *far* to his right and that he had a chance to escape, he gave it a little more and touched bottom and came plunging up out of the water.

To his right was a motel, its spotlighted pool area adjoining the beach and casting light on the beach itself. In front of him was the massive blackness of a hotel abutment and he ran right at it, toward the shadows that would hide him from Golden. Between abutment and motel was the stairs-to-street arrangement of a public beach.

He heard Golden's *heyeyeyeyey!* and turned his head to see the shape rising up out of the water.

If only he'd had his gun! One shot . . .

He was still running as hard as he could and water was still splashing around his shins and he didn't realize how close he was to the abutment. Golden gave another yell, and Jerry glanced back again, pumping his legs even harder. As he turned his eyes forward, he smashed face first into the concrete. He fell. The beach sloped and he rolled over, once, and came to rest face down, hidden in wavelets and shadows.

By the time Golden found him, he had drowned in four inches of water.

Traffic was even slower than usual. It took the cab carrying Ivan Lamas a good ten minutes to get over the bridge past the Americana and at least as long to pass through Haulover Beach Park. The driver said, "I knew it," pointing ahead at the lights of 163rd Street and the Castaways Motel complex. "Something's happened. People slowing and *gawking* . . ."

They slowed and gawked themselves when they reached the Wreck Bar. Looking out across the southbound lanes, Lamas saw people crowded onto the canal docking area adjoining the bar. Strung lights illuminated the scene. One of a dozen cabin cruisers had smashed decking and railing.

The driver leaned out and called to a policeman helplessly waving at traffic from the divider. "Cheney! Hey, it's me!"

The officer came over. Lamas settled back in his seat. The officer merely glanced at him as he bent to the front window. "Never seen anything like it," he said. "She came up Collins like a runaway locomotive. There was traffic waiting at the light and I thought sure she was going to plow right into it. But she turned left, went across the southbound, just missed a car, then onto the dock and over."

Lamas wanted to tell the driver to move on. The driver asked how many in the car. "Just the one woman. We can see her. Went halfway through the windshield . . ."

They finally drove off. He would have said something to the fool of a driver. He would have eliminated his tip and told him why. But he paid without a word and tipped normally. He couldn't afford to be remembered for anything out of the ordinary.

In the house, he poured a brandy and sat down at the radio to learn the full extent of the disaster.

No one had come for him. Tonto hadn't returned and accused him of anything. They'd bought the story of his being used by those nuts. So he'd gone down and prepared for the show, his last show in the Platinum Room. There'd been a half-hour postponement and Wally had welcomed it. Now he was waiting, about five minutes to go, the door of his dressing room locked against all.

But the door of his mind, of his heart, was wide open. Everything was coming in that door—and lots going out too.

Hate was going out. Not because it wasn't justified. Jesus, yes, it was justified, and he had never been Tom enough to ignore it. *Anything* was justified. But hate was another slave-chain, more trouble piled on the trouble already there.

And hate turned a man into a fool. Like that call he'd made. Had people died because of that call? Had the speechwriter died because of that call?

He got up, hands clenched at his breast, and realized he was looking at himself in the mirror. He was suffering and posing both at the same time.

Show biz. He was more show biz than he was Negro.

Maybe that was the answer. Everyone was more something than Negro, more something than white. They just had to find that something and then they forgot to concentrate on black and white and Jew and Gentile and vegetarian and meat-eater.

The knock sounded and the voice called, "Time, Mr. Jones!"

He felt himself crying. He watched the performance in the mirror, and couldn't watch any more, and turned his back on his image.

"Mr. Jones?"

He wiped his eyes with a tissue and tried to bring order to his mind, and realized he was thinking of one thing and one thing only. With his whole insides. With his gut.

That audience out there.

"Mr. Jones, is everything all right?"

"All *right?*" he answered. "Why baby, all right is death. *Great* is kinda nice. Wild and terrific are cool. Fabulous is getting there."

He came out and put an arm around the fat, sad-sack kid and liked him for his pleased, embarrassed smile and went onto that stage. And with the most distracted audience of his career still buzzing away about the kidnap attempt, and with a trio that hadn't been allowed to say boo to him in a week and was feeling the chill, and with a stomach that still wanted to upchuck and a throat too tight with too much emotion, he did a job, reached his audience, scored solidly if not the great big smasheroo he'd wanted opening night, gave these people what he hadn't been able to give until now—and, as always, gave himself even more.

Ruthie boarded the jet at twelve-ten Sunday morning. The door closed immediately behind her and the stewardess put her into an aisle seat beside a thin old lady who kept her eyes fixed out the window. There were instructions about seat belts and no-smoking and they taxied into position and then they were surging up the runway.

Airborne, and on her way to San Juan with nothing but a little canvas bag and some stuff from the airport pharmacy. And three grand in her purse, tapped from the stake in Jerry's car, just in case.

She wondered if he'd taken a few thousand, too. She wondered if he was pro enough to figure just-in-case was usually-happens. She hoped he'd made it somehow, wished him the best, but didn't dwell on him.

She had taken a cab from the Metropole to the Algiers, and from the Algiers to Lincoln Road, and from there to Miami International. A cancellation—two, in fact—had been available and she'd rushed and made it. Now the next big hurdle was San Juan itself. If they were waiting at the airport . . .

No use thinking of that. The odds were that they wouldn't be. The odds were that it would take time to identify her, and even more time to trace her escape route. If and when they came looking, she wouldn't be anywhere near the places Americans hung out; she'd be as far from the ocean-front strip of hotels as she could get. Maybe she'd find herself a nice guy and set him up in some sort of business. Three grand wasn't much, but it should go quite a ways among the Puerto Ricans themselves.

Yes, a sweet, dark, hot little lover boy. Like the kid in Reno who swept out the motel and had eyes for everything in skirts. She'd given him a standing go-round that last night when Leo was at the tables. Just ten minutes, but God he'd been wild and he'd made those ten minutes count.

She sighed. Even a few weeks of that wouldn't be bad. What the hell else was there?

She had a Manhattan and some hors d'oeuvres and another Manhattan. She lit a cigarette and glanced at the old lady and the old lady was asleep. She sighed, feeling kinda happy, kinda sad.

Imagine, kinda happy! But she did. San Juan was new and new places were fun.

Anything was fun when you stayed out of the electric chair or gas chamber or however they did it in Florida.

She decided to remain awake until they landed, but after a while the rumble and shudder and two cocktails got to her and she closed her eyes. Well, she'd soon find out. Maybe she'd had it, and maybe it was another shuffle, another deal. Nice Puerto Rican guy . . . fall in love with her . . . children . . .

Violetta returned to the Metropole at two A.M. She'd been walking, and sitting on benches staring at the sea, and walking some more, trying to think of what to do. Finally, she'd decided that there was no sense running away. She would go back and see whether anyone was looking for her. Only the waiter . . .

There were two police officers sitting in the lobby facing the doors. Except for looking at her miniskirt and one smiling a little, they didn't do anything. The lobby still had a few couples— no more than the usual weekend amount. She went past the desk and up the corridor, and only then did she allow herself to shiver. She hadn't been wearing nearly enough clothing for such a chill evening.

She came into her office, and noticed light showing under Mc-Kensil's closed door. He wouldn't be here so late, would he?

She opened the door. He was at his desk staring at her. She said, "Were you up there?"

He motioned her in. "Close the door. Speak low."

She took the chair beside the desk. "A man died, didn't he?" She didn't have the strength to ask directly.

"A man?" He laughed and shook his head. "Six men died, that I know of, and Michael Wheeler might make it seven."

She asked for a cigarette. He served her from a box on the desk and lit it and said, "You look frozen. I have some brandy."

"Yes. Please. Those men . . ."

He went to a cabinet. "First a man outside Wally Jones's apartment. Then the speechwriter, shot by your friend Jorge. Then Jorge, who seems to have killed himself before he could die of—" He must have seen her face then because he stopped speaking and brought her a water glass half-filled with straight brandy. She sipped, shuddered, sipped again.

"Then an officer in the garage. Mr. Krasmer, the one they tied up. And finally that beach boy, drowned."

She drank it all down, shaking and coughing and letting the tears fill her eyes because it was the alcohol and not her feelings—the alcohol.

He touched her shoulder lightly. He went back to the desk, lit a cigarette, and looked at it. "A simple robbery, you said."

She smoked. The heat spread from her stomach throughout her body. She leaned back, crossed her legs, said, "What about me?"

He was staring. She remembered she wore no pants. He said, "There was a waiter, but he couldn't remember anything beyond a woman. He didn't even say a girl—just a woman who opened the Senator's door for him. He might recognize you, so of course . . ."

"I'm leaving this job," she said wearily. "I have a better offer."

He smiled slightly. "I think you'll be all right."

"And you?"

"As long as no one says anything . . ." He shrugged. "I guess I'm all right, too. At least for the while. That's why I've been waiting here. To be available. To know the minute I'm *not* all right."

"You can go home now? I can go home now?"

He nodded.

She crossed her legs again, sighing, eyes suddenly heavy. He was quiet. She focused on him. He was looking at her, the way he had looked in his car that first day. She said, "You mustn't worry about the pictures. I will see they are destroyed."

"Thank you." He couldn't seem to drag his eyes away from her legs. She uncrossed them, stretched them straight out before her, yawned. She knew how much the miniskirt showed; knew what he was beginning to want. She said, "I will wait with you. I want to be sure, too."

"Well, why don't you . . . get more comfortable?" He was up, reaching for her hand. She allowed him to lead her to the couch. When she sat down, he went to the door and locked it. "So the cleaning people won't disturb you," he said, and returned, and hesitated.

She smiled. He sat down. "You'll think I'm insane," he said, "but as long as we're waiting to find out whether or not we're destroyed, why not wait . . . pleasantly?"

"Yes. Why not?"

He kissed her hand. She touched his face, gently. All those people dead. Their own little Bay of Pigs, and who was there to blame, to hate, this time?

He kissed her cheek. She leaned back. He kissed her lips, cleared his throat, began to speak. Then he said, "What the devil am I afraid of!" and ran his hand up between her legs.

Only once during the two hours they spent together in that office did she allow herself any foolishness. That was when she pressed her lips to his neck, dreaming, whispering so low she barely heard it herself, "*Ai, Jorge.*"

7

The doorbell was ringing and Bruce sat up in bed, awake on the instant. It was six o'clock. He hurried through the living room, hoping to see Ellie. He'd found the suitcase on returning to the garage, but not the girl. And there'd been no answer from the suite.

He opened the door. Claude DeWyant looked as if he hadn't slept all night. The always-dapper hotel man was rumpled and unshaven.

"Where is she? The boys say she drove away like a maniac. What happened? What did you do to her?"

"Wait a minute. Isn't she at the hotel? I thought she went to bed and wouldn't answer—"

"Then she isn't here?" DeWyant suddenly looked worse. "I hold you responsible," he whispered. "I warned you and you wouldn't listen. Now I can't find her and she was driving wild and if she's done anything—"

"Come in," Bruce said, stepping aside.

DeWyant shook his head violently. "There'll be no weeping together, if that's what you think. We have nothing to say to each other. We're enemies. I warned you. I hold you responsible." He turned away. "You'd better start running! I'll let a contract on you! I can't find her and she was driving—" His voice cracked. He rushed toward the elevators, head down and shoulders shaking.

Bruce went to the kitchen and made coffee. He carried a cup to the phone and called the *Herald*'s news desk. He spoke to a friend and learned two things; one immediately and one after five minutes' wait. The first: Claude DeWyant's threats weren't to be taken lightly. He *did* have Mafia partners. He had told the truth about himself. (Had he also told the truth about Ellie?)

Two cups of coffee later, Bruce learned the second bit of news, and was shocked clear through. There *had* been a major auto accident in Miami Beach last night.

Heart hammering, he asked for the particulars.

"Woman named Lois Degano, killed in her Volkswagen. Here's what's going to make our front page. She was completely nude . . ."

He left the apartment and went to the garage and got in his Jaguar. He didn't think of the suitcase in the trunk. He thought of Lou—and prayed that Ellie hadn't ended up the same way, somewhere else. He had to make sure she *never* ended up that way.

How, he didn't know. Perhaps by giving her up . . .

Not until nine o'clock did Dr. Cormond suggest that Eve leave Mr. Wheeler. "You need food and rest," he murmured. She didn't argue. She had been beside her patient with the hotel doctor, with the ambulance intern and his pulmotor, and the last four hours with Wheeler's Philadelphia specialist. She rose. Mr. Wheeler stopped her. "Eve . . . don't go."

"She's exhausted," Cormond said. "I'm ordering her to—"

"No one orders . . . her but me. Want to talk . . . to her . . . alone."

Dr. Cormond hesitated. Mr. Wheeler, right eye again dimmer than the left, glared at him. Dr. Cormond went out of the bedroom, closing the door.

"You had something . . . with that . . . thug."

He meant Jerry. She nodded.

"It's over now?"

Again she nodded. Jerry was dead. And even if he'd been alive and on his knees before her, it was over.

Used. Again, always, *used.*

"Don't look . . . like that. Nothing's . . . changed." He took her hand. "You and me . . . Eve, on to . . . Palm Beach . . . as planned. You and me . . . and a good life . . . you'll see."

She said yes, and wanted to go now. She needed some moments to herself. Ever since the insanity of last night, she had belonged to others. Now she needed to belong to herself, and to think a little. Certainly, she would go with Mr. Wheeler. Where else *was* there to go? It would mean money and position and soon he would be better, as he'd been before last night. . . .

She stood up, pulling her hand free.

"Eve?" He was worried.

She said, "I'll be back as soon as I'm rested," and went out.

Dr. Cormond was standing near the couch amidst a cluster of men. He was speaking, and then he nodded at her, motioning her over to him. The two men sitting on the couch stood up. There was the Senator, and then there was the smaller, slighter man whom she recognized as the President of the United States. The Senator spoke before the President could. He introduced her, and he seemed a different man—a stronger, surer man. A much *happier* man, though that made little sense, considering what had happened last night.

The President said, "Thank you, Eve. Dick and the doctor told me what you did for my father-in-law." She murmured it was just her job, and the others smiled, and she knew they thought she was overwhelmed. But somehow she wasn't. She was terribly tired, and not in a purely physical sense. The doctor said, "She's really exhausted . . . all night long . . ." and the Senator took her arm and walked with her to the kitchen. "You're part of the family," he said, and whether or not he meant it he said it in a nice way. "My father-in-law wants you to stay on—" he paused— "as something more than just a nurse, with salary to match. I'm glad he feels that way." He suggested she use the second bedroom in his suite for her nap, and left.

She made coffee and sat down at the table. Bryan Whitelock came in. "Got an extra cup?" he asked. She poured for both of them and they drank and she was grateful for his silence. He finished and stood up.

"You know something? You've got it made."

"You, too," she said.

He nodded. "That's right. We struck a home. The best there is."

She opened the refrigerator. "The Senator, too," she said, to be saying something, to show she was becoming aware of things.

"You noticed that, did you?" He dropped his voice. "Last night he finally got out from under Poppa's heavy hand, by saving Poppa's bacon."

"That's not very nice," she murmured.

He smiled. "I've been with him five years, with the family eight. I've never seen him the way he is now. He's top dog. Not the President. Not old Mike. But Dickie-boy. And it's going to stay that way."

She sat down and began peeling an orange.

He stood there. She finally looked up at him. "Take a lesson from that," he said. "You saved some bacon, too. Like me. In our own ways, two more top dogs." He was watching her closely, and she suddenly felt he saw more than Michael Wheeler and the Senator; he saw more than she herself did. He was still working for the family, selling her on something. Except that she didn't need to be sold—did she?

He left. She sat at the table, the orange peeled and uneaten before her, wanting to leave, yet not wanting to go next door and sleep. She wanted . . . she wanted . . .

She went out and the men looked at her and she had never had so much acceptance from so many men. And *such* men! She went to the hall closet and got the little beach bag with her bathing suit and towel robe.

It was still gray outside, but beginning to warm up. She stopped at the deck booth and asked if she could rent a cabana. The boy inside said, "They're all taken, but you can *use* one. Number Sixty's gonna be empty today."

She changed into the bikini Mr. Wheeler had bought her in Palm Beach and came back to the booth to tip the boy. He thanked her, his eyes moving over her body in casual examination. "Hey, wild about Jerry, huh? I mean, you used to talk to him when you and your patient came down."

She said yes and turned toward the beach and caught his eyes sliding to her bottom. She remembered how Jerry had liked it . . .

He'd used her. He'd lied to her.

But was it *all* lies?

She waded, moving up the beach in ankle-deep water. She looked out at the horizon, at the broadening patch of blue and growing area of sunshine. By staying with Mr. Wheeler, she would stay in the sunshine. As Bryan Whitelock had said, she'd struck a home.

But something bothered her. Something . . .

Wasn't staying with Mr. Wheeler staying still, perhaps going back to what she had been before Miami? Wasn't it another way of hiding behind the old and the sick, finding security with a patient again?

She turned back to the hotel, telling herself she was exhausted, she needed sleep, by tomorrow all doubt would be gone.

When she entered the cabana and saw the phone, she hesitated—then placed the call to Bannesville, Pennsylvania. Alice Andrews was as agitated, and as tearful, as she'd been during the first call. And again, what she most wanted to know was when she would be seeing Eve.

"I told you before," Eve said. "I don't know. I . . . just wanted to say hello."

"But you can't mean you'll *never*? . . ." She didn't finish. Except for the sound of her tears, there was silence. Eve refused to break it, waiting for something that would change things.

Alice Andrews finally spoke, the tears gone, her voice quite steady. "I don't blame you for not staying for the funeral."

Eve maintained her silence, but something began aching inside her. She covered the mouthpiece and cleared her throat and shook her head. No reason for *her* to cry. None at all.

"I was married to him for twenty-three years, but I never knew how cruel he could be."

Eve took deep breaths. She fought the aching, the tearing, the *changing* going on. Too many changes since last night—too many changes and much too quickly.

"He was my husband and I thought I loved him, but at the end, well, I just couldn't love him. I kept telling myself it was

448

the sickness, the pain, and maybe it was. I pray it was. I pray he was out of his mind and that was why he acted as he did to you."

Eve began to cry, silently, pressing the phone to her ear.

"But I can't forgive it. And I can't forgive myself. All the time it was happening—every night in bed—I prayed he would change the next day so I wouldn't have to tell you this. And before I could tell you this, you were gone."

Eve fought for control. "It's all right."

"No, it's not. You must hate him."

"No—not really." She wept and held to her voice. "Not any more."

"Do you—" The voice grew uncertain and hesitant. "Do you hate me, too?"

"Of course not. I never . . . no . . ." She covered the mouthpiece, sobbing.

"Then come home, Evie. At least for a while. At least to visit. Please, darling, I miss you so. You're my life now. You were, from the day I got you."

Eve's sobs ended. She remembered her father saying Alice hadn't wanted to adopt her, had wanted one of the adorable babies . . .

"I never knew I could love a child so much, Evie. Especially one almost grown before I met her. I wanted a two- or three-year-old. Caspar insisted on you. For that, at least, I thank him. I don't care about his reasons. I thank him. You've been everything a mother could want."

"I can't talk any more," Eve whispered, and she couldn't.

"All right. You do whatever makes you happy. You'll call again, Evie?"

"Yes. Good-bye."

"Good-bye, Evie."

And then Eve said, "Wait . . . Mother! I want to come home. I want to come home, Mother!"

She swam in the pool. A new muscle boy kidded her and she smiled a little and went to the cabana and changed. She was still tired, still needed sleep, but confusion was gone. She was going back to Bannesville General Hospital and the men and women she knew. She wasn't afraid of those men and women any more. She wasn't hiding behind the old and the sick any more. They were her job, not her life. She had finally grown up.

Eve Andrews, adult. That was all it amounted to. Now she had to go back to that suite where all those men waited, all those important men, and prove that Eve Andrews, adult, could hold to a decision.

May was on a two o'clock jet to Chicago. Harold was following, in a railroad baggage car. She had said good-bye to Al at five this morning, and returned to learn she was a widow. It still hadn't caught up with her, not all of it. Too much to do. Too many arrangements to make.

The plane swung north in its pattern, and she looked out over Miami Beach, at the blue sea and the sugarcube hotels. She was going home, but only for a funeral. She was going home, but only to make the right sounds in the right places for the right people. Then she would get away from everything and solace her grief and rest her frayed nerves—and whatever else it was people said at times like this.

But what she would be doing was returning to Miami Beach. Not to the same hotel, but to the sun and the boys—to the *men*, next time. Returning to the satisfaction of her senses, so long denied her. Returning because whatever else she might find in herself during the days to come, she had already found a vast gratitude, a vast liking for this swinging strip of sand, this Kosher Riviera, as Harold had once called it.

He had mocked it. There was plenty to mock. She watched it as long as she could and didn't mock it. She watched it and thought only of the day she would fly back to it again.

It was six o'clock before he reached Sanibel. He had checked hospitals in Miami Beach and Miami—until he'd thought of the island near Fort Myers.

He parked near the Gulf-front cabins of the Trade Winds and

saw a middle-aged couple and infant child on the beach. He walked over and asked for the owner and they didn't know where he was. He considered describing Ellie, but then he saw a figure far beyond the tree-strewn sanctuary—a figure small with distance, a female figure in yellow.

Ellie had been wearing a yellow dress last night.

He began to run even while the middle-aged couple was talking to him. He ran hard, until he was certain. Then he walked.

They met and stopped. He said, "Call your father. He's sick with worry."

"I did. About an hour ago." She didn't look at him.

She began to walk again. He walked beside her. She looked at the Gulf. He said, "You're a very perceptive person. Quite right in running. Quite right in everything . . ."

"Don't," she whispered, but she still didn't look at him and he felt she never would.

"No *mea culpa*, Ellie. Just a statement of fact. No engagement. No commitment. We're free as birds, right?"

"Yes." It was a whisper lost in the surf.

"Well, then . . ." He took her hand. "At least look at me and say we're friends."

She shook her head. "No," she whispered. "Not friends."

He let the hand go. Something gripped his insides, hurting him. He began to say a flip farewell, then gave it up and walked faster, leaving her behind.

"You threw me first, the money second."

He didn't get it, and turned. She was looking at him. Her face was drawn, wan, far from the beautiful face it could be. Her face reflected the tortured mind, and a man had to be nuts to let himself in for a lifetime of *that*.

"I remember now," she said, looking at him so hard he felt exposed, open to a vision beyond sight. "A small thing, but first you threw *me* to the side, to the floor. Only then you threw the money. You saved *me* first, the money second."

He shrugged. He wouldn't take the cop-out. "I don't remember."

"But I do. I remember nothing else."

Her eyes begged him, and he couldn't turn away from them, from the girl who needed him. He was afraid of the wan look and the mind behind the wan look. He was afraid of the father who hated him and whose threats could no longer be ignored. He was afraid that the life of leisure and joy would turn out to be one of struggle for survival, his as well as hers. But he couldn't turn away.

The something gripping his insides got rough and he said, "Oh Christ," and reached for her and held her. He finally loved the girl, but he wouldn't tell her until she knew it without his telling her. He loved the girl and he held the girl and the something gripping his insides let up only after he'd kissed the girl.

They walked until it was dark. Then they went to her cabin. Then the Golden Boy began to learn what it was all about.

CUBAN EPILOGUE

At ten o'clock, after he had almost given up, Lamas heard the car in the driveway. He put down his cigar and placed a mint in his mouth. He was combing his hair in front of the gold-frame antique mirror when there was a knock at the study door. "Come in."

The young chauffeur walked, or rather strolled, inside. Lamas told himself to ignore it. "The girl is here, *patrón*." He spoke in English, and badly.

"What took so long, Mateo?"

"She wasn't home."

No "*patrón*." No explanation.

"And so you waited?"

"Sure. Like you told me . . . *patrón*."

Maybe it would be better if Mateo dropped the "*patrón*." From him, it sounded ridiculous.

"The mother was there? You talked to her?"

"Sure, like you told me."

"She said anything? You know, was she—curious?"

Mateo shrugged. "An old *madre*. Older than I thought a young girl like that would have. An old woman and all she asked was how rich you were and your house. Like that."

"All right. She can come in now for her interview."

Had Mateo's lips twisted in a smile as he turned? If he dared! . . .

She came in, and he hurried over to take her hand and kiss it. He closed the door and spoke in Spanish. "It is good to see you, Violetta. Almost a month, and you never contacted me."

"I was waiting, Mr. Lamas."

"Ivan, please."

"I was waiting to find out whether I was safe or not. You

wouldn't have wanted me coming here if I wasn't safe, would you?"

He waved a hand. "That you and the manager were safe was obvious from the second or third day afterward. Very fortunate. Or was it that you were more clever than the others?"

"This is very nice," she said, looking around the study.

"I practically live here."

"You're lucky."

He smiled. She couldn't know how careful he'd had to be since the disaster of January twenty-eighth. Or that he'd been ostracized by most of his acquaintances in the Cuban liberation movements. Or that Matilde Humes, the woman he had considered marrying if all went well, had refused to see him after the news of his chauffeur's complicity. And those three long periods of questioning by the FBI. Humiliation piled on humiliation!

Still, he smiled. She was a pretty thing and her short skirt tantalized him. Cheap, certainly, but he would teach her to dress in time.

He led her to a chair. "A drink?"

She shook her head.

"You smoke?"

"Yes, but not now, thanks."

"Ah . . . would you mind telling me why you weren't at home at the appointed time? We agreed my car would pick you up at eight."

She shrugged. "I was at a movie. The picture was longer than I thought."

A poor lie. She had obviously had second thoughts. He went to his desk and opened the top drawer. "After what happened, I felt I owed you a little something." He took out the box and brought it to her. "Not that the plan wasn't correct. But I've since come to see that I trusted a man . . . well, let us say an uneducated man, in order not to speak ill of the dead."

She was opening the box. She looked at the string of medium pearls, worth at least three thousand dollars, which he had picked up for eighteen hundred. It would stun her, of course, but it would more than pay for itself in the months to come. She would move in as a maid . . .

She snapped the lid closed. "It is beautiful, but not what I was to be paid."

He was surprised. "Payment was incumbent upon success. And you were one, I thought, who did not do such a thing for money."

"Ten thousand dollars, Mr. Lamas."

"Ivan, please. The money, well, we can discuss it."

She held out the box.

"Keep it, won't you?"

"I prefer the money."

He felt a twinge of anger, but held it down. The little doxie had an inflated view of her worth!

Still, she was young, she was desirable . . .

He went to the desk, wrote out the check, and brought it to her. She murmured, "Thank you, Ivan," and opened her purse. He tapped the box of pearls. "That too, my dear." She dropped it in with the check.

"And now," he said, "perhaps you'll reconsider having that drink?"

"No, but a cigarette."

He placed one between her lips and lit it, then drew up a small black chair close to her armchair. "You were very clever, Violetta. If I'd had *men* like you, things would certainly have been different."

She said nothing, inhaling smoke.

"The next time, I'll have men of brain as well as action. Intelligent men to carry out *exactly* what I—"

She stood up, interrupting him in a cold, insulting voice. "They died, Jorge and Vidal and Leech. You made plans and they died. They rot in the ground and you talk of *next time*."

He rose swiftly, slapping her as hard as he could. She staggered, and he prepared to lecture her on respecting her betters. Suddenly, she was reaching out. He fought a scream as her nails raked his left cheek—raked deep. He leaped back, trembling. The girl was insane!

Voice still cold, still insulting, she said, "I think I know now why Fidel succeeded. I think I know now how hopeless it is to talk of changing things in Cuba. The people must remember *patrones* like you." She turned to the door.

"You *dare?*" he whispered, feeling blood trickling off his chin. "You think I will allow you to remain unpunished? You think that check? . . ."

She opened the door wide, and he fell silent. She spoke softly, yet he feared that Maria and Mateo would hear.

"Be careful, *patrón*. Remember what I know about you and your *plans*. Understand that it is written down in case I have an *accident*. Perhaps the best thing I could do for the memory of my father, brother, and uncle would be to see you in jail."

He dabbed at his face and was still. The girl looked at him, waiting. He refused to answer, refused to be drawn into anything with such . . . *filth*.

She walked out. The front door slammed. At the same moment, Maria came to the study. "Your face!" she gasped.

"Go to bed!" He twisted away. "Close the door!"

He went to the bathroom and doctored his cheek. The bitch! The stupid little peasant bitch! As if he cared what such *campesinas* thought of him! His plans were being formed. He had several, and one was growing stronger by the hour. A strange plan, and therefore unlikely to be detected by the authorities. A simple plan, dependent upon his finding a very special man—one willing to accept certain death for his cause.

Say he found such a man. Latorre's second cousin, for example, who fancied himself the heir of Ché Guevara—an embarrassment to Latorre and the entire family, he'd once been certified insane and placed in a mental institution. He was free now, supposedly better now, but still known to make speeches that could get anyone else killed in the Cuban section.

Say he convinced such a man that he would be avenging Guevara and doing a general service to humanity by killing the President of the United States. Say he paid the Latorre family heavily (through emissaries, of course—everything through emis-

456

saries), while making them understand that it was on the altar of their *own* cause that they were allowing the cousin to be sacrificed.

Say the cousin could be helped to assassinate the President, and then allowed to confess in court that he was an agent of Castro's Cuba. Wouldn't a war fever sweep this country that could be cured only by invasion? Wouldn't reason give way to passion and words to weapons?

He returned to the study and sat down to work with pencil and paper. It seemed farfetched, but so had the plan of January twenty-eighth—and even in failure, look how close they had come to capturing the prize!

And this would *not* fail! This would show that little peasant bitch, show the fools in the liberation movements, show Matilde Humes, show them all!

Show them who Ivan Cesar Lamas was!

About the Author

HERBERT KASTLE has been a high-school teacher, and editor, a film writer, an advertising copywriter, and —always—a novelist. Previous novels included *Camera* and the highly praised *Koptic Court*. Then, in 1968, he distilled his Hollywood years into *The Movie Maker*, considered by many the most ambitious and sensational novel ever written about the film world and its strange inhabitants. Mr. Kastle travels extensively to research locales for his novels (several months were spent in Miami Beach in preparation for *Miami Golden Boy*) and recently completed an extended jaunt to Switzerland and other European countries absorbing color for a new novel.